THE
WRITING
CIRCLE

THE
WRITING CIRCLE

Corinne Demas

voice

HYPERION   NEW YORK

Library of Congress Cataloging-in-Publication Data has been applied for.

ISBN: 978-1-4013-4114-5

Hyperion books are available for special promotions and premiums. For details contact the HarperCollins Special Markets Department in the New York office at 212-207-7528, fax 212-207-7222, or email spsales@harpercollins.com.

FIRST EDITION

10 9 8 7 6 5 4 3 2 1

SUSTAINABLE FORESTRY INITIATIVE
Certified Fiber Sourcing
www.sfiprogram.org

THIS LABEL APPLIES TO TEXT STOCK

We try to produce the most beautiful books possible, and we are also extremely concerned about the impact of our manufacturing process on the forests of the world and the environment as a whole. Accordingly, we've made sure that all of the paper we use has been certified as coming from forests that are managed to ensure the protection of the people and wildlife dependent upon them.

For Matt

$\mathscr{P}$REFACE

THE HOUSE IS SET ON A HILLSIDE, WITH A LONG DRIVEWAY THAT leads up to it and disappears around the back. It's after dinner-time, already dark. A garage door at the rear of the house opens, and a pickup truck backs out and turns around. Whoever is driving has not turned the headlights on, and if you were viewing the scene from above, you would barely make out the truck as it comes around the side of the house, as it heads down the driveway.

A figure cuts across the sloping front lawn and starts down the drive-way, towards the road. It's probably a woman, but she's dressed in black, and almost invisible in the dark. A young man is standing by the house, watching her. Light spills out of the doorway behind him. He hears the pickup truck as it emerges around the corner of the house, and he turns towards the sound. Then he cries out something—the woman's name perhaps—but she does not hear him. She's halfway down the driveway, just at the point where it takes a sharp turn. He flies down the hillside, plunges towards her, towards the point of intersection.

PART ONE

PART ONE

Upstairs, in a room in the hospital, were a man and a woman and a dead baby. You would not realize, at first, that the baby was dead. The woman had bobby pins holding her brown hair back off her face. The man wore glasses with tortoiseshell plastic frames, cloudy over the bridge of his nose. Those were the only details the doctor could bear to picture now.

Years later the couple would have two more children—both boys—but at the time neither they nor the young doctor had any way to know that. They would adore those sons, and anyone who hadn't known about the first child they might have had, a little girl, would think them so content as parents that they wanted for nothing. But that night, as the doctor walked out through the lobby of the hospital, the future, which would in fact hold a reasonable share of blessings, was unimaginable.

It was a small country hospital, and the doctor, who was older than he looked, had come back to the area where he had grown up to join a local practice. His parents had moved to Arizona and sold the house where he had spent the early years of his life, but he still knew people in town, though not many, since he had always been a shy kid and had gone away to boarding school and then college.

The hospital had recently opened its new wing, the result of a surprisingly successful capital campaign, and the lobby had been in use for only three weeks. It was designed along the lines of a grand hotel, with high ceilings, art deco light fixtures, and upholstered armchairs placed in conversation clusters along its length. The floor was carpeted in purple and the walls

were paneled in honey-colored wood, and the effect was soothing and de-
ceiving, though no one was entirely fooled because the smell of the hospital
seeped out from the rooms and corridors beyond. It was a façade that
seemed fragile, because just beyond it the real business of the hospital—
carried out in rooms with white linoleum floors—seemed as if it might burst
through. But that was during the day. Now, at 2:30 A.M., even that world
beyond the wood veneer was quiet, too, the lights all dimmed.

A woman wheeled a carpet sweeper in front of the bank of elevators and
disappeared behind a doorway. And then the lobby was absolutely still until
the doctor appeared around the partition at the far end. He had changed
from his scrubs into his street clothes, and he wore running shoes and a
black leather jacket that didn't seem like the style of clothing a doctor would
choose. From a distance, the jacket made him look like a teenager. He
walked with his shoulders slung forward and his chin against his chest, and
he didn't look up until he passed the glass doors of the gift shop and snack
bar. He paused for a moment and looked into the room, which was illuminated only by the lights in the refrigerated unit that held juice and bottled
water. It had been nearly two days since he had slept and hours since he had
eaten. He ran his hand along the brass door handle, and, although he knew
the door was locked, when his hand reached the end he jiggled it anyway.
He leaned against the door, pressing the side of his unshaved face against
the cool glass, and closed his eyes for a second.

It was clear to him that he could not go on this way. He had allowed
grief to enter into a realm where grief had no place, and the result was that
he could no longer function as he needed to. He was absolutely certain
about this—more certain than he had been when he had decided to go to
medical school, more certain than when he had completed his residency and
decided to join a practice in the place where he had grown up. He was certain that he could not recover the kind of distance that he knew he needed
to have, that he had trespassed into an emotional territory where even the
greatest amount of resolve couldn't lead him out. He had no idea what else
he would do with himself, but he knew it couldn't be this.

The revolving doors in the center of the entrance had been locked. He let himself out from the smaller door on the side. The staff parking lot was on the far side of the building, farthest from the main road. There were white pines in the lot that must have been planted when the original hospital building had been erected, and now they were forest giants, several stories high. He breathed in the smell of them. He walked to his car at the far end of the lot and brushed the pine needles from the windshield. He started up the car and drove out to the semicircle of road that went past the emergency room entrance and under the porte cochere outside the main lobby. He looked back at the brick front of the hospital. Most of the rooms were dark. He was certain their room was dark, the room where the couple and the dead baby were, and he counted off the floors and windows and located which one was theirs. He forced himself to look at it, but his head soon jerked as he twitched himself awake. He put on his headlights, which he had neglected to do before, and pulled out into the road that would take him home.

$\mathcal{N}$ANCY

I T WAS THE DAY OF TESTICULAR CANCER. NANCY (A NAME THAT no one was given anymore) had laid out the offprints from various medical journals on her desk the night before, but she hadn't looked at any of them yet. The monthly newsletter she edited had a dozen articles an issue, and she usually spent a day collecting material for each article, and a day reading through it, boiling it down, and writing it up. The newsletter was published under the name of a university medical school, but Nancy was its major author. An editorial board of physicians at the hospital—whose names were used for PR—sometimes suggested subjects for her, but mostly it was she who came up with the topics covered each month. She kept her ear out for what people were worried about, health crises that hit the local news (like the deadly strain of *E. coli* bacteria that had contaminated baby spinach) and the usual seasonal concerns. She did articles about lower back pain when spring gardening season arrived, articles about skin cancer as summer approached, and articles about frostbite at the start of winter. She farmed out some of the work to freelance writers (she had once been one of them), but she rewrote all the articles herself. The narrative voice she had perfected was professional but jaunty. She sounded like an authority, but her tone was upbeat, even when the article was ultimately informing the reader about some hideous condition that involved suffering, disfigurement, and certain early death.

"We are not in the business of scaring people" is what the physician who had started the newsletter and hired her years before had said. "We're in the business of informing them and helping them make wise choices about their health."

The wise choice about testicular cancer, Nancy knew from an article she'd done a year before, was to wear boxers rather than briefs and to be wary of bicycling. But there was now some new information about tumors and heat, and it was time for a follow-up. The word *cancer* in the headline was a certain draw for readers.

She was making herself a cup of tea when the phone rang. It was Bernard.

"I'm just calling to remind you about Sunday," he said.

"I remembered."

"Good. It would have been embarrassing if you hadn't shown up."

"For you?"

Bernard laughed. "Yes. They would all have thought I had told you the wrong day. I did give you directions, didn't I?"

"You did, Bernard."

"But I neglected to tell you that sometimes Adam's buzzer doesn't work. If you ring and no one appears, go around the side of the building and tap on the window."

"Oh come on," said Nancy. "I'm not going to tap on windows!"

"Then if you meet me there at precisely three o'clock and the buzzer doesn't work, *I'll* go around and tap on the window."

"That will be very gracious of you," said Nancy. "By the way, I know something about all the members, except for Adam Freytoch."

"He's been with us only a few years. He designs running shoes for a living but has been working on a novel. He doesn't signify."

"Bernard!" Nancy cried. "How can you say that about someone?"

"He tries hard," said Bernard. "But he's very young."

"You are cruel," said Nancy. "You were young once, yourself."

"Too long ago for anyone to remember," said Bernard, so softly that Nancy couldn't tell if the wistfulness in his voice was authentic or ironic.

"I'll see you Sunday, then," said Nancy.

"Yes," said Bernard. "And no need to be worried. I'm sure they will all take to you."

"What makes you think I'm worried?" asked Nancy.

"Because you worry," said Bernard. "That's the sort of person you are."

"You don't know me that well," said Nancy.

"It's in your face," said Bernard. "Your perpetually knitted brow." And with that he hung up.

Nancy poured the hot water onto the waiting tea bag in her mug and angled the glass cabinet door so she could see her reflection. She was someone who worried, though less so now that her daughter, Aliki, was grown, but she had never thought it was so obvious. Bernard was like that. He said disturbing things, tossed them off, and whether they were true or not, they rankled. Once after he had made a particularly blunt remark about a jacket she wore—"sadly misshapen," she remembered he called it—she had accused him of being tactless.

"Tact, my dear," he had replied, "is merely a ploy of the unimaginative."

He was impossible, and she'd told him so. But she liked him, nevertheless, though she knew many people who didn't. She couldn't imagine being married to him, though, and she found it remarkable that two women, Virginia, in his past, and Aimee, now, had taken him on.

But he was right about her being worried. She hadn't published anything in years, and she was afraid Bernard—to whom she had foolishly confessed she was working on something new—had pressured the others to invite her to join them. She was not anxious about Virginia, who was unfailingly kind, or Christopher Billingsley, who wrote thrillers and whom Bernard had once described as "hopelessly seeking literary approval." But Gillian Coit was another story. Gillian was a poet who had been getting a lot of press recently. Nancy had met her twice in the past, and the second time Gillian hadn't remembered they'd been introduced before.

Nancy rescued the tea bag from the now almost too dark tea and carried the mug to her study. It had originally been a glass-enclosed porch, an addition to the back of the antique Greek Revival house, and she had renovated it and installed a heating system. The house was large and there were other rooms that would have been more sensible to use as a study, but she liked the way this room was far from the heart of the house yet still linked to it—an extremity—like a hand from the body itself. When the snow banked up in winter, she could get to her work without putting on her boots. She was away from her domestic life but still connected. She was away from her bedroom, where she and Oates made love, and she was away from Aliki's bedroom. When Aliki left for college, Nancy didn't want to alter anything in the room, as if ensuring that Aliki's departure was only temporary, yet each time Nancy passed the room and looked in, the uncharacteristic tidiness spoke only of absence.

Once, for the fun of it, Nancy had written an article on empty nest syndrome, *a condition that parents—a higher percentage of females than males—suffer when their children go away to college, particularly acute if the child in question is the person's only progeny,* but of course she could never publish it in the medical newsletter. Although the intensity of the emotion was palpable, *not a melancholia brought about simply because of a change in the timbre of the dwelling place, but a response to a cluster of factors: loss of occupation (on-duty parent), loss of youth, awareness of mortality,* it was hardly a legitimate medical condition. The name conjured an image of a quizzical robin perched by a nest of twigs. Nancy could write about depression or menopause, but she knew you had no business complaining because your child had made it through high school, gotten into college, and was thriving at that same college rather than hanging around under your roof.

Nancy's study was the room closest to the river, and she had a view of it, this lovely, moving body of water, from her desk. The house itself faced the road with its best front and then straggled out behind, summer kitchen, shed, added on over the decades and then incorporated into the house, one by one. The porch was the last link. From the point of view of historic preservationists, it should have been torn down, since it was tacked on in the 1920s, added by people who liked, as Nancy did, to look at the river but who didn't like to be bitten by mosquitoes while they did so. Presumably the generation that had built the original house was not so inclined. For them the river's value was utilitarian rather than aesthetic. If the original owners sat anywhere, it would have been in front of the house, so they could observe what passed on the road. The road was busier now, and cars sped by. Far at the back of the house, Nancy was protected from their noise, protected even from awareness of them.

She set her mug on her desk and settled into her chair. She started flipping through the articles awaiting her from *The Journal of the American Medical Association* and *The New England Journal of Medicine*, the *Mayo Clinic Proceedings*, the *British Medical Journal*. She nudged them to the side and looked out her window—the goldenrod at the edge of the mowed field, the just oranging maples, the brown river, low after the summer.

She thought about her father and wondered how he would view what she did for a living. All those years of his secret life when he had studied and practiced medicine, delving into the peculiarities of the human body and the way it went awry, and here she was writing about medical conditions without the slightest training herself, without a single encounter with a real patient. She did not delude herself that she was doing a noble thing. Perhaps people were desperate for information like this, but she was part of an enterprise whose interests were commercial, not altruistic. And for her own part, she did it because it was a way to make a living. It was, by all accounts, an enviable job for a writer. She was paid well, and her hours were flexible. She was her own boss. And presumably she had time for her own writing—for certainly the writing she did for the health newsletter was not her own. Her own, now, was the novel about her father, which she had been working on, bit by bit, for the past year.

It wasn't really about her father, of course, it was fiction after all, but the main character was based on her father. She felt close to him, as if he were still alive, as if by writing about his youth she had given that youth back to him. And it was a way to explore the mystery of the choice her father had made in his life, the secret that had been kept from her most of her childhood. The secret that, when revealed, gave her insight into a man whom she had thought she knew.

She had had to wait until he died to write about him. She could not have intruded on the privacy of his past knowing that he would witness this intrusion. She could not bear his knowing what she imagined about him, for imagining takes a liberty with someone's life, and although her father loved her, would grant her anything, it would have embarrassed them both.

Bernard's phone call had thrown her off course this morning. It had reminded her that she had committed herself to a next step. It was one thing to probe into her father's story in the intimacy of her manuscript, in the safety of her study. It was another thing to expose it to anyone else. What was she doing laying it bare before someone like Gillian Coit?

There was a circle of brown liquid in the bottom of Nancy's mug now, but it was cold. She spun the mug around once, so the white stars blurred on the blue ceramic background, then she pushed the mug to the back of her desk. She had to get to work now. She turned to the articles in front of her. She began reading through the stack, marking useful paragraphs with a blue felt-tipped pen and processing the information, summarizing it in a few simple sentences. *Male testes are located in the scrotum outside the body cavity because it's cooler there. When testicular cancer cells spread to parts of the body that are warmer environments (like the brain and the liver), they don't thrive as well and are therefore less resistant to the drugs that combat them. The idea of using heat to help combat cancer is already meeting some success in cases of prostate cancer.*

Who reading this would imagine its author here now, sitting with her feet tucked up under her, a woman in sweatpants and a T-shirt, a sweater with worn-out elbows slung around her neck? Who would imagine the scene from her window, the monarchs clustered on the purple asters, the river in the distance turning blue-green in the morning sunshine?

BERNARD

SMALL, AND SLENDER AS A BOY, BERNARD'S WIFE, AIMEE, HAD struggled most of her adult life to have people take her seriously. From a distance, she looked like a child. Up close, she looked twenty rather than forty. Her voice was soft, too, a little girl's voice, though she spoke with a care and deliberateness, and when you entered into a conversation with her you thought her smarter than in fact she was. She was a quarter Japanese, a quarter French, and when it suited her, she exploited one or the other.

Bernard was inclined to clutter and messiness. His home with Virginia had been filled with old books, old sofas, and old velvet drapes. Aimee changed all that. Bernard had ended up with the house after his divorce, and Aimee transformed it when she moved in. Not so much to exorcise Virginia (she *liked* Virginia) or make her mark as second wife, but because the place depressed her as it was. The house was practically gutted. All the woodwork was painted white—including the mantel in the living room and the stair railing, which Bernard, in a previous life, had spent days stripping of its old paint. And the furniture was spare and modern. Aimee transformed Bernard's wardrobe as well, but when he could, he still wore the old clothes he had salvaged.

"He looks," Virginia told her husband, Joe, "like a man sitting in a furniture showroom. But he doesn't complain. He's in love with her, he'll put up with anything." Virginia smiled and shook her head. "The old fool," she added, kindly.

Bernard worked late at night—every night—and slept late in the morning. Aimee couldn't sleep past eight, and the only way she could get Bernard to come to bed before midnight was to make a bath for him, in the large, claw-footed tub, slip in behind him, and soap his broad, white back. He wouldn't return to his study after that.

He was sleeping late, as usual, this Sunday morning, and Aimee had already jogged her requisite three miles, gotten the paper and croissants, and showered before she woke him. She slipped, naked, into bed beside him and lay with half her body across his. His breath in the morning was usually a turnoff, so she avoided his mouth and instead left a trail of kisses from his ear across his cheek, down the side of his neck, settling her lips finally in the corner of his collarbone, the soft stretch of skin that, when she pressed against it, seemed to have nothing below it but air.

Bernard stirred in his sleep, woke, and smiled. He reached up one hand and stroked Aimee's head. The bottom edge of her hair was wet, and he knew she had just come from the shower.

"I wish you didn't have to go anywhere," she said. "I wish we could have the whole day together."

"We have most of the day," said Bernard. His hand moved down from Aimee's head to her shoulder, to her back.

"Three. You have to be there at three. That's the middle of the afternoon."

"Sh," said Bernard. He held her against him and moved his body back and forth so her small breasts rubbed against his chest.

"Where are you meeting?"

"Adam's."

"At least that's nearby."

"Sh," whispered Bernard. His hand progressed now to Aimee's buttocks. He cupped one cheek and then moved his hand towards the center, slipping his forefinger into the fold. He pressed against her anus. There was a moment when she began to relax and his finger started to push inside her, but her muscles tightened suddenly.

"I wanted to drive up to Cranford Orchards today," she said. "If you have to go to Adam's, then we better get going now or it won't be worth driving all the way up there."

Bernard opened his eyes. He patted Aimee and smiled. The erection, which he had nearly achieved, subsided, painlessly.

"All right," he said.

He didn't think Aimee did this consciously, but this wasn't the first time she had begun to arouse him on a Sunday morning only to withdraw, as if to punish him for the transgression he was about to commit: going to a meeting that she was excluded from, taking their weekend time, which she felt belonged to them rightfully as a couple, and using it for an activity that didn't include her. She had no concern about activities he was involved in during the week. She worked at an architectural design firm and put in long hours.

She also sometimes attempted to sabotage—well, perhaps that was too strong a word—influence? his going to the meeting. A romantic encounter on an early Sunday afternoon, so he might forget about the meeting entirely (he didn't) or an emergency that arose. Bernard never called her on this, never confronted it directly. He took her jealousy of his time away as a sign of her affection for him. He thought she was transparent, but he smiled at her in private, for he knew she would be furious if he pointed this out to her, would see it as a sign of his paternalism. He wasn't afraid of her, but he was afraid of her anger, which was the anger of a small person, sharp and intense.

At Cranford Orchards the trees looked almost artificial, the apples round and red against all the green, like ornaments that had been placed on the branches, that could not possibly have emerged from those brown, knotty stems.

"A jubilant sight," said Bernard as they stood on the edge of the gravel parking area, looking out at a hillside of apple trees.

"This would be a perfect place for a house," said Aimee. "Can you imagine?"

"If there were a house here, we wouldn't be able to stand here."

"You say that all the time," said Aimee, "whenever we're somewhere with a great view. But, Bern, wouldn't you like to wake up in the morning and step out on a deck off your bedroom and see this?"

"I like waking up in the morning in my bedroom at home and driving up here and standing with you and looking out at the view."

Aimee punched the side of his shoulder and started walking towards the farm-stand building. It was an old barn that had been turned into a seasonal shop, selling not just apples but, as Bernard described it, "all things apple," including apple pies, apple butter, pot holders and dishcloths with apple print fabric, wooden apple refrigerator magnets, and stationery with apple motifs. Bernard stood studying the barn siding while Aimee darted about in the shop. Bernard was impatient with anything that resembled a gift shop, but he loved the old building, the dark wood of the inside of the barn. He did not mind that Aimee covered every piece of wood in his house with a glare of white, but he missed the grain. The nature, the origin of all the trim details of his house—the moldings and mantels and window frames—was now completely hidden. It could have all been made out of plaster.

"Should we get a bag of Macouns?" asked Aimee.

"Whatever you like, my dear," said Bernard.

The question was somewhat rhetorical. Aimee already had the bag in her hand. In her other hand was a cluster of orange. She saw him looking at it and held it up, as if it were a bouquet.

"Japanese lanterns," she said, smiling.

"I know."

"We have just the vase for them."

Bernard nodded. He had no idea what vase she was referring to, had no idea about their stock of vases—some had probably always been in the house (Virginia took few things with her), several Aimee had brought to their marriage, and one he remembered they'd received as a wedding present from some relative of his, which had pleased

Aimee. They had been married by a justice of the peace in a small ceremony at home, and although Aimee had claimed at the time it was what she wanted, he sometimes wondered if she had secretly longed for a wedding with all the trappings and had hoped he would insist on it. The vase had come in an excessively large white box from some expensive store, and Aimee had opened it with excitement. He thought she saw it as a token that their union had been accepted by his family. But maybe he was reading something into it that wasn't there, maybe it was just that she had liked the vase for its clean, crystal lines, liked it for itself.

The woman at the cash register moved her eyes from Aimee to Bernard and back again. She was, no doubt, trying to ascertain their relationship. It had happened on several occasions that someone had mistaken them for father and daughter—even though they didn't look at all related, Aimee with her straight, nearly black hair and dark eyes and her small, taut body, and Bernard with pale eyes and curly hair that had once been blond, and a corpulent, puffy look. Aimee was particularly sensitive to this and at times like these would convey by a touch or a word something that put things straight.

Bernard started reaching into the back pocket of his baggy corduroy pants to extract his wallet, but Aimee quickly laid her credit card on the counter. "We're all set, dear," she said. Her voice said: *wife*.

The woman picked up the card and went about her business, and Bernard imagined what she might be thinking. His daughter, Rachel, had been fine about his marrying a woman closer to her age than Virginia's, but he hadn't forgotten her comment at the time.

"You'll just have to get used to people looking at you like a cradle robber," she'd said.

"It's only because Aimee looks young for her age."

"Aimee *is* young," Rachel said. "She's young enough to be your daughter."

"Not really," Bernard insisted.

"Daddy!" Rachel had cried, "do the math! Unless you were sexually retarded—"

"No," said Bernard.

"Well?"

"I concede your point," Bernard said. "You're not angry at me, are you, Peachie?"

"Of course not," said Rachel, and she kissed him loudly on the cheek. "You deserve to be happy. And Aimee's fine. Even Mommy likes her."

His son, Teddy, had been less generous. He refused to attend the wedding and, even before their more recent falling-out, adopted an injured, somewhat aggrieved air whenever they were together. Bernard guessed that Teddy thought Aimee had been seduced and pressured into marriage by Bernard (although it was quite the other way around) and that he ran her life. The rest of the world, Bernard was sure, viewed it that Aimee ran his.

Back at the house, Aimee arranged the Japanese lanterns in a clay crock Bernard wasn't sure he'd seen before (he was certain, however, that it was not the wedding gift vase) and set it on the mantel in the room she called the library. The orange was bright against the white wall.

"What do you think?" asked Aimee.

"I like them very much," said Bernard.

Aimee nodded, satisfied, and went back to the kitchen to lay out the luncheon food they had picked up at the deli on their way home. She had not been fishing for a compliment, Bernard knew this. Her question had been more pro forma.

Bernard stood for a while, looking at the Japanese lanterns. In the spare setting, their intricacy was remarkable. If they had been set on that mantel in the old house, they would have been lost in the midst of everything else. Bernard didn't share Aimee's taste, but he admired the conviction of it. He was more comfortable, aesthetically, with Victorianism than Modernism, but he didn't care enough about aesthetics to have it matter. And for Aimee it mattered greatly. She was passionate—obsessive, Bernard sometimes thought—about her surroundings, her ambiance. She'd redesign the world, if she could.

"Did you want me to heat up the bread?" Aimee called.

"No," said Bernard, heading to the kitchen. "It's getting late. I need to be leaving soon."

"It was your idea to buy all this," said Aimee.

That had been true, but it was only because Aimee had wanted to eat lunch in a restaurant and it had seemed it would take less time to pick up something and eat at the house.

Aimee had set the table in the bay window with blue place mats and blue napkins. Now she was placing the food on the glass plates. To his alarm he saw that two wineglasses had been set on the counter. He glanced at his watch surreptitiously.

"I don't think I'll have anything to drink," he said.

"We have a half-opened Pinot Grigio," said Aimee, and she went to the refrigerator and brought it out. "It would be so nice with the antipasto."

"All right," said Bernard. "A small glass, then."

He resigned himself to a more leisurely lunch than he wanted. Towards the end he suddenly remembered that he had promised Nancy he would meet her on Adam's front porch. Even if he left right now, he would be late.

He pushed back his chair and stood up.

"I need to go," he told Aimee. "Leave the dishes, I'll get them when I'm back." He leaned down and kissed her on the mouth before she could speak. "I'll be back before you know it," he said.

VIRGINIA

VIRGINIA DIDN'T DRIVE. SOMEONE OFTEN GAVE HER A RIDE home after the meetings, saving Joe a trip, but Joe always brought her there. Virginia had attempted to get a driver's license twice, when she was young, and both times she had failed. The first time it had been more the fault of the car, a broken emergency brake on a rusty Peugeot she had borrowed for the test. The second time, nervous after her aborted attempt, she had sailed through a stop sign without even touching her foot to the brake. She resigned herself to depending on public transportation or the men in her life to chauffeur her around. Bernard loved to drive, and during the decades they were married, the thought of her trying again to get a license never came up. Joe, who had not learned to drive till he was thirty-five, the consequence of growing up in New York City, where no one in his family owned a car, was an insecure driver. It was too late, Virginia thought, for her to try to get a license now. Highways frightened her, traffic made her nervous, and her night vision wasn't very good. So Joe chauffeured, stoically, pleased there was something he could do for Virginia.

They had not seen each other for fifty years when they met again, but that didn't mean they hadn't thought about each other. Joe had followed Virginia's career, bought multiple copies of all her books, read them with more care than even her editors, and written her an admiring note for each one. She treasured these notes. They were cautious and chivalrous, even after he was a widower and Virginia was divorced and there was no need for caution on either side.

They had gone to elementary school together, a progressive private school in Manhattan. The tuition had been a stretch for Joe's family. He was the only kid who had to commute from Brooklyn. Virginia's family was wealthy but bohemian, so even Joe hadn't realized at the time how rich they were. After sixth grade, they'd gone to different schools and lost touch. Joe had invited Virginia to his high school senior prom, but she was at a boarding school and hadn't been able to get to the city for it, although she had wanted to. Joe hadn't known that, had thought perhaps she hadn't really wanted to. But, oh, how she had wanted to!

"It's a miracle you're here," he told Virginia when she was seated beside him at the restaurant where their elementary school class had gathered for its reunion.

"No miracle," said Virginia. "You wrote, and made an excellent point. You said it was an event that would be unlikely to occur again. And"—she smiled—"you shamed me into it."

"Shamed you?" asked Joe.

"You made it sound as if you thought I might think myself too important to come to a reunion. Me, important! So to prove to you how ridiculous that notion was, here I am." Virginia raised her hand in emphasis, and the silver bangles on her wrist slid down and settled in a clump on the fatter part of her arm.

"I'm glad," said Joe.

"Besides," said Virginia, "I had to see what became of you."

"I went to graduate school in history," said Joe. "I ended up selling mattresses." He had flattened the white linen napkin that had been folded in a cone at his place, and now he tried, unsuccessfully, to restore it to its proper shape.

"Your family's business, right?" asked Virginia.

"You remembered that, Ginny?"

Nobody in her life now called her that. It was the name from her childhood, the name that was reserved for her family and for friends she had made before she went off to boarding school, where she was only "Virginia." Later, with her friends in college, she was sometimes called "Gin."

"I remember everything about you," said Virginia. "I was in love with you back then."

Joe looked up at her. And then, as if he might not trust the expression on his face, looked down again. He'd had a crew cut when they were in elementary school—all the boys did back then, they looked like shorn little military recruits. His hair was longer now, and grey. His eyebrows were still dark, exactly as she remembered them, thick and straight across his brow, which had given him a serious look, even when he was a little boy.

"But tell me more," said Virginia, gently. "I lost track of you after you left Columbia."

"When my father died, someone had to take over the business. There's money in mattresses, not just under them; that's what he used to say. Eventually I partnered with a British company. We made all-natural latex mattresses with wool toppings from sheep who ate only organic hay. Still, they were just mattresses."

Joe reached forward and lifted his wineglass. He took a long sip.

"After you got married—you see, I followed what you were up to—I eventually married, too. I had two sons. My wife died when the boys were in college. Recently I sold the business and retired. Now I read. I travel and I read. Mostly, I read."

Joe had been looking down at the table. He looked up now. "I knew you were divorced, and I thought about trying to get together with you, but—"

"Why didn't you?"

"Not brave enough, I guess. I didn't think you'd be interested." Joe gave a little laugh, then he paused before he spoke again. "I've never stopped being in love with you, Ginny," he said.

Virginia put her hand on his arm. "Let's get out of here," she said.

As they were ducking out of the restaurant, a heavyset man with a tuft of hair on either side of his otherwise bald head was just coming in. He grabbed Joe by the shoulders.

"Joey Sussman!" he cried. "I bet I'm right!"

Joe removed one of the man's hands from his shoulder, gave it a vigorous shake, and clapped him on the back.

"You're on!" he said. "Gotta go, though," and without giving the man a chance to recover, he pushed Virginia out ahead of him. They fled down the steps. He grabbed her hand, and they ran down the sidewalk to the corner, catching their breath while they waited for the light to change.

"Who *was* that?" asked Virginia.

"I think it was Barry—what was his name? The kid who was allergic to everything."

"Barry Din-something. Dinsdale?"

"Dinsdorf?"

"That's it!" said Virginia. She looked back towards the restaurant. "God, he looked old," she said. "We don't look that old, do we?"

"I don't know about *us*," said Joe, "but you look just the same."

Virginia was about to say something joking, but the light changed, and as they crossed the street they held hands tighter. They were walking north, and a wind was coming along the avenue. Virginia shivered, and Joe released her hand and put his arm around her. She ducked her head and leaned closer against him.

It was a Sunday evening and the street was nearly deserted. Halfway down the block they stepped into the entranceway of an office building so they were blocked from the wind. Virginia leaned back against the granite wall.

The last time they had kissed, it had been spin the bottle at a birthday party. For a second Virginia was back there, standing close to Joe in the dark of her parents' bedroom while the other kids were in the living room, sitting in a circle on the floor. But then she was here, with Joe, in a sheltered corner next to glass revolving doors stilled for the night, the wind sweeping up the avenue, tossing pages of an old newspaper along the sidewalk. She closed her eyes.

JOE PULLED UP INTO A SPACE by a fire hydrant in front of Adam's house. He had never mastered parallel parking, and he nosed into the space, the tail of his car sticking out farther than it should have.

"I'll be here to pick you up around five," he told Virginia. "Unless you call me if you get a ride."

"Thank you, darling," said Virginia. She had her hand on the car door handle and turned so that she could kiss Joe good-bye. The kiss, which had begun as a brief touch of lips to lips, slowed into a real kiss. Virginia let go of the door handle and put her arms around Joe's neck. His hands slid up under the back of her hair and held her head close against his.

"That's better," he said, when he released her.

Virginia gave him a quick kiss of farewell and got out of the car. She closed the door and stood on the curb watching until Joe had backed out into the street. He gave a toot of the horn as he drove away. Then she turned towards Adam's house and started up the front stairs.

There was a woman waiting on the front porch. She was in her forties, Virginia guessed, with blond hair cut just below her ears. She looked at Virginia questioningly.

In an instant Virginia realized who she must be. "Are you trying to get to the meeting at Adam's place?" she asked.

"Oh, thanks, yes," the woman said. "I was supposed to be meeting Bernard here at three, but I don't think he's come."

Virginia laughed. "Bernard is never on time," she said. She held out her hand. "I'm Virginia," she said. "I was married to Bernard for twenty years. And you must be Nancy. He said he was bringing you today."

"Yes." Nancy took Virginia's hand. They clasped rather than shook. Virginia remembered Bernard telling her that Nancy wasn't married but had a relationship with someone who traveled a lot. Gillian won't like her, she thought, but Chris will.

"Stay right here," said Virginia. "I'll go rap on Adam's window so he can let us in. The buzzer doesn't work."

Virginia disappeared down the steps and around the side of the building. She was back in a moment. And soon the door was unlocked and Adam held it open. He was a tall, solid young man with a lot of hair and heavy-framed glasses, which might have been either entirely out of date or highly in style.

"This is Nancy," said Virginia. "Bernie's late as usual and she was left standing here waiting for him."

"It wasn't long," said Nancy. "And then you came to my rescue."

"I'm Adam," said the young man. He didn't hold out his hand. "Come on in."

Adam's apartment was half of the first floor of a house that had once been an elegant single-family residence. It had suffered numerous indignities since, including the partitioning off of its larger rooms to divide into apartments, the removal of its stained-glass windows (sold to an antiques dealer), and the covering of its beautiful painted ceilings with acoustical tiles. Nancy followed Virginia back to the living room while Adam went to put a piece of wood in the outside door to prop it open till everyone had arrived.

The living room looked, at first glance, like a typical graduate student's lair, but the two armchairs were Stickley. Virginia wasn't a fan of Mission furniture, but she knew that it had no doubt cost Adam a big chunk of his salary. He came from a working-class family; this was not stuff he would have inherited.

Virginia led Nancy towards the window, where Gillian was standing, wineglass in hand, looking out. Her braid of hair reached far below her waist, and Virginia resisted an urge to give it a tug. Gillian turned as she heard them approach.

"Gillian, this is Nancy, Bernard's new recruit," she said.

"Oh, yes," said Gillian. "I'm Gillian Coit. Pleased to meet you."

"We've already met," said Nancy. "At the Achesons', last Christmas."

"Oh," said Gillian. She looked perplexed.

Virginia hadn't expected they would hit it off. Now she was sure of it.

"In fact, we'd actually met once years before that," said Nancy. "We were both guests at a writing festival at the University of Michigan."

"I'm so sorry," said Gillian. "I chose not to remember much about that time. I got caught in a snowstorm on my way home and had to spend a night in the Atlanta airport."

"The perils of holding writing festivals in the winter," said Virginia. "Is Chris here yet?" she asked Gillian in an attempt to change the subject.

"He's back in the kitchen, I think," she said.

"That's where the drinks are," said Virginia. "Why don't we go get something?"

"Sure," said Nancy.

In the kitchen, Chris was wrestling with a corkscrew. He put the bottle down on the counter to shake Nancy's hand. He was a man many women found attractive, though Virginia didn't. He was tan and smooth shaven, and smelled like a cologne that was advertised in a scented strip inserted in an issue of *The New Yorker*. Virginia had called the magazine to complain.

"So, you're the replacement candidate for Helene," he said.

"Helene?" asked Nancy. "Who's Helene?"

Virginia tried to give Chris a look, but he refused to make eye contact with her. "Helene Spivack," she said. "She had been a member."

"She died," said Chris, bluntly. "Lung cancer."

"I see," said Nancy.

"Bernie didn't tell you?" asked Virginia.

Nancy shook her head.

"I'm sorry," said Virginia. She would have to talk to Bernie about this. She wondered what else he hadn't told Nancy.

"Wine?" asked Chris, holding up a bottle.

"There's coffee and tea," said Virginia.

"I wouldn't mind a cup of tea," said Nancy.

"Help yourself," said Virginia. She gestured towards the electric kettle, some boxes of tea bags, and a collection of mugs sitting on the counter. They were all injured in some way, chipped or stained. Nancy selected one with an image of Charlie Chaplin and made herself a cup of tea.

"I hear Bernard," said Virginia. "I guess we'll be able to start."

They headed back into the living room. Bernard greeted Virginia with a kiss on the cheek. He took Nancy's hand and clasped his other over it.

"I hope you'll forgive me for my tardiness," he said.

"Of course," said Nancy.

"It's all right, Bernie," said Virginia. "Nobody expects you to be on time. Nancy will learn like the rest of us."

Bernard seemed genuinely surprised. "I didn't realize it was per-ceived as a chronic flaw," he said.

"Don't look so sorrowful," said Virginia, and she slipped her arm into his. "We love you just the same."

And she did love Bernard. Not the way she loved Joe, and not the way she'd loved Bernard when they were young and newly married. Then, she had loved him fiercely. She'd loved him, but she'd also been infuriated by him. He had been verbally passionate, but in bed he was lethargic. He was pompous, babyish about basic things, impractical, slovenly, and selectively unworldly. Oh—the list went on. But now that she was no longer married to him, now that she was happily married to Joe, the love she felt for Bernard was undamaged by frustration. Everything she didn't like about Bernard was Aimee's to deal with. No marriage counseling could have ironed out all their difficulties as a couple as neatly, as successfully as their divorce and realignment had done.

In the living room Bernard sat on the sofa with Nancy, Virginia took the chair beside him, and Gillian positioned herself across from them. Adam pulled two more chairs up to the circle.

"Perhaps it's time for us to get going," said Gillian. "Chris," she called into the kitchen, "could you honor us with your presence?"

Chris came into the room and took the chair next to Gillian's, sliding it close so the wooden arms touched. "Here I am," he said.

Virginia looked at Nancy's face to see her reaction, but Nancy had her eyes on Bernard.

NANCY

NANCY SETTLED BACK INTO ADAM'S SOFA AND SET HER CUP on the table at the side. The sofa was covered in a paisley print spread that looked like a remnant from the seventies. She could almost smell the marijuana of her youth in the fabric.

Nancy had brought part of the manuscript of her novel, but she immediately realized it was a mistake: she was not going to be asked to read any of it. She tucked the tote bag in close against her feet. She didn't want anyone to know how presumptuous she'd been. This was the first time any part of the novel had been out of her house, and it seemed defenseless, vulnerable. She pressed her calves against the tote bag, sheltered the pages inside between her legs and the skirt of the sofa.

She wished now that she had taken a glass of wine. The warmth of the tea was comforting in her hands, but seeing Gillian in the chair across from her, her long fingers banding the stem of her wineglass, made Nancy feel like a kid in comparison, clutching her clunky mug.

Bernard might have explained to Nancy how things worked, how they took turns in a particular order, presenting their work, but he hadn't. One more thing he had failed to do. He passed around copies of his manuscript, a chapter from a biography he was writing on George Frideric Handel. Handel was, Nancy thought, a perfect subject for Bernard, an anglophile who liked the Baroque period so much he once tried to learn (without great success) the viola da gamba. The pages were not clipped, and there was a general flurry of papers.

"Good God, Bernie," said Virginia, "it would be nice if you gave us something more manageable." On the opposite side of the paper was what was obviously a draft of another manuscript of Bernard's, so that the words of one were soaking into the words of the other. Stereo Bernard. Bernard had won acclaim, though not enormous financial compensation, for two previous biographies. Nancy admired his writing, though she would never have read either by choice. The study of John Donne was sufferable, but a ponderous tome on the philosopher Hegel?—please!

Bernard began reading aloud from his chapter while people scribbled in the margins. His voice had the timbre of a voice-over on a radio commercial. It could make anything sound better, being read with that authority.

> Though it is unquestionably logical to consider deafness as the sensory loss of greatest tragic dimension for a composer—and how could we not, with the image so imprinted on us all of Beethoven, in a near rage of desperation, churning out a torrent of music while struggling with his deafness?—for a composer artist like Handel, the loss of vision had a profound effect. We can hear his anguish in a note entered on the score of his oratorio *Jephtha* while he was immersed in composition: "Got as far as this on Wednesday, 13th February, 1751, unable to go on owing to weakening of the sight of my left eye."

Bernard paused in his reading and looked around at the group. He leaned forward and took in an unnecessarily large breath. "Unable to go on!" he repeated, emphasizing the words even more dramatically than when he first read them, his freckled, high forehead shiny with the sweat of his exertion. "Think of that!" he implored them, before turning back to his manuscript.

> Enforced separation from the visual world would be an impairment
> of serious consequence for any musician, but to a composer like

Handel, so connected to and inspired by his observations of the world, it could be catastrophic. Think for a moment of the visual necessity behind one of the most admired of his works, *Music for the Royal Fireworks* (written only several years before the impending blindness), music written to accompany a display that was created specifically as an entertainment for the eyes.

"If we had this ahead of time," said Gillian when Bernard was finally done, "we'd be able to give it more than a cursory reading."

"Nobody's got that kind of time, Gillian," said Chris. "Maybe you do, but I sure as hell don't." He was a man who was just short of being handsome, Nancy thought. A bit too heavy in the face.

"You'd make the time," said Gillian.

"We've discussed this ad nauseam," said Virginia. "We're not going to change things now. Can we just move ahead for the moment?" She looked around for confirmation. It was obvious to Nancy that Adam was the least important one of them. He nodded, but nobody looked at him.

"Of course, let's go on," said Gillian. "We always do."

Nancy could see Virginia begin a retort, then stop herself.

"Before we do," said Bernard, "I beg your indulgence for a moment. Adam, if I may make use of your equipment—" Bernard had produced a CD from his bag and was making his way over to Adam's bookcase. "I want you all to be able to fully appreciate the significance of the theory I've been developing."

"What is this?" asked Gillian. "Show-and-tell time?"

Bernard held up his palm. "Two minutes, just the fourth movement, 'La Réjouissance,' from the *Fireworks Music* is all I ask you to listen to," said Bernard.

"Please," said Gillian. "I'm sure we've all heard it before."

"But not in this context," said Bernard.

"Speak for yourself, Gillian," said Chris. "Why don't you just get on with it?" he asked Bernard. Which Bernard tried to do. It did not surprise Nancy that Bernard had difficulty working Adam's CD player and, after finally succeeding in inserting his disk, was unable to decipher, even with his reading glasses, the buttons on the remote. Adam came to his rescue and started the track. Bernard leaned back in his chair and, with an expression of beatific rapture, conducted with his two forefingers.

When the demonstration was over, Virginia flipped through Bernard's manuscript and began to comment. Chris followed, then Gillian, then Adam. They all started with some words of praise—that seemed to be the acknowledged format—before taking stabs at the manuscript. When they were through they turned, almost in unison, to Nancy.

She hadn't been sure she actually would be participating in the discussion, that they would ask her opinion this first time, but she had made some notes. She began as they had, with some general words of praise. "I wonder, though, about that line about Beethoven," she said. "It's, perhaps, a touch hyperbolic, but more important, I think it draws our attention away from Handel. Beethoven sort of eclipses him here." She said this cautiously, watching Bernard's face as she spoke. She was afraid he might be affronted. In fact, it was quite the opposite; he looked around at the others as if he were the proud parent of a child who had just said something clever, as if she had lived up to his recommendation.

"Beethoven does have the capacity of eclipsing everyone. I will see to it that he doesn't." He smiled at Nancy.

What she hadn't realized until this moment was that she was on trial. She had thought she had been invited to join them, and hadn't realized that this was just a meeting where they were going to look her over and then decide whether she would be invited back. She would never have consented to come on those terms, never have subjected herself to such humiliation if she had known. She wanted to get up and collect her coat and walk out on them. She pictured herself doing this, her tote bag close against her hip, but she didn't move.

Gillian's turn was next. She passed out a poem, apologizing that she had forgotten Nancy would be coming and had made only five copies.

"No problem," said Bernard. "We'll look on together." He moved closer to Nancy; the foam in the pillow cushion contracted under his weight. He crossed his leg and rested the pages on his knee.

The poem was in six parts. Gillian read in a whispery voice, her chin held up, like a heron holding something in its beak. The point of the poem eluded Nancy, and she didn't get many of the allusions, but there were lines that were rich and intelligent, so it was impossible to dismiss the poem as merely pretentious. Nancy had never read a collection of Gillian's poems, but she had read selections from them that had been included in reviews. She had read them looking forward to finding fault, but the fault she found was her own inadequacy, not the poems'. Still, Gillian could be more accessible if she chose. Instead, she had indulged herself in exclusivity. She wrote to please no one, wrote for no audience. Nancy admired this. In her own work, she wrote for herself first, but she also had a desire to please, befriend the reader, make the reader see things her way.

When it came her turn to comment, she chose to simply praise something she found to praise, an image that she could make sense of:

When all flesh and fat is gone
dolphin's sleek skin, ship's white sails
only bones remain:
the secret, ineffable structure

She could tell, in a second, that she had confused Gillian, thrown her off. Nancy guessed that Gillian had been prepared to dislike her, yet she was as vulnerable to praise as anyone. Nancy knew she had disarmed Gillian, outmaneuvered her.

When Adam's work was discussed next—a novel that involved a young American businessman and a Russian woman who might or might not be a prostitute—Nancy felt she was on safer ground. Adam's novel was probably brilliant, but it was verbose, and verbosity is an easy thing to point out. Adam's naïveté, his effusiveness, his insecurity were so palpable that Nancy felt a protective urge towards him. He was in love with everything he wrote, and Nancy could see he suffered viscerally at the mere thought of cutting or revising. She put her suggestions as delicately as she could, making sure that her praise was extreme, her criticism paltry. Even so, she could see Adam cringe under the weight of it. Clearly, he had been told to hack away at his prose many times before. He looked up at her, and his eyes were so large and brown, his lashes girlishly long, his mouth held firmly against any betrayal of emotion.

"Sonia is fascinating," she said in conclusion. "She's not like any character I've ever met before. I want to read more about her."

Adam swallowed and gave a little nod.

"Well," said Virginia, "that's such a nice note to end on. I suggest we stop here."

"I'm on for next week," said Chris.

"Yes, Chris," said Gillian, "we know."

Everyone stood and began gathering their papers, but Nancy saw that she was the only one actually leaving. They had planned to stay and talk about her after she was gone, but Bernard had neglected to tell her that, too. To spare herself further humiliation, she pretended that she had known this all along.

Bernard walked her to her car, but it was obvious he was going back in to join the others.

"Virginia says I have bungled dreadfully," he said. "I should have explained."

"Don't worry, Bernard," said Nancy. "It's okay. I get it. No need to explain."

"I just find all this rather awkward, you know. And don't worry, I'm absolutely certain there will be no question about everyone wanting you. You're first rate, you know."

"I know," said Nancy, smiling.

"Of course you may not want to be part of us, now that you've seen us, seen who we are and all the foolishness we're prey to." He waited for a moment, expecting forgiveness? Nancy wondered, but she didn't say anything.

"Good-bye, now, Nancy," he said.

"Good-bye, Bernard." She had her hand out, ready to give it to him, but he took her face in his hands and kissed her on both cheeks. That European double kiss, the artfulness of it, made it seem even more formal than a handshake.

It was a cool afternoon, cooler, too, now that the sun was going down. She turned on the heater of her car and sat with the engine running, and looked across the street. She could see the heads in the lighted window of Adam's living room. Virginia had her back to the window. Her hair was dyed black, and although it wasn't visible at this distance, Nancy knew there was a small balding patch on the top of Virginia's head.

They were there, inside the warm living room, discussing her. Her spot on the sofa was empty, but they would each be picturing her among them still, as they talked about whether they wanted her to continue with them or not. Bernard, yes; Virginia, yes; Adam, probably yes. Chris, she had no idea. And Gillian? Nancy guessed that Gillian did not want her but would have difficulty coming up with a legitimate reason to vote against her. Did it have to be unanimous? Nancy had no idea. With votes like this, there were always surprises. Someone whom she had been counting on for support would turn out to be harboring resentment towards her. And someone whom she had felt was an enemy would prove to be a supporter.

She was angry that she had given them the right to judge her. In a second of empowerment, she decided that if they offered her membership, she would turn them down. But just as quickly she knew that she would not. If they asked her to join, she would be flattered and honored.

Hating herself for being this way, she shifted the car into drive and pulled out into the street. All the way home she switched from one radio station to another, unable to find anything interesting enough to distract her from her thoughts. Back at the house, she called Oates, knowing she would get his voice mail but wanting to hear the sound of his voice. She left a message. Then she called Aliki, at college.

"Hey, you've reached my cell. You know what to do," said the message. Nancy hung up quickly.

She took the folder with the pages of her novel out of her tote bag and laid it on her desk. She read over the pages she had brought with her, read them to herself as she would have read them aloud. They were hers still, unshared, private. No one there knew what she was writing about. No one knew about the young doctor leaving the hospital late at night, looking up at the window of the room where there was a dead baby.

Out behind her house, on the darkening riverbank, Nancy closed her eyes and listened to the water move past. *Daddy, Daddy, Daddy,* she thought.

NANCY EXPECTED BERNARD TO CALL HER, but he didn't. He drove by and came rushing up to the front door, the door that almost no one ever used.

"I have been asked to invite you to be part of the Leopardi Circle," he said.

"Leopardi Circle?"

"It's what we call ourselves, strictly among ourselves, of course," said Bernard. "Helene bestowed the name on us. She was an Italophile and loved Leopardi." In response to Nancy's blank stare he added, gently, "Leopardi, the poet."

Nancy smiled as if she might have known.

"Will you give us the honor of joining us?" asked Bernard.

"I think I will," Nancy said. But as his face began to register relief, she asked, because she felt she had to, "Tell me, though, was it unanimous?"

"Everyone is onboard, Nancy," he said firmly.

"Only someone—or perhaps more than one—needed a little persuasion?"

"There are some people who always require persuasion," said Bernard. "That's the way they operate. But everyone is terribly enthusiastic about having you be part of us."

"Thank you, Bernard," she said. "You're a good soul." And she kissed him European style, on both of his cheeks, high enough on his face so her lips touched pink, hairless skin, and not the grey beard below.

$\mathcal{P}$AUL

PAUL TRAUB, GILLIAN'S STEPSON, WAS WAITING FOR HER TO pick him up outside the ice hockey rink. Ordinarily his dad picked him up after Sunday practice, but his dad was on call at the hospital this weekend and Gillian had said she'd do it. He should have known she'd be late. He just hoped she hadn't forgotten. When his friend Mike—the only friend he'd made this miserable year at The Academy—had been picked up, Mike's mother had offered him a ride, but he'd assured her he didn't need one. It was a toss-up: risk being stuck here if Gillian had forgotten or taking the ride from Mike's mom and having Gillian show up after he left. He chose the former. If Gillian turned up and couldn't find him, his dad would give him hell.

Paul called the house, but no one was home. He guessed Gillian was coming straight from something else—those writers she hung out with on Sundays. Anyone else—anyone else who was normal, that is—would have a cell phone. But Gillian refused to own one, refused to even use one. How the hell was he supposed to get in touch with her if there was no place to call her?

It was getting cold, and Paul pulled the hood of his sweatshirt up over his head. When he'd dropped him off in the morning, his dad had asked, "No jacket?" and he'd said, "Naw, don't need one," and it had ended there. If it had been his mother, there would have been an argument and she would have pushed his jacket at him as he got out of the car. As for Gillian, she didn't notice what he wore, and if she did she didn't have any opinions about it. Or maybe she did have opinions, but she didn't express them. It was hard to tell. She didn't comment about much of anything he did. He liked that, mostly, but sometimes it seemed weird, too. Sometimes he missed his mother's constant intrusion, constant worrying—obsessing, yes, that's what it was, obsessing—over every detail of his life. He stepped back into the doorway to get out of the wind. He was afraid to go inside in case Gillian drove up, didn't see him, and drove away. He couldn't imagine she'd actually get out of the car to look for him.

Mr. O'Connor, who ran the ice arena, came out with a bunch of keys in his hand. "You still here?" he asked.

"Just waiting for my ride," said Paul.

"I'm turning out the lights now, locking up," said Mr. O'Connor. "You going to be okay?"

"Sure," said Paul. "They'll be here any minute." The word *they* was a nice, neutral word.

Mr. O'Connor was a red-faced man who, Paul had heard, had once been a professional hockey player but who looked as if he hadn't done anything athletic in a few decades. He seemed to like Paul, but Paul didn't know why. He didn't know why anyone would ever like him.

"I'll be heading over to Morse Hall after I'm done closing up here. So if you get stuck, come by and find me."

"Thanks, Mr. O'Connor," said Paul. Maybe Mr. O'Connor felt sorry for him. Maybe everyone did.

Paul watched the lights go out in the high windows of the arena. Mr. O'Connor came out and locked the doors behind him.

"See you later," he said, and he waved at Paul.

"See you later," said Paul. He watched Mr. O'Connor walk across the street. There were few cars coming at this time on a Sunday, so he didn't go down to the crosswalk, just darted across the road as students were never supposed to do. Paul thought he might turn back and wave again, but he didn't. He just raised his collar to the wind and kept walking.

The hockey rink was at the far end of the campus, and the campus now looked like a small, tidy village in the distance, with the chapel bell tower at the center of the green. It looked idyllic, as it did in the photographs in the brochure they sent out to prospective students. The buildings farther around on the campus were in a variety of styles, some modern, some just plain ugly, but the four original buildings around the quadrangle were Federal style, brick, lined up like officers in a military formation.

The Academy was a school that was half boarders, half day students, and Paul envied the boarders, not so much their being at The Academy 24/7 but their freedom from their families, and all that entailed. He'd never have been admitted as a boarder, though—those places were competitive and limited—and it was only because Gillian had connections—she'd been a guest writer there once—that he'd gotten in at all. If he stuck around for eleventh and twelfth grades, he'd want to be a boarder, for sure.

But it didn't look as if he'd be there next year anyway, so it didn't matter. He was pretty sure his mom would take him back, once she got over being so hurt that he'd chosen to spend this year with his dad and Gillian. But, hey, he might not have any choice anyway; his dad might decide he wouldn't keep him for another year even if he wanted to stay. It all depended on Gillian, what she wanted, Paul knew that much. And he couldn't tell about Gillian. Sometimes she was really nice to him, and sometimes she was kind of mean. Mostly she didn't seem to notice him that much. They lived in the same house, but sometimes she seemed surprised by his presence.

Dried oak leaves blew across the parking lot, their pointed ends clawing across the pavement. Paul pulled his sleeves down over his hands. He imagined his dad getting home this evening and asking Gillian, "Where's Paul?" and Gillian looking vague and confused and saying something like "Paul? I have no idea," and his dad realizing it had been stupid of him to count on her to pick him up. By the time his dad got here, he'd be frozen, dead. Or maybe Mr. O'Connor would have come back to the building because he'd forgotten something and found his body just in time. Or maybe not. His mom would scream at his dad that it was all his fault. And although it was really Gillian's fault, his dad would never yell at her. He never yelled at her about anything, just sometimes shook his head as if he should have known better.

Just then Paul recognized Gillian's black pickup truck coming into the parking lot. It slowed by the entrance to the arena, and Paul leaped towards it and got in.

"You'd expect they'd leave some lights on," said Gillian. "I almost drove past here."

"They turned them off when everyone left, after practice," said Paul.

Still Gillian didn't get it. She obviously didn't have any idea what time she was supposed to pick him up. No idea how long he had been waiting. No idea how cold it was.

"Your father certainly pays enough to this elite establishment," said Gillian. "They could spend some of it on electricity."

In the dark of the car, Paul looked at Gillian's profile. Almost as if she sensed his eyes on her, she turned to him, and gave him a small smile. He couldn't help himself; he smiled back.

"Were you waiting for me very long?" she asked.

"It's okay," said Paul. And, strangely, he meant it. It was okay. Because she did come. Because she hadn't forgotten him. Because—because she smiled.

"You were, weren't you?" asked Gillian.

"It wasn't that long," said Paul.

"I'm so sorry," said Gillian. She leaned forward and touched the side of his cheek with three fingertips. Then she pulled out into the road.

"Once, when I was a child, I was waiting for my father to pick me up after a school play," she said. "I waited until it got dark, but he never came, and I walked home. I was used to it. My father often didn't turn up for things. It was a considerable walk, and as I walked my anger grew. When I got home, I discovered he had been taken to the hospital with a kidney stone attack, and I felt guilty, as if my anger had in some way contributed to his suffering. Guilt, the most complex of emotions." Gillian was quiet for moment. Then she added, softly, "Do you know I've never told anyone else about this before."

Paul wasn't sure what to say, so he didn't say anything. He didn't know what to make of the story itself, how it connected to Gillian's being late this time—she hadn't offered him an excuse, and certainly she wasn't in the hospital. He also didn't know what to make of her confidence. It wasn't the first time she'd told him something she said she'd never told anyone else. Her confidences were like gifts, and whatever irritation he had felt towards Gillian disappeared.

Gillian didn't seem to expect an answer. She turned on the CD player. "Vivaldi's *Gloria*," she said.

They drove home listening to *Laudamus te*—he knew it was Latin, but he wasn't sure what it meant. The music pumped inside him, shook his bones. He felt, as he had on the previous occasions, privileged by her confession, and also unworthy of it. No one else in his life talked to him the way Gillian did. No one else talked like her at all.

THE NEXT MORNING, Monday, when Paul and his dad, Jerry, were eating breakfast together, his dad set aside the newspaper and asked him about hockey practice.

"I'm still the worst one on the team," said Paul.

"I wasn't even good enough to make it on a team," said Jerry.

"It's not like they pick people for the team," said Paul. "Everyone is put on some team. It's like gym."

"Even so," said Jerry. "You know what you're doing out there. I've seen you play."

"Even a moron can know what they're doing in hockey," said Paul.

Jerry looked at Paul over the top of his reading glasses. "Maybe so, but let me tell you, not everyone can stay upright on those tricky skates."

Paul didn't tell his father that Gillian had been late picking him up. There was no point in it. Early that morning, even before he'd left for school, Gillian had driven off to her house on Cape Cod. She did this a lot—went off to write, either on the Cape or at various writers' colonies. Jerry was always depressed when she left. He didn't usually eat breakfast with Paul, but this morning he seemed eager for Paul's company.

When Gillian returned from her writing retreats, Jerry was shamelessly happy. He'd bring home a bunch of flowers and set them in the vase on the side table, a vase that Paul's mother had noticed once when she dropped Paul off and said, "So that's where that vase went. I thought it had gotten broken when we sold the house, but I guess your father had it all these years."

Jerry would cook a fancy dinner, humming to himself while he stirred pots on the stove, splattering the glass stove top with tomato sauce and wiping it off with a sponge so the water hissed. Once he'd had dinner all ready and then Gillian had called to say she wasn't coming home that night.

"She's involved in working on something, and if she takes a break from it she'll lose it," Jerry said. His voice had no anger in it, just a touch of disappointment. It wasn't so much that he resigned himself to the tyranny of Gillian's poetry but that he encouraged it. He protected Gillian's writing time and inspiration as much as he protected Gillian herself. Paul and Jerry ate the dinner in the den that night while they watched a movie, and when Gillian got home, two days later, she and Jerry went out to eat.

A small van picked Paul up in the morning and brought him back from school in the afternoon. The only problem was, when there was a late after-school activity, he needed to get a ride. If Gillian was gone for the week and Jerry couldn't get him, Paul had to get a classmate's parent to give him a ride. He was already indebted to too many of them.

Monday, Paul got home a few hours before his father. Jerry called to say he would pick up Chinese takeout on his way home and asked Paul to phone in the order. Paul found the menu in the drawer in the kitchen and was looking through it, trying to decide between moo-shi pork and moo-shi chicken, when the phone rang again.

"Is this Gillian Coit's home?" asked a male voice.

"Uh-huh."

"May I speak with her?"

"She's not here," said Paul.

"This is Adam Freytoch, a friend of hers. Who's this?"

"Paul."

It was obvious that Adam didn't recognize the name, so Paul added, "Her stepson."

"Oh. Do you know when she'll be back?"

"Not for a few days," he said.

"She left something here at my house after a meeting on Sunday. Know how I can get in touch with her? I know she doesn't have a cell phone."

"She's gone to the Cape," said Paul. "There's a phone at the house. I could give you that number if I can find it."

"That would be great," said Adam.

The number, in his dad's handwriting, was written across the front page of the leather address book Paul found in the drawer. It said "Cottage:" and the phone number. Gillian called it her cottage, but in fact it was more like a house.

Paul read the number off to Adam.

"Do you know where it is exactly?" asked Adam.

"In Truro," said Paul. "I don't know the street. I don't think it has a street, just some dirt road. Kind of on a marsh I think."

He had been there only once, when he was younger, when Gillian and his dad had gotten married. He and his dad and his sister, Jennifer, had stayed in a motel and then gone to the house for the wedding.

Jennifer had cried the whole time. That's what he remembered most: Jennifer crying, and his dad getting pissed at her and finally yelling, "Enough! Stop, please," and Jennifer saying, "You can't make me!" He had to go get her out of the bathroom when it was time for the ceremony. The house was really old, and there was a moldy smell in the bathroom. There were vases of lilacs everywhere, and the house smelled of lilacs, but there was still a moldy smell in the bathroom.

"Well, thanks," said Adam. "If she calls, please let her know that I'm trying to get in touch with her. Tell her she left a folder by the side of her chair. I'm sure she'll want it."

"Okay," said Paul. "But she usually doesn't call."

GILLIAN

THE DIRT ROAD THAT LED TO GILLIAN'S HOUSE RAN PERIL-
ously between a steep hillside and the edge of a marsh. It was so
narrow and so tortuous and so desolate that no one who didn't know
for sure would believe that there was a house at the end of it, that it led
to anywhere. Gillian could have driven it blindfolded. She knew the
curves, the ruts, the rocks, the soggy places where a tire would get
stuck. No one could find her here, unless she wanted to be found.

Gillian avoided driving on highways, and this morning, as she so
often did, she took back roads on her way to the Cape, even though it
added hours to her trip. When she finally got to Truro, the tide was
out. She opened the car window and sucked in the smell as she drove
along the dirt road. Her little house was there, waiting for her as always. She stepped out of the truck and leaned against the fender, taking in the scene, holding herself back from entering it, as if not wanting
to break a spell. The house was set in a hollow, cupped by hills on
three sides. It faced the marsh squarely. Door in the center, two windows on each side, and a squat brick chimney. There were twelve panes
of glass in each window, and the sun, now low in the sky, glinted on
selected panes, turning them into mirrors.

"Hello, Button," Gillian said. It was her secret name for the house,
short for Buttonfield, a name only Jerry knew. Houses on the Cape often sported nautical names, names referring to wind or sea or mist. If
she were to give her house a public name, it would have to be something

literary, a pun or allusion, but she found such cleverness wearisome. People in town simply called it "that house on the marsh." When she was growing up, she lived near a field where a button factory had once stood. The kids called it the buttonfield, because they sometimes found buttons among the weeds. When Gillian was young, she imagined that buttons grew on plants and fell, when ripe, like seedpods. The smaller children believed her when she told them this. It might make good material for a poem, but she had never used it. She did not like to mine her childhood. She did not like to mine much of her personal life either—although she was happy to make use of what she heard of others'.

Gillian had never had a room to herself when she was young, and Button was not just a room, but an entire house. She and Jerry owned the other house together, but Button was all hers. In the rural New Hampshire town where she'd grown up, the restored antique houses were owned by wealthy people who lived elsewhere and just vacationed there. People like her family were left behind to make it through the bleak winter in houses that were just plain old. Here, in Truro, she was the one to come and go, whenever she pleased.

Gillian unlocked the front door and pushed against it with her shoulder to get it to open. Inside, everything looked exactly as she had last left it. She walked the downstairs circle of rooms around the center chimney: living room, dining room, kitchen, and study. The study was painted a pale blue, the color the sea is in children's paintings but never in real life. There were two bedrooms upstairs, but she wouldn't go up there. When she was at the house alone, she slept on the daybed in the study. She pulled off the white sheet that covered it and tossed it on the floor. She turned the thermostat up and waited until she heard the furnace turn on. The new heating system was one of the few alterations she had let Jerry make to the house. She'd had to admit that it was magical to be able to come to the house and have it warm within hours.

Before she carried in anything from the car, she walked to the edge of the marsh and looked out across it, towards the bay. A strip of low dune separated the marsh from the bay and obscured the house's view of open water. The house would have been worth more than twice what it was if that sand were not there, but Gillian didn't mind. The idea of a view not seen, of something known about but denied was more interesting than an open view. And the marsh held more for her than the bay. Here, in her marsh, a great blue heron perched still as a tree stump. Here, it hunted, lifting each slender leg with the articulation of a dancer, then swooping so quickly to snatch its prey in its beak that her eye couldn't follow. Here the great blue heron lifted off into the sky, pumping its huge wings until the air received it, let it glide. It was her bird, her muse. It did not appear in all her poems, but it was often what got them going. It got one going now. The images swarmed in her mind, mixed with words, some evaporating before she could get a fix on them, others growing firmer, larger. For no reason whatsoever the word *avuncular* came to the foreground. "Avuncular," she said aloud, and she smiled. It wasn't a word that would take her anyplace. She let it go, and the word that took its place in her mind was *still*, with its double meaning. Triple meaning, actually, though she had no use for it as a noun. It was a word worth playing with; she needed to sit down with a pen in hand.

She carried her duffel bag and briefcase in from the car and made a second trip for the bag of groceries. She'd have to go to town to get food eventually, but she had brought enough so that could wait two days, at least. She always did her best writing when she first came to the house, when she had no contact with the outside world, when she could feel that she had slipped into this world unnoticed.

Gillian put the grocery bag on the counter and then noticed a trail of tiny black seeds. They weren't seeds, though, she realized, they were mouse droppings. She grabbed up the bag of groceries and set it down on the kitchen stool, then wiped the counter with a wad of wet paper towels. She opened the cabinet under the sink and was about to throw the paper towels into the plastic garbage can when she saw what was there: a field mouse lay curled up in death in the bottom of the can. It must have climbed in, looking for food, and been unable to get out. Gillian screamed and slammed the cabinet shut with her knee. Her heart was thumping so wildly she could not move at first. She was shaky, but she was afraid to grab on to the edge of the counter to steady herself, afraid to have her hand that close to the dead mouse. Breathe, she told herself, just breathe. She stumbled out of the room, out of the house, then broke into a run. At the edge of the marsh, she sank to the ground and huddled there, her arms around her knees. She stared out at the darkening marsh, working the view against the image she wanted to drive from her mind: the small creature who had circled frantically, struggled to scale the impossibly slick plastic walls, and died of hunger, thirst, exhaustion, loss of hope.

She didn't know what she was going to do. She'd driven all the way out here because she needed to be here to write. She was desperate to write. She couldn't just shut up the house and drive all the way back again. But she couldn't go into the kitchen again while the small corpse lay there, under the sink.

The only thing to do, she decided, was to close the door to the kitchen and camp out in the study. She'd have to go to town to buy food, but she could wait for that until morning. She had an apple in the car; that would get her through till then.

She stood up slowly and forced herself to go back inside the house. She closed the kitchen door without looking inside. From the phone in the study, she called Jerry. She expected to get his voice mail, and she did, but she had been hoping that miraculously he might answer. She wanted to talk to him so he would help calm her, but she could not have him paged for this: a dead mouse in the garbage can. And though she wanted to talk to him, she was afraid of what he'd say. He would tell her to come home. Impossible. Or, worse, he would tell her he would drive out and take care of it. He would drive all night, after getting someone to cover for him at the office the next day, after making arrangements about Paul. When he had arrived and taken care of the mouse, he'd start worrying about all the things he felt were wrong with the house—Jerry had no affection or patience for antique houses—and he'd worry about her staying here alone. When Christa Worthington, a single mother, had been murdered in her Truro house not that far away, Jerry had been nearly frantic when Gillian had stayed here. But Gillian had never been frightened in her house alone at night, even before the murderer—Christa's garbageman—had been found and brought to trial.

Gillian stood for a moment, phone in hand, when the obvious solution occurred to her: the handyman, Pete Ambrose, who drained the pipes and checked on the house in the winter. She got his answering machine and left a message.

As night approached, Gillian turned on all the lights. Usually she found the darkness in her house comforting. She liked the smell of the old pine paneling and the ash from the fireplace. She liked the texture of things, the velvet of chair coverings, the fuzzy mohair throw. But she needed lots of light now. The mouse in the kitchen expanded, bloated, in the confines of the garbage can.

Fortunately, there was enough wood for a fire. Gillian rolled sections of old newspaper and tied them in knots. She laid them in the fireplace, arranged kindling and logs on top. It took her three tries to get a corner of the newspaper to catch on fire, but soon it burst into orange, and for a moment the fire actually roared. They always called it a "roaring" fire, and yet she didn't think she'd ever heard that sound before.

Gillian got a pencil and a large pad of plain white paper from the desk, moved an armchair close to the fire, and sat there, tucking her feet up under her. Although she typed her poems up later, she always composed them by hand on unlined paper. Lines on paper were like prison bars. Now and then the stirrings of the logs in the fire sounded like the pattering of mice, but she was not afraid of live mice. Only dead ones.

When the phone rang, she sprang to get it. It had to be Pete. The phone was unlisted, and the only other person who had the number was Jerry. And this wouldn't be Jerry. She had trained him never to call unless she left a message asking him to. She said it infantilized her when he called to see that she had arrived safely, to check up on her. It ruined her concentration, her solitude, spoiled the whole point of her going away. "Assume I am alive and well enough, until you hear otherwise," she said.

She was so certain it would be Pete Ambrose calling that even when the caller said, "Hello, Gillian. It's Adam," she didn't focus on what he said.

"Thank God you got my message," she said.

"What?"

"Who is this?" she asked. Fear suddenly flooded her. It didn't sound like Pete's voice. Who was this man?

"It's me, Adam," he said. "Adam Freytoch."

"Adam?" she asked. "Why are you calling?"

"You left a folder at my house. Poems, handwritten. I thought you might be wondering what happened to them."

She realized she hadn't checked her briefcase when she got home from the meeting on Sunday. She hadn't known she was missing a folder of drafts of new poems, scraps and ideas she had no other copies of. How could she have left them there?

"How in God's name did you ever get this number?" she asked.

"Your son, Paul. I called your house."

"My stepson. He gave it to you?" Her voice rose.

"I told him I needed to get in touch with you." Adam said this as if he was afraid he had gotten the boy in trouble. She hadn't realized how angry she'd sounded.

"I see," she said.

"I'm here. I mean I'm out on the Cape. I brought them with me. I could drop them off for you."

"You're where exactly?"

"In Orleans. I have a friend out here."

"I'm not in Orleans," she said. "I'm in Truro."

"I could zip out there. No trouble," he said.

She did not believe for a moment that he had a friend in Orleans. Well, maybe he did, but he hadn't come out to visit a friend, that was just an excuse. He'd come out to return her poems to her. From the first, when he'd joined the Leopardi Circle, Adam had been obsequious. He'd been a prodigy of Helene's. Helene had convinced the others to take him on, and soon after, she had died, abandoning him among them. Gillian had always suspected he was infatuated with her, but he tried hard not to show it, sometimes being brusque and then apologetic for his brusqueness. He was young and awkward and sweet, and if he was in love with her, she was used to that. Every time she'd done a stint as a writer in residence, she'd acquired any number of admirers. Adam wasn't an MFA student anymore—he actually had a job, made a good living—but he still had a graduate student's demeanor. Once he got published—and she thought he had as good a chance as anyone of getting published—that would probably change. It usually did.

Gillian never invited anyone to Button, but the circumstances argued for an exception. First, Adam had her poems, and she couldn't bear to think of them being out of her possession, being touched by anyone else. And then there was the dead mouse. It was possible Pete wouldn't return her call for a long time. He might not even return it at all.

"Perhaps you could do me a small favor," said Gillian. "How are you with dead rodents?"

"What do you need done?"

"I need one to be buried," said Gillian.

"Buried?" said Adam. "Sure. No problem."

"It's very difficult to find this house," said Gillian.

"I'm great at finding places," said Adam. "Just give me directions and I'll get there."

"All right," said Gillian.

GILLIAN THOUGHT OF IT AS A LITTLE TRIAL. If Adam gave up and had to call her for additional help, that would be the end of it. She'd wait for Pete to come and deal with the mouse, and she'd leave her folder of poems with Adam until she saw him next.

But Adam did manage to find the house. She heard his car before she saw it, picking its way along the dirt road. Then the headlights darted out across the marsh. He pulled up beside her truck and walked up to meet her in the doorway, holding her folder out to her as an offering. She had forgotten how tall he was, tall enough so she didn't feel tall herself.

"You're really way out here," he said.

"Yes, I am."

Adam followed Gillian through the front hall into the study. She laid the folder on the desk beneath the window and smiled at him. "Thank you for bringing this," she said.

"My pleasure," said Adam. It obviously was. If she'd had any doubt about how Adam felt about her, she didn't now. The muscles in his neck tightened as he swallowed. A streak of sweat glistened along the side of his face.

"You're still willing to help out with the little problem in the kitchen?" she asked.

"Sure," he said. "It's no big deal. You want me to get rid of a dead mouse in a trap?"

Gillian shuddered. "It's in the garbage can," she said. "Under the sink. It died there. It must have fallen in and then not been able to climb out."

"I'll take care of it," said Adam. He had placed his hand on her shoulder, as if to steady her. "Just sit right here and it will be gone before you know it."

"The kitchen is around there," she said, pointing. "I closed the door."

He pushed her gently, and she sat on the footstool by the armchair. She felt a flicker of fear again when he left the room, wanted his hand back on her shoulder.

A few minutes later he called from the kitchen. "Can I go out through the back door?" he asked. "That way I won't have to come through the house."

"Yes!" she cried. "Do that."

"Is there a flashlight somewhere around here?" he asked.

"In the drawer to the right of the stove."

It seemed as if he was gone for a long time. She was glad the windows in the study didn't face behind the house so she couldn't see him carrying the mouse off. She heard him running water in the kitchen when he came back into the house. Washing the garbage can out, she thought, washing his hands.

When he returned to the study, he squatted beside her. "All done," he said.

"Did you bury it?"

"Not exactly. I dumped it back in the woods."

"Dumped it?"

"Don't worry. It's far away from the house and you'll never find it."

"Promise?" she asked.

"Promise," he said. She allowed him to take her head and press it against his chest. She allowed him to stroke her hair.

After a while he stood up. "Have you had any dinner yet?" he asked.

"No," she said. "I couldn't go into the kitchen."

"Do you have any food in the house?"

"I brought some."

"Would you like me to cook some dinner for you? I'm a great cook."

"Who says so?" Her voice was different now. Still soft as a child's, but with a hint of irony.

"Everyone says so," said Adam. "My girlfriend, my friends."

"You have a girlfriend?"

"Yeah, but it's not all that serious really. She doesn't live with me, and . . ."

Gillian smiled. "It's all right for you to have a girlfriend, Adam," she said. But she could tell from his face that he felt apologetic, as if this in some way compromised his presence here in her house.

"Come, let's go into the kitchen," she said. "I'll show you where things are and you'll cook for me. For us. I'd like that." She got up and started walking towards the kitchen, but she hesitated at the doorway.

"It's all right," said Adam. "There's nothing here." He opened the cabinet under the sink and tilted the garbage can to show her. She flinched.

"Please, close that," she cried.

Adam closed the door and patted it twice to show it was firm. He unpacked the food from the shopping bag. He put the rigatoni in a pot to boil, chopped vegetables, and sautéed them in olive oil. He made a salad. Gillian opened a bottle of wine and selected two glasses from the ceiling rack. She rinsed the dust off and set them on the counter so their rims touched. While Adam watched, she poured wine into both of them so they were exactly level. She lifted hers and took a sip.

"I don't believe in toasts," she said. When the Leopardi Circle met, Adam drank coffee rather than wine, but she guessed he would drink wine now. Neither of them said anything about him driving anywhere later that night.

The telephone's ring startled them both. Again, Gillian assumed it had to be Pete, but it was a woman's voice.

"Mrs. Coit?" she asked. "This is Marie Ambrose, Pete's wife. He's out of town until Thursday, but I can give you the number of somebody else to call if there's a problem with the house."

"Thank you so much," said Gillian. "But it's been taken care of. It was very considerate of you to call."

She hung up and smiled at Adam. "The handyman is out of town," she said. "I must have been prescient when I left that folder at your house."

Adam grinned. He seemed more sure of himself now. The cooking. Or maybe the glass of wine.

"Tell me about your girlfriend," Gillian said.

"What's to tell?"

"What does she do?"

"She's a senior, in college, going into comp sci." He noticed the question on Gillian's face. "Sorry, computer science."

"And her name?"

"Kim. Kimberly."

Gillian smiled. "I keep forgetting how young you are."

"What do you mean?"

"There was a time, not so long ago, when every baby girl was named Kimberly."

Adam poked at the slices of squash in the frying pan, flipped them so their browned sides were up.

"What does she look like, this Kim?"

Adam shrugged. "I don't know."

"You're a writer, Adam," said Gillian, leaning towards him. "You wouldn't say that about your character, Sonia."

"Hey, novels are different."

"Dark hair or blond?"

"Blond, I guess."

Gillian shook her head and laughed. "Hopeless," she said, and she rested her hand on his arm for a second. She went to set the table in the dining room. For some reason, the word *blond* had made her think of Nancy, and this was disquieting, just as the idea of Adam's girlfriend had been, though she wasn't sure why.

There was no electricity in the dining room, just candles, which she stored in a tin box to keep safe from mice. Mice would eat anything once winter came. For a moment she paused, silverware in her hand, fighting off the image of the small, still body in the bottom of the garbage can. *Still.* There was that intriguing word. The poem hardly begun. She'd gotten off track, allowed Adam to interrupt her. But she couldn't have been at peace in the house with something dead, right there in the kitchen. She inhaled the aroma of garlic. She needed a good dinner. She'd start fresh in the morning.

AFTER DINNER they brought their wineglasses and the bottle into the study. Adam rekindled the fire, and they sat by it in the armchairs, sharing the footstool between them. Adam's socks were red, woolly, with a handmade look. Gillian wondered if his girlfriend had made them, but she didn't ask.

"Tell me," she said. "What do you think of the new addition?"

"Nancy?"

Gillian nodded. Then she laughed. "You're still used to thinking of yourself as the newest member, aren't you? But now you're one of us old-timers."

"I guess you're right," said Adam, and he laughed, too. "I hadn't thought of it that way. Still, she's published two novels and I haven't published any."

"You've published short stories," said Gillian. "And as for Nancy, she hasn't published a novel for a long time."

"Yeah, well, so far my total earnings from my career as a short story writer are less than a hundred dollars, oh yes, and a few contributors' copies of some literary magazines."

"Writing isn't about making money," said Gillian. "As if you didn't know." She tapped the side of her foot against Adam's. Her socks were black cashmere. Ordinary wool made her toes itch.

"Designing sports shoes *is* about making money. And let me tell you, it sucks."

"You still haven't told me what you think about Nancy," said Gillian.

It was Bernard who had proposed Nancy to the Leopardis. Gillian would have preferred a man to a woman—she always got along better with men—but the two men proposed had been poets, and Gillian didn't like poets. She didn't like their desperate intensity, the impossibility of their dreams. She didn't want a poet less successful than herself because she didn't want to be resented. But she also didn't want a poet more successful (though there were very few who were) because she didn't want to feel jealousy. Jealousy sapped her emotion, took it away from her poetry. She'd gone along with Nancy as a gift to Bernard, and she made sure he knew it. Everyone had gone along with Nancy, except for Chris. Chris had nominated a friend of his who was a poet—not a real poet, more of a songwriter, guitar-strumming coffeehouse figure—but no one else supported him. Chris opposed Nancy, claiming she was "not a good fit," but Gillian thought it was out of pique, though in the end he bowed to the wishes of the others.

"Nancy seems nice," said Adam.

"Nice?" she asked. "Is that all you can say about her?"

"Okay," said Adam, smiling. "How's this: She's an agile critic, a keen observer, and a refreshing counter to Chris's self-importance. I found her affable."

As soon as Nancy had turned up at the meeting on Sunday, Gillian realized she'd made a mistake, but it was already too late. Nancy was small and tidy, and Gillian felt, as she often did in the presence of petite women, too tall; her feet felt too big. She studied Nancy, seeking some imperfection to fasten on, some way to reduce her, and her eyes had fastened on Nancy's ears. Nancy had attached earlobes, and they seemed to slide off the sides of her face. They made you think of flesh, in an unpleasant way, a clitoris that had been stunted in growth or, worse, amputated. Obtusely—or was it brazenly?—Nancy wore stud earrings and tucked her hair behind her ears, calling attention to them. If Gillian had had ears like that, she would have kept them covered by her hair.

"Affable, I'll buy that," said Gillian. "But please, Adam, she may seem affable, but you of all of us need to be a little wary of her."

"Why me?"

"Because you're the only other novelist."

"And Chris is what?"

"Correction, the only other literary novelist."

"So why should that matter?"

"You're young, you have a glittering future. First novels generate the kind of excitement that third novels never do."

"Soooo." Adam drew the word out. "Why should I be wary?"

"Because writers are inherently competitive. We're not supposed to be, we pretend we aren't, but we're actually vicious. Poets are the worst, of course, because we have to fight over the very few people in the world who read poetry, but serious novelists are just as bad. Nancy can't help but be jealous of you. She'll pretend to support you—she may even *believe* that she wants to support you—but she really can't bear to see you succeed."

Adam looked at Gillian. He laughed a little. "You make her sound ruthless."

"Not ruthless, just protecting her own work from the threat of competition. You just can't trust her, that's all."

"Can I trust you?" Adam asked.

"I'll leave you to decide that," said Gillian, smiling.

"Can I kiss you? Or rather, *may* I kiss you?"

"Do you ordinarily ask women if you can kiss them before you do so?"

"You're not an ordinary woman," said Adam.

"No," said Gillian, "I suppose not." She leaned forward a little in her chair so her long braid of hair was freed from the weight of her back and pulled it over her shoulder. She undid the elastic that was coiled around the end and took Adam's hand and slipped the elastic onto his wrist. She slowly unbraided her hair, leaning towards the fire as if she were opening the braid up for the fire, as if she were revealing its secret interior to the flames. When it was all loose, she ran her fingers through the rippled hair, then stood up and shook it out behind her. She watched Adam's face. He looked as if he was afraid to breathe.

𝒜 D A M

ADAM'S FIRST NOVEL WEIGHED FIVE POUNDS, SEVEN OUNCES (not including the manuscript box) and covered three generations of a prosperous Wyoming ranch family. Adam had visited Wyoming only once in his life and knew no one who had ever lived there, but he'd read everything he could get his hands on that had to do with the area. He couldn't interest any publisher or agent in the novel, but it did fulfill the thesis requirement for his MFA. His mentor, Helene, had never produced a novel that weighed more than two pounds. Although she hadn't succeeded in curing Adam of his verbosity, she had managed to steer him to write about something more familiar for his second try. His new novel included a scene set in Moscow, even farther from home, but at least he'd spent his junior year of college there, and the narrator (involved in a knotty relationship with a Russian woman) was a young American male, not unlike himself.

In high school Adam had been a victim of competing talents. He was a natural in math and science but harbored literary pretensions (he was editor of the literary magazine) and was serious enough about the viola that he considered applying to a conservatory. In college—where he majored in engineering—the viola lay forgotten under his lofted dorm room bed, but he submitted more than three times as many pages as anyone else in his fiction writing workshop. After graduation he got a job in engineering but completed a low-residency MFA program in creative writing as well. The longer he continued at his job, the more alien it felt to him. He carried his new novel around in his head with him at all times, working on it whenever he was free from thinking of something else. It was his alternate, secret life. Sometimes it seemed like the only life he really had.

After he'd been orphaned in the Leopardi Circle at the death of Helene, Adam had been taken under the wing of Virginia. Her maternal instincts, Adam noticed, were juiced up anytime she was in the proximity of anyone under forty. When he had first joined them, he thought Virginia might be someone who wrote romance or science fiction, not what he considered a serious writer. She was portly and wore pants with elastic waistbands, and she had a grandmotherly manner. But as soon as he first heard her read from her manuscript, he realized he had misjudged her and, embarrassed, he read all her previously published books. It was a sobering venture. He felt he was not even remotely in her league. He felt that way about all the Leopardis—especially Gillian. Gillian above all. As for Chris, Adam didn't exactly respect what he did, but he recognized that Chris was good at it, and he couldn't ignore the fact that Chris not only made a living as a writer but made enough money to buy the kind of sports car Adam could only dream of, while Adam made nothing from his writing. Absolutely nothing at all.

THE FIRE HAD GONE OUT. The wall was cold against his naked back. When Adam turned his head to the left, a muscle twanged in his neck, no doubt from sleeping on his side in this narrow bed. He could tell from the absolute quiet that he was alone in the room. There was a purple hair elastic biting into his wrist. He pulled it away from his skin, then let it snap back against his wrist bone.

He did not need to close his eyes to see Gillian's naked back, the long inward curve of her spine leading down to her smooth buttocks, the surprising black curls of her pubic hair as she turned towards him, that small hill, like a child's head, the dab of pink in the cleft.

Morning sunlight made its way through the windows on one side and fell on the quilt. The colored triangles of fabric were bleached almost as pale as the white background, but it was not this morning's sun that had accomplished it, it had taken decades; the quilt looked a hundred years old. The glass in the windowpanes was antique, too, imperfect, like ice on the pond just after a night's freeze. He sat up in bed and squinted in the sunlight. Through the front windows of the room he could see the marsh, and his car and Gillian's truck parked at the edge of the rough lawn. He sat up farther.

There was a figure in the distance, someone walking along the edge of the marsh: Gillian. Her back was towards him, the hood of her grey sweater pulled up over her head. He wanted to reach across the distance between them and pull the hood back, freeing her hair. He wanted to see what the wind would do with it.

Adam found his clothes in a pile on the floor and got dressed. He could not decide what he should do. He didn't know what Gillian expected of him, didn't know what she wanted, and he was afraid of doing the wrong thing. He sat on the footstool and looked at the wide floorboards beneath his bare feet. They had been painted once, he could tell, then later stripped so the honey-colored pine was once again open to the light. But that had been years before; the surface was dull now. He traced a curve of grain with his big toe, circled a knothole. He felt certain, though, that Gillian didn't want him sticking around. He guessed that she would hope he was gone before she returned from her walk, so she could sit in the study and work on whatever poem she was beginning right now—he was sure she was working on a poem as she walked—but he also could not bear to leave without seeing her. He would not kiss her good-bye—he wasn't so foolish—but he would just touch her: her hair, her arm, anything. Surely she would grant him that. He thought, fleetingly, about writing Gillian a note, leaving it out on the counter, but he couldn't imagine what to say, nor what tone he should take. Something cute about his gratitude towards the mouse?

No, all wrong. Something about the quality of light in the study when he awoke, the narrow bed where they had slept, her head so close against him that her hair covered his mouth? No, wrong, too. Here he was a writer and he had nothing to say, or so much to say he couldn't say anything at all.

In the kitchen Adam found a bagel from the grocery bag he'd unpacked the night before. He put it in his pocket. He would pick up a cup of coffee when he stopped for gas along the road. The dishes from their dinner the night before were stacked, still, by the sink. He thought about washing them, but he didn't want to remove the evidence of that dinner; he wanted to leave something behind of himself so she might think of him after he was gone.

He took a last look at the study: the two pillows squashed together at the head of the bed, the two armchairs pulled close to the fireplace, the ash in the fireplace, feathery, the color of doves. He closed the front door behind him and stood on the doorstep looking out at the marsh. He watched Gillian as she walked along, head bowed as if she were studying the ground. She bent to pick something up, a shell perhaps? Before she had straightened up again to examine it in her hand, he had begun running towards her. He had stopped thinking now, stopped trying to decide what to do; he just moved.

She turned when she heard him approaching. He was out of breath, and she gave him a little smile, her head cocked, while she waited for him to speak. But it wasn't just the running that kept him from speaking. He had no words, all he had was images: Gillian's long, slender thigh, his own fingers running from her knee up to the curve where the pale skin stretched tight across her hip. His hand moved now, to touch the hair on the side of her face that had gotten free of the sweater's hood, but it moved too slowly. He rushed ahead and kissed her mouth—kissed her without asking if he could—and then turned and started running back towards his car. He got in and started it up without looking towards the marsh. But after he had turned the car around and was ready to drive off, he stopped and looked back at the whole scene. Gillian was walking towards the house now, her hands in her pockets. She looked so small against the wide marsh. The last thing in the world he wanted to be doing was to drive off, to leave her there. But that's what he knew he had to do.

KIM HAD LEFT HIM SEVERAL MESSAGES on his cell phone, as well as his voice mail at work. Her voice, perky and familiar, grew more querulous with each call.

"I got offered free tickets to the Natalie MacMaster concert last night," she said when he got back to her. "I was so frustrated I couldn't get ahold of you."

"So, did you go?"

"Yup. Sandy went with me."

"How was it?"

"Amazing," said Kim. "You would have loved it."

To make up for his initial annoyance at the persistence of Kim's messages, Adam took her out for dinner at Peking Garden, the more expensive of the two Chinese restaurants in town. Across the booth from him, Kim unwound her long scarf and laid it on the seat next to her. Her soft blond hair was puffed out on one side of her head with static electricity. She leaned back against the banquette and smiled at him. She had a round face, and her eyes were set wide apart, which gave her, Adam felt, a slightly bovine look.

"How come you turned your cell phone off?" Kim asked.

"I didn't," said Adam. "Battery must have run out." The lie came to him so quickly, so easily, it startled him. He wasn't a skilled liar, wasn't used to lying. He couldn't remember ever having lied to Kim. He had never had any reason to lie to her before.

"Where were you yesterday?" asked Kim after their food had arrived and they'd started eating.

"Helping out a friend."

Kim's eyebrows went up.

"No one you know," said Adam. "Just an old friend who was in a bit of trouble." He said this in a tone designed to lead Kim to believe it was someone who had gotten themselves into something possibly illegal and it was best for all involved not to discuss it further.

"Okay," said Kim, and she didn't ask anything more. She wasn't a prying person. Also, she trusted him. He'd never given her any reason not to.

"Here," she said. "Open up. I know you love these." She held her chopsticks out towards him, a piece of slick, black mushroom pinched between the ends.

"You like them, too."

"Not as much as you," said Kim. "Besides, I've had some." The mushroom was out of focus now, close to his face. He opened in compliance, felt the slimy surface against his lips. Kim pushed it into his mouth.

"Good?" she asked.

He chewed and nodded, but it was hard for him to swallow.

They went back to her apartment after dinner. He didn't want to stay the night, but she looked so hurt when he said he had to leave, he ended up staying anyway. The bathroom Kim shared with her two housemates was filled with hair products, gels, makeup, and lotions that smelled cloyingly of fruit. A hair dryer rested like a pistol across the cluttered counter. He thought of the bathroom in Gillian's house, an oval of bone-colored soap in a clamshell beside the blue basin. When he came back to the bedroom, Kim was standing by the bed, setting her alarm. She'd taken out her contacts earlier, and she had her eyeglasses on. She was wearing an oversized T-shirt and fuzzy slippers, and the heavy-framed eyeglasses made her look like a precocious child.

Adam took off his clothes and slipped under the bedcovers. Kim laid her glasses on the bedside table and lifted her arms to take her

T-shirt off. There was still a pink semicircle under each small breast, a mark from her underwire bra. She turned off the light, darted under the covers, and cuddled next to him.

"I missed you," she said. She stretched her neck up and planted a series of loud kisses on his mouth.

He didn't say anything in return, but he put his arm under her and drew her close.

"Tired?" she asked.

"Yeah, I'm beat," he said.

"That's okay," she said. "I'm pretty tired, too."

He reached over with his free arm and rested his hand on her shoulder. She lifted it to her face and gave it a kiss. Her fingers touched the band around his wrist.

"What's this?" she asked.

Grateful for the dark so that Kim could not see his face, Adam struggled to figure out what to say. "Just something someone left on my desk at work."

"Why are you wearing it?" asked Kim.

"I don't know," he said. "Just fiddling with it."

"It's not good to have something tight around your wrist like that," said Kim. She slid her finger under the band and began to pull it off.

He pushed her hand away. "Hey, leave that, will you?"

"Okay," she said. She moved away from him a little. "Adam?" she asked after a moment. "Is something the matter?"

"No, everything's fine," he said. "I've just had kind of a hard day."

"I'm sorry," said Kim. "You want to talk about it?"

"No, I just want to go to sleep."

"Sure," said Kim. "It's just nice to have you here." She snuggled close. Her hair smelled of strawberry-scented shampoo.

Adam closed his eyes, but he did not sleep. He didn't want to think about the night before, didn't want to touch any of that here, now. He was afraid he might injure it in some way. But there was nothing else he could fix his mind on, and images of Gillian kept intruding. He forced himself to think about things in her house instead—the wax pooling around the bases of the candlesticks at dinner, the logs settling in the fireplace in the study. His arm, pinned under Kim's body, ached, but he felt obligated to keep it there.

NANCY

ON THE MORNING OF THE NIGHT THAT ROBERT OATES MULL-ingford asked her to marry him, Nancy put fresh linens on their bed. With luck, he'd be home for dinner, but even if his flight were delayed, he'd certainly be home by that night. Nancy never changed the sheets while Oates was gone—she wanted to sleep with the nap of the flannel matted down by his warm body, with the scent of his breath and his sweat. But before he came home, she always made the bed up with clean sheets. Ever since they'd started living together, she'd done it every time he was gone for a business trip; it had become a ritual, a way of ensuring his safe return.

Nancy pulled the duvet cover off the down quilt, stripped the sheet off the mattress, and shook the pillows free from their pillowcases. A small white feather rose on a draft of air. She watched it float past the bedpost, then settle on the floor. She laid the folded fresh linens on the bed. They smelled of the lavender sachet from the closet, but she knew the smell wouldn't last long. Oates had been gone for two weeks, and now, so close to the time of his return, she didn't mind being alone. She wondered what it would be like if he no longer had to travel for his business. Maybe he would have to go away somewhere just so she could suffer their separation, the price she paid so she could savor the anticipation of his returning, so she could feel the relief and joy—no, it wasn't hyperbolic to call it joy—of their reunions.

They'd bought the bed at an auction on impulse. It was their first purchase together, only three weeks after they met. By then Nancy didn't want them sleeping in a bed she had slept in with other men, or worse, a bed he had slept in with other women.

On their first night in their bed, Nancy had said, "I guess I own this side, and you own your side," but Oates had laughed.

"You don't divide beds sideways," he said. "You divide them across the middle."

"And who gets which half?"

"You get the heads, of course," said Oates. "And I get everything from the waist down."

Nancy worked the corners of the quilt up inside the duvet cover—always a trick—and held it tight on the bottom edge while she shook it. Lofting, that's what the saleswoman in the shop had called it when she and Oates had bought the quilt together. The saleswoman had given them a demonstration, expertly fluffing the quilt till it was inflated to three times its size. Then she had compressed it and stuffed it back into the cotton storage bag, tightening the drawstring top, a conjurer undoing her trick. It had made Nancy uncomfortable to have this strange woman handle their quilt, touch something intimate, something that would float on their naked bodies, that they would make love under.

Before she went downstairs, Nancy put on perfume Oates had given her for her birthday, Je Reviens, *I will return*. Strangely, she had never thought before that he might have selected it for its name rather than its scent. She touched the glass stopper to her wrists and neck, then ran it down her chest to the hollow between her breasts, stretching the neckline of her sweater. She dabbed her belly button and reached down inside her pants to the crease of her thigh. But she did not touch herself more, as she might have done if Oates were not coming home that night.

She looked at the bed and readjusted the pillows. It seemed important that the bed be perfectly symmetrical, the pillows aligned. When the phone rang, she held her breath for a moment before answering, afraid it was Oates saying he was delayed. But to her surprise it was Chris.

"By any chance are you free for lunch?" he asked.

"Today?"

"Yes, today. I know people usually schedule lunches weeks in advance, but then they're always canceling and rescheduling. So I thought I'd see if you could join me at the last minute."

"I suppose I could," said Nancy.

"I'll take that for a 'yes,'" said Chris, "though I'd hoped for a bit more enthusiasm."

"I'm sorry," said Nancy. It was the expression she used so often it came out automatically, whether she was actually sorry or not. "I didn't mean to convey a lack of enthusiasm."

"It's okay," said Chris. "I'm sure you're wondering why is this guy asking me for lunch? Am I right?"

Nancy couldn't help laughing. "Yes, you're right."

"I thought it would be nice for us to get acquainted. You're new. Others know you, but I don't."

They settled on a time and a place, a new restaurant in town called Xantha's, which she hadn't been to yet, but Chris obviously had. She did wonder what the real reason was for him asking her for lunch. He didn't seem like a man who would waste a lunch on something as inconsequential as getting acquainted.

Nancy hung up the phone carefully. So far Oates's return was still safe. She went downstairs to her study. She wanted to work on her novel this morning, but she had a deadline for the newsletter. She finished an article she'd been doing on the disappointing news about virtual colonoscopies and turned her attention to licorice, which had

recently been implicated in a study on hypertension. It caused salt re-
tention, contributed to weight gain, and raised the risk of heart ar-
rhythmia. Still, the very word *licorice* made her salivate. She loved all
kinds of licorice: the soft twisties you had to peel apart, the disks
stamped to resemble coins, the bean-size pastilles that came in a little
tin. Her mother hated licorice, but her father relished it as she did.
He'd buy a bag of licorice shoestrings and they'd eat them together,
twirling them around their tongues, dangling them into their mouths
like black spaghetti. One time they'd started at opposite ends of a long
strand and chewed towards each other until they were nose to nose.
Nancy's father's top drawer always smelled of Black Jack gum. You didn't
see it around anymore, that blue package with the black oval.

Condemning licorice in her newsletter made Nancy feel like a trai-
tor to the pleasure of her past. After all, she had eaten licorice all her
life and hadn't suffered any ill effects. At least not that she knew of.
Old loyalty made her suspicious that maybe it wasn't licorice but something else that would prove to be the culprit, licorice merely the innocent bystander. Studies were always contradicting previous studies,
though it could take years for a reversal. All her newsletter did was
alert people to the latest findings. But it was all so pathetic, really. In
spite of all the fancy technology, they were still naïve about the myster-
ies of the human body. She could forgive the medical community its
innocence, but she had more trouble forgiving it its arrogance. The so-
called wisdom doctors dispensed was just the theory of the moment.
Her father had known this. In his early life as a doctor, he had learned
about it firsthand.

Nancy pushed her laptop towards the back of her desk and closed
the lid. She realized she'd lost the proper narrative tone for her article.
Lost faith, for the moment, in the voice she had created, that friendly,
authoritative voice, the pseudophysician who informed, illuminated,
reassured. She needed to get away from her desk, get out of the house.
She often took a walk in the late morning as a break from work. She

grabbed a jacket and went outside. Few cars came along her road at this time of day. The road paralleled the river, and she walked upstream, as she usually did, towards the Kleinholz farm.

Teresa Kleinholz was Nancy's friend, though their friendship was constrained by their political differences. Nancy liked everything else about Teresa. Teresa was instinctively generous and worked hard without talking about it. She had a pudgy face, little blue eyes, and wore itchy-looking sweaters and scarves that she knit herself. Although they'd dexterously avoided talking about politics all the years they'd known each other, the bumper sticker Teresa put on her car at the last election ended any possibility they would ever be close. Even now, the bumper sticker, dirty and torn at the edges, made Nancy tighten her lips each time she saw it.

The Kleinholzes owned two horses, bought for Teresa's daughter, Kate. Kate was busy in high school now and no longer enchanted by equines, and Teresa had inherited the horses and their care. One of the horses was a mare with an attitude, the other an old gelding named Jackie, whom Nancy had ridden a number of times. He had a white patch on the front of his face that looked as if he had leaned against a freshly painted fence. He was slow, gentle, and partially blind in one eye. When Nancy took care of the horses when the Kleinholzes were out of town, she was partial to Jackie, sneaking him an extra apple. Today, as she climbed the hill towards the farm, she recognized the vet's black pickup truck in the driveway and walked faster. When she got closer, she saw a little tableau in the far corner of the field: Jackie was lying on the ground, with Teresa and the vet bent over him. The mare stood eyeing things from a safe distance.

Nancy leaned on the fence and tried to make out what was going on. Teresa and the vet were intent on what they were doing and didn't look up. Nancy debated going across the field, but it seemed wrong to disturb them. Also, she was afraid to get any closer. Whatever was happening there in the field, it didn't look good. Horses didn't lie down like that unless there was something really the matter. Nancy turned and started walking back home again. Then she broke into a run. The road had a lot of sand in the pavement. Slivers of mica glinted in the sunlight. Nancy ran until she was far enough from the Kleinholzes' farm, far enough so she didn't have to see if Jackie was dying.

WHEN SHE GOT TO THE RESTAURANT, Nancy found Chris already seated at a table by the window. She would never have chosen that table, where they were on display to everyone walking by. The glass came right down to the floor, so even their feet, under the table, had no privacy.

Chris had a pink, freshly shaved look, and his dark hair looked as if it had just been professionally styled. Oates's hair was grey, and Nancy cut it herself while Oates sat on a stool in the kitchen, an old bedsheet draped around him.

"It's great you were able to come," said Chris. "I thought I should get to know you a little, not rely on what others said about you."

"And what did they say?"

"Only good things," he said. "What a valuable addition you'd be to the Leopardi Circle. What a magnificent writer you are." He leaned towards her over the table. He smiled and sniffed. "Nice!" he said.

How much perfume had she put on, anyway? It had been a while ago, but perhaps sweating had brought it out again. She had a horrible thought that Chris might think she had perfumed herself for him. Was it possible that he thought she was available, that this lunch was a prelude to a date? She would have to work Oates into the conversation as quickly as she could.

But Chris was a step ahead of her. "Just so you know," he said, "there are no rules about people seeing each other outside of class."

"Do you mean seeing each other, as in having lunch together, or do you mean something more?"

"Either," he said.

The waitress appeared to take their order. Chris had obviously already studied the menu and knew what he wanted. Nancy looked at it quickly and ordered a turkey sandwich, usually a safe choice.

"Aside from Bernard and Virginia, who were actually married to each other," she said, "are there pairings I should know about?"

"Nothing currently," said Chris. "Though I'm sure you know that Gillian and Bernard had their moment. Gillian and I, appearances to the contrary—and I am speaking ironically here—have yet to have our moment."

Nancy hadn't known about Gillian and Bernard, though it did not surprise her. She was probably one of the few women she knew whom Bernard had not slept with.

"In case you or anyone wondered," said Nancy, "I'm happy to see people outside of class. But I do live with someone."

"Of course I wondered. I knew you weren't married and thought it would help to set things straight, right at the start."

"So that's why you invited me out for lunch?"

"Not exactly," said Chris. "Though, to be honest with you, it's better to know these things than to make a fool of oneself, which, as you may have heard, I've done more than once in my life."

"No," said Nancy, smiling. "I haven't heard. But I'm still waiting to hear the real reason you invited me."

"I just wanted you to know that, in spite of whatever Bernard may have told you, I'm really happy to have you in the Leopardi Circle."

Bernard *had* told her that the decision to accept her hadn't been unanimous, but he *hadn't* told her that Chris was the holdout.

"Then tell me," said Nancy, "just between us, as new friends now, how come you voted against me?"

Chris smiled a big smile. It was obviously a smile that had served him well in the past in his dealings with women. The waitress had come with their order, and Chris waited until she left before speaking again.

"Truth is," he began, "it had nothing to do with you personally. I just thought we had enough highfalutin literary types, and I wanted a better balance."

"Who's weighing in on the highfalutin side?" asked Nancy.

"Gillian, obviously. It would take a warehouse of ordinary folks to balance her. And Bernard—I know he's your buddy, but you have to admit he is a literary icon. And Virginia, although she's a sweetie."

"I gather you don't like Gillian."

"Nobody *likes* Gillian," said Chris. "She isn't someone to like. She's someone to revere. And I, along with everyone else, revere her."

"But you do like Virginia."

"Virginia is the real thing, but thoroughly unpretentious. She's the one who brought me into the clan—did you know that?"

"No," said Nancy. She had wondered about Chris; he seemed so professionally at odds with everyone else. "I didn't realize you knew her."

"I lived in the same house as her daughter, Rachel. First-floor apartment, Rachel was upstairs. It was right when I'd moved to the area after marriage number two tanked. Rachel and her husband took pity on me when they found out I was alone for Thanksgiving and invited me to join them for their family dinner."

Chris was quiet for a moment, poked at the quesadilla on his plate. He looked up at Nancy. "I had tried to call my boys to wish them a happy Thanksgiving, and their bitch of a mother wouldn't let me talk to them. I was pretty shaken up, and Virginia put her plump arm around my shoulder and did one of her 'there, theres.' Very comforting."

"Yes," said Nancy, "I can see Virginia doing that."

"Virginia and Helene—she's the one who, how shall we say, dropped out for good?—had talked about starting something. They asked Bernard, and he asked Gillian. There was another guy—named Dick Smollett of all things—who came onboard. He nabbed a MacArthur, stopped writing, but that's another story. Then Virginia asked me. Felt sorry for me, no doubt. I think it was a shock to all when they found out the kind of thing I write. But by then it was too late, I was one of them."

"But do you like being 'one of them'?"

"I feel I am among the elect. As you will, too, now that you are also 'one of them.' But I want to warn you, Nancy, protect your heart, because they will undermine your confidence in your writing, in yourself."

"That sounds ominous," said Nancy, laughing a little. "Who is this 'they'? Anyone in particular?"

"It's just the way it works. But Gillian's the one you need to watch out for especially."

"So, that's another reason you invited me to lunch: to warn me?"

"You seem like a good person, Nancy. You deserve to be warned."

"If it's so bad, then why be part of the Leopardi Circle?" asked Nancy.

"Ah—that's the mystery, isn't it?" said Chris. "Because it's the crème de la crème of the local literati. Because of its pretentious name. Not my choice, in case you wondered; it was Helene's."

"Yes, Bernard told me."

"People indulge the dying," said Chris. "Even Gillian came onboard with the name, though she initially resisted since the suggestion hadn't originated with her. I've come to appreciate the irony of such an erudite mascot for a bunch of hacks like us. And this fellow, Giacomo Leopardi, was, appropriately—as Helene pointed out—tortured, pessimistic, and, above all, passionate."

"Pessimistic hacks?" asked Nancy, smiling.

"Not you, of course," said Chris.

Nancy moved her plate to the side of the table so the waitress would know she was done.

"You haven't finished your sandwich," said Chris.

"Chipotle sauce on the turkey," said Nancy in a low voice. "Not a success."

"You should have asked for something else," said Chris. "Or are you the sort who doesn't like to make fusses in restaurants?"

"I'm the sort," said Nancy.

"I could have guessed," said Chris. "In that case, why don't you let me pick up the tab?"

Nancy's face betrayed her surprise. She had assumed from the start that Chris was picking up the tab. Chris smiled. "I was just kidding," he said. "Did you think I'm the kind of guy who asks someone out to lunch and then expects them to pay?"

"Frankly," said Nancy, "I didn't know."

Chris just shook his head, his mouth turned down like a little boy's. Nancy could see why women—other women, that is—would find him appealing. When they left the restaurant, he walked her to her car. He wasn't a tall man—only a few inches taller than she. Sitting down, he looked as if he might be as tall as Oates, who was just over six feet.

"Mind if I ask you something?" he asked.

"No," said Nancy.

"You seemed, how shall I describe it, somewhat depressed at lunch."

"I did?"

"The look on your face, in those odd moments when you didn't think I was looking at you."

"Oh."

"And I couldn't help wondering if it was something I'd said, or done. Or maybe just me, my presence . . . ?"

Had she been depressed? She realized she had been. It surprised her that Chris had noticed. "Not you at all," she said. "It's just that I passed by a friend's farm before lunch. The vet was there, and her horse—a horse I've grown somewhat attached to—was lying down in the field. I'm afraid he's not going to make it."

"I'm sorry," said Chris. He did not say, as any number of people might have, "Oh, just a horse."

"Are you an equestrian?" he asked after a moment.

"Nothing like that," said Nancy. "I rode when I was young, but I don't much anymore."

Chris stopped on the sidewalk and tilted his head to look at her. "I can picture you," he said, "one of those wealthy little girls in a riding habit and flesh-colored jodhpurs going over jumps, your blond hair flipping up on the sides." Chris ran his finger along the bottom edge of her hair so it rose and fell.

"My hair was under my helmet," said Nancy. "And we weren't wealthy, my father was a schoolteacher. And the jumps weren't very high."

"Thank you for lunch," said Chris. And before she had a chance to worry about whether he was going to lean forward and kiss her good-bye, he held out his hand for her to shake.

TO HELP COVER THE EXPENSE of her horseback riding when she was a girl, Nancy worked at the stable. She was allowed unlimited riding on a horse named Star, an old gelding with a lopsided trot and a habit of shying at jumps. It was almost like having her own horse, but she knew the difference. There were other girls who owned horses they boarded at the barn—horses worth thousands of dollars—and they didn't do stable work.

The school bus dropped Nancy off at the barn, and then one of her parents picked her up before dinner. If she was running late, her mother would wait for her in the car, but her father would always come in and give her a hand finishing up. On weekend mornings when Nancy's father drove her to the barn, she'd turn out Star in the fenced pasture, and then her father would help with her chores. They'd work in companionable quiet, dividing up what needed to be done—raking up manure, spreading fresh wood chips, filling water buckets—without ever discussing it. It was a secret between them. Not that Nancy's mother had ever stated that the chores should all be done by Nancy herself, but there was an unspoken understanding between Nancy and her father that her mother might not approve of his doing any of the work.

One late afternoon in winter, after they'd given Star his grain and hay, they lingered for a while, leaning on the half door of Star's stall. They stood together, Nancy's father's arm around her, listening to Star eat, to the swish of his tail, and the occasional soft whinnies from other horses in the barn.

"We should be pushing on," her father said, "it's about time for dinner." But they hadn't left just then; they just stood there, smelling the comforting smells of hay and wood chips and warm manure, and listening to the sweet peacefulness of the barn.

Most often when Nancy thought about her father, she thought of things he said. But strangely, he was most present in memories like this one, when nothing was said and when nothing much was happening— just a horse eating his hay, and darkness settling in around a lighted barn.

WHEN NANCY GOT BACK TO HER HOUSE, she started turning in to her driveway, then backed out again and kept going along the road. She slowed as she neared the Kleinholz farm. The vet's black pickup was gone from the driveway. There was a raw, brown rectangle in the far corner of the field where Jackie had been lying, as if someone had just prepared the ground for a new garden.

"No!" Nancy cried out. "No, no, no, no, no."

She drove up to the Kleinholzes' house and ran up to the back door. Teresa was in the kitchen baking pumpkin muffins. The first batch, on a cooling rack on the counter, had been overdone, and the kitchen smelled of burned pumpkin.

"What happened to Jackie?" Nancy asked.

"A virus of some kind," said Teresa. "He got so weak he couldn't stand. So the vet put him down."

"And he was buried, right there?"

"That's the way it's done," said Teresa. She laid her fingers on Nancy's forearm. "Herb Miller came over with his backhoe. We were lucky to get him to come right over."

It was Nancy who was crying.

"He was an old horse," said Teresa.

OATES'S FLIGHT WAS DELAYED, so Nancy ate dinner by herself, leftover ravioli that she didn't bother to heat up. When his car finally pulled up in the driveway, it was almost eleven. They didn't even make it upstairs; they made love in the kitchen, standing up, Nancy with her back against the counter.

In bed, later, on the clean sheets that still carried a hint of lavender, Nancy told Oates about Jackie dying and being buried, about lunch with Chris, who warned her about the jeopardy of joining the Leopardi Circle, about licorice (which Oates liked as much as she did), now a pariah of candies.

"That's a lot to think about," said Oates. "Do you think you can add one more thing?"

"It depends what it is," said Nancy.

"It's that I want you to marry me," said Oates.

"We've talked about this before," said Nancy.

"We've talked about it," said Oates, "but I've never formally asked you before. So I'm asking you tonight."

"Why tonight?"

"Flying in tonight, I was looking out at the lights in the distance—little yellow lights, houses, towns—wondering if I could see yours. They were the only lights that mattered to me. I thought, if you are all that matters to me, shouldn't we be everything, shouldn't we be married?"

"It still frightens me a little," said Nancy. "I like us the way we are."

"You're afraid if I become your husband, you'll lose me?"

"Uh-huh," said Nancy softly.

"That was someone else, a long time ago," said Oates. "Not me. I'm not going to leave you. I promise."

"Do you want an answer tonight?" asked Nancy.

"If it's 'yes,' then I would like to know as soon as possible. I'd like to go to sleep knowing that."

Nancy curled up in the crook of Oates's arm. "It's yes," she said.

It was so quiet she could hear the river straining against its banks behind the house. She could hear the sweet thump, thump, thump, thump of Oates's heart. So quiet, she could almost hear the Kleinholzes' mare pawing at the wood chips in her stall.

$\mathscr{C}$HRIS

WHILE HE WAS MANAGING EDITOR OF THE *YORKTOWN TRI-bune*, Chris had contributed a preface for a collection of articles written by one of their columnists. The book had a small print run, but it was handsomely published in a blue cloth binding with gold letters, and the jacket featured a Vermeer print. Chris had never paid attention to book quality before this, but the heft and well-craftedness of this book pleased him. And he was excited by its longevity. For over a year the book presided on the table beside the sofa, the cover solid, the pages still white. In contrast, the pages of the *Trib* yellowed, dried up on the edges and curled, like leaves. Even the issues saved in their morgue aged poorly.

Chris had always been attracted to journalism because of its presence, its energy, its speed. When he first came to the *Trib* as a reporter, he had covered town meetings, zoning board meetings, planning board meetings, and it was a thrill that he could attend a meeting, distill everything that happened, and the next afternoon it was there in print: solid, news. It was as if his brain was pulling the world together for his readers. His take on things was there on people's doorsteps the next morning. And every news item was followed by another. Everything was always new.

It was only after the publication of the book of articles that the evanescence of newspapers began to depress him. A brilliant series he'd done on rural poverty (a series that *should* have won a Pulitzer) ended up in the recycling bin along with everything else. On newsprint it was no different from the weekly horoscope, from the engagement announcements, from the ads for Prime Foods' sale of capons. The pages of the *Trib*, his words, his thoughts, lined parakeet cages, were shat on by gerbils, peed on by incontinent puppies, were crumpled up and used to start fires in woodstoves. Sometimes—more often than not—they were not even read. Sometimes, when subscribers went on vacation and neglected to inform the circulation department, the paper sat in sodden piles on doorsteps.

Books, Chris imagined, lasted forever. Or at least as good as forever. He was smart, he was a crackerjack writer, so why squander his talent on newsprint? With fiction, you were supposed to write about something familiar. He knew about a suburban New York newspaper. He knew about small-town politics. He knew about small-town crime. It was all there for him—all he needed to do was put it together.

It was around this time that his marriage to his first wife, his college girlfriend, faltered, then came to an end. Valerie was a social worker in a teenage residential facility and often worked the weekend shift, the only time that he was off. They rarely spent time together and came to realize they didn't mind. Not that he exited gracefully. A brief and stupid affair with a friend of hers at the very time he and Valerie were making a halfhearted attempt at reconciliation guaranteed that Valerie would feel resentful towards him the rest of their post-married life. Valerie's friend patched things up with Valerie but turned nasty towards him, even though it was she who had pushed their indiscretion and he who had merely consented, consented because—well, because he wanted to please her. He liked pleasing women. And this is what befuddled him. How was it that, although he loved women so much, his relationships with them inevitably ended with them turning against him? He marveled at Bernard and Virginia.

Alone, Chris wrote his first novel. He sold it after only six months of trying. The advance was small, but, heady with his success, he ditched his job at the *Trib*. He was a writer now, a *real* writer. He sublet a friend's vacation house in rural Massachusetts for a month, then decided to stay put in the area. From the profit on the sale of the house in Westchester, even split two ways, he had enough to live on for more than a year. After Valerie, he had three intense relationships in quick succession, each one begun with the conviction that this was the woman he would spend the rest of his life with.

The first, Julie, was in the landscaping business. She gave him wonderful massages, but she took astrology seriously. The relationship lasted only a few months. The next, Simone, was a reference librarian. She was overqualified for her job at the local library, underpaid, and insufficiently ambitious. That lasted somewhat longer. The third, Susan Pratt, was a rising vice president in the mortgage department of a commercial bank. She had lots of drive, which in hindsight he realized he mistook for passion. Although initially she seemed attracted by the fact that he was a writer, after they were married she grew increasing irritated with his unstructured work schedule and the unpredictability of his income. Within three years they had produced two sons, he had produced two more novels, and he had acquired yet another ex-wife who (unfathomably, he felt) despised him. Susan was more venomous than Valerie, and unlike Valerie she had two weapons to use against him. Samuel and Benjamin (Susan refused to allow them to go by the nicknames Sam and Ben) had inherited their mother's thin face, but they had his dark, big eyes. It surprised Chris how much he loved them. How unequivocally.

THE MORNING OF HIS COLONOSCOPY, Chris waited in the living room for his sister, Lydia, to turn up. She lived in Boston, two hours away, but had volunteered to pick him up after the procedure. They would only release him into the care of someone who undertook responsibility for him, and one of the excuses he had used to postpone the procedure was he had no one he could ask to do that. And because she didn't trust that he wouldn't come up with a last-minute excuse to cancel the appointment, Lydia had planned to drive him to it as well. The sacrifice of time and all the planning required to make this possible should have endeared Lydia to Chris. Certainly she loved him and had his best interests at heart. But Chris—in spite of being something of a hypochondriac—was phobic about medical procedures, and now that he was facing what he believed was one of the world's most dreaded, he blamed Lydia entirely. He didn't like the idea of some wire probe snaking itself up inside his body, a miniature light lighting the way and a miniature camera recording everything it saw, invading the privacy of his intestines. Certainly there were dark recesses of his body that were meant to remain mysterious. On their own, they functioned in perfect synchrony. Why provoke them?

Chris's golden retriever, Maybe, raced to the door, tail wagging, when Lydia arrived. Chris had bought Maybe as a gift for Sam and Ben, but Susan's response to the puppy had been to call Chris irresponsible within earshot of the boys and to make him take it home with him.

"How are you holding up?" Lydia asked Chris after she had paid attention to Maybe and wiped the dog drool off on her jeans.

"How do you think?" asked Chris.

"Oh, poor baby," said Lydia. She gave Chris a hug. "You'll see, it will be over in no time and you'll feel silly for having been so worried about it."

"If I am still alive," said Chris.

"Really, Chris, people don't usually die because of a colonoscopy."

"No, Lyddie, they die because of the humiliation."

Lydia's eyes narrowed. "Get your coat," she said.

AT THE MEDICAL FACILITY (at least it wasn't a hospital), Lydia waved good-bye to Chris as he went through the door to the ominous back quarters when his name was called. In an overbrightly lit dressing room, he took off his clothes, as required, and put on a thoroughly inadequate smock and a pair of socks with rubber treads on their soles. Ben and Sam had worn socks like that when they were little. A nurse instructed him to put his clothing in a small locker and helped him lock it up and put the elastic key chain on his wrist. He hadn't realized his hands were shaking.

"You might want to give me that watch of yours," she said, pointing at his other wrist. "I'll bring it out to your wife for safekeeping."

"My sister," said Chris, as he removed the watch and surrendered it to her. Since their last names were the same, it was a reasonable mistake, though they looked enough alike that most observant people guessed they were related. And now, once again, Chris felt a pang of wifelessness. While he was fortunate to have a sister who cared for him enough to accompany him to his colonoscopy, it was pitiable that he had no one else in his life whom he could ask. No wife, no lover. Not even a good friend.

The room Chris was led to had reclining lounge chairs lined up all around it, each in an area partitioned off with curtains. The linoleum floor was so highly polished the surface looked wet. In a wild second he fantasized dashing across to the exit and was grateful for the no-skid socks. But it was already too late. He was seated in the reclining chair and a nurse with a soothing voice was going over his medical history, asking him questions he was certain he had already answered on the form. She'd introduced herself as Julie, and while she went over in more detail than he cared to know what exactly he had in store for him, he kept his terror at bay by thinking about the Other Julie, the one he'd been in love with, briefly, a decade ago. The Other Julie wore khaki shorts rolled up high on her thighs, and heavy boots. She had long, frizzy blond hair, which she held back with a bandanna. She shaved her armpits for him, but not her legs.

"This will just be a little pinch," said This Julie, and she stuck a needle into the top of his hand and threaded a slender plastic tube into his vein.

The chair, he discovered, was like a giant baby carriage. He was wheeled through swinging doors, down a corridor to an operating room, where he was hoisted up on a table under a light that glared. There was a television screen hooked up to a lot of equipment. A doctor who looked like an overweight Woody Allen repeated information about the procedure. There were other nurses around, talking, but he couldn't hear what they were saying, and he was in a reclining chair again, in a curtained cubicle, though not the one he had been in before. A nurse he wasn't sure if he had seen before was offering him juice and crackers.

"Everything was fine," said the doctor, leaning over him. But then it was Lydia who was leaning over him, saying, "See, I was right, wasn't I? It wasn't much of anything at all."

"*I* was right," said Chris. "They didn't find anything wrong, so this whole thing was unnecessary."

Later, home on his sofa with Maybe lying on the floor beside him, Chris argued with Lydia about what he had said in the recovery area.

"You told the doctor you had found it fascinating to watch the procedure on the screen and were planning to use the experience in your next novel."

"I never said anything like that," insisted Chris. "And I didn't watch anything on the screen. I was out, asleep, before they even began."

"That drug plays with your memory," said Lydia. "I wasn't there during the procedure, so I can't tell you what you saw. But I was there in the recovery area, and I heard your long conversation with the doctor."

"I can't believe it," said Chris. "I can't believe I was conscious and don't remember a thing."

"That's why they recommend you not sign any legal documents for a day after, so the drug can wear off."

Lydia leaned down and smoothed Chris's hair back off his forehead. "I'm going to make you something to eat," she said.

While she was in the kitchen, Chris started to doze, but shook himself awake. He had always known there were drugs that produced such potent forgetfulness, but experiencing it himself, a drug that could make part of his own life inaccessible to him, the one person who should have access to it, was a different matter. He would use this in his new book.

Lydia brought him lunch, walked Maybe, and then got ready to go back to her own life, to her husband and her daughter.

"Will you be all right on your own?" Lydia asked him.

"Sure," said Chris.

"You promise you'll take it easy and won't do anything stupid?"

"I promise, Lyddie," said Chris. "I'm beat. I'll probably just watch a movie, then go to bed. And if I have any energy, the most I'll do is work on the chapter I'm bringing to my coven on Sunday."

"How's that been going?" asked Lydia.

"We got a new member. A fiction writer named Nancy Markopolis."

"I don't think I've heard of her."

"Not many people have," said Chris. "I took her to lunch yesterday. Nice woman. She has a slightly prissy look and a patrician manner, but I like her."

"Oh no, Chris. Don't get involved with one of your writer friends," said Lydia. "You yourself said it would be messy."

"Who's getting involved?" asked Chris.

"That's what you always say," said Lydia.

"You can relax this time. Apparently Nancy is spoken for."

"I wish I could trust you," said Lydia. "Look, I better get on the road. Give me a call tomorrow and let me know how you're feeling."

"I'll be fine," said Chris. "And tomorrow I get to take the boys to dinner."

"What was this business you were telling me about Susan's lawyer going after you about the child support?"

"Susan heard somewhere that I'd been offered six figures for my next book deal and convinced her lawyer that I've been in cahoots with my agent to hide assets from her. I had to come up with tax returns, letters from the publisher, affidavits, you name it, so Dave can get it all squared away by the judge's deadline."

"I know that Dave is your old college buddy, Chris," said Lydia, "but I'm not sure he's on top of things. It may be time to get yourself a better lawyer."

"Don't worry about me, Lyddie. I trust Dave to get this mess all cleared up in time."

Lydia sighed and rested her hand on Chris's foot. She gave it a shake. She hadn't liked Susan when Chris first started going out with her and had urged him not to marry her. Chris was grateful that she was kind enough not to remind him of that now.

THE NEXT DAY CHRIS FELT TIRED OUT but elated by the realization he had survived his colonoscopy. He was grateful to his colon, all thousand feet of it. He was proud of himself for having actually gone through with the procedure, and only a little ashamed of what a hard time he had given Lydia. He sent her a lavish bouquet of flowers.

At Susan's house, Chris waited in the car in the driveway for Sam and Ben to come out. He would have liked to have gotten out of the car to embrace his sons, to open the car doors for them, but Susan's lawyer had been explicit that he was forbidden to set foot on her property, and his lawyer, who agreed this was preposterous, urged him to comply. Ben and Sam were wearing matching navy blue jackets that looked too big for them. At the car door they turned to look back at the house—where Chris saw a head at the window—but they did not wave.

When the boys first got in the car, they were always subdued. It took a while before Chris could get a smile out of each of them. Chris thought of it as his sons thawing out after he removed them from Susan's icehouse.

"So, guys, where do you want to go?" he asked.

"Jimmy's!" they cried, together. It was their opening routine. Chris always asked, and they always went to Jimmy's. Originally, their pre-ferred places were fast-food restaurants near the mall, but Chris had managed to win them over to Jimmy's, a triumph he was particularly happy about. McDonald's and Friendly's were the places Susan brought the boys to as a rare treat.

Jimmy's was a diner run by Greeks. They had a favorite booth, which they called "our" booth, and Jimmy, the owner, whom Chris had struck up a friendship with, always remembered them by name. Sometimes, when Chris was missing his sons more than he could bear, he drove the eighty miles to Jimmy's for dinner. He didn't sit in "our" booth, he sat at the counter, on one of the red Naugahyde, swiveling chairs, and schmoozed with Jimmy when Jimmy wasn't working the register.

Chris was always trying to get the boys to try Greek food, but both Sam and Ben were unadventurous eaters. Ben was particularly picky. Once a restaurant had served him a turkey sandwich and had neglected to hold the mayonnaise, and Ben wouldn't touch the turkey, even after Chris had rubbed all the mayonnaise off with his paper napkin.

"So how did things go with your poster?" Chris asked Sam. Both boys were sitting across from him in the booth. Ben was pushing the buttons on the jukebox mounted there. Chris had given him a quarter for it, but he couldn't choose.

"Okay," said Sam.

"Did Ms. Cornwell put it up on the bulletin board?"

"Yup," said Sam.

"That's great," said Chris.

"She puts them all up on the bulletin board," said Sam. "Even the stupid ones."

"Mom wouldn't let Sam get new markers," said Ben.

"How were the old ones?" asked Chris.

"All dried out," said Ben.

"Just the blue and the yellow," said Sam.

Chris kept notes on everything the boys told him at these dinners. As a reporter, he'd trained himself to listen well and then quickly write down everything he'd heard as soon as he had a chance. He kept a notebook in his car, and as soon as he dropped his sons off he'd fill a page or two. The note-taking served two purposes. First, he wanted to keep track of all the details of his sons' lives so they'd feel he was really connected with them, and he didn't trust himself to remember things. He also wanted to document anything they said that might be useful to him in legal negotiations. He never grilled them about Susan, but some of what he'd picked up would, he felt, make any reasonable judge award him custody. Would make any judge with a heart break down and weep.

People always commented on how well-behaved Ben and Sam were, and while this gave Chris a moment of pride, it worried him as well.

"I believe in raising little gentlemen," Susan had once said. But he was afraid they were too docile, too repressed.

They had sundaes for dessert—a specialty of the diner. The sundaes were so big Chris always ended up finishing Ben's, and sometimes Sam's, too. Both boys were too skinny, Chris thought.

Ben was bouncing around in his seat.

"Want to hit the bathroom before we go?" Chris asked him.

Ben nodded and scooted out from the booth.

"You all set?" he asked Sam.

"Uh-huh," said Sam.

Sam had saved some of his fries in a paper napkin for Chris to bring back to Maybe, and although Chris knew that they weren't good for the dog, he took the offering and promised he'd give it to him. He reached across the table and ruffled Sam's hair, which was cut short and stuck up in front. He wanted to take Sam's head in both his hands and kiss him on his brow, the way Chris's father used to kiss him when he was a kid. But he was afraid he might get all teary-eyed. Driving back home after leaving the boys at Susan's house, he often cried in the car, but he didn't ever want to cry in front of Sam or Ben.

Chris had noticed a police cruiser off the side of the road near the entrance to Susan's driveway, but he didn't make anything of it. He drove up the driveway and turned off the engine so he could give the boys a good-bye hug. They sat in the back, and he had to reach around the front seat to hug them. He watched the boys run into the house. The door on the breezeway slammed shut after them, but he waited, knowing they'd run through the house and wave good-bye to him from the living room window. He had his eyes on them, their faces framed by the mullions of the bay window, when he realized the police car had come up the driveway behind him and a cop was getting out.

Chris was fairly certain he hadn't been speeding—he always drove carefully when the boys were in the car—but maybe this crazy town had a speed trap that he'd missed. He produced his driver's license for the cop, as requested, and was surprised he wasn't asked for the car registration as well.

"Would you please get out of your car," said the cop. He was a young cop, a foot taller than Chris at least, with large ears that stuck out. The cop asked Chris his name, then studied his face and the photo on the license.

"What's going on?" asked Chris.

"I have a warrant here for your arrest," said the cop.

"You're kidding me, right?" asked Chris.

"I'm afraid not," said the cop. "You're being arrested for failure to pay back child support." And he showed Chris an official-looking document.

"Oh, that's no problem, then," said Chris. "Everything's been taken care of. It was all a misunderstanding. My lawyer worked things out with my ex-wife's lawyer, and I'm in the clear."

"Apparently not," said the cop.

"But this is crazy," said Chris. "I gave my lawyer all the necessary papers. I spent days digging out my old tax records to prove I wasn't hiding secret assets."

"I'm sorry," said the cop. "The governor is cracking down on 'dead-beat dads,' and so it's our job to round them up."

"But I'm not a deadbeat dad," said Chris. "I pay through the nose, every month. I've never missed a month."

"I'm sorry," said the cop, again, "but there's nothing I can do. I have to bring you in to the county jail, and once you're there, you can get in touch with your lawyer."

"I can't believe this," said Chris.

"You might want to leave all your valuables in your car," said the cop, "because things have a way of disappearing in the jail. And leave your belt, because they'll just take it away from you."

"You got kids?" Chris asked.

The cop nodded.

"Then you'll understand," said Chris. "I've got two boys, Ben and Sam." He pointed at Susan's house. "I hadn't seen them for a week. I drove eighty miles to get here. I got to take them out to dinner, then I had to bring them right back. I won't get to see them again for another week."

"I wish I could help you out," said the cop, "but I have no choice except to take you in."

Chris left his watch and most of the contents of his wallet in the glove compartment of his car. He took off his belt and laid it on the seat. On the console was the paper napkin filled with French fries. The oil had seeped through in places, leaving translucent stains on the paper.

Chris held the fries out to the cop. "I promised my son I'd bring these back to the dog," he said.

The cop shook his head in sympathy. "I'm sorry," he said.

But although he was required to put Chris in handcuffs, he waited till he had backed out of the driveway and they were out of sight of the two small faces in the window.

NANCY

SUNDAY MORNING, NANCY FOUND OATES IN THE KITCHEN when she came downstairs. Sunlight from the window divided the room into half brightness, half shadow. Oates stood at the stove, his hand and arm in sunlight. He was humming while he stirred scrambled eggs. He rested the spatula on the edge of the frying pan and turned to kiss her.

"My bride," he said.

"Did I make any promises last night?" asked Nancy.

"You sure did," said Oates.

"Maybe it was like one of those drugs they give you—you say things but have no memory of it the next day."

"I don't think so," said Oates.

She untied her bathrobe and pushed up his T-shirt so she could nuzzle against him, her skin against his skin.

"And you'll love me still, even after we're married?" she asked.

"I love you now, and I'll love you then," he said.

"It's probably too early to call Aliki, don't you think?"

Oates looked up at the clock and then at Nancy. "We could have breakfast first," he said. "But I bet Aliki won't mind being woken up for this." Oates gave the eggs a last prod, covered the pan, and turned off the stove.

"Let's call her right now."

Aliki's voice was full of sleep, but when Nancy said, "We've got some news for you," she immediately perked up. "Hooray!" she shouted. "It's about time. Put Oates on."

"I'm on," said Oates. "It's the speakerphone."

"How did you finally persuade Mom to come to her senses?" asked Aliki.

"There was no persuasion necessary," said Nancy. "It's just that it seemed the right time."

"At last!" said Aliki.

"So you're happy for us?" asked Nancy.

"Duh," said Aliki.

There were other people to call with the news. But that could wait till after breakfast. Oates put the eggs on the plates, and Nancy got the toast. They sat across from each other, and Nancy rested the soles of her feet on top of Oates's warm feet. When she was a little girl, she'd waltzed with her father at a cousin's wedding reception, with her feet (black patent-leather shoes) on top of his feet. How they'd flown around the room! She hadn't had to know the steps, all she had to do was keep her balance, keep from sliding off.

The breakfast table was beside the window, and the sun caught the facets of the glass butter dish, setting them aglow. The butter on the toast melted in puddles, the shape of continents. The minute hand on the clock clicked from one designated minute to the next. It would go on like that all hour, all day. Forever. This is what happiness is, thought Nancy. And while so much of what she thought and felt went into her writing, she knew she'd never make use of this moment. It was hers to be remembered, hers alone.

LATER IN THE DAY Oates was sprawled on the sofa in the den, eating a cinnamon bun and reading the "Week in Review" section of the

Sunday *New York Times*. The rest of the paper was spread out on the floor beside him. A piece of gummy walnut was stuck to the corner of his lip. He nabbed it with his tongue.

"I feel guilty leaving you this afternoon," Nancy told him. "You've been back only a day."

"I'll be fine," said Oates. "I rarely have the house to myself. I'll putter to my heart's content."

"I don't have to go," said Nancy. "It's Sunday. We should be spending it together." The room was all sunshine now. It smelled of coffee and morning.

"Go," said Oates. He looked up over the top of his glasses at her. "I know you've been worrying about reading anything to them, sweetheart, but believe me, they'll love your work."

"They'll shred my chapter," said Nancy.

"I doubt it," said Oates, but Nancy interrupted him.

"And then I'll lose heart in the entire project," she said.

"You're not going to lose heart in your book, Nancy. You believe in it. I believe in it."

"I don't have to be doing this," said Nancy. "I can call Bernard and tell him I've changed my mind."

"Nancy. Just go," said Oates. "Have fun at your Leo Party, or whatever it is they call themselves."

"The Leopardi Circle," said Nancy. "Named for a famous early-nineteenth-century Italian poet and philosopher."

"Oops," said Oates. "I never heard of him. Do you want to reconsider what you promised last night?"

Nancy bent to kiss him. "It's all right, darling," she said. "I had to look him up, myself. I'm sure I shocked Bernard when I displayed my ignorance, but he was uncharacteristically nonjudgmental."

Nancy straightened the waistband of her long, grey skirt. "How do I look?" she asked.

"Fine," said Oates.

"You don't think I'm too dressed up?"

"You look fine."

Nancy bent down again to kiss him good-bye. "Why do you put up with me?" she asked.

"I can't imagine," said Oates.

"Still want to marry me?"

"What do you think?" asked Oates, and he pulled her down again for another kiss.

NANCY'S FATHER graded his students' papers at the table in the middle of the kitchen. He had a desk—a mahogany desk with its green leather top protected by a piece of glass—but Nancy couldn't recall him ever sitting there. The desk had come from the office of his father, a cardiologist, and Nancy wondered later if that was the reason it went unused. Nancy liked having her father work in the kitchen, his glasses perched cockeyed on his face, an extra red pencil tucked behind his ear. He was part of the hum of the family: her mother stirring lentil soup on the stove, her little brother, Nick, racing his Matchbox cars along the floorboards, and she reading on the old sofa under the window. When her father needed his pencil sharpened, she'd jump up to do it. He had a pencil sharpener in a clear plastic case, so she could watch the red-tipped curls of wood peel off the pencil as she turned it against the blade.

When Nancy was little she'd been told that her grandfather, Papou, was a heart doctor, and even when she was old enough to know better, she still connected him with the paper hearts of valentines. She understood he was eminent because he treated the most important organ of the body, the one that determined life. But even so, what he did seemed removed from people. He attended to a particular part of the human body, not to the person herself. He was not someone you went to when you were throwing up or had a fever or broke out in hives. When she got a splinter at the boardwalk on the beach, it was her grandmother who removed it. And when she had to have surgery on the arm she broke falling off a horse, her Papou came to her hospital room carrying a stuffed bear. He wasn't wearing a white doctor's coat; he looked like any visitor.

Nancy's father loved his students. Not as much as he loved his own children, but sometimes, Nancy felt, almost as much. Not in a gushy way, like her own fifth-grade teacher, Mrs. O'Reilly, a cooer, but in a serious, almost reverent way. Every child, even the most obdurate of the boys, was worthy of his infinite patience, of his kindness. He worked tirelessly for them, but he wasn't one of the popular teachers, the cool ones who went by their first names and gave kids high fives in the hallway. In time, Nancy believed now, his students would all appreciate him in retrospect. She'd never been assigned to her father's class, and she avoided running into him at school as much as possible. At school she aimed to be invisible. Once she had been in the toilet stall when she overheard two girls in his class complaining about a paper they'd just gotten back.

"He took off five points just because I didn't do the outline right," said one girl. "He's so unfair!"

"Yeah," said the other girl.

Nancy wanted to rush out at them. Her father was never unfair. He was the fairest person in the world. She waited in the stall until they had left the bathroom, afraid to flush, afraid to let them know she had been in there, her hands pressed against the grey marble.

Nancy dreaded anyone thinking she got special treatment because her father taught at her school, and she was an obsessively conscientious student to dispel any accusation of favoritism. Even in high school and in college, where her father could have had no possible influence, even years after he retired, she was still burdened by a little fear that she had to do everything right, that the A she got (and she usually did get A's) had to be a grade she had truly earned. It was not just that she was worried she'd be accused of having an unfair advantage. It was that secretly she was worried that perhaps she did have one.

Nick, two years younger, never shared these worries. He hated to read and was a screwup in school, though he excelled at standardized tests. As an adult he'd made a success of himself in Silicon Valley. He'd redeemed himself, but their father hadn't lived to see that redemption. Yet their father hadn't worried over Nick. He had trusted that Nick, once mature, would thrive.

It was clear to Nancy, though it was never spoken of directly, that her father's career choice was a disappointment to his parents. It was as if they had expected him to do something more with himself, as if he was meant for better things than to minister to the learning of eleven-year-olds. Nancy's grandmother spoke, always hopefully, as if Nancy's father were in some temporary job and would then move on to something better.

"There's an opening for principal in our district," Nancy remembered her grandmother saying, but her father just shook his head gently and placed his hand on her shoulder. "Thanks, Ma," he said, nothing more. Nancy's grandmother let out an exaggerated sigh that conveyed in its exhale an entire litany of disappointment and resignation.

Nancy's mother was a teacher, too, an art teacher, but that wasn't seen to be a disappointment to *her* parents. Nancy wasn't sure if that's because expectations were different if you were a woman or if it was because her mother's family wasn't Greek. But while her father was content with what he did, in fact treated it like a calling, teaching seemed a job Nancy's mother had settled for. There was a restlessness about her. She wanted something more than teaching—she wanted a career as an artist. She blamed the failure of her career on fashion, on the politics of the art community, but certainly not on her talent, which she believed in always, even now, when she lived in a Florida condominium and never put it into practice. She constantly bemoaned the limited resources the public school put into art and the fact that her program was considered dispensable. In her last years teaching, her art room was turned into a classroom to deal with overcrowding. She was reduced to a peripatetic status, all of her supplies housed in a cart.

"Like a hotel maid," she complained.

Nancy could picture her aggrieved mother, cart in front of her, steaming through the Middlebrook Elementary School hallways, colored markers and jars of poster paint flying off in her wake.

Nancy's father believed in her mother's art career as much as she did. He made over the breezeway into a studio. He took Nancy and Nick off to excursions on weekends so Nancy's mother could have undisturbed time. She worked in silverpoint pencil, meticulous grey drawings of things that were themselves ordinary but that were transformed, that took on a luminescence. A drawing of simple oak leaf gall would take her months to complete. She occasionally showed her work, occasionally sold a few drawings, but she would never be reimbursed for all the hours she put into those infinite, hair-fine lines. She chose not to draw lovely things—which might have been more popular—but instead those with asymmetry and flaws. She scorned commissions. In her drawings of people, even those she loved, everything was slightly distorted—in the way a bad snapshot changes things. She drew Nick with a scowl, Nancy's hair unwashed. It was a portrait of how you feared you might look, rather than a portrait of what you wanted to look like. And although Nancy was actually quite pretty, she never thought of herself as such, and her mother's drawings of her only confirmed this.

With her father, Nancy never felt it mattered what she looked like. He just wanted to know what she thought. Her father never cared about what anything looked like. Nancy's mother cared about shape. She cared about line. She cared about shadow and light. Nancy's father cared about how things worked. He cared about the why.

.   .   .

FICTION, NANCY THOUGHT, was like a block of ice, created out of nothing more than water, and inside was a pebble, which was the real story, the truth that everything was built up around. If the ice melted, you'd have that left. In the novel she was writing, the true little story, the nugget within the fiction, came from a moment in a conversation with her father, their last long car trip together before he died.

He'd picked her up at the airport when she came home for Christmas her second year in graduate school. It was raining, and the side windows of the car were steamed up, insulating them from the outside world. The car felt snug and private. Only in a car, when something else was being accomplished—the moving from one place to another—was it possible to talk about difficult things. If you sat down face-to-face in a room, it didn't happen. Perhaps it was the soothing motion. Or the fact that they weren't looking at each other, that her father was looking forward, that all she saw of him was his profile, the right half his face.

They'd been on the road for half an hour before she steered the conversation to what she had planned to tell him. It was easier to bring something up to her father alone than tell both her parents at once, and he'd always been the one she could confide in, and the one whose judgment she trusted. She took in a breath, then started talking, quickly, before she could think about it. "Here's the thing," she said. "I decided I'm not going to continue in the program after this year."

"Oh," said Nancy's father. "When did this happen?"

"I've been thinking about it since the start of the semester."

"Michigan's not the place for you?"

"It's not the university. I just don't want to do a Ph.D. I'll stay through spring semester since I have my teaching fellowship, but that's it."

"You don't like math anymore?"

"It's not that—"

"You're not giving up on it because it's getting hard?"

"No. Actually, it's not really hard. I'm good at it, Daddy." She looked at him, and he took his eyes off the road to turn towards her full face. "It's just that it's not what I want to be doing with my life."

"I see," he said. Then he asked, "Is there something else you'd rather be doing?"

"I'd like to write."

He didn't speak right away. "Do you have something in particular you'd like write?"

"A novel." And then, when he didn't say anything, she added, "I'm not sure what it's about yet, but there are some characters I began writing about in my short story course in college. I want to do more with them." She hesitated for a moment, then said, quickly, "I'm applying to MFA programs."

He didn't respond right away.

"Is that okay?" she asked.

"Of course it's okay."

"Mom won't be happy."

"It's not her decision," said Nancy's father. "It's yours."

Nancy cleared a small porthole on the window so she could look out. They were driving on an overpass over a river, but the gorge was thick with mist, and she knew a river curled below only because she'd seen it before.

"Was being a doctor Yiya and Papou's decision? Is that why you weren't happy with it?" she asked.

"No, it was my decision," said her father. "They'd always hoped I'd be a doctor—but they didn't push me; I was the one who pushed myself. I was so uncertain of what I myself wanted, it was easy to be guided by their certainty, by what they wanted for me."

"So when did you realize you wanted to do something else?"

"It wasn't until I was actually in a practice. It was all right being pre-med in college. I hated medical school, but I managed to get through it, and I got through my residency. And after all that work, it made sense to just keep going. So I did."

And then he told her about the dead baby. About the night that his life changed. She'd never heard anything about it before. For most of her childhood she'd had only a vague idea that sometime in his past her father had had a different job, that when he'd been young, before he married her mother, he'd been a doctor. It wasn't discussed. All she knew was that being a doctor hadn't suited him.

She didn't know then that she would ever write about it. She didn't file it away thinking: someday I'll use this, there's a novel here. She didn't know then she would ever write about her father. All she knew then was that her father had told her something about himself that she had never guessed at, that he had revealed something that illuminated so much of him, the way he was.

"You left medicine because you'd made a mistake," she said. "But don't a lot of doctors make a mistake sometime in their career, especially when they're young?"

"Oh no," said her father. "That wasn't it at all. I hadn't made a mistake. I could have lived with that. I could, eventually, have forgiven myself if it had been my fault. It might even have made me a better doctor. I was young and would have learned from it. Its grief could have served me. No, it was that it was not my fault, it was the fault of medicine itself. The baby could not have been saved. And that's why I left."

"I don't get it," said Nancy. "If it wasn't your fault—"

"I was up against something too big. I felt powerless. I realized there would be conditions—not just that one—that could never be cured. Babies would die. People would suffer. And even the most brilliant, the most diligent, even the luckiest doctor could not save them." His voice rose on the word *luckiest*.

He paused for a moment. His voice was softer now. "We think we know so much about the human body, but we know so little. Most of it is a mystery, still. I couldn't spend my life in a profession where I toiled against such odds."

She understood then why he was the kind of teacher he was. Why he'd gone off each day with the leather satchel with the repaired handle, his head not square over his shoulders but nosing forward, eager at the prospect of what lay ahead. Why, when he had settled at the kitchen table with a pile of yellow test papers before him, he ruffled through them and straightened the pile like a cardplayer handling a deck of cards, pushed the sleeves of his plaid shirt up on his wrists, took a sip of coffee, and gave a little grunt of pleasure at the enterprise that awaited him. Why he had beamed when the clerk at the hardware store who got up on the ladder to reach a dehumidifier for them turned out to be a former student, and said, "Hey, Mr. Markopolis, great to see you!"

But her father's story of the dead baby was there, growing in secret, waiting for her. Waiting for her to get years away from it. Waiting for her to have become a mother and held her own live baby in her arms, imagined what it would be like to lose it. Waiting for her father to die and for her to have gotten past the sharp grief of losing him.

It wasn't until Nancy had deposited Aliki at college freshman year and come home to confront what her life had become that her new novel began to emerge.

In Aliki's bedroom, she turned right-side-out a sweatshirt abandoned on the back of a chair, folded it, and put it in a drawer. She straightened a mobile of paper birds that had been knocked off-balance, and collected a shoe that had been left half under the bed and reunited it with its mate in the closet. But the room, tidied, seemed robbed of its last bit of life, and Nancy was immediately sorry she'd touched anything. She retreated down the hall to her study. She sat at her desk and looked out towards the river.

When Nancy had gone away to college, her mother had made quite a fuss about how much she would be missing her, but it was only recently that Nancy learned how her father had felt then.

"He was simply undone," Nancy's mother told her. "I thought he was with your brother out in the garage. When I went to call them to dinner, your father wasn't there. I found him upstairs in your bedroom. He was sitting there, at the foot of your bed. He'd been sitting, just looking at your empty room, ever since we'd gotten back to the house. 'I'm trying to get used to this new phase of my life' is what he told me."

"This new phase of my life." The words hovered in Nancy's mind. One grief tugged at another. Her new loss compounded her old one. Aliki had defected—as Nancy certainly wanted her to—by growing up. Her father had defected by dying. He was not here for her now, to listen to her, to help her come to terms with what her life had become.

She thought about that car ride they'd taken together years before, the way he'd listened to her as she told him she'd decided to change her life. She began thinking about the story he'd told her, about the decision he had made and the way his own life had changed. She'd never quite thought of it as a story before, but now it began to take the shape of one. She'd never separated her father from a character that might be drawn from him, but slowly this character began to emerge for her. His story pulled her in. She started to picture the character as a young doctor, leaving the hospital that night. She began to imagine the jacket he might be wearing, the feel of the glass door he leaned against, the overgrown pine trees in the hospital parking lot. She started to write.

VIRGINIA'S HOUSE, where the meeting took place, was the only house in the neighborhood of large, gracious homes that was in need of a paint job, that had a shutter askew. English ivy had claimed part of the brick façade and gotten a stronghold on the gutters. Junipers, which had been intended as foundation plantings, had been allowed to grow in whatever direction they pleased. Nancy had to stick to the far side of the path to escape their itchy branches as she walked up to the front door.

The man who answered the door introduced himself as Virginia's husband, Joe.

"Don't worry," he said, "I'm not joining you folks today. I'm just on doorman duty. You can leave your things in the library." The room he showed her to had bookcases on each wall, but they were inadequate for the job. Books were wedged in sideways and were piled up on the floor. The edges of the drapes and the arms of the sofas looked as if they had been clawed, and the room smelled of cat.

She was the first one to arrive, but Gillian and Bernard came soon after. Nancy took a chair with a high back and wooden armrests. She thought she would feel more confident reading if she was propped upright rather than low on a sofa. She was sorry now she had chosen the skirt. Virginia was wearing slacks (short enough so her brightly colored socks were revealed when she sat down), and Gillian was wearing jeans and scuffed, though obviously expensive, boots.

"Chris may be delayed," said Virginia. "He spent last night in jail."

Gillian let out a hoot. "Jail! This is too good," she said. "What did he do? Wait, let me guess—"

"It's nothing Chris did," said Virginia. "His lawyer missed a deadline for filing some papers about child support. And there was a backup at the prison getting bail."

"Chris in jail," said Gillian, and she gave a broad smile. One of her front teeth was a little crooked. She must not have had braces as a kid, thought Nancy. Although she had always assumed Gillian came from a background of wealth, she wondered now if that was true.

"Be kind," said Bernard, and he wagged his finger at Gillian.

"You know I'm never kind," said Gillian.

When Chris arrived, he didn't look as pink as he had when Nancy had met him for lunch.

"I spent the night in a prison gymnasium," Chris told them. "Cots in three rows running from one basketball hoop to the other. Fluorescent lights glaring. Must have been a few hundred guys in there."

"It sounds as if you have acquired some tidbits for your new book," said Gillian.

"More than enough," said Chris. "And if you don't mind, I'd rather not talk any more about it now."

"Of course," said Virginia. "Chris, I believe you have a chapter for us. And Nancy will be reading from her new book. And I have a chapter, myself."

"I don't think we should wait any longer for Adam," said Bernard. But they didn't have to, because Adam turned up, as if on cue. He sat down on the other side of Virginia. He, more than Chris, looked as if he had spent the night in a gymnasium in a jail.

"Everything all right?" Virginia asked.

"Sure," said Adam, but he didn't say he was sorry for being late. He looked around the circle, and Nancy noticed him pause at Gillian, then pull his glance away. Oh no, she thought, poor guy's in love with Gillian. It didn't surprise her.

"Nancy, would you like to begin," Virginia asked, "or would you prefer someone else to?"

"Oh, someone else," said Nancy. She wanted to go first to get it over with, but she didn't feel ready to read yet.

"Then why don't we begin with Chris," said Virginia.

"Fine by me," said Chris. He was obviously eager to read, had already removed the paper clip from his sheaf of pages.

"Sorry, folks, I didn't make copies for you," he said. "This is first draft, hot off the press. Just wrote it." He summarized the plot of his novel so far for Nancy's benefit, then launched his new chapter. It was fast-paced, but Nancy was worried about her own reading and had to force herself to pay close attention. Chris's main character, a retired journalist on a small-town newspaper, was the same in all Chris's novels, and Nancy could see why they were a success. He would have just the right appeal for a certain kind of female reader—a tough guy on the surface but with the requisite introspective quality and some necessary flaws. Someone had once pointed out that the only narrator you can't create is one who is more intelligent than yourself, but what surprised Nancy was that Chris's narrator showed a sensitivity she would never have guessed Chris capable of.

"There's certainly plenty of action," said Gillian when Chris seemed to be done reading, "but, once again, I have to question if the violence is gratuitous or if it serves to enhance the novel."

"It does serve to further the plot," said Bernard.

"Perhaps, then, we should talk about the plot," said Gillian.

"Hold on," said Chris, "I'm not done yet." He turned back to his manuscript.

He found Jurack's dog first. Even if you didn't like dogs, you'd feel bad for this one. The poor bastard had been so thirsty he'd tried to drink from a vase of flowers. Gotten nothing more than a muzzle full of glass for his efforts.

"Hey, buddy," Dreever said, "how'd you get yourself stuck in a place like this?" He saw a bowl on the table and filled it with water. Set it on the floor. It looked like a bowl that cost a hundred grand at least. Nothing in the place looked cheap. The table was solid cherry, not veneer. His years with Claire had taught him that you can get away with cheap at three feet away, but not any closer. Jurack managed to find girlfriends who had taste and money. In the time he'd been on his own, Dreever hadn't managed to find one with either.

Dreever didn't know for sure that it was Alfie Jurack's dog, but that was a good guess. Not many people crazy enough to own beagles.

"One question I have, Chris," said Bernard, when Chris was done reading, "what do you have against beagles?"

"Nothing," said Chris.

"Than why make a deprecatory statement about them?"

"What are you, some kind of defender of beagles?" asked Chris.

Bernard did one of his exaggerated inhales, as if he were a baritone about to favor them with a cadenza from the *Messiah*. "A beagle was a part of my family when I was a boy," he said. "It was a reliable and handsomely patterned dog. Not a breed to be ridiculed."

"I didn't know you had a beagle!" exclaimed Virginia. "All those years! The only dog you ever spoke of from your childhood was that dog Maisie."

"Maisie *was* a beagle," said Bernard.

Virginia smiled, but not so Bernard could see. "I would never have guessed," she said.

"What kind of dog do we all picture with the young Bernard?" asked Gillian.

Chris waved his arms as if he were an umpire calling a foul. "I believe we were discussing my novel," he said.

"Oh, Chris," said Gillian. "You can cede the limelight for a minute."

"I imagined a dog with"—Virginia chose her words carefully— "stature. A komondor, perhaps, or a Great Pyrenees or a Russian wolf-hound."

"But it was called Maisie," said Adam. People seemed surprised to hear him speak. "That's kind of a commonplace name."

"If I recall, it was named for the Henry James character, so it did have literary pretensions," said Virginia. When Adam looked as if he wasn't sure what she was referring to, she added, kindly, "the novel *What Maisie Knew*."

"I always liked that novel," said Nancy. "It's a manageable size for Henry James."

"Of his shorter works, *The Spoils of Poynton* is by far his best," said Gillian. "And Bernard could have named his dog Fleda Vetch."

"No canine should be named Fleda Vetch," said Bernard, and turning to Virginia he said, "A beagle may be a dog of modest size, but it does have stature."

"I'd like to remind you all that it is currently my turn," said Chris. "Does anyone have a comment about what I recently read?"

"I have a comment about your notions of taste and wealth," Gillian said. "They seem—well—somewhat predictable."

"What are you talking about?" asked Chris.

"Solid cherry table, not veneer."

"Veneer can convey taste and wealth," said Bernard. "Think of the detailing in those magnificent Federal highboys."

"Oh, for God's sake," said Chris. He looked around at the group, as if for help, and fastened his gaze on Nancy.

"I thought the description of the thirsty dog was quite effective," she said. "About the table—I wonder whether your character Dreever would notice that sort of detail."

"I think he would," said Adam. "He's a detective, he's trained himself to observe detail."

"What I'm asking is not so much does he notice detail," said Nancy, "but is he the kind of man who would know the distinction between veneer and solid wood?"

"I think he is," said Virginia. "Part of the appeal of Chris's character is that he has an artistic, more feminine side."

"I should ask you to write a blurb for me," said Chris.

"I'd certainly be happy to," said Virginia, "but my name wouldn't carry much weight on your book jacket—and besides, you hardly need blurbs. Dreever seems to have a fan club of his own."

Chris looked pleased but was trying not to show that he was.

"Stop preening, Chris," said Gillian. "The success of your series proves only that people will read anything these days."

Virginia gave Gillian a look of reproach, but Chris grinned. "I love it when Gillian's envy flares," he said.

"Nancy, you're new to the group," said Bernard, "and I would be distressed if you took this childish competitiveness as a sign that we aren't all deeply supportive of each other's literary"—and at this word he gave Gillian a severe look—"efforts."

"Hear, hear!" said Chris.

"Perhaps it's time we moved ahead," said Virginia. "Nancy?"

Nancy gave a barely perceptible shake of her head. "Would you prefer it if I went next?" Virginia asked gently. Nancy nodded. Gratitude rose inside her. She hadn't realized how it could be an actual physical sensation, but now it spread through her like warmth; she could feel it in her thighs, in her hands, in her fingers. It wasn't just the question of having them listen to and comment on her prose, it was the question of opening her book up to them, this secret part of her life, which no one except Oates had been privy to. It was laying bare all the labor of her making things up—for writing fiction was that, an exhausting amount of fabrication, as if you were a criminal on the stand, spinning lies, each one linked to another.

Virginia's previous and successful book had been about the Middle Ages, and Nancy was amazed to realize that Virginia, whom she had assumed would spend the rest of her writing career embedded in the period in which she'd invested so many years of research, had moved on to Ancient Greece, an entirely different culture, place, and century. But there was a clarity and sureness—is that what it was?—to Virginia's prose that made it seem as if she had devoted her entire life to the world of Agamemnon.

The heat would come later in the day, embrace the plains of Argos, the fortified city of Mycenae, the fields and olive groves around it, but now the air was rich with the cool intricacies of morning. Thirty-two centuries later it would progress this same way, claiming, as the morning eased towards noon, first the rocks at the top of the arch-way, then the flanks of the carved lions at the gate to the citadel. It would move from stone, to wood, to earth, to every living thing. The leaves of each olive tree would struggle to preserve the small territory of shade below it.

In the evening, the heat would recede in the same way. Only hours after the sun had descended into the cleft of the mountains would the stone begin to cool. The stone archway at the gate to the palace would be last of all, as if the two lions who rose in mirror image on their hind legs, reaching for the gods, were flesh themselves.

It was clear to Nancy from the discussion afterwards that everyone admired Virginia's work. Everyone, except Adam, had something to say. Nancy couldn't help wondering if they really knew about Ancient Greece or had boned up in anticipation of Virginia reading her chapter so they could show off at the meeting.

"You know, Ginny, I don't remember our doing Mycenae. Was it on that trip to Crete?" asked Bernard.

"I never went to Mycenae with you," said Virginia. "I went with my mother when I was eighteen. And I went with Joe, two years ago."

"Oh," said Bernard, his face still puzzled. "But we did Delphi, didn't we?"

"Yes," said Virginia. "Though it's not like lunch, Bernie. One doesn't *do* Delphi."

Bernard ignored Virginia's comment and looked at Adam. "We haven't heard anything from you," he said.

"It all sounded great," said Adam. "Nothing to suggest changing."

Nancy turned towards a sound coming from Gillian. It was her boot rubbing against the leg of her chair. Nancy looked up and caught a small, calm smile on Gillian's face, then looked quickly back at Adam. She'd been wrong earlier, she realized. It wasn't that Adam was hopelessly in love with Gillian; there was definitely something between them.

"Let's go on to Nancy, then, why don't we?" said Virginia.

When Nancy was in sixth grade she gave an oral report to her class on the solar system. Behind her, leaning against the blackboard, was the poster board she had made, which featured all the planets in cutout silver paper stapled (the glue hadn't held) on the black background. When she'd practiced reading it at home, the pages flapped in her unsteady hands, and her father had suggested she hold her notebook underneath them. In front of the classroom, the taste of her poorly digested breakfast in her mouth, she'd dutifully lectured her classmates on Jupiter, Neptune, and Pluto, her finger pinched between the metal spirals of the notebook, the secret way she'd discovered to keep herself from panic.

She thought of that now. She held her manuscript on top of the folder she'd brought and pressed her fingertip against the sharp end of the paper clip. As she read, she saw it all, as if she were in a movie theater and had plunged through the two dimensions of the screen into the world beyond it. She was in the hospital lobby, lurking in the dark against the wall, watching the young doctor walk past. He did not see her. He had her father's stature, but his face, which may have originally been based on a photograph of her father when he'd been young, was a face that she had shaped in her mind so it became the face of a different man, a man she had never seen except in her imagination. She watched him as he passed through the door at the side of the hospital's revolving doors, and, invisible still, she followed him and watched as he walked out to his car in the parking lot, got in, and drove away.

She looked up when she was done reading, and the scene in her novel was replaced by the room around her, the faces of Virginia, Bernard, Chris, Adam, and Gillian. She looked down again quickly. It was too late now. There was no taking back what she had laid out. No way of making her novel her secret again.

Bernard was the first to speak. "Compelling," he said. "You drew me right in."

"Got me, too," said Chris. "It's a great opening. Getting that dead baby onstage right at the start."

"You write so beautifully," said Virginia. "We can picture the scene exactly. And we feel empathy for your character. Which is, of course, the most important thing."

Gillian seemed about to speak, and the comfort Nancy had accrued from Bernard's, Chris's, and Virginia's words evaporated in an instant. "Gillian's the one you need to watch out for especially," Chris had said.

"Yes, we do feel some empathy," said Gillian, "but we're left with only a suggestion of what went wrong. Not that the narrator's a tease—I wouldn't accuse you of such a cheap trick—but there's something withheld here that seems artificially withheld. The narrator knows what went on, how this baby died, but isn't saying."

"Isn't saying *yet*," said Chris. "This is only the first chapter, right, Nancy?" He looked at her. Nancy nodded.

"I understand that," said Gillian, "but while Chris talks about getting the dead baby onstage, I think we need to get the main issue onstage."

"What do you think the main issue is?" asked Bernard.

"Guilt," said Gillian. "We need to know what this doctor did that went wrong. We need to understand why he's tormented, why he feels so guilty."

"But he doesn't feel guilty," said Nancy.

"That's even better," said Gillian. "But we still need to know why he *should* feel guilty, we need to know how he messed up."

"But the reason he doesn't feel guilty," said Nancy, "is that he didn't mess up. It's not his fault at all."

"Then whose fault is it?" asked Gillian.

"It's no one's fault," said Nancy. "It just happened."

"Is there a malpractice suit?"

"No, nothing like that," said Nancy.

"Then where's your story?" asked Gillian.

"That's a Chris question," said Bernard, "isn't it?"

"I think there's the start of a story here," said Chris.

"Maybe Nancy isn't interested in a conventional plot," said Virginia. "Maybe this is really a novel about character."

"But if, as Nancy says, 'it just happened,' then we're not really talking about character, are we?" said Gillian.

"Of course we could be talking about character," said Virginia. "We could be interested in how the character responds to what happened."

"Guilt," said Gillian, "is the most interesting emotion. If there's no guilt here, I don't know what drives the character, what drives the narrative."

"You know, you amaze me, Gillian," said Chris. "You're a great poet—we all know that—but you've never written a line of fiction. How can you sit there and talk about driving a narrative?"

"I may be a poet rather than a fiction writer, but that doesn't mean I don't understand fiction," said Gillian. "Perhaps you don't read beyond your genre, Chris, but please entertain the possibility that some of the rest of us do."

"Could we all be less contentious, please?" asked Bernard. "This is getting into an old battleground, and I don't think it's beneficial to Nancy."

"It might be useful for us to know what stage the book is at," said Virginia. "It's different if we're hearing a first chapter of a novel that is already finished in draft, or if it's a novel that has just been begun. Nancy?"

"I haven't finished the book," said Nancy. "But I've thought it through to the end. I mean, I know where it's headed. I know who my main character is and what he's going to do."

"You're writing about a doctor," said Chris. "Do you know anything about that world?"

"My husband's a doctor," said Gillian. "And I can tell you, it certainly is a special world."

"My grandfather was a doctor," said Nancy, "and my father had been a doctor when he was young."

Gillian smiled. "Ah, I see," she said.

Nancy felt as if she had been trapped. The last thing she wanted to reveal to them was that the character in her novel had anything to do with her real father; that she knew what he was going to do because he had, in fact, done it.

"This is a novel," said Nancy. "Fiction." But Gillian was still smiling.

Bernard cleared his throat ostentatiously. He turned to Adam. "Adam," he said. "We've hardly heard from you today. Would you care to inject something new into the discourse?"

Adam stood up, abruptly. "You know, actually, I'm not feeling too great. I'm going to take off now." He picked up his folder from the floor, grabbed the leather jacket he'd slung on the back of his chair, and left the room. He didn't quite slam the front door behind him, but he certainly could have closed it more gently.

"What was that all about?" asked Chris.

"I can't imagine," said Bernard.

"He didn't seem well," said Virginia.

Nancy looked to where Gillian was watching out the window. Adam had gotten into his car and started the engine. Because he was the last to arrive, he had had to park in the driveway rather than the turn-around at the end. He backed out onto the street, his arm slung across the seat back. Nancy noticed that Gillian was still watching out the window even after his car was out of sight.

RACHEL

RACHEL (PEACHIE TO INTIMATES), BERNARD AND VIRGINIA'S daughter, had been a precocious, angelic-looking child with flaxen curls. Now she was an unremarkable-looking, bony young woman, with glasses and brown hair. Precocity, with Bernard and Virginia as parents, had always been taken for granted.

Rachel was a born peacemaker. She was the compliant kindergartner who gave up her turn on the swing set to avoid confrontation, the little sister who relinquished the window seat on the airplane to her brother, the college roommate who took the undesirable upper bunk. But, in spite of all her best efforts, she had been unable to keep her parents' marriage intact. She did her best to be nonjudgmental of all of her father's romantic liaisons that he let her know about, and kept purposefully ignorant about the others. Her brother, Teddy, was less forgiving of their father.

"Please," Rachel had pleaded with him at the time of Bernard's wedding, "Aimee's not that bad."

"It's not because he's marrying someone young enough to be his kid," said Teddy, "it's because he's such a hypocrite."

When Teddy had married a colleague at the research lab, a Russian eleven years older than he, Bernard had said he blamed himself that his son had so little self-esteem that he thought he couldn't do better than a "postmenopausal" woman. But Rachel could understand why Teddy might find Marika attractive. She not only shared Teddy's enthusiasm for fungi, but she had the bright look of a marmoset. If she was mute on the occasion of meeting Bernard, Rachel guessed it was simple terror, not, as Bernard thought, dullness. But Bernard had no appreciation of the mind of a scientist and treated Teddy's choice of a career in biology as a grave disappointment.

Rachel, herself, had been dismayed about her father's marriage to Aimee, but she summoned enthusiasm for both the occasion and the bride. Although she voiced her true feelings about Aimee to Virginia, she never spoke to anyone of her pain at Aimee's transformation of her childhood home—the whitening of everything, as if Aimee were cleansing the house of its past.

"No matter how nice I am," said Rachel, "she's always wary of me, as if she suspects I'm trying to find a wedge between her and Bernard. She's not that way with you."

"She perceives me as old and dumpy, no threat."

"How am I a threat?" asked Rachel.

"You have a claim on Bernard," said Virginia. "You always will."

"And you don't?"

"No," said Virginia. "Not anymore."

When Rachel discovered she was pregnant, she decided to try to gather all her family together for Thanksgiving, in the hope that an announcement of the coming of the next generation might bring about reconciliation. Her husband, Dennis, typically laconic, smiled at her and shook his head. "Easier to bring about world peace," he said.

But Rachel was optimistic. When Virginia and Joe said they would come, she called Bernard. Rachel knew it certainly wasn't something Aimee would choose to do, but she must have been shamed into it by Virginia's good-spiritness, and so Bernard called back to say they would accept, too. Then Rachel was left with the more difficult task of persuading her brother. He was an early riser, and she decided to call him first thing in the morning, before his mind had been taken over by *Rhizopogon occidentalis*.

"We'll have a turkey," said Rachel. "A big turkey." She and Dennis were vegetarians, but she had decided they wouldn't have to eat the turkey, just serve it, and her mother would certainly cook it for them.

"It's not that I don't think you're terrific to take on something like this," said Teddy. "But I just don't want to eat with Bernie."

"He's apologized for what he said," said Rachel. "Can't you ever get past that?"

"It's not just about me and Marika. What about the way he's treated Mom? And I don't mean just in marrying Aimee. I mean for all the shit that came before."

"But if Mommy can forgive him for his foolishness, I don't see why you can't."

"If it suits Mom to forget the past and be chummy with Bernie, that's her business," said Teddy. "But frankly I find it a little weird. Don't you?"

"No," said Rachel. "I find it marvelous, really. And you have it wrong, Teddy. It's not that she's forgotten the past, it's that she's put it in its proper prospective. She's very happy now. She and Joe are really in love with each other."

"Ah, the King of Mattresses!"

"I thought you liked Joe."

"Of course I like Joe," said Teddy in a kinder voice.

"You'll think about it, then? You'll ask Marika?"

"I'll think about it," said Teddy.

RACHEL DROVE OFF HAPPILY to work that day, her mind busy with fantasies. She pictured the long table (two tables pulled together, actually, the split hidden under a white linen cloth) and a cornucopia of food. Heaping platters of roasted root vegetables, tureens of cranberry sauce, two-liter bottles of wine. She pictured Dennis tinging a fork against the side of his glass, putting his arm around her, and announcing, "Peachie and I are going to be having a baby." And then everyone would hug everyone, and her father, not bothering to wipe tears from his cheeks, would embrace Teddy, his only son.

Rachel taught English at The Academy. Her field of interest was the Metaphysical poets, but she had no hope of teaching John Donne. The curriculum was determined by the senior members of her department, and she didn't even get to select which books to read.

"We don't teach literature anymore," she had complained to Bernard. "It's all about multiculturalism. I'm teaching Zora Neale Hurston and Amy Tan."

"Amy Tan?" asked Bernard.

"Don't even ask," said Rachel.

"No Shakespeare?" asked Bernard.

"We did *The Merchant of Venice*," said Rachel. "But we focused on the issue of anti-Semitism. We're doing *Sense and Sensibility*, but the only reason I get to teach a Jane Austen novel is that she's hot right now."

"Jane Austen, hot?" asked Bernard.

"Yes, Daddy," said Rachel. Dennis thought Bernard was sometimes deliberately obtuse, but Rachel believed in what she called her father's "innocence of popular culture."

"What about Aimee?" asked Dennis. "She's hip, and they live together. A little of it must rub off on him."

Rachel always chose her words carefully when she was discussing Aimee, even when it was with Dennis.

"Aimee can accomplish only so much," she said.

RACHEL'S GOOD MOOD lasted until lunchtime, when she was summoned to an unexpected meeting in the headmaster's office. She'd just sat down at the desk in her office, hoping to catch up on grading some papers while she ate. She slipped her half-eaten avocado wrap back into its plastic container, grabbed her jacket, and went across the quadrangle.

The headmaster, Donald Bruer, who liked to be called "Bru" by both colleagues and students, had pulled his chair around to the front of his desk. He was a small, excessively clean man. Beside him sat Stewart Joralemon, in the English Department. Rachel didn't know Stewart well, but she did know he'd been at The Academy for many years. He was paunchy and hairy, and had eyes that didn't line up properly so you never knew which one to look at.

"We have a little situation here," began Bru.

"A case of plagiarism," said Stewart. "There's no point in using a euphemism."

Bru swallowed, nodded, and went on. "Stewart got two papers turned in that are a cause of concern. There were paragraphs in both of them that seemed beyond the skill of the students—not, of course, that students here don't often produce superlative work—but these seemed, ah, extraordinary."

"Plagiarized," said Stewart.

"After questioning the two students separately," continued Bru, "he concluded that one of the students had provided a paper for the other. And that both papers had relied heavily on sources that had not been perfectly attributed."

"Goddamn it," said Stewart, and he slapped the table beside him. "We're not talking about imperfect attribution here. We're talking about plagiarism."

Rachel pulled back into her wing chair, as if she could find protection between its upholstered flanks.

Bru didn't move, but Rachel could see the muscles under his chin tighten up.

"According to our honor code, certain infractions might well result in a student's suspension or even dismissal. Often, however, there are mitigating circumstances. And that's where your help would come in."

Stewart stood up and pushed his chair back. "Suspension, dismissal—it's your call," he said. "But both of these boys are getting failing grades in my course. And if it ruins their chances for Harvard, all the better." He left the office door open behind him, and Bru had to get up to close it.

"I'm sorry you had to be a witness to any unpleasantness," he said to Rachel when he resumed his seat. "I know you're wondering what any of this has to do with you. One of the students involved, Paul Traub, is, I believe, in your advisory group."

"Who's the other student?" asked Rachel.

"Thayer Henniman." His face betrayed almost nothing. But Rachel understood it all in an instant. Thayer, scion of the family that had endowed The Academy with its new dormitory complex, was a slow-witted, lazy student, and a bully. He would no doubt be president of the country someday.

She didn't need to ask, but she did anyway. "Who wrote the paper for whom?"

"It seems Paul wrote it for Thayer," said Bru. "Paul wouldn't say anything about it, but Thayer confessed. Actually, he used it as an excuse to counter Stewart's charge of plagiarism. He was angry that Paul had given him what he described as a 'crappy' paper." Anyone but Bru would have smiled.

"And what do you want me to do?" asked Rachel.

"I'd like you to talk to Paul. Get his confidence. Find out what went on here. Is he selling papers to other students?"

"And when would you like me to do this?" asked Rachel.

"Today," said Bru. "I'll have a note sent to Paul that he should skip hockey practice this afternoon and meet you in your office after class."

"I see," said Rachel.

"And then you and I could have a meeting here about it afterwards."

Rachel's head swam. Her immediate inclination was to say, "Yes, of course," but the sight of the firm crease in Bru's chinos made her pause.

She couldn't have an honest meeting with Paul and then trot over and report everything she'd learned to Bru. "I'll stay late to meet with Paul today, as you requested," said Rachel, "but I'm afraid I'll need to leave right after that."

Bru blinked. "Then we'll meet tomorrow," he said.

IN HER OFFICE, at the end of the day, Rachel waited for Paul to turn up. She didn't know him very well. He was quiet, unobtrusive, and he'd never come to talk with her about anything beyond the official advising meetings that were required. She looked through the manila file folder with his name on it once again, but there was nothing revealing there. He was a day student, not a boarder, as were all the students who had been assigned to her. He had distinguished himself neither by achievement nor disgrace. His grades were respectable. He had chosen hockey for his outside sport. He played the clarinet.

Rachel knew from Virginia that he was the stepson of Gillian Coit, a writer friend of her parents', but she didn't know much more about him. She looked again through the folder. He'd previously gone to a public school in Connecticut, where his mother, whose name was Linda, now lived. Rachel wondered why Paul wasn't living with her. Rachel laid her arms across her belly. It was unimaginable to her that she would ever turn the rearing of her future child over to a stepmother. Even if the child turned out to be an impossible teenager— and as far as she knew, Paul was rather nice, for a teenager. But it was also unimaginable to Rachel that she and Dennis would ever not be together, that Dennis would have another woman for a wife, that she would have another husband. That her divorced parents might have once felt that way about their own union, she acknowledged. But she and Dennis were different. She was certain of that.

Paul had been standing by her half-open office door for a minute or two before she turned and realized he was there. She had expected him to knock, but obviously that was foolish of her. Boys like Paul didn't knock, they just waited. The somewhat more courageous ones coughed or cleared their throats.

"Hi," she said, "come have a seat."

Paul had dark hair, left long perhaps to hide his face and his acne—though it possibly contributed to the acne problem. Rachel remembered from her own, not so far away, acned youth. He was flushed from jaw to cheekbone, either from the outdoors (he probably ran to get to her office) or embarrassment, or some combination of both. He slumped into the chair beside her desk, his shoulders so curled, his legs so sprawled, it was if he were a boneless creature who had been poured onto the seat.

"I thought I might start by asking you about things like hockey and what bands you're listening to these days," said Rachel, "but then I figured you know why you're here, so we might as well deal with it right away and get it over with." Rachel gave a sigh. "Bet you don't want to be talking about any of this," she said.

Paul looked up at her. What she'd said had obviously surprised him.

Rachel leaned in closer to him, her voice just a note above a whisper. "Actually," she said, "I don't really want to be talking about this either. But Mr. Bruer"—she couldn't bring herself to call him Bru—"asked me to—since I guess you weren't particularly forthcoming with him, and since it's my job . . . well, here we are." She smiled at Paul, but he wasn't ready to smile back.

"What I heard," said Rachel, "is that there are two issues in your case. One, that you turned in a paper that wasn't entirely original work. And the other that you gave—or maybe sold—a paper to another student. Or at least that's what he said."

"I didn't sell it," said Paul.

"I didn't think so," said Rachel. "But why did you write it for him?"

Paul looked down.

"Okay," said Rachel. "Guess we should talk about the first issue. Here's what I don't understand. You're a pretty good student. And English is one of your better subjects, isn't it?"

Paul nodded.

"So why did you need to copy stuff from the Internet? It's not like you couldn't come up with some ideas for yourself."

"I don't know," said Paul.

"Have you done something like this before?" asked Rachel.

"No," said Paul.

"Mr. Joralemon takes things like that pretty seriously." Rachel caught herself. "Actually, I take things like that seriously, too," she said. "Everyone here does. Do you think maybe you just weren't clear about how to attribute things? Is this maybe just a case of your not knowing how to handle secondary material properly?"

Paul was looking at his lap, studying a speck on his jeans. His hair fell forward on his shoulders. His scalp, visible along his crooked part, was painfully white. Rachel wanted to brush his hair back, cover it.

"No," said Paul. He spoke so softly Rachel had to lean closer to hear him. She felt relieved hearing him say that. There wasn't a student at The Academy who could honestly claim innocence about attributing material properly, certainly none in Stewart Joralemon's class, but half of the kids in Paul's situation would have seized that as an excuse.

"You know plagiarism can result in a student's suspension or dismissal," said Rachel. "Don't you?"

"Yes."

"Is that why you did it?"

"Huh?" asked Paul.

"You're a smart kid, Paul, you knew what the consequences were," said Rachel. "I have to guess that you did it for a reason. That maybe you wanted to be caught."

"Why would I want that?" asked Paul. He looked up at her without lifting his head.

"So you would get suspended and you wouldn't have to go to this school anymore?"

"You think I wanted to be kicked out?"

Rachel shrugged. "I was just guessing that maybe you wanted a reason to move back and live with your mother."

Paul's head jerked up. He looked straight at her. "That's all wrong," he said. "If I didn't want to be here, I wouldn't be here. I could be living with my mom. I don't need a reason."

"Then why did you do it?"

"I didn't have time to write two papers. I had to do something."

Rachel turned back to her desk for a moment. She straightened the lid on her plastic sandwich container, then aligned the container with the notebook on her desk.

She looked back at Paul. "Why did you have to write two papers? I can't believe Thayer Henniman is a friend of yours. Why would you do a paper for him? Did he threaten you, Paul? Or did you owe him something?" As soon as she said that, she was sorry. Paul's face looked suddenly like the face of an old man. He turned away, towards the window, but not in time. He blinked but could not stem the flow of tears.

"It's not like that," he said. "It's just that he asked me, 'cause he knows I've been doing okay in that class. And it didn't seem like such a big deal."

"But what did you hope to get out of it?" asked Rachel.

"I just wanted him to like me. He's really popular. Now he's pissed at me because he got caught because I screwed up on the paper. And now all his friends will be pissed at me, too."

"He deserved to get caught," said Rachel. "And I can't imagine that his friendship is worth very much in any case."

"That's easy for you to say," said Paul. He turned back to Rachel. "It's not like I have any real friends here."

"I'm sorry," said Rachel, and she had to fight her instinct to touch Paul's arm. She was fairly sure he would not want to be touched.

"So is Bru going to kick me out?" asked Paul.

"I don't know," said Rachel.

"My dad's going to hit the roof," said Paul. "He'll probably send me back to my mom's even if they don't kick me out. Unless Gillian—my dad's wife—doesn't want him to."

It seemed to Rachel that they were straying into an area she probably would be happier not knowing about, but still, she was curious.

"Are you and Gillian buddies?" she asked.

"No way!" said Paul. "But Gillian likes it that I chose to live this year with Dad instead of Mom. She likes beating my mom at things. Jennifer, my sister, is living with Mom. She and Gillian don't get along at all."

"And you do."

"Sometimes," said Paul.

Outside, through the window, the photosensitive bulbs in the lights along the campus walkway turned on. It was still light enough so the lamps seemed pale, but Rachel knew it would get dark quickly. She looked over at the clock on her wall.

"I think we've talked enough for one afternoon," said Rachel. "You're still in time for the van home, aren't you?"

Paul's eyes followed hers to the clock, then he checked the pocket watch hanging from his backpack. "Yeah, I'll make it," he said. "No problem."

She wanted to cradle him in her arms. She wanted to tell him that it wouldn't be that long before he was grown up, and this place and all the petty things about it would be safely stowed in his past. She wanted to tell him that Thayer Henniman wasn't worthy of being his friend, that he was worth a dozen Thayer Hennimans. She watched him out her window as he ran along the path and cut across the lawn down towards the hockey rink, his backpack slung over one shoulder. In the distance, in the shadow, he looked like a boy with a misshapen back.

$\mathcal{P}$AUL

PAUL STARTED WALKING TOWARDS THE HOCKEY RINK, BUT when he reached the road, he hesitated before he crossed it. It was quiet on the street, and no noise came from the rink, although Paul could instantly hear the noise in his head, the swoosh of skates against ice, the hammering of puck against stick, the double tweet of the coach's whistle. The windows of the building were set high, under the curve of the roof. Lit up now, against the white of the walls, they looked like two upside-down, glowing smiles. Practice would be over soon, and the double doors would open, spilling boys out into a parking lot beside the building. In just a few minutes, parents' cars and the school vans would start arriving.

Paul slung his backpack farther up on his shoulder. Instead of crossing the street, he turned left and headed away from The Academy. There was no way he'd make it back to campus in time for the van, and he had no idea how he'd ever get home, but he didn't care. He was already in such deep trouble that one more thing could hardly matter. It felt for a second wondrously light, the not caring, but then terrifying, too. He wasn't used to the lightness. He had little experience with just doing something without running through all of the possible consequences, worrying over each one.

The sidewalk had recently been upgraded from concrete to brick, with granite curbs, but it petered out dismally, and without warning, at the end of The Academy's property. From there on Paul had to walk along the side of the road on the uneven gravel shoulder. Most of the traffic was on the opposite side of the road, cars heading away from town at the end of the workday, but they came along fast. There was a squirrel lying in the road, squashed and bloodied. Paul didn't want to look as he passed close to it but couldn't stop himself from looking. Its tail was moving, and Paul thought at first it was waving it in a gro-tesque gesture of agony—but that was crazy, because how could the squirrel have all its insides squished out of it and still be alive? Then Paul realized it was the wind that was blowing the squirrel's tail, and the squirrel was most certainly dead. That seemed a lot better. He shifted his backpack to his other shoulder and tried jogging along for a while, but the books in his backpack were heavy, and he was tired, and he slowed to a walk again. It was edging towards dusk.

A few miles later he turned off on a side street, just past a church set up on a hill. The street was wide, with an island up the middle. It was planted with rhododendrons and azaleas and must have had its pine bark mulch recently applied. The smell was intoxicating, and Paul wanted to lie down there and bury his nose in the mulch. He wanted to bury himself in it completely. I could do that, he thought, I could just do that. But he didn't; he kept walking along the street, his eye on a house close to the next corner.

It was a large, Tudor-style house, old enough so the ornamental trees and shrubs had grown up around it, softened its corners. Paul had lived here when he was a child, when his parents were still together. He'd been here once before this year. He and his father had come out this way, and his father had decided to just drive by. No one was around now; nothing moved. Paul crossed over to the lot and stood by a hemlock tree on the side. He looked up at the brick wall. There was a small, mullioned window in the curved brick façade. It was on the landing of the staircase, set low enough so when he was little he could look out of it. He'd loved that corner of the house, a little carpeted room neither upstairs nor downstairs, with its own small window that let him see all the way down the street. Through the turned walnut spindles of the stair railings he could see across the foyer of the house to the front door and, to the right, into the living room.

When his parents had split up, his mother hadn't been able to keep the house because she couldn't afford it, and then she'd moved to Connecticut for work and bought a house half the size. Paul's father had liked the house, but Gillian wouldn't live in it. They'd built their new house farther out in the country, a modern house where all the windows were big open spaces of undivided glass and the floors were great stretches of pale, bare wood with only a few flat woven rugs scattered here and there.

A spotlight went on in the yard, and Paul jumped back against the branches. But no one emerged from the back door, and Paul guessed it was a light on a timer. Still, he was afraid of being caught there, and he crossed the street to the island and stood for a moment, looking at the front of the house. He hadn't lived there since he was six or seven, but he remembered the layout of the rooms, knew which windows were which. On the left of the house was a new addition, a glass conservatory, that looked all wrong. If Paul had had a stone in his hand, he would have wanted to lob it through one of the panes. In the kitchen, on the wall behind the door to the basement, every year his mother marked his height and his sister, Jennifer's. His mother had cried when they were leaving the house and she'd seen the pencil markings there with all the dates.

In August, when he'd left his mother's house in Connecticut to come live with his father, his mother had cried, too.

"You can come home anytime you want, Paul," she'd told him. "Just give me a call, anytime, and I'll come and get you." But she probably wouldn't mean that now, not after he'd been expelled from The Academy, not after what he'd done.

He hadn't wanted to see her crying then, and he'd gone out to his father's car in the driveway, leaving his father to grab the last suitcase.

But he'd turned back to look. His mother's face was all blotchy and red, like a little kid's.

"Come on, Linda," his father had said, "give the boy a break."

And his mother had slapped his father across the face, slapped him hard.

Now the weight of consequence, which Paul had been spared for the past hour, came back to him heavier than before. He had to get back to The Academy. He had to call his father and hope he would come and pick him up. He couldn't call him from here because he couldn't let anyone know that he'd come to look at the house. He didn't even know why it was important, but he knew it was a secret he wanted to keep.

He walked back up to the main road and started hiking back towards The Academy. His backpack felt heavier than ever, and he opened it and considered which book he might chuck. His science book was the heaviest, but he got it only halfway out of the zippered opening before he lost courage and stuffed it back in again. He had his back to the traffic now, and every time a car passed him, he felt its whoosh and smelled its exhaust. He was so tired now, and it was already dark. He wondered if he would ever make it back. He'd never hitchhiked before in his life, never dared to, but at the next cross street, where there was a circle of light, he turned to face the oncoming cars and held out his thumb. If he were caught hitchhiking, that would be one more crime added to the list. He'd been warned enough about the dangers—he knew boys could be victims, too, not just girls—but he didn't know what else to do; he didn't think he'd make it walking back.

Three cars and a truck passed him by, but then a pickup truck slowed down and pulled over. Paul had been half hoping no one would, that he wouldn't actually have to carry through with his wild idea of hitchhiking. There was a pile of demolition material in the back of the truck and a black Lab sticking its head out of the window.

"Where you headed?" a guy called out to him.

"Just up the road a few miles," said Paul.

"Hop in," the guy said. He had frizzy brown hair and a thick, frizzy beard that so engulfed his face you'd think he'd suffocate behind it. Paul paused for a moment. The guy didn't look like those pictures you saw in the paper of kidnappers or murderers, but with all that hair, it was hard to read the expression on his face. He didn't seem drunk, though, and the dog seemed like a good sign. Murderers didn't usually have dogs with them. Or did they?

"You coming?" asked the guy.

Paul swallowed and climbed up into the truck. The guy pushed the dog back into the small space behind the seat. There didn't seem to be any seat belt, and Paul didn't dare ask about it. The dog sniffed Paul's neck and clawed the seat.

"That's Nero," said the guy.

"Nice dog," said Paul. It seemed like the right thing to say.

The guy didn't say anything more. He drove fast, but he didn't pass the car in front of them. They passed some woods, and Paul couldn't stop himself from thinking it looked like the sort of place someone would dump a body. But soon, more quickly than Paul had expected, they were approaching the grounds of The Academy. The distance had seemed so much longer when he had been walking.

"Anyplace along here," said Paul.

"You got it," said the guy. He pulled over not far from the hockey rink and looked out across the lawns. Paul could tell that he was taking it all in, taking in the kid he'd given a lift to.

"Thanks a lot," Paul said, and he got out of the truck and grabbed his backpack. The dog jumped back up into the seat, wagging its tail furiously.

"Right," said the guy, and he drove off. Paul felt weepy with relief. He climbed the rise and dropped his backpack on the ground. He called his father's cell phone, and his luck still held, his father answered. He told his father he'd had to stick around late to work on a project with a kid who lived on campus. He wasn't good at lying, but his father didn't question him. Half an hour later he picked up Paul. He talked all the way home about a patient of his who had been a professional baseball player, a southpaw who had played a few seasons with the Red Sox. It was obvious that Bru hadn't gotten through to him yet. Maybe Bru had spoken to Gillian. Though when they got home, she greeted them both in her pleasant, cool way, and she made no move to take Jerry aside to have a word with him before they sat down to dinner.

But you could never tell about Gillian. She was inscrutable. She could be thinking anything, harboring anything, waiting to spring it on you, and you wouldn't know.

They were eating Chinese food for dinner. The table had been set with chopsticks, but Paul used a fork. He kept stealing glances at Gillian. Her chopsticks were shiny red as finger nail polish, and she was eating cautiously, the fine tips of the chopsticks pinching a mushroom, a few grains of rice. Long after Paul was finished eating, she was still working on her small portion, her arm moving slowly from plate to mouth, the chopsticks like extensions of her slender fingers.

AFTER DINNER PAUL RETREATED TO HIS ROOM. The house was built into the side of a hill, and his bedroom and Jennifer's were on the lowest level, with an adjoining bathroom and a large recreation room. The master bedroom was on the second floor, above the main living level, far enough away so no child could hear the sounds of adult love-making or, as Linda had pointed out when he and Jennifer were younger, too far away for any adult to hear if a sick child called out in the night. Paul's and Jennifer's bedrooms had large windows looking out across the meadow, but they had a basement smell that even dehumidifiers couldn't successfully combat. Jennifer refused to sleep in her room, and so Jerry had persuaded Gillian to relinquish the guest room on the main level to Jennifer. Not that it mattered much, since Jennifer almost never came to stay. Linda, who was concerned about mold and allergies, said she didn't want her son sleeping in a cellar while he was living with his father, but Paul liked his room, liked the fact that it was tucked deep in the house, out of the way of everybody. There were sliding glass doors that led directly outside, so Paul could come in and out as he pleased without really having to let anyone know. Not that he ever did.

Paul figured that if Gillian had heard anything, she would have brought it up at dinner, or just after. But when he'd announced he was going downstairs to his room, nothing was said. Here, in his room, Paul felt he was safe, at least for a while. His father and Gillian hardly ever came down here. He had homework to do, but he didn't feel like doing any of it. He had a book to read for Mr. Joralemon's class, but what was the point of reading it if he was going to fail the class anyway? What was the point of him doing any schoolwork if he was going to be suspended or expelled? He didn't know what he was going to do the next day. It seemed odd that he would just go to school in the morning, same as always. Still, nobody had told him to do anything different. And he had to go back to the school anyway, since he had stuff in his gym locker and books he'd borrowed from the library. His good Nalgene bottle was in his locker at school. He wasn't just going to leave it there forever. He grabbed his sketchbook and pen, put his headphones on, and settled back on his bed, drawing while he listened to a band that an old friend of his in Connecticut had told him about and no one at The Academy had ever heard of. The drummer was too loud and not very inventive, but that was okay. Loud was good.

In the art class Paul had once taken, the teacher said you should always sit properly at a table when you drew, but Paul liked to work stretched out on his bed. He had always been good at art—his mom still had the self-portrait he did in sixth grade framed on the wall—but he hadn't liked the art class much. He wanted to draw the stories inside his head, not some fruit in a bowl. His friends back in Connecticut thought he'd be a great superhero comic book artist someday, but he hadn't let anyone at The Academy see his drawings.

They must have knocked, but Paul didn't hear the knock on his door. He was startled when he saw it opening slowly and his father's head suddenly pop into his room, like the clown in his old jack-in-the-box, which had frightened him as a child. He sat up in bed and fumbled to turn down the volume on his speakers.

"May we speak with you for a moment, please?" said Jerry.

Paul didn't need to ask what it was about. He slid his sketchbook behind the pillow and pulled his knees up and hugged them close to his body. His father entered the room, Gillian just behind him. He saw them looking around, trying to find a place to sit. The bed was piled with stuff, which was a good thing. Paul didn't want either of them that close to him, didn't want either of them sitting on his bed. Jerry moved some clothes from the desk chair to the desk and offered the chair to Gillian. She sat, and Jerry stood beside her, one hand on her shoulder, linking them together, making it clear to Paul that whatever they were going to say to him had been worked out in advance, that they were a team. Paul's navy blue Academy sweatshirt was still draped over the chair back, one arm hanging limply.

Jerry's face looked bloated, the way it did just before he started yelling at Paul's mother. Gillian's face was serene, unsmiling. She looked straight at Paul.

"Gillian received a call today from the headmaster of your school," began Jerry. "What she heard from him was upsetting to both her and to me."

Paul pulled back closer to the wall. He looked down at his feet. He had a hole in his sock, and his toe stuck out like a little white, bald head.

"I'm waiting for you to say something," said Jerry. His voice was louder now. "What's been going on with you? What the hell did you think you were doing?"

Paul didn't say anything.

"Look at me!" shouted Jerry.

Paul looked up. Gillian's hand moved and rested on top of Jerry's hand on her shoulder. Her voice was soft and cool.

"Paul," she said, "we don't really understand what could have motivated you to do something so"—she paused for a second, not so much to search for the perfect word as to lay emphasis on it—"so dishonorable," she said. "It's puzzling to both of us, since it seems previously you had been doing perfectly acceptable work in that course. And it's particularly distressing to me, since you live here, with me, and should know to value the words of any writer. The Internet may make things easy, but it's no excuse."

"I didn't say it was," mumbled Paul.

"What was that?" asked Jerry.

"Nothing," said Paul. He moved closer to the wall, but he was in the corner; there wasn't anyplace to go.

"If you ever borrow anything from another writer," said Gillian, "you need to transform it, make it better. You need to make it yours."

"Here's what you're going to do, young man," said Jerry. His voice was rising again. "You're going to sit down tonight and rewrite that paper. And you're going to bring it to school with you tomorrow and turn it in to your teacher."

"I'm going to fail the course anyway," said Paul.

"It's not a question of failing or not failing," said Jerry. "It's a question of doing things right."

"What about Thayer's paper? Do I have to do that one, too?"

"Thayer?" asked Jerry.

"The other kid."

Jerry looked at Gillian. "What's this all about?" he asked.

Gillian shrugged. "I don't know," she said. "All that was discussed with me was the question of plagiarism, and the possible consequences the school is considering for Paul."

"Let's not get offtrack here, then," said Jerry. "And, Paul, I don't want you trying to lay any of the blame for this on some other kid."

"That's not what I was trying to do," said Paul.

"If you're expelled from The Academy," said Jerry, "we're going to have to hustle and get you enrolled in the public high school, you know that, don't you? And you know what a disappointment this is to Gillian and to me? It was no easy trick getting you admitted to The Academy. Gillian had to really pull strings to get you in."

"I can go live with Mom," Paul said. "I can go to school there."

"That certainly occurred to me," said Jerry. "But Gillian thinks you should be allowed to continue living here with us. She wants us to give you another chance. I'd like to hear you say thank you to her."

"Paul doesn't need to thank me," said Gillian. "I know how remorseful he must be feeling right now about all of this." She stood up and started walking towards the door, her hand around Jerry's arm.

Jerry sighed. "All right, then," he said. He followed Gillian, but before he left the room he stopped and took a hard look at Paul. "What I want you to do is get up right now and sit at your desk and get to work rewriting that paper. I expect it done before you go to sleep tonight." He thumped his knuckles on the footboard of the bed.

Paul closed his eyes, but his lids didn't hold back his tears. He didn't open his eyes until his father and Gillian were gone, until his room was his again.

$\mathcal{V}$IRGINIA

IN THE UNDERSIZED, OVERHEATED KITCHEN OF RACHEL'S APART-
ment, Virginia basted the turkey while Rachel stirred the vegetarian
stuffing, which was sequestered in a pot, a safe distance from the roasting
bird. Rachel had assigned Joe and Dennis to look after the guests in the
living room. Bernard and Teddy would both be on good behavior, but
the tension between them was so palpable it was safer to keep them apart
until the meal was served. While Teddy could be counted on to avoid
Bernard, Virginia wasn't sure Bernard could be trusted to avoid Teddy.

Rachel was wearing a hot angora sweater. Her face was flushed, and
her wire-rimmed glasses had slipped down on her moist nose. Virginia
knew that the sweater had been a gift from Bernard and Aimee, selected no doubt by Aimee, and that Rachel was wearing it even though
she was uneasy about the possible mistreatment of rabbits that had gone
into its creation. Aimee herself wore only tailored, expensive clothes in
greys and black, and although Rachel's style was less severe, she would
never have selected a sweater like this, pink, with sequins and a scal-
loped neckline. Virginia wondered if this was how Aimee saw Rachel,
or if there was just a touch of condescension in the gift. Not charitable
of me, she thought. And she was too happy not to have charitable feelings, even about Aimee.

Virginia pushed the turkey back into the oven and turned to Rachel.
"Would you like me to take over for you, Peachie?" she asked. "You
look like you could use some fresh air."

"Thanks, Mommy," said Rachel. "I'm fine. Really."

Virginia smiled, and because she was so happy, because she couldn't contain herself, she leaned forward and kissed Rachel on her glistening brow.

"Oh, darling," said Virginia. She had learned Rachel's secret two weeks ago and knew that Rachel had planned this occasion to share it with all the family. When Rachel had called to confide in her— and that in itself was a miracle, it was only in the past few years that Rachel was so open with her—Virginia laid her head down on her desk and cried with happiness and relief. She'd never let Rachel know, but she'd been afraid that Rachel, serious and hardworking as she was, might never get around to thinking about motherhood until it was too late or that, because Rachel and Dennis were poor but re- luctant to accept monetary aid, they would feel they couldn't afford to be parents.

Rachel had asked Virginia to keep the news a secret from everyone, even from Joe, but Virginia had pleaded. "He'll see me going around the house with a besotted look on my face," she'd said, "and what am I to tell him when he wants to know why I'm so happy? I'm really quite incapable of lying to Joe."

"You're hopeless, Mommy," Rachel had said. "But Dennis and I did want to surprise everyone with this at Thanksgiving, and now if Joe knows, he won't act surprised, and then Daddy will know that I told you and not him."

"I'll make Joe swear ahead that he will act suitably surprised," said Virginia.

In fact, Virginia hadn't told Joe, not exactly. Eager to prove wor- thy of her daughter's confidence, yet disinclined to have any secret from her husband, she'd solved her moral quandary with a semantic trick.

"Rachel has confided in me something quite wonderful," she'd told Joe, "but would prefer that I keep it a secret for the moment. I'm sure you can guess what it is, but would you mind very much if I left the telling of it to Rachel herself?"

Joe's answer had been to take Virginia in his arms. "Oh, Ginny," he'd whispered. "What happy news!"

Dennis came into the kitchen, ostensibly to see how things were going, but Virginia guessed it was probably to escape from Bernard, who tended to patronize him, and Aimee, who tended to ignore him. He kissed the back of Rachel's neck.

Rachel turned around towards him suddenly. "You're not leaving certain parties unchaperoned out there together, are you?" she asked.

"Joe's talking to Teddy and Marika," said Dennis, "and Aimee's out on the porch making calls on her cell, and Bernie's somewhere, I don't know where, but a safe distance from Teddy."

"Go look after him, please," said Rachel.

"Don't you need some help in the kitchen?" asked Dennis.

"Mommy and I have dinner under control," said Rachel. "You menfolk are on cleanup detail, remember?"

"Does that include me?" asked Bernard, who had come into the kitchen, wineglass in hand.

"Sure, Daddy, you're included. We have an apron in your size."

"I like washing up, Peachie," said Bernard. "I'm an expert with crystal that doesn't go in the dishwasher, and I always did the pots for your mother, didn't I, Virginia?"

"You did not do the pots for *me*," said Virginia. "They were your dirty pots just as much as they were mine." But she gave Bernard a friendly little poke on the arm. They were going to be grandparents together. Just wait, she wanted to tell him, there's something marvelous in store for you.

"Maybe Aimee would help you set the table," said Rachel, "when she's done with her calls. I left the seating chart on top of the piano."

"All right," said Dennis, and he went off to the dining room. Virginia was fairly sure he wouldn't seek Aimee's help.

When Dennis was gone, Bernard made himself comfortable on a stool by the kitchen counter, unfazed by the chaos around him and, it seemed to Virginia, remarkably unaffected by the heat. He'd always been able to tolerate extremes of temperature, and now he made no move to loosen the cravat around his neck, or remove the new cashmere blazer that Virginia guessed Aimee had outfitted him in.

"So, Peachie, tell me what's been going on at The Academy with Gillian's stepson," said Bernard. "She made some mention of his being on probation there—I gather he's something of a problem at home—and I figured you'd know more of the story."

"Oh, that!" cried Rachel. She turned the heat off under the pot of stuffing and covered it with a lid. "That poor kid, Paul. He got bulldozed into writing a paper for an odious boy named Thayer, whose family's a major Academy donor, and when Stewart Joralemon figured out there were some parts that had been lifted from articles on the Internet, he hauled in Thayer. And do you know what Thayer said in his own defense?" Rachel paused, and Virginia shook her head and smiled at her daughter. She admired the passion Rachel brought to her work, but she did worry sometimes about Rachel's intensity.

"He claimed he wasn't guilty of plagiarism because he hadn't written the paper at all, Paul Traub had written it. And here's the kicker: he was actually indignant that Paul had given him what he called a 'crappy' paper!"

"Why was Paul writing a paper for another student?" asked Virginia.

Rachel pushed her hair back off her face and took a deep breath. "That's what makes it such a heartbreaking story," she said. "Paul's one of those shy, unpopular kids. He wanted Thayer to be his friend."

Bernard cleared his throat. "Maybe, Peachie, Paul is more clever than you think. Maybe he felt pressured to produce a paper for this

Thayer character and inserted plagiarized sections with the hopes that Thayer would be exposed. The perfect revenge."

"Oh no, Daddy, not at all," said Rachel. "Paul's the kind of kid who would never imagine doing anything like that. He's innocent— pathetically so. And his own paper had unacknowledged quotes in it as well. He was stuck trying to produce two papers in a short time and didn't know what else to do. You said Gillian suggested he was a problem at home. I can't believe that. My guess is that Gillian is a problem."

Bernard raised his eyebrows. Virginia had to smile. She had guessed that once, most probably after she and Bernard were no longer together, there had been something brief between Bernard and Gillian, but she was fairly certain that Rachel had no idea.

"You like this boy, don't you," said Virginia.

Rachel sighed. "I hate to see any kid get treated unfairly," she said.

"If all he got was being put on probation, it sounds as if he was treated rather leniently," said Bernard.

"But that's only because I knew about Thayer," said Rachel. Her face was red now. "Donald Bruer wanted to suspend Paul and let Thayer off. But that would be unconscionably inequitable. How could I keep silent about that?"

"Is that what you told him?" asked Virginia.

Rachel nodded and shrugged. "Something like that."

Virginia smiled. She could just see her slender daughter, her slender *pregnant* daughter, rising to the defense of this hapless boy.

"I know Stewart Joralemon," said Bernard. "I always took him for a rather square, honest chap."

"Oh, *he* was fair. He was going to fail both boys in his course. But Donald Bruer couldn't have Thayer Henniman fail a course. So he arranged it so both boys dropped the course so it wouldn't appear on their records."

"And Joralemon went along with that?"

"Not exactly," said Rachel. "He took an unexpected early retirement. At least that's the official word. But he was forced out. They're paying him well, but they won't let him teach anymore."

"Oh, Peachie," said Virginia, "I'm so sorry you have to work at a place like that!" She wanted to say that maybe, once the baby was there, Rachel could leave that job.

"I like the students, though," said Rachel. "Well, most of them, that is."

"You should be teaching at the college level," said Bernard. "You should be teaching Donne and Marvell."

"There aren't a lot of jobs around here, Daddy, you know that," said Rachel. "I'm lucky to have the job I've got."

Teddy, with Marika so close behind him her head seemed perched on his shoulder, was standing in the narrow kitchen doorway.

"What's the prognosis for dinner, Peachie?" he asked. "We've got a long drive home."

"I think we're just about ready," said Rachel. "Aren't we, Mommy?"

"I think so," said Virginia. She looked back and forth between her two offspring. "I love having the two of you both together," she said, and then, because she noticed Marika, quickly added, "I love having us all together for Thanksgiving."

THERE WAS A PLACE CARD FOR EACH GUEST, hand-lettered, Virginia could tell, by Rachel. Rachel had put Teddy and Marika at one end of the table and Bernard and Aimee at the other. She and Joe were across from Rachel and Dennis. There was such an abundance of food and drink laid out that Virginia knew, even if they sat there for a week, they'd never eat it all. It was Virginia who had carved the turkey, and, in deference to Rachel and Dennis, the carcass of the bird resided in the kitchen and only a platter of sliced meat was out on the table. Joe, as instructed by Virginia ahead of time, lifted his glass and proposed a toast. "Here's to Peachie and Dennis for hosting this sumptuous feast, and for bringing us together. And here's to a happy Thanksgiving to all."

Marika had her head down, eyes shut, as if in preprandial prayer, but no one else seemed to miss a more religious invocation. "Huzzah!" cried out Bernard, and there was a raising of glasses, although the table was too broad for people actually to touch glasses with anyone except the person sitting on either side. Bernard attempted to clink his with Teddy's and Marika's across the table, then rather ostentatiously got up from his seat and walked over to their side so he could do it properly. He had tucked his white linen napkin (a wedding gift set) in under his chin. He always did this in restaurants, which made him look like a giant baby with a bib. It was one of the quirks that had annoyed Virginia when she had been married to Bernard but that now seemed not only harmless but mildly amusing.

Thinking of babies, Virginia looked over at Rachel, sitting catty-cornered to Bernard. She looked a little worn-out but beatific. She leaned her head on Dennis's shoulder. They'd probably be making their announcement once everyone had had a first run on the food.

"I've done it!" said Joe, and Virginia turned to him.

"What?" she asked.

Joe pointed to a glob of cranberry sauce on the white tablecloth.

"I'll soak it in cold water later," said Virginia, "but for now—" She looked around the table and saw that everyone was absorbed in what they were doing, covered the spot with her bread plate, and gave Joe a conspiratorial smile.

There was the sound of a knife tinging against a glass. Virginia looked towards the sound. It was Bernard. Virginia wanted to think it was sweet of Rachel to have given this honor to her father. But she couldn't help feeling surprised that Dennis had ceded the privilege to

Bernard, and she was disappointed Rachel had conspired with Bernard when all along Virginia had been feeling so privileged by what she'd believed was her special prior knowledge.

Once he had everyone's attention, Bernard cleared his throat.

"Since we are all gathered here, Pilgrim style, on this rare occasion, there is an announcement of a coming joyous event which it is my great pleasure to share with you."

Virginia settled back in her seat; her moment of displeasure had passed. It hardly mattered who made the announcement; the important thing was that Rachel was going to be a mother. She looked at Rachel, but the look of contentment had vanished from Rachel's face. Rachel held her fork midway between her plate and mouth, a piece of sweet potato speared on the tines.

"Aimee and I," said Bernard, and he paused for just a second, "are going to be having a baby."

Virginia heard what Bernard was saying, but the meaning eluded her until she saw Rachel's fork drop to her plate.

"Oh my," said Rachel softly.

"What?" asked Teddy. Virginia turned to look at her son, who was seated beside her. He threw down his napkin, pushed back his chair, and stood up from the table. "You've got to be kidding!" he said.

"Please, Teddy, sit down. Please!" cried Marika.

"Well," said Joe after a moment had passed. "Congratulations are certainly in order." He held up his glass.

"I'm sorry, Peachie," said Teddy, "but I'm afraid I can't deal with this. Come on, Marika, we're leaving."

"Please, Teddy, we can't leave here now. We can't leave all of this!" Marika gestured to the table, to the food, to the circle of people.

Bernard, his arm around Aimee, stared at his son. Aimee had her eyes pinched shut. Virginia knew Aimee was wishing that she was anywhere else except at this dinner table, with these people. She would have liked to have felt sorry for Aimee, but her heart was entirely focused on Rachel. She and Dennis would never make their announcement now. Bernard had stolen her moment from her, stolen not just that. Bernie, Virginia thought, how could you do this to her? How could you do this to our Peachie?

Rachel was looking at her father sitting next to her. Virginia could see how hard she was working to arrange her face so she wouldn't betray how she was feeling.

$\mathscr{A}$DAM

$\mathbf{A}$DAM HADN'T PLANNED ON GOING HOME FOR THANKS-giving, but Kim had invited him to spend the holiday with her family, who lived nearby, and he needed an excuse to avoid going. He was afraid if he stayed in his apartment he might feel so sorry for himself he'd end up accepting Kim's invitation, or worse, she'd discover he was alone and arrive on his doorstep with a platter of stuffing, gravy-soaked mashed potatoes, and turkey smeared with cranberry sauce, covered in tinfoil.

It was too late to get a plane reservation, so Adam drove out to Western Pennsylvania, calling his folks to let them know he was coming when he stopped for gas along the interstate. His parents still lived in the brick farmhouse where he'd grown up. They'd chosen to live out in the country, rather than in Pittsburgh, where his father worked, because they felt it was healthier for children, but the farmland around them had ended up being strip-mined. As a kid Adam had been fascinated by the excavation project, and sorry when the land was finally restored. But he'd taken a different view of strip mining when he began working on his new novel, which was set in the area. Though the hills had been returned to something resembling their original gentle contours, the landscape had been irrevocably altered. He'd first described the coal as a cancer that had been hollowed out of the earth, the skin then folded back over the incision. But that metaphor made the mining seem curative rather than exploitative. Coal was an intrinsic and ancient part of the earth. And though the fields had been reseeded, they were like scar tissue, covering the place where a vital—and in this case healthy—organ had been removed. Driving through these hills now, he felt as if the landscape he had been conjuring in his mind had been waiting for his return. It was vividly corroborating the sorrowful past he'd been trying to document.

When he arrived at his parents' house, Adam made his way through the gauntlet of relatives and deposited his duffel bag on the twin bed in his old bedroom. While the room his two sisters had shared had been turned into a study, his bedroom had been preserved intact, a shrine to his adolescence. The wall over his desk displayed a mortifying collection of documents testifying to his supposedly exemplary youth: his science fair award, his commendation from the youth symphony orchestra, his literary contest honorable mention. He thought he'd stack them all in the closet, but when he lifted the first framed certificate off the wall, it left a rectangle whiter than the wall surrounding it, a ghost of his achievement. At the family dinner, he bore up as well as he could under his parents' undiluted approbation, their enthusiasm for his girlfriend, Kim, whom they had seen pictures of, and their admiration for his job. He made more money than either of his parents ever did—a source of embarrassment for him and pleasure for them. He put up with numerous jokes about shoes. Several relatives wanted to know when they could read "this book" of his, and he cornered his mother in the kitchen to set this straight.

"I'm not even done writing it," he told her. "And even if I do finish it, I don't know that I'll get anyone to publish it."

His mother wiped her hand on her apron before laying it on the side on his cheek. "Of course you will," she said.

At night, after a halfhearted attempt to help with dishes, he went out with his cousin Rick and got so drunk that he confessed his job sucked and all he wanted to do was work on his novel, but he didn't breathe a word about Gillian. Even if he was totally wasted, he wouldn't breathe a word about her.

THE LEOPARDIS had planned only one meeting after Thanksgiving. Then there would be a long break until after Christmas. Adam would have been happy to meet every week, but everyone else, except possibly Chris, had too much going on over the holiday season. It was unbearable for Adam to think of going so long without seeing Gillian, but seeing her at the group's meetings was unbearable as well.

Kim believed he had been what she called "moody" because of problems at work, and he did not correct her. Things at work were shitty— Phil, a guy whom he had once thought of as a friend, had edged him out on a project—but he didn't really care. He just wanted to write, and when he sold his novel (dared he even think that? shouldn't it be *if?*) he'd tell his job to go to hell and never look at another cross trainer again. Kim cleaned out his refrigerator for him, she bought a gizmo with wooden balls to massage his back, she made him pancakes, arranging the blueberries into a face with two eyes and a smile, the color of a bruise. It was easier to make love to her than not.

He went with Kim, Christmas shopping at the mall. She wanted him to buy new jeans.

"The ones I've got are fine," he told her.

"I'd like you to get some that really fit," she said. "Something a little stylish."

"They're just jeans," he said, but he tried on various pairs for her: boot cut, straight leg, wide leg, and bought two, to please her. He kept thinking about what Gillian might like—if she noticed something like the fit of jeans. He wasn't sure.

Kim was knitting him a sweater for Christmas. It was a complicated pattern, which involved a lot of needles with points at both ends and seemed to require more than her two hands. He knew he had to get her a Christmas gift, and he slowed as they walked past a kiosk displaying silver jewelry. Earrings were safe: they didn't seem like a commitment of any sort. Adam ran his finger along a row, setting the dangling shapes in motion.

"Do you like any?" he asked Kim.

"These are nice," she said. She was looking at a row of studs with nautical themes: starfish, dolphins, scallop shells. "Who are they for?"

Adam didn't say anything, but he smiled, and Kim gave a little "ooh" when she realized he meant her. He bought her dolphins impaled on silver posts.

"Do I have to wait until Christmas?" she asked.

"Nah," he said.

She took off the earrings she was wearing and inserted the new ones, admiring them in the mirror by the display. From a distance they looked more like crescent moons than tiny dolphins, perpetually leaping up in the air, over Kim's soft earlobes.

THE LEOPARDIS MET AT NANCY'S HOUSE. It was the first time Nancy had hosted a meeting, and it was clear that she'd gone to great lengths, baking a coffee ring, cranberry bread, and lemon squares. Mugs, glasses, and spoons were lined up evenly along the counter, a stack of cocktail napkins fanned out beside them. There was coffee, tea, cider, beer, and wine. Adam helped himself to a beer and was about to drink from the bottle when he thought better of it and poured it into a glass.

"We're not accustomed to such splendor," said Bernard. "Nancy, you'll make someone a fine little wife someday."

Adam thought Virginia looked as if she might smack him.

Nancy was obviously used to Bernard. "I intend to do just that," she said. "And if you're good, you'll be invited to the wedding."

"Who's getting married?" asked Chris, who had just come into the room.

"Our beloved Nancy," said Bernard.

"Will I be invited to the wedding?" asked Chris.

"I'll invite you all," said Nancy.

"Ignore Chris," said Virginia. "You're too gracious. You're not obliged to invite any of us."

"I don't see it as an obligation," said Nancy, but Adam guessed that, in fact, she might.

Gillian didn't turn up until they were about ready to begin. He watched her cast her eyes around Nancy's living room, appraising it, and wondered what the source was of the look of faint amusement on her face—the coasters laid out on the coffee table? the bowl of pine-cones? the crocheted pillow that was probably a kid's craft project?

"Hello, Adam," Gillian said when she saw him. You would think there had never been anything between them.

Chris had a revised section of his novel that he wanted to read.

"It's the courtroom event that was referred to in the version I read a few weeks ago," he said. "You all suggested I develop it as a scene. So here it is."

"I don't believe I remember that," said Bernard.

"It was my suggestion," said Gillian. "As you once put it so persuasively, Bernard, we're all deeply supportive of each other's literary efforts."

Chris cleared his throat ostentatiously.

Outside the Westshire County Courthouse, it felt more like August than April. Tulips, planted by the city, had succumbed to the heat a week before. The area around the ashtray by the door was scattered with butts that had missed their mark.

"As you see, there's a break here," said Chris. "I'm not sure if I want to leave it this way or connect the narrative better."

"Just read," said Gillian.

Chris started to say something, then went back to his manuscript:

No one would have picked him out. In the overheated third-floor room of the courthouse, fifty citizens waited to see if they were stuck with jury duty. It was only 8:30, but already hot. The chairs were set in rows facing a TV at the front, tuned to a cooking show. The reception was so bad it looked like it had been filmed in a snow squall. Two ceiling fans struggled to stir the warm air.

Some of the people dozed, some watched TV, some read. No one paid particular attention to the man in the second row. If they noticed anyone, it would have been the woman with tattoos banding her flabby arm. Or the kid with the chains who looked more likely to be on trial than judging one. The man had an Ivy League look. The kind of tan you get on a sailboat, not working in a field. He wore a blue striped shirt and neat, navy slacks. But the shoes were all wrong—hiking boots with mud still on them. Mud not more than a day old. He appeared to be dozing, but he wasn't dozing.

Chris continued reading at his usual speed but slowed for the last part of the chapter, when the whole jury pool was sent to a courtroom for possible impaneling.

One by one the jurors were called up to the bench and the judge decided who to excuse. The defendant's lawyer stood between him and the court stenographer. The defendant wore a suit obviously bought for the trial. He had a recent haircut.

The prosecuting attorney was a blonde in a lime green dress. Her dress clashed with the blue curtains and the American flag by the window. Both attorneys eyed each potential juror. No one eyed them more intently than the defendant, the man accused of a dozen rape charges and sixteen counts of indecent assault and battery.

"I think I must be missing something," said Virginia. "Is the defendant Alfie Jurack?"

"Not Alfie," said Chris, "his buddy."

"Refresh me, please," said Bernard. "Who is the gentleman with the tan. Not Dreever?"

"You're not supposed to know yet," said Chris.

"But he is relevant, I presume," said Bernard.

"You bet," said Chris.

"It should be *whom*, not *who*," said Gillian.

"*Whom* is the gentleman with the tan?" asked Chris.

"One by one the jurors were called up to the bench and the judge decided *whom* to excuse," said Gillian irritably.

"I was kidding, Gillian," said Chris. "I knew what line you meant. And although you might not believe I know a direct object when I see one, I'd like to defend my word choice as an acceptable colloquialism."

"Shabby grammar is never acceptable," said Gillian.

"But we do need to be sensitive to narrative voice," said Bernard. "In this case *who*—though I admit it makes me uncomfortable—might be a reasonable alternative. It's the author's call."

"My guess is a copy editor will catch it," said Nancy, "and request you change it."

"I spend half my life defending my prose against copy editors," said Chris.

"I'd like to address the overall effect of the scene," said Virginia. "It catches our attention. We want to find out who this man is, and what he's plotting. It does seem as if something's going to occur as a result of his presence at this trial. Chris, as always, you create suspense quite beautifully. The descriptions have your usual economy. I might suggest the references to the heat at the beginning seem redundant."

Chris flipped back to the first page of his manuscript. "I guess I might not need *warm* air," he said. "*Stale?*"

"Just *air* would suffice," said Virginia.

"I agree with Virginia," said Nancy. "The scene does arouse our interest. And that jury room seems so real—I was stuck on a jury recently; I wasn't actually called, though. I wonder if you might reconsider the word *blonde* for the attorney."

"She is blond," said Chris.

"That's hair color," said Nancy. "You called her 'a blonde,' which has a different tone than 'she was blond.'"

"I think the tone's intentional," said Adam. He hadn't planned on saying anything, but he wanted Gillian to notice him, to acknowledge he was there. "It's the narrator's attitude—cheeky."

"If that's what Chris intends," said Nancy, "that's one thing. But I thought the narrator was more neutral."

"I'd like to comment on the stereotype of the 'Ivy League look,'" said Gillian.

"It is a look," said Chris.

"Then describe it, and we'll know."

"You've been teaching too many writing workshops," said Chris, "doing the old 'show me don't tell me' routine."

"For the regrettable duration of my undergraduate career, I was a member of the Ivy League," said Bernard, "yet I certainly don't see myself as a stereotype."

"You did sail, though," snapped Virginia. Adam was surprised by her uncharacteristic sharpness. She turned to the others and added, more gently, "When I first met Bernie, he referred to a 'yawl' and I thought it was a southern affectation rather than a boat."

"I'd like to see something more distinctive about him," said Gillian. "I'm referring to the character, not Bernard."

"I think that's the point," said Nancy. "There is nothing distinctive about him. That's why we notice the mud on his boots."

"An ominous detail," said Bernard.

"I don't think it's ominous," said Adam. "I think it's meant to show he's an outdoors guy. Maybe he's really a farmer."

"In a blue striped shirt?" asked Gillian. She looked at him now.

"Even a farmer might own a blue striped shirt," said Adam. "And he's not going to wear his work clothes on jury duty."

"That's a good point," said Nancy. "But I think the mud is supposed to be ominous. Some crime . . ."

"You've been reading too many detective novels, Nancy," said Adam.

"As long as she reads all of mine," said Chris.

"I think it's time we moved along," said Virginia. "Adam, you have something for us this week, don't you?"

Adam nodded. He pulled out copies of his chapter and passed them around. He watched Gillian while she set a paper-clipped packet on her lap and passed the sheaf on to Bernard. Even if he had no choice but to give up on ever having anything more with her, what he wanted, at the very least, was that she take him seriously as a writer. He looked at her for a minute longer, then he turned his attention to what he was going to read.

It wasn't until April, a vicious April with hailstorms that knocked out power, and rain so heavy the already-sodden ground turned to mush, that I took Sonia to hear my old friend Mickey's band play at a club in a part of town that had missed out when there had been a halfhearted attempt at urban renewal.

"Fallen Archangels?" Sonia asked, laying the pronunciation firmly on the wrong syllable. "What does that mean, Bill?"

"It doesn't mean shit," I said. "Every band tonight has a name dumber than the next."

When we got there, Mickey was hanging around the bar, trying to pick up either one of two girls who looked so young they must have had fake IDs, his drumsticks sticking out of his back pocket, his jeans pulling down in the back so you couldn't miss seeing three inches of boxers imprinted with blue penguins on skateboards, and a swath of pale, nearly hairless ass. I introduced Sonia, but the band that was finishing its last number was deafening and I could have been just moving my lips, not saying anything at all. I got two beers quickly, not even asking Sonia what she might want to order, and herded her over to a stretch of seating along the wall. She was wearing the four-inch, toeless heels—orange canvas with laces that wrapped up around her shins—she'd bought the day before, even though the sidewalks were still a minefield of puddles from the day's rain, and even though I'd warned her that she might be spending the night on her feet, and knowing that she'd be having trouble staying upright but would be afraid to complain, I took pity on her now. She sank, gratefully, onto the bench, which was upholstered with fabric so beer-stained and worn you would never guess that it had once been red velvet, and pointed to the sign above our heads, which read "Earphones $1."

"Joke?" she asked.

"No joke," I said.

There were four guys in Mickey's band and a girl named Viv, who did vocals and keyboard, whom Mickey had once tried to fix me up with, but it had gone nowhere pretty fast. Viv was the size of a ten-year-old, with bleached hair pulled into a dozen little pigtails, fierce, dark eyes set too close to her nose, skinny thighs, and tiny breasts, which I'd had no desire to touch, either then or now. Sonia, who had been trying to lose weight ever since I'd met her, even though I kept telling her I liked her the way she was, beside me now seemed, in comparison, as lushly endowed as Rubens' Angelica, a virtual continent of flesh.

Sonia, as Adam had originally described her, had been plump and voluptuous, an incarnation of the sort of woman he had once desired, or thought he desired. But later, with the image of Gillian's slender body in his mind, he felt he was betraying that beauty by having Bill, his narrator, salivate over Sonia's well-endowed body. He'd rewritten that whole section, switching body types between Viv and Sonia, though keeping their heads intact, and planned to go through the entire novel and alter Sonia's body so it was more his current ideal. But Sonia, the character whom he had created, didn't work with a double A cup size. And Viv, whom he had first imagined as having an undernourished, little girl look, was no longer Viv when he deposited another fifty pounds on her. The problem with fiction was that, once you created the characters, they had a way of taking off on their own, and they resisted—just as adamantly as real live people—any attempts to assign them a new head or body.

Adam finished reading his chapter, then looked up slowly from his manuscript. Virginia was beaming at him. Thank God for Virginia.

"Fine scene, fine scene," said Bernard. "What is this group the Fallen Archangels?"

"It's not a real band," said Adam, "I just made it up."

"Good name," said Chris.

It did not surprise Adam that, while they praised his dialogue, once again he found himself under attack for his verbosity. Virginia zeroed in on Sonia's shoes.

"You don't need to tell us they were 'four-inch, toeless heels—orange canvas with laces that wrapped up around her shins,'" she said. "Four-inch heels would suffice."

"But the reader might picture the wrong thing entirely—black patent leather," said Adam.

"It's too many details," said Virginia.

"I think *orange* matters," said Nancy. "It tells us something about Sonia."

"Then keep *orange*," said Virginia, "but we don't need to know they're canvas and open-toed."

"Adam designs shoes for a living," said Chris. "You're never going to get him to relinquish anything in that department. I think what needs some trimming is Mickey."

"I rather like Mickey," said Bernard.

"I think the paragraph about the April weather and the 'part of town that had missed out when there had been a halfhearted attempt at urban renewal' could be tighter," said Nancy. She'd read his lines in a way that made them sound verbose, thought Adam. "Could you just say *seedy?*" Nancy asked.

"*Seedy* is so seedy," said Chris.

"You're all talking about details," said Gillian. At last, she was entering the discussion. "There's one major problem with Adam's novel, and it's time we focused on that."

"So, are you planning to reveal what it is," asked Chris, "or keep us guessing?"

"It's the first-person point of view," said Gillian. "Bill may be the main character in this novel, but he's not a good choice for a narrator."

"His voice is credible," said Virginia.

"His credibility is not the issue," said Gillian. "It's the texture of his voice. He's verbose because he's self-absorbed. He can't relinquish any of his observations because he cares too much about them. He's mired in his point of view."

"But so much of this novel depends on his special perspective on things—it's essential that we see Sonia through his eyes," said Virginia.

"A third-person, limited-omniscient narrator can handle it all," said Gillian. "And spare us Bill's claustrophobic voice."

"Well, well, well," said Bernard. "That's quite a tall order. Adam's already written several hundred pages."

"Switching point of view isn't that difficult," said Gillian. She picked up Adam's chapter. "Here, for starters:

There were four guys in Mickey's band and a girl named Viv, who did vocals and keyboard, whom Mickey had once tried to fix up with Bill, but it had gone nowhere pretty fast. Viv was the size of a ten-year-old, with bleached hair pulled into a dozen little pigtails, fierce, dark eyes set too close to her nose, skinny thighs, and tiny breasts, which Bill had had no desire to touch, either then or now.

Isn't that better?"

Adam could not lift his head to look at her. "Self-absorbed," "mired," "claustrophobic"—the words she'd used were describing his character, Bill, but she was really telling everyone what she thought of him.

GILLIAN

GILLIAN'S CHRISTMAS TREE, SET UP BY THE WINDOW IN THE front hall, was so lush and symmetrical it looked artificial. All of her childhood, Gillian had longed for the kind of tree she'd seen in the homes of her friends, trees laden with colored lights, glittering balls, and a profusion of ornaments, but now that she could have any kind of tree she wanted, she let her old fantasy rest in the past, unfulfilled. Her tree was chaste, with tiny, clear lights, blown glass balls that looked like soap bubbles, and a sprinkling of silver ornaments. No angels— Gillian hated angels—no Santas, no reindeer.

Gillian's parents always said they didn't have the money to waste on a Christmas tree and settled for a wreath, with a droopy bow and little artificial apples with their glaze chipping off. Her aunt, the one who had underwritten her college education, who could have mounted an impressive tree, never bothered. The Christmas that Gillian was eleven she'd persuaded her brother, Ned—he was in the merchant marine now and she hadn't seen him in years—to venture out to the woods with her and cut down a tree. She held back the branches so Ned could crawl underneath and get to the trunk with his saw. The pine needles pricked her bare wrists and her toes froze, but she felt dreamy embed- ded in the scent of the pine needles. She didn't move until Ned cried, "Watch out, Gilly!" and the tree swooshed to the ground. They carried the tree back home and set it up on a makeshift stand. In the forest, in the company of other white pines, it had seemed full and green, but alone in the living room, it proved to be a scraggly thing, and its puny branches sagged under the weight of the bread-dough ornaments Gillian had made. Her father actually laughed at it.

"Now why'd you want to drag something like that into the house?" he asked.

Although Gillian would have been content to ignore Christmas entirely, every year since they had been married, she and Jerry had installed a tree and given a holiday party, a way to reciprocate for a year of party invitations. The guest list was a disharmonious combination of Jerry's colleagues from the hospital and Gillian's literary acquaintances. Fortunately, the house was spacious enough so they didn't have to mix. Gillian's agent, prestigious and somewhat doddering, and her editor, prestigious and rather youthful (though not as young as he looked), came up from New York, an obligation they suffered manfully. Gillian did her best to insulate them from the more sycophantic of the guests—which included not only writers but doctors who, within sniffing distance of a New York editor, remembered their brilliant idea for a book.

Paul had been excused from helping Jerry and Gillian decorate the tree, but Jerry had made it clear that his attendance at the party was required. Since the plagiarism incident at The Academy, Jerry had been trying to be firm about his expectations for Paul. Gillian didn't really care if Paul was at the party or not, but she understood why Jerry wanted him there, this pretense of them being a family. As for next year, she knew if she suggested Paul return to live with his mother, Jerry would agree. What she didn't want was Paul, on his own, choosing Linda over them.

"Could I do the bartending?" Paul asked.

"Since when do you know anything about bartending?" Jerry asked.

"I don't, yet," said Paul. "But I could learn. I've got a book. It's just formulas for mixing things, like chem lab."

"The caterers have a professional bartender," said Jerry. "What I'd like you to do is be sociable with the guests."

"Actually, there is something particular I could use your help with," said Gillian. "Chris, one of the writers who's coming, is bringing his two sons with him, and I was hoping you might entertain them."

"How old are they?" asked Paul.

"I'm not sure," said Gillian. "Six or eight?"

"You want me to babysit!" Paul sat up straight in his chair.

"It's not exactly babysitting," said Gillian. "Their father will be here."

"So can't they just watch a video or something?"

Gillian tilted her head and smiled at Paul. "You've always had an affinity for children," she said. "I thought it would lovely if you could do something more engaging with them."

Paul sighed and slumped in his chair.

Gillian smiled at him again. "Thank you, Paul," she said. "I really appreciate your helping out."

In exchange for this favor, Gillian sided with Paul that he be allowed to wear jeans to the party, but Jerry insisted he put on a tie and blazer. Although Jerry and Paul were dressed similarly, when they stood near each other in the kitchen before the party, they didn't look much like father and son. Gillian guessed they never would. Even if Paul filled out so he had Jerry's bulk, he had his mother's long neck and narrow nose. It was Jennifer who resembled her father.

Gillian thought that Adam would probably not come to the party, but there was always the chance that he might. He had been avoiding her for weeks—not so dramatically anyone else would notice, but Gillian noticed. She thought it was probably a good thing that he was keeping his distance. And yet she hoped he would come to the party. She wanted him to see this house. The Leopardis met at the homes of members who lived closer to town, and he'd been away and missed her party last year. She wanted him to see her with Jerry.

She selected an ankle-length black velvet dress with a slit that revealed a stretch of long, slender leg. Gillian had small breasts, but the dress was sleeveless and cut low, and it was tight enough so you could see the jut of her hip bones. She didn't like jewelry, but to please Jerry, she wore a hammered silver bracelet he'd had made for her. Her thin, white arm looked like the appendage of a banded bird.

Jerry's friends came to the party on the early side and quickly congregated close to the bar. The writers always drifted in later. Nancy was the first to arrive, with the man she was now apparently engaged to, whom she introduced as Oates. He had a wide expanse of forehead and pale eyebrows, and his features seemed crowded in the lower half of his face. Gillian could imagine him rolling up his sleeves and washing pots in the kitchen after dinner, but he was not the kind of man she could imagine in bed. Nancy was wearing a frilly white blouse, a red skirt, and earrings that dangled little golden bells. Gillian had an urge to strike one with her fingernail, set it dinging close to Nancy's ear.

Gillian could tell that Nancy was studying Jerry, trying to make out something about him, trying to figure out what had drawn him and Gillian together. Nancy was holding Oates's hand, and Gillian wondered if she was going to remain attached to him that way all night. She had something she wanted to ask Nancy. She'd have to get her aside later, when Nancy might have disentangled herself from Oates.

Gillian kept an eye on the front door, watching the arriving guests. She didn't want to be watching for Adam, but she couldn't help herself. Just when she had succeeded in convincing herself that he wouldn't come and had turned her attention away from the front door, he must have arrived. The next time she looked that way she saw him standing near the door, a girl leaning on his arm so she could unzip her boots. Adam gazed at her, and even when she smiled at him, his mouth remained a fixed line.

The girl had slipped a pair of dress shoes on her feet, high heels with pointy toes. She stood up now and looked at Gillian. She was astonishingly young. Even in her high heels, she was inches shorter than Gillian. She looked like a little girl playing dress-up.

"This is Kim," said Adam.

Kim. So, thought Gillian, they had stayed together.

"Hi!" said Kim. "Thanks so much for inviting Adam and me." She had a round face and long, silky blond hair. And she was so young! It had taken Gillian by surprise, and yet why was she surprised? At Button, Adam had told her that Kim was a college student. "Comp sci," he had said, so though she looked sweet, she must be reasonably intelligent.

"I'm pleased you could come," said Gillian. She looked at Adam, but now he was looking at Kim.

"I love your tree!" said Kim. "Is it real?"

"Oh yes, it's real," said Gillian.

Kim stepped closer to the tree and reached out to touch a branch. Given a harp and a halo, she'd make a credible angel.

"Why don't you come inside and get yourselves something to drink?" said Gillian. She rested her fingers on Adam's shoulder as they walked to the living room. She knew Adam was looking everything over hard, taking everything in.

"I love your house!" said Kim. "Adam, don't you just love their house?"

Adam nodded and gave a grunt of assent. Kim had slipped her arm through his. Gillian saw her give it a squeeze.

"Thank you," said Gillian. "Please, make yourselves at home."

A waiter came up with a tray of hors d'oeuvres. Gillian heard the doorbell ring again and watched Jerry go to greet the next guests, Chris and his sons. She looked around and spotted Paul, who was hanging out beside the bar.

"Paul!" she called softly, and when he looked up, she beckoned to him. He came ambling over.

"This is my stepson, Paul," she said. "Paul, this is Adam and Kim. Kim is interested in the house, and I wondered if you'd show her around?"

"Sure," said Paul. He looked dazzled, as if he'd been asked to escort a movie star.

"Adam, I need your help," Gillian said. "Nancy is standing over there with her fiancé, Oates. They don't know anyone here. Would you be kind and go talk with them for me? Chris has just arrived, and I have to find something to keep his little boys entertained." She steered Adam across the living room to where Nancy and Oates stood, wineglasses in hand, making conversation with each other. Adam looked back towards Kim, and Gillian looked back, too. Kim, safely across the room, waved. Anyone might have mistaken her for a high school kid, a friend of Paul's.

CHRIS'S SONS—one was a Sam, the other, a Ben, but Gillian wasn't sure which was which—looked meek and unadventurous. Chris had come prepared with a movie, and Gillian felt no qualms about leaving them on their own to watch it in the den.

"Is everyone else here already?" asked Chris.

"Virginia and Bernard haven't come yet, but Adam and Nancy are here."

"Is that the famous fiancé?" asked Chris, pointing across the living room.

"His name is Oates," said Gillian.

"I'll grab myself something to drink and check him out," said Chris. "Is that the usual gaggle of physicians by the bar?"

"It is."

"You should bring Nancy over to introduce to them. She can pick up some tidbits for that novel of hers."

"I don't know that Nancy is interested in picking anything up. She seems to be fairly set on what she wants to do."

Chris thrust his finger at Gillian. "You just don't like it when people don't snap up your advice," he said.

"Maybe so," said Gillian, "but there's not much point in taking our time to consider a manuscript if you don't want to listen to what we have to say."

"Oh, Nancy listens, all right," said Chris. "But you and she have different visions of what her novel is."

"You thought it was presumptuous of me, didn't you, a mere poet trying to tell a novelist how to redirect her novel?"

Chris laughed. "I don't think I dared call you presumptuous," he said. "And I know I'd never call any poet 'mere.'"

"But you did tell me, didn't you, that if I thought writing a novel was as easy as instructing someone else to write a novel, I should try it myself?"

"I said something like that," said Chris, "but I believe I qualified it with the word *condescend*. You should *condescend* to try it yourself."

"*Condescend* used ironically, of course."

"Of course," said Chris.

Virginia and Joe joined them now, Joe with a bottle of wine, Virginia with a basket of Christmas cookies.

"Are we the last ones to arrive?" she asked.

"Bernard hasn't made an appearance yet," said Gillian.

"Oh, Bernie," said Virginia. Gillian thought she looked relieved.

"Where are those little boys of yours?" Virginia asked Chris. "I've made enough cookies so they can bring some home with them."

"Ensconced with *Miracle on 34th Street*," said Chris, and he pointed down the hallway towards the den. Paul was just returning with Kim. He had a ridiculous expression on his face. He was obviously smitten.

"Does Paul have a girlfriend now?" Virginia asked Gillian.

"That's Adam's little girlfriend," said Gillian. "Paul was just showing her around."

Gillian introduced Kim around and introduced Paul to those who didn't already know him; then she moved close to Adam.

"Paul's given Kim her house tour. Would you like me to give you one?" she asked.

Adam nodded. He didn't say anything to Kim; he followed Gillian. She had expected that he would. She showed him around the lower floor first: Paul's room, the bedroom Jennifer had abandoned, the rec room with the exercise equipment no one used. On the first floor they toured the kitchen, the pantry, the laundry room, the guest room, and Jerry's study. Gillian pointed to a glass-fronted bookcase. "Jerry is my archivist," she said. "He keeps a copy of every edition of my books." Adam tilted his head to read some of the titles, but he didn't comment.

Chris's sons looked up when they came into the den, said "Hi," then went back to watching their movie. Someone had given them a tray with a bowl of chips and something to drink.

"My study is upstairs," said Gillian. Her bare feet made soft pattering sounds on the wood steps. Adam followed more noisily behind her. Gillian walked into the bedroom. The bed in the center was low and white. Her black skirt dragged along the edge of the duvet as she crossed the room. She pushed the half-open door of the bathroom fully open, so he could look in. The marble countertop was so highly polished it looked wet. Her study was through the bedroom. The desk was placed under a window that looked out over the meadow.

"Sit here," said Gillian, and she pulled out the chair at the desk. Adam sat.

"This desk was made for me by a young man who was a student of mine when I taught at Harvard one summer. He gave up poetry and turned to carpentry instead."

Gillian stroked the surface. "Smell the wood," she said. "It's cherry, and it has a special beeswax polish."

Adam bent towards the desk, and closed his eyes, and smelled.

"You've seen my writing place in Truro," said Gillian. "And this is where I write when I am here. Now you've seen everything important about me."

Adam laid the side of his face on the surface of the desk. Gillian ran her finger along the side of his ear and down around the curve of his cheekbone. It was so quiet in the room she could hear her fingertip moving along the fine hairs on the edge of his ear and the stubble on his face.

"Sometime, when I'm in Truro, you can come have supper with me again," she said.

BERNARD

GILLIAN'S CHRISTMAS TREE CAST A SWATH OF LIGHT ON THE gravel driveway through the tall window of the front hall. Bernard stopped the car in the driveway just short of the light and turned to Aimee.

"We won't stay long," he said, and he smoothed her sleek, dark hair back behind her ear. "I promise you."

"That's exactly what you said last year," said Aimee. "Then you drank too much brandy, got mired in a debate with your writing buddies, and I had to extricate you and drive you home."

"Was I really that bad?" asked Bernard.

"Yes," said Aimee.

"Well, that was last year," said Bernard. "Now I'm going to be a father. I'll be on my best behavior."

"If I recall," said Aimee without a touch of humor, "you've been a father for several decades."

Bernard sighed, drove up closer to the house, and parked near the front door. For some reason none of the other guests had claimed that space; they had all parked at a respectful distance. Aimee had already gotten out of the car when he came around to help her.

"I'm fine," she said, "no need to be solicitous."

"The gravel's so deep here I thought you might need a hand."

"I'm wearing flats," said Aimee. "And I'm not yet so heavy I sink in." Aimee, in fact, didn't look any heavier than before she was pregnant.

Virginia, Bernard recalled, had been enormous when she was pregnant with Teddy, and even when she'd been pregnant with Peachie, who had been a runt.

When Peachie had called him to tell him she was pregnant, he'd had a moment's pause. He had not yet fully accustomed himself to the idea that his little daughter was an adult, that she was married. "That's just grand!" he had told Peachie. But all he could think was, How had this happened? How had all those years gone by so fast? And if Peachie was a mother, that would make him a grandfather. Him, a grandfather! He'd have to make the best of it. Actually, he'd have to do better than that; he'd have to embrace the idea.

"Virginia will be so happy," he'd told Peachie.

"She is," said Peachie. There was a moment's silence. If she had just said "yes," then he wouldn't have known she had told Virginia ahead of him. But Peachie had simply spoken the truth, the way Peachie always did. It wasn't so strange, was it, that a girl should tell her mother first about these things? Still, Bernard had been hurt.

He hadn't had an opportunity to speak alone with Virginia since he'd heard Peachie' s news, hadn't in fact talked with her (aside from the meeting of the Leopardi Circle) since that disastrous Thanksgiving dinner, when Teddy had been so unimaginably rude to him. At the Leopardi meeting, Virginia hadn't been as pleasant as usual—there had been something changed in her manner towards him. He wondered what might have caused her to feel less than her customary warmth. Could it be she was hurt that he hadn't told her about Aimee's pregnancy ahead of telling everyone else? Perhaps at Gillian's party he could get her aside and talk with her. He would just have to figure out a delicate way of detaching himself from Aimee. Aimee wouldn't detach easily; she was always wary at gatherings with members of the Leopardi Circle, and now, pregnant, she had gotten unpredictable and easily irritated.

"At least you approve of Gillian's house," said Bernard as they paused on the front porch.

"I approve of Duncan as an architect," said Aimee. "I think he let the client have too much say in this particular case."

"You are a hard lady to please," said Bernard.

Dinner had already been served by the time Bernard and Aimee entered the living room, and everyone had found a spot to eat—chairs, sofas, the arms of sofas, pillows on the floor.

"I'm so glad you were able to come," said Gillian, her eye on Aimee as she greeted them, but she did not congratulate Aimee on her pregnancy as Bernard had hoped she might. When he had announced the news to the Leopardis at the end of their meeting, Gillian had simply said, "Well, well, Bernard. That should keep you busy."

"Would you like to sit down and have me make up a plate for you?" Bernard asked Aimee.

"I can serve myself," she said. "And I'd appreciate it if you didn't treat me like an invalid."

"I was just trying to be gallant," said Bernard.

"Well, don't," said Aimee. Bernard watched her spoon up a large helping of artichoke hearts, think better of it, and return half to the serving dish.

Once they'd gotten their dinner, Bernard looked around the room to find the best place for them to settle. Not with Virginia, for sure, and not with Gillian. For some reason Aimee always seemed on guard around Gillian. Then Bernard spotted Nancy. She could be counted on not to say anything provoking. And she was there with that man named Oates, whom, presumably, she was going to marry, so Aimee wouldn't feel threatened by her, as she might if Nancy were single. Aimee found all single women predatory.

Nancy seemed pleased to see him. "I don't think the two of you have met before," said Nancy, and she introduced Oates and Aimee. Then she added, addressing Oates, "Aimee is Bernard's wife." Oates had a wide, unguarded face, and Bernard could chart his thought progression as he tried to figure out the relationship between him and Aimee, then learned that Bernard was her husband. Bernard was used to this response in people, and it amused more than annoyed him.

It wasn't until well after dessert had been served that Bernard was able to move away from Aimee. He'd seen Virginia heading on her own towards the front hall, and he maneuvered his way across the room so it wouldn't be obvious he was following her. He found her in the guest room, where the coats were piled on the bed. She was rummaging through them, looking for something. The fabric of her blouse, a peacock blue, was taut over her back, so Bernard could see the indentation of her bra. Virginia was capacious and large-bosomed, her flesh soft, and Bernard had a little pang of sadness that it wasn't his anymore, that flesh, to touch. When Virginia looked up, she was startled to find him standing in the doorway, watching her.

"Bernie!" she said.

"I was hoping to catch a moment with you," he began.

"I just came to get my reading glasses," said Virginia, and she held them up for him. "I couldn't find them in my purse, and then I remembered I'd left them in my coat pocket."

Bernard leaned against the wall. He set his coffee cup on the dresser.

"I've been feeling as if you haven't been wanting to talk with me," said Bernard. "Are you angry at me about something?"

Virginia tilted her head and shook it slightly at him.

"What is it, Virginia?"

"Oh, Bernie," she said, and she sighed. Bernard waited for her to go on, but she didn't.

"That was quite a display that Teddy treated us to at Thanksgiving," he said.

"Teddy was upset," said Virginia. "You can't entirely blame him."

Bernard stood up straight. "Of course I blame him," he said. "He was rude. He was hostile."

"He was hurt," said Virginia.

Bernard's eyes widened. "*He* was hurt! How do you think I was left feeling? I'd been trying so hard to reach out to him."

Virginia sighed again. "Listen to yourself, Bernie," she said. "All you can consider is your own feelings."

"I certainly took Aimee's feelings into account," said Bernard.

"I felt sorry for Aimee, of course," said Virginia. "But I wish you'd think a little more about the impact of your announcement on your two children, on Teddy and Peachie."

"Peachie?" said Bernard. "Why are you bringing up Peachie? Peachie said she was happy for me."

"Peachie would say that," said Virginia.

"Why shouldn't she be happy for me?" asked Bernard.

"Here's what puzzles me, Bernie," said Virginia. "As a writer you have an unerring ability to get into the minds of your subjects, but in your dealings with the people around you, you seem unable—or is it reluctant?—to imagine things from their perspective."

"And what is this perspective that you claim I can't imagine?"

"Bernie," said Virginia, and she started towards the door. "I don't want to be having this conversation with you."

Bernard caught her arm. "Please, Virginia," he said. "Don't walk out on me!"

Virginia turned and looked at him. "I'm sorry, Bernie," she said. "I don't want to argue with you. I'm not married to you anymore. It's not my job to elucidate things for you. Nor is it my job to try to convince you about anything or influence what you do. Let's just be friends."

"What was I to do, Virginia?" asked Bernard. "Shouldn't I have told everyone about Aimee being pregnant?"

"You rather sprung it on us," said Virginia.

"It was sprung on me!" said Bernard.

Virginia raised her eyebrows.

"I wasn't going to say anything," said Bernard, "but that's the truth. You may have been thinking that I had planned to enter the world of fatherhood for a third time, but it wasn't the case at all. It just happened."

Virginia shook her head at him. "You're a grown man, Bernie. Babies don't just happen. You know that."

"Apparently Aimee had wanted a baby and didn't believe that I did. I wasn't actually consulted."

"Bernie, I don't want to know this. If your wife gets pregnant when you had made it clear you didn't want to be a father, then it seems as if there's a major problem in your marriage."

"I didn't make it exactly clear," said Bernard. "I had just assumed that Aimee had no interest in being a mother."

"Bernie, I'm sorry for you—if that's what you want me to be—but I'm really not the one to be talking to about this. I can talk to you, if necessary, about your relationship with Teddy and Peachie, but I can't talk to you about your relationship with Aimee."

She was starting out the door again, beyond his reach.

"Tell me, Virginia, one thing—is it that you're jealous of Aimee?"

Virginia turned around. "Why would I be jealous of Aimee?" she asked. "I don't want to be your wife, Bernie. I am truly happy married to Joe."

"Because she's pregnant," said Bernard. "Because she's going to be a mother."

Virginia came up close to Bernard and put her hands on his two arms, as if she were holding him in place so she could lecture him.

"Bernie," she said. "I *am* a mother. I am the mother of two grown children. I have absolutely no desire to be pregnant again. I am about to become a grandmother. That's where I am in my life now. That's what's appropriate for me, at my age. And just so you know, I find it, unequivocally, the most wonderful thing in the world." She dropped her hold on him and turned and walked from the room.

Bernard pushed some of the coats aside and sat down at the foot of the bed. He reached for his cup of coffee, but there wasn't much coffee left, and it was cold. Slowly he got up from the bed and started to make his way back towards the party. Gillian and Nancy were talking near the doorway to the kitchen. Bernard had left Aimee with Nancy, and he didn't spot her anywhere in the room.

"Have you seen Aimee around?" he asked Nancy.

"I think she's over by the window, talking to Chris and Adam," said Nancy.

"Bernard's so sweet and old-fashioned," said Gillian, "he needs to keep his wife in sight at all times."

"What are you two plotting?" asked Bernard, to change the subject.

"Gillian wanted a sneak preview of the final chapters of my novel," said Nancy. "But I'm afraid it's not that easy to summarize what I'm trying to do."

"I'd take that as a compliment, Nancy," said Bernard. "If Gillian cares enough about your characters to want to know their fate, that means you've accomplished a great deal."

"It's always been a problem with people reading parts of novels," said Gillian. "With a poem you see the entire entity, so you can judge it for what it is. But with a novel it's difficult to place the piece you hear each week into the whole. I found it hard to see what the chapter Nancy last read was actually contributing to the novel without knowing what Nancy's design is for the entire story."

Bernard was trying to be engaged in the conversation, but sometimes Gillian did have a way of going on about things. This was a party, after all, not a literary analysis. He had noticed that Aimee was hurrying out of the living room.

"Excuse me, ladies," he said.

He found Aimee in the guest room. She had unearthed her coat and was slipping her arms into the sleeves.

"What's up?" he asked.

Aimee's face was tight. Her eyes were shiny beads, so black he couldn't see the pupils.

"Just tell me one thing," she said. "Is there any woman at this party you haven't slept with?"

"What?" asked Bernard. "What are you talking about?"

"I just want the truth, Bernard," said Aimee. "Have you had sex with every female in that writing group of yours?"

"Aimee, what is this all about? What has anyone said to you?"

"Your friend Chris assumed I already knew that you and Gillian had had what he called a 'thing' in the past. He was making a joke about writers and incest. Am I the only one here who didn't know that, in addition to Virginia, you'd had an affair with Gillian and probably Nancy, too?"

"Oh, Aimee—" began Bernard.

"Don't lie to me, Bernard. Whatever you do, don't lie to me."

"I never had a relationship with Nancy," said Bernard. "We've been friends since we met at Bread Loaf, but never anything more."

"But you did have an affair with Gillian."

"It was years ago," said Bernard. He was about to say, "before you were born," but stopped himself in time.

"How could you?" asked Aimee. "How could you have wanted to have an affair with *her*? She's so—" Aimee broke off, unable to speak.

"It wasn't very successful," said Bernard. "And it was very brief."

"But you decided to keep it from me."

"No, nothing like that. I just didn't tell you."

"And why was that?"

Bernard shrugged. "It wasn't very important," he said.

"It's important to me," said Aimee.

"It was long before I met you," he said. "What was the purpose?"

Aimee's face looked bloated now, red and bloated.

"I came to her party," she said. "I ate her food. The two of you make me sick!"

"Please, Aimee," said Bernard—he knew enough not to call her by any term of endearment—"I just didn't want to make more of anything. I just wanted to—"

"I've had it with you," said Aimee. "I'm leaving. I'm taking the car, and I'm leaving. And don't think you're coming with me."

She pushed past Bernard, and when he tried to catch her, she thrashed at him with her fists and dashed out. He started after her down the gravel driveway, but she got into the car quickly and slammed the door. She looked fierce sitting there as she started the engine and waited for the electric seat to rise sufficiently for her to drive. He stood for a moment in front of the car to plead with her, but when Aimee revved the engine, he stepped back and let her pass.

PART TWO

𝒩ANCY

IN THE WEEKS BEFORE THE WEDDING, NANCY LAY AWAKE LONG after Oates had fallen asleep. She strained to listen for the sound of the river beyond the house, going about its steady business, its certain, predictable presence. She pictured it in its spring high, swollen with brown water, charging along, carrying, indiscriminately, everything it was given, bearing the weight of everything it could bear, and dropping to the bottom only those few things too heavy for it: rocks and metal. Glass.

On a pad of paper on her bedside table, Nancy scribbled notes of things she was afraid she wouldn't remember. When she read them in the morning, her handwriting was large and foreign, as if it had been written by a stranger. Sometimes the messages were indecipherable, and whatever she had hoped to retrieve was lost forever. She was certain about Oates, certain that she wanted to marry him, and yet she felt a sense of peril. She could put no image to it, it took no shape in her imagination, but it was with her, catching in her chest when she took in her breath before she could fill her lungs.

"Maybe it's that I'm afraid if we're married we'll change," she said to Oates. "That you'll love me less. That we won't be as happy as we are."

"I won't love you less," said Oates. "And we'll still be us, just as we are, just as happy."

"Maybe it's that I'm afraid you'll leave me," she said.

"That was some other guy," said Oates. "That isn't me. I'll never leave you—you're already part of me."

She knew he was right, knew that it wasn't Oates she was worried about, it was something else. At night she couldn't sleep, and as the date approached, she woke early in the morning, before it was quite daylight, and couldn't fall back asleep. She went through the day tired and anxious. Finally she decided to consult a psychiatrist whom she had seen briefly years ago, while she was suffering through her divorce.

The bathroom off the waiting room at Dr. Veifreck's office had Venetian blinds tilted so that you could look out at the parking lot without people outside being able to see in. There was a bathtub that obviously no one used. An old curtain still hung there. The vinyl was brittle and cloudy. It was a vestige of when a family had taken showers there, when the building had been a home inhabited with normal lives rather than a collection of therapists who listened to fifty-minute-long summaries of lives, unhappy person after unhappy person. Suddenly it seemed ridiculous to her that she had come to consult Dr. Viefreck. She was happy. She had everything she wanted—a kind man who was going to be her husband. A wonderful daughter. She had some prewedding jitters. She'd been single for fifteen years, who wouldn't? Nancy accepted the prescription for anti-anxiety medication that Dr. Viefreck gave her and slipped it into her wallet. She knew she wouldn't use it— she wanted to feel what she was feeling, she wanted the authentic experience—but it seemed rude to decline to take the prescription. Outside of the office Nancy felt freed, vindicated. She opened the sunroof as she drove away, exulted in what seemed like an escape. Oates was in the backyard when she got home, painting the door to the garden shed, where the bar for the reception would be set up.

He held his paintbrush out to the side when she came up and embraced her with one arm. "What's this all about?" he asked.

She kissed him hard on the mouth. "I think we need to go upstairs," she said. She took the paintbrush from him and laid it on the ground.

"Let me at least close the paint can," he said. She watched him take the lid and place it on the can. He thumped it down. Paint oozed up around it, a white halo.

Upstairs in their bedroom, they dropped their clothes in two piles on the floor. Nancy pulled back the spread and lay down across the bed. The skylight above her gave her a square of unblemished blue. She turned towards Oates. He had paint in his hair and sweat in the creases of his brow. She kissed his brow, and his nose, and his neck. She closed her eyes and pressed against him. She was off duty now. She was out of reach of all her thoughts. She wasn't Nancy anymore. She was skin and sweat. She was tongue against tongue. She was body enclosing body. She was gasps and yelps and shudders and sighs.

NANCY'S MOTHER, DEIRDRE, came to stay with them the week before the wedding. She said she wanted to be of help. Nancy knew she would be no help at all, but there was no way to tell her without hurting her feelings.

Deirdre's hair, once blond like Nancy's, was grey now. She wore it pulled back with a velvet scrunchie, but hair escaped around her face. Unlike Nancy and her father, Deirdre was not a tidy person. In Nancy's house she left a wake of disarray. When she made an attempt to clean up or put things away, she created more disorder. She rearranged things to suit herself, adding artistic touches that seemed somehow critical of Nancy's home decoration.

When Nancy was growing up, her mother was always misplacing things—the keys to the car, her handbag—and the rest of the family was constantly involved in archaeological expeditions. Now old age had exacerbated this tendency, and in the few days with them Deirdre had lost her eyeglasses, her cell phone, her wallet, her pills, and, most puzzling, the dress she had planned to wear to the wedding. (She'd hung it on the back of the door to the guest room.) To keep her out of trouble, Nancy asked her to make the place cards for the tables at the reception. Her mother had always been good at crafts projects, making elaborate Halloween costumes for Nancy and Nick, and decorations for their birthday parties. Deirdre threw herself into this project with considerable energy. She went to town and bought wisteria-colored paper (it was her idea of a color scheme for the wedding—Nancy hadn't thought to have one), then made another trip for a paper cutter and a calligraphy pen. She took over the entire dining room table for the enterprise.

"She's making such a big to-do about this," Nancy whispered to Oates in their bed at night. "I wish I hadn't gotten her involved."

But when Nancy watched Deirdre bent over her work the next day, she felt sorry for her. Deirdre, her eyesight bad, had attached an extension cord to the floor lamp so she could pull it over to give her more light, and she had a pillow wedged behind her hurting back. She labored over the place cards she had cut, lettering them and drawing a delicate border on each one. Nancy wondered if any of the guests would appreciate her artistic efforts.

"Why don't you come for a walk with me?" she asked her mother.

"Shouldn't I finish these first?"

"It's nice out now," said Nancy. "Take a break, and you can finish later."

Deirdre held up the list of guests who had accepted. "Some of the names here on your side I don't recognize at all," she said.

Nancy looked at the list. "Those are people in this writing circle I've joined," she said. Bernard was coming on his own, now that Aimee had moved out. Adam wasn't coming, but Chris was. Virginia and Joe were coming, and, to Nancy's surprise, Gillian and her husband were coming. Nancy had been hoping, she realized, that Gillian would not come.

"I thought this was going to be a small wedding, just close friends," said Deirdre.

"I had to bend that a little in this case. I wanted to invite my old friend Bernard, but he's one of the writers, and I couldn't really invite him without inviting the others."

"I'm surprised you joined a writing group," said Deirdre. "I thought you didn't like such things."

"I don't in general," said Nancy. "But these are pretty high-powered writers, and I was flattered they wanted me."

"Oh, flattery gets us into all sorts of things, doesn't it?" said Deirdre. "Still, I wouldn't think you'd want a bunch of other writers telling you what to write."

"They don't exactly tell me what to write," said Nancy, laughing.

"*Criticizing* what you write, then," said Deirdre. "So have they all become your friends now?"

Nancy pointed at the list. "Virginia, certainly—you'll like her, Mom—and Chris, maybe. Gillian, no, not at all."

"Oh dear," said Deirdre. "Why not?"

"She's ambitious, egotistical, and . . . I just don't trust her," said Nancy. "She's always perfectly nice to me, but there's something about her . . ."

"And she's coming to your wedding!" exclaimed Deirdre.

"I have no real reason to distrust her," said Nancy, "and she's a close friend of Bernard's."

"Bernard!" said Deirdre. "There's someone I hope you don't trust."

"Bernard's fine, Mom," said Nancy. "He's absolutely harmless. And he's in low spirits now, so go out of your way to be nice to him. His wife—that's Aimee, his most recent wife—left him."

"I'm not surprised," said Deirdre.

Deirdre put on her running shoes, new, too-white shoes with gigantic soles. She looked with concern at Nancy's worn sneakers. "Those don't look like they're giving you enough support," she said.

"They're fine," said Nancy.

"Would you like me to buy you a pair of decent shoes while I'm here?" asked Deirdre.

"Mom," said Nancy, "if I want new shoes, I can buy them for myself."

"All right," said Deirdre. And she held up her hands in a sign of truce. Nancy felt sorry she had spoken sharply. She slipped her arm around her mother's shoulder, gave it a squeeze. Nancy was small, like her mother. Now Deirdre had shrunk, so she was an inch shorter than Nancy, but the thick soles of her shoes made her almost the same height.

They hadn't gone very far up the road before Deirdre turned to Nancy. "How is that novel of yours coming along?" she asked.

"It's done," said Nancy. "I wanted it off my desk so I could turn my attention to my wedding. So I worked like crazy to finish it and send it off."

"Bravo!" said Deirdre. "When do I get to read it?"

"It's not a book yet, Mom," said Nancy. "I just sent it to my agent."

"What did she say?"

"She said she loved it, but it was a quiet, elegiac—that was her word, elegiac—novel and would probably be a tough sell."

"Why doesn't she just send it to that old editor of yours. What was his name?"

"Gareth," said Nancy. "But he's not at Simon and Schuster anymore, and all he's doing now are celebrity memoirs."

Deirdre sighed. "Well, I know you'll find someone who will feel lucky to publish it. Don't worry about it."

"Actually, I'm not," said Nancy. "I've had so much to think about for the wedding, I haven't had room left for anxiety about my novel."

"Why don't you let me read the manuscript in the meantime?"

"I don't know," said Nancy. "It's sweet of you to want to read it, but I think I'd rather wait till it was actually published before I show it to anyone."

"You always were a bit touchy about your work," said Deirdre.

"Touchy?" Nancy asked.

"Didn't want anyone to see it until it was all done. You never showed me your papers until you had gotten them back from the teacher. You showed your father, but you never showed me."

They had walked nearly all the way to the Kleinholz farm. In spite of her high-tech running shoes, Deirdre was showing signs of fatigue.

"Want to turn back now?" Nancy asked.

"We could," said Deirdre. "I have those place cards that need to be finished." Deirdre turned to Nancy. "You know you haven't even told me what this novel is about," she said.

Nancy took a moment to form her answer. It had been difficult for her to share her novel with the Leopardi Circle. Showing it to her mother was a different problem. Her novel *was* fiction, after all, but her mother would dig right through to the base of the story, cast aside the artistry, and seize on the central portrait, which was based on Nancy's father. What was true about the character in the novel would disturb her only somewhat less than what wasn't true, than the liberties Nancy had taken.

"It's about the changes people make in their lives," said Nancy. "The choices they don't realize they have, and the choices they take advantage of."

Fortunately Deirdre was drawn away from the subject of the novel. "Changes!" she said. "Big changes for my Nancy! Happy ones! Oates is such a nice man."

"Obviously I think so," said Nancy.

They were at a place where the road came close to a bend in the river, and they stood on the high bank, looking downstream. Aliki had suggested that Nancy and Oates travel to the wedding by canoe, float with the current down to the guests, who'd be waiting to greet them on the riverbank. It was such a romantic idea that Nancy had actually considered it before she ruled it out as entirely impractical.

"Of course Douglas seemed like a nice man, too, when you married him," said Deirdre.

Nancy didn't say anything, hoping that Deirdre would move on to something else. But after a moment Deirdre asked, "By the way, didn't you tell me Douglas developed some sort of strange neurological condition after he left you?"

"Trigeminal neuralgia, also known as tic douloureux," said Nancy. "It causes episodes of severe facial pain. I did an article on it in the newsletter."

"Everyone wished him ill, and I'm happy to hear we were not disappointed."

"I didn't wish him ill," said Nancy. Though at the time she had thought it was entirely appropriate that he should develop a condition which caused him to flinch as if in response to the deceits of his life.

"The trouble with you, sweetheart," said Deirdre, "is that you're too nice. You should enjoy your revenge."

"I'll save revenge for when I really need it," said Nancy, laughing. "And you know, Mom, I really don't regret Douglas at all. I got Aliki. And now I have Oates. It's all worked out just fine."

They started walking again back to the house. Nancy hoped they were done with the subject of Douglas, but just by the rhododendrons at the side of the road, Deirdre reached out for Nancy's shoulder.

"You know, I blamed myself at the time," she said.

"Blamed yourself? What for?"

"For Douglas. For not seeing into his character better, for not warning you against marrying him."

"Seeing into his character was my job, Mom. I was the one who was marrying him."

"But you were blinded by love," said Deirdre. "I wasn't. I should have seen him more clearly. Your father saw him. He had lots of doubts about him, but unfortunately I put his fears to rest."

"What do you mean?" asked Nancy. "I don't remember him saying anything about Douglas at the time."

"He was very upset at the wedding, and everyone thought it was because his little girl was getting married. But it was because he didn't really like Douglas. Your father saw things quite clearly," said Deirdre. "It was because he was a teacher, he was always looking into the souls of his students. We usually think of women as having intuition, but your father was a very intuitive man."

Deirdre sighed. "You can't imagine how much pain it causes me not to have him here. Not to have him here at your wedding. Not to have him know that things turned out all right for you."

Nancy leaned against the bushes. She felt dizzy hearing this, as if her mother had pulled out from her the very thing that had been hurting so much, laid it outside for her to see.

That was it: her father wasn't going to be here. It wasn't just that she wanted him here to give her away—give her away better than before—it wasn't just that she wanted Oates to know him, him to know Oates, but that she wanted him to know that, in spite of everything, things had worked out all right. He had died worrying about her, his daughter, a young, single parent, abandoned by her husband, and worrying about his granddaughter growing up with an absent father. And there was no way that Nancy could shout up to him, say, "See, Daddy, I made it. Everything's okay now."

"I've got to get to the place cards," said Deirdre. "I'm up to *L*. I have about twenty to go."

She scurried on ahead into the house, and Nancy followed, numbly, behind her.

IT WAS RAINING THE MORNING OF THE WEDDING. They had planned on having the ceremony outdoors by the river and had to set things up inside instead.

"Don't worry, Mom, I'll take care of everything," said Aliki. "You go upstairs and get dressed."

"Aliki, go help your mother," said Oates. "Deirdre and I will take care of everything down here."

Nancy smiled at Oates in gratitude. Deirdre had been all set to head upstairs with her, but he'd put his hand on her arm.

Nancy's long dress was laid out on the bed, her shoes set on the floor before it. She sat on the side of the bed and let Aliki brush her hair and do her makeup. No one had brushed her hair for her this way since Aliki was a little girl and used to play "beauty shop."

She had intended to buy a dress that would have practical uses later on, but Aliki had encouraged her to buy this one, although Nancy couldn't imagine another occasion when she might wear it. The shoes, bone-colored pumps, would be ones she could probably wear again.

Aliki had made her a crown of wildflowers. "I'm afraid they're already wilted," she said.

"I'm a bit wilted myself," said Nancy.

"No, Mom, you look absolutely gorgeous." Aliki took Nancy's shoulders and turned her so she was facing the mirror. Nancy took herself in quickly—this bride in a pale blue sleeveless dress—and she then studied the face of Aliki, whose chin rested on her shoulder. She turned and kissed her.

"My beautiful daughter," she said.

Downstairs the string quartet was tuning up. "I guess this is really happening," said Nancy.

"It's about time," said Aliki.

"You think I'm doing the right thing?"

But Aliki didn't answer. She broke into tears, and then laughed at herself for crying. She hugged Nancy. "Oh, Mommy," she said, "I'm so happy." Her voice was muffled, her face warm against Nancy's neck.

. . .

THE CEREMONY was held in front of the fireplace in the living room. Guests spilled out into the dining room, the front hall, and some sat on the staircase, watching through the banisters. They were an unlikely mix of relatives and friends of hers and Oates's, representatives of each phase of her life—from her best friend from elementary school, to her college roommate, to the writers in the Leopardi Circle. Nancy imagined that her father was there, among them somewhere, bearing witness to it all.

The reception was under a tent in the backyard. The rain had stopped, and the braver guests ventured out on the wet lawn. The flower arrangements, which Teresa Kleinholz had done as a wedding gift (Nancy had requested no presents, but Teresa had insisted), had blown over in the wind, leaving wet stains across the tablecloths. Nancy and Oates, hand in hand, made their way around the guests, who were clustered, champagne flutes in hand. Chris's two sons had not been invited, but Chris had brought them anyway.

"I had the boys for the weekend, at the last minute," he told Nancy. "I was sure you didn't mind."

Nancy did mind, but didn't say so. Gillian's husband had had an emergency at the hospital and hadn't made it, so Nancy suggested they squeeze in at his place. She assumed the numbers would turn out all right for the caterers (two kids who ate little and consumed no alcohol in lieu of one adult who did), and it amused her to think of Gillian stuck sitting next to two little boys.

Deirdre, Nancy saw, was going around introducing herself to everyone she didn't know and making introductions among the people she knew. She had taken Oates's Midwestern relatives in tow. At one point after dinner, Nancy noticed that Deirdre had planted herself at the table where the Leopardis were sitting. Later, after the cake had been cut and everyone was enjoying dessert, she settled back in her seat at Nancy and Oates's table.

"I'd keep my eye on the person we were talking about," she whispered to Nancy. "She's smart and she's sly."

"Thanks, Mom," said Nancy. But she wasn't worrying about Gillian. She was suffused with good feeling for everyone. She was linked now, forever, with Oates. She felt safe from all the possible treacheries of the world.

$\mathcal{R}$ACHEL

IN THE EARLY AFTERNOON SUN CRADLED BETWEEN THE DOWN-town buildings, Rachel stood for a moment deciding which way to turn. She was small and pregnant, and from a distance looked too young to be an expectant mother. But up closer you could see that she was older, and her face, although delicate, was clearly that of an intelligent woman who had her life firmly in hand.

She had come from an appointment with her obstetrician and had been told that everything was going fine. She already knew this. She was in tune with her baby, his rhythms, his movements. If there had been anything wrong, she would have felt his distress. She knew him as well as she knew anyone in the world, as well as she knew herself. She had not wanted to know in advance the sex of her baby, but a distinctive anatomical part on the ultrasound had made this impossible, so she now thought of the baby as a "he." She didn't want to name him before she could see his face. She and Dennis had decided not to tell anyone the baby's sex. Her father had announced to everyone that Aimee had informed him their coming baby was male, and it had seemed strange knowing something that intimate about anyone before they were born. Rachel felt all babies in utero were owed a degree of privacy.

She was meeting Virginia later for a late lunch, treating herself to a few hours of browsing in old bookshops beforehand, but she felt hungry now. She headed to a place that sold homemade ice cream and lingered by the glass counter, looking up at the painted menu and at the vats of ice cream. In the end she decided on some frozen yogurt, a virtuous choice. She was paying for her dessert when she heard a familiar voice ordering behind her. It was Paul. She might not have recognized him here, out of the school setting, but she knew the voice.

"Hi, Paul," she said.

He looked up at her, surprised, confused. "Hey."

"How are you doing?"

"All right," said Paul. The girl behind the counter tapped the ice cream scoop. "Oh, yeah, um, double chocolate fudge," he said. "Sorry about that."

Rachel still had her wallet in her hand. "I'll get it," she said. "My treat."

"You don't have to," said Paul.

"I know," said Rachel. "But I'd like to."

Paul walked beside her out of the ice cream shop, and, when she suggested they sit on a bench in the park nearby, he sat with her. When he bent his face to his ice cream cone, his hair fell down on both sides, and Rachel suppressed a desire to push it back. He looked up at her, a crooked chocolate mustache across his upper lip.

"Thanks for this," he said.

"It was my pleasure. I would have ordered it myself, but I'm trying to be prudent. This way I get to vicariously enjoy yours."

She'd trapped him, she knew. But she had a feeling he wasn't sorry to have a chance to talk with her.

"What do you have there?" she asked, pointing to the sketchbook she noticed he had tucked under his arm.

"Just a book I draw things in," he said.

"May I see?"

He paused for a second, then he shrugged and handed it over to her. The drawings startled her, they were so vivid, and the figures were expertly drawn. In one, an armed man riding a pterodactyl circled over a landscape that looked like a mix of Italy and the rain forest. In the next, he'd swooped down and seemed to be lifting to safety a round-faced woman with long, pale hair. There were pages of drawings, an epic adventure, a million fine black lines.

"These are quite good," she said. "I didn't know you were an artist."

"I just like to draw things," he said.

"Well, you should draw things, you're remarkably talented," she said. "Are you taking any art courses?"

"No. I just like to do it on my own."

"You know, your style reminds me a bit of Escher," she said. "Are you familiar with his work?"

"Never heard of him," he said.

Rachel brightened. "M. C. Escher. He was a graphic artist, Dutch. Oh, you'll love him," she said. "He did this wonderful lithograph of two hands drawing each other. I'll get you a book of his art. You'll see!"

"That would be cool," he said.

"Thank you for letting me see these," she said. She handed the sketchbook back to him, and he secured it protectively back under his arm. He was still flushed with embarrassment over the unexpected praise.

"How are things going otherwise?" she asked him.

"Okay, I guess."

"I haven't heard what you're doing next year. Are you staying at The Academy?"

"I'm not sure," he said. "Here's the thing. My mom wants me to come back with her, but my dad wants me to stay here. He says I stand a better chance of getting into college from The Academy than from my high school back home."

"What do you want to do?"

"I don't know. It's kind of weird having them both want me—you know?—sometimes neither of them wants me."

"I can't imagine that's the case," said Rachel quickly.

"Well, probably my mom always wants me, but you can't really tell about my dad. He's weird. And Gillian is weirder." Paul dipped his head down into his ice cream again. It seemed like a true pleasure, and Rachel felt happy to be able to give it to him. She guessed he didn't have much in his life that was this pleasurable, this simple. He looked up at her again, and his tongue darted out to catch a gob of ice cream off his lip. "When your parents are divorced, a lot of things get screwed up," he said.

"I know it can sometimes confuse things," said Rachel. "My parents are divorced."

The look on Paul's face suggested that he had forgotten it was possible she even had parents. "They are?" he said.

Rachel nodded.

"Do they get along okay?" asked Paul.

"They do," said Rachel. "But even so, there are complications."

"Right," said Paul. "Complications. My dad's remarried, but my mom isn't. She had a boyfriend for a while, but that didn't last. And now she's really lonely. She'd hate anyone my dad married, but she especially hates Gillian. I think my dad hooked up with her while he was still living with my mom."

"That's hard," said Rachel.

Paul dipped down and worked on his ice cream cone for a few minutes. Then he looked up. "Did your parents get remarried?" he asked.

"Yes, both of them," said Rachel. "In fact, my father and his wife are having a baby." She didn't expect to be confiding anything in Paul, it just slipped out.

"They are?" asked Paul. "Aren't they kind of old?"

Rachel wondered how old Paul thought she was. "My father is, but his wife is a lot younger."

"Oh, one of those!" said Paul.

Rachel laughed. "My parents were both at Gillian's Christmas party—my father is Bernard, my mother is Virginia," she said. "You may have met them. They're in Gillian's writing group." She wondered if Paul had witnessed or heard about Aimee's dramatic exit from the party.

Paul shrugged.

"I guess you wouldn't pay much attention to them," said Rachel, "they're old." She grinned at him. "I'm sure you'd consider everyone in the writing group 'old.'"

"There's one guy who's a lot younger," said Paul. "He brought his girlfriend to the party. Her name's Kim. She's really hot, but she's really nice, too."

Paul had reached the bottom of his cone. He stuffed it all in his mouth and crunched. When he had swallowed the last bit, he wiped the sleeve of his denim jacket across his face.

"Jennifer—that's my sister—had this idea that my dad and Gillian would have a baby—Gillian doesn't have any kids—and then, soon as that happened, my dad would just dump us. But it hasn't happened, at least it hasn't happened yet," he added. "My dad's always disappointing me. He pretends that I matter to him, and then he acts like I don't matter to him at all. Gillian matters to him, though. He'd drop everything for her."

Rachel waited. She was good at listening.

"I keep looking at Gillian to see if she's pregnant maybe. But now I think it's never going to happen. I don't think she's interested in having kids. She's all into her writing."

"That's certainly the way it is for some writers," Rachel said. "Not all," she added—she thought of her own parents—"but some."

"She's been working on this new book," said Paul. "It's kind of a secret, she doesn't talk about it. I don't think even my dad knows."

"It's not a secret, Paul," said Rachel. "She's supposed to be coming out with a new collection of poems in the fall. It's been long awaited. Even I know about it."

"Oh yeah, I know about *that* book," said Paul. "But I don't mean her poetry book, I mean she's been writing a novel. It's all hidden in the back of her file drawer. I only know about it because once I came up there unexpectedly and she was working on it and acted like she wasn't. But she saw that I'd seen something, so she asked me not to tell my dad about it—I guess she wanted it to be a surprise for him—so I told her I wouldn't. And then later I found it in her file."

"Paul, you shouldn't be looking through people's files," said Rachel.

"I wasn't looking for her stuff," said Paul. "I was looking to see if she'd gotten a letter from The Academy about me. You know, back when that happened with the paper for Thayer."

"Even so," said Rachel.

Paul shrugged. "Yeah, maybe," he said.

"Speaking of The Academy," said Rachel, "do you think you could stick it out another two years till graduation?"

"I don't know," said Paul. "My mom really misses me. And I kind of miss living home, with her. And I don't really have any friends at The Academy and you're the only faculty member there I like, and you're not going to be there anymore."

"I'm not?" asked Rachel.

"You're having a baby, aren't you?" asked Paul.

"My baby's going to be born at the start of the summer, and I was planning on teaching again in the fall."

"Oh," said Paul, and he seemed embarrassed.

"If you decide to stay," said Rachel, "I'll see you in the fall then. And you know, Paul, I like you, too."

After they said good-bye, Rachel sat for a little while longer, watching Paul slouch off in the distance, his backpack slung from one shoulder. A child of divorce, she thought. She was surprised at herself for having told him that she was a child of divorce as well. She was usually scrupulous about not telling students much about her personal life; there was enough about her—the fact that she was having a baby— that they were already privy to. But she felt different about Paul. And knowing that she had divorced parents and survived might make it easier for him to believe in his own survival. She had a quick fantasy of taking Paul in for the year, giving him a better home than his father and Gillian. But it was ridiculous. They'd barely have room for the new baby in their small apartment.

AT LUNCH Virginia produced a bag with several CDs she had just purchased. "They're for the baby," she said. "They sell classical music packaged for infants, but it's just Mozart, and not the best musicians, either. So I got these. Why not the Guarneri String Quartet?"

"Thank you," said Rachel, and she got up to give her mother a kiss.

"Those who knit, knit for babies," said Virginia. "Those who can't knit, purchase CDs."

The restaurant was in a converted factory building, in an austere, high-ceilinged room with bare wood floors. Rachel studied the menu, but she didn't feel hungry, and nothing appealed to her. She didn't want Virginia to be concerned, though, that she wasn't eating, so she ordered fish and hoped the serving would be small.

"Dad came over for dinner with us on Sunday," she said.

Virginia tilted her head.

"I'm worried about him," said Rachel.

"Why is that?" asked Virginia.

"He's all alone in that big house. He's miserable and lonely."

"Is that what he told you?" asked Virginia.

"Not exactly," admitted Rachel.

"Bernie has always overdramatized whatever it is he's going through. My guess is a lot of the time he's quite content. I'm sure he's leaving his clothes all over the furniture and his papers all over the table and is thoroughly enjoying not being on Aimee's short leash."

"Still, he does seem depressed," insisted Rachel. "I feel I should be doing something for him."

"Peachie," said Virginia, and she leaned across the table and looked Rachel straight in the face, "you cannot worry about your father. Bernie is a grown man, and he doesn't need you looking after him."

"I'm not looking after him," said Rachel, "I'm just feeling sorry for him."

"Oh, sweetheart," said Virginia, and she settled back in her chair. "Please, take care of yourself, take care of that dear little baby inside you, take care of your lovely husband. Let Bernie take care of himself. It's wrong of him to come whining to you. He should be taking caring of *you*."

"He wasn't exactly whining," said Rachel.

Virginia raised her eyebrows, and Rachel smiled. "Well, only a little," she said.

"Bernie should have been a novelist," said Virginia. "Biography lets him escape himself to some degree, but it doesn't give him the latitude of fiction, doesn't give him the necessary drama."

The fish came with a mound of couscous and some scrawny green beans. Rachel scraped the almond breading off to the side and squeezed the lemon so it pooled in the groove down the center of the fillet.

"This is just between us," said, Rachel, "but do you know who's writing a novel?"

"Who?" asked Virginia.

"Gillian Coit," said Rachel.

Virginia frowned. "Where did you get that from?"

"Her stepson, Paul, told me. I know I'm breaking his confidence, but it's different telling you."

"Oh, he must have that wrong," said Virginia. "Gillian's a poet. She doesn't write fiction."

"I guess she does now."

"I'd be surprised," said Virginia. "She's never brought a page of it to our group."

"Paul says she's writing it in secret."

"Well," said Virginia, "every poet fancies they can turn out prose with no trouble. Of course, they're extremely territorial if one of us prose writers dares to write poetry."

"Did you ever write poetry, Mom?" asked Rachel.

"That's *my* secret," said Virginia. "But I do intend to write poetry for my grandchild. I'll write Mother Gooseish, Dr. Seussish rhymes to cover all events and occasions."

"Dad wrote a poem for me once," said Rachel.

"He did?" asked Virginia.

"That summer I went to that dreadful Quaker camp in upstate New York and was so homesick."

"Oh," said Virginia, "I've always felt guilty about sending you there. But Teddy liked it, and you'd wanted to go."

"Dad wrote me a rhyming poem that was very silly, but pompous, too, if you know what I mean. He was trying to cheer me up."

"I didn't know," said Virginia. "Well, that was very sweet of him."

"It was," said Rachel.

The waitress clearing the table next to them knocked a platter off. It crashed to the floor but did not break. Rachel jumped, and without warning, her eyes blurred with tears. She remembered the camp dining hall with the plates stacked at the end of the long table, the cabin with the metal bed frame with the springs that trembled under her weight. She remembered the girl with pimples who handed out the mail, and the unexpected envelope from her father, his squat, black-ink handwriting. But was she crying for that, for herself then, small and homesick, or for something else? How rare it was that her father really thought about her, cared about how she was feeling, how rare it was that he actually went out of his way for her. There was so much she wanted from him, but he was always disappointing her. He had been disappointing her for most of her life.

Virginia was out of her seat and had come to put her arms around her. Rachel pressed her face against her mother's belly.

$\mathcal{V}$IRGINIA

$\mathbf{G}$ILLIAN HAD THANKED THEM ALL IN THE ACKNOWLEDG-
ments of her new poetry collection, *Transcendence*, and Virginia
felt this obligated them to go to New York for the launching of the
book. The Leopardis had a tradition of attending events when any of
their books were published, but they had slackened off a little when it
came to Chris, as he pointed out to the others when Gillian's book
event was discussed.

"You're so wonderfully prolific, Chris," said Virginia. "We can't possibly make all of your events, but we have gone to more of yours than
anyone else's."

"Since I publish only once a decade," said Bernard, "you are all required to turn out for me."

"This is an important book for Gillian," said Virginia, "and the
poems in the collection are ones she worked on in our group. I think it
would be"—she paused a moment, searching for the right word—
"*ungenerous* if we weren't there to support her."

"We could always skip the reading and turn up for the party afterwards," said Chris, but Bernard leveled him with such a look of ad-
monition that he quickly added, "Just kidding. Okay, go ahead, count
me in."

They drove into the city together in Bernard's old Mercedes—
Virginia in the back with Nancy, Adam next to Bernard in the front.
Chris was coming on his own because he was going directly to visit his

sons the next day. It was unlikely that he would have been willing to drive in Bernard's car in any case—he drove a new, sporty-looking thing that was either much more expensive than it looked or much cheaper, Virginia wasn't sure which—and it was just as well. Not only would five of them have been a little tight, but which of the males would have been content to squeeze in with the ladies in the back?

The Mercedes was a dark blue Virginia associated with yachts, and had blue leather seats. It was an old, thoroughly impractical car, but Bernard had never been a man who was attracted to the practical. Aimee and their baby, Horace (who but Bernard, thought Virginia, would name a baby Horace?), had moved back into the house, and Bernard had become a ridiculously doting father. He changed diapers and prepared formula (Aimee had not wanted to breast-feed), things he had never done when Rachel and Teddy were babies. Virginia guessed that the few months Aimee had spent on her own had made her realize a good thing when she had it, and she had come back to Bernard (extracting from him innumerable concessions) not so much out of love as out of practicality. Once young Horace was in school, Virginia predicted that Aimee would move off on her own again. How unkind I am, thought Virginia.

Bernard's enthusiasm for babies was now global, but the actual attention he paid to his grandson, Peter, Rachel's baby, born a few weeks before Horace, was scant compared with what he lavished on his new son. Virginia was sure Rachel felt the slight, though Rachel did not say so, and, as with other things, Virginia lamented his obtuseness and was aggrieved on Rachel's behalf. While she admitted she was prejudiced, there was no question that Peter was infinitely more attractive a baby than Horace, a squinty little Buddha, but Bernard bragged about his son (the miracle of his own prowess) shamelessly and mentioned Peter only in passing.

Bernard had been willing to go on this trip to New York only because Aimee had taken Horace to visit her parents in Seattle. Though

Bernard liked to be within cooing distance of his son, the thought of his in-laws was sobering enough that when Aimee had suggested making the trip on her own, he had heartily agreed.

"It will be a Leopardi Circle field trip," Bernard had proposed gaily. "And I will play chauffeur." Virginia would have felt more comfortable with Adam driving, but Adam's car was small for four. And it did make sense for them to drive down all together.

Virginia had pulled down the armrest between her and Nancy and settled back in her seat. She could smell Nancy's perfume, or was it her shampoo? Nancy always smelled—Virginia thought about the word and settled on *pretty*, a word she rarely used.

The group had taken a break over the summer, since so many of them were out of town for long stretches—Nancy on her honeymoon in Greece, Gillian on the Cape, Virginia in Maine. They'd met only once since the fall had begun.

"You were such a lovely bride," said Virginia. "Did I tell you that?"

Nancy laughed. "I think you did," she said. "But I don't mind hearing it again."

"It's good to see you looking so happy," said Virginia.

"Didn't I look happy before?" asked Nancy.

"You always looked a bit—how shall I describe it?—anxious about something. But perhaps you were anxious about us?"

"Who's anxious about us?" asked Bernard from the front seat.

"No one, Bernie," said Virginia in a louder voice. "We're just talking back here. Girl talk. Concentrate on your driving."

Nancy smiled faintly. "I think I was anxious about reading any of my novel to you. I'd been alone with it for so long, it was hard to go public."

"Have you heard anything?" asked Virginia softly.

Nancy shook her head. "My agent is sending it out, but no one seems to be snapping it up yet."

Virginia patted her hand. "Someone will. It's a remarkable, deeply felt novel."

"Thank you," said Nancy.

"You're not starting a new one yet?"

Nancy shook her head.

"I know," said Virginia. "You're still with this one. But you'll keep coming to our meetings, I hope. I count on your feedback. "

"Of course she'll be coming," said Bernard. Virginia hadn't thought he could hear above the sound of the traffic, but apparently he could. "When you're part of the Leopardi Circle, you have to come to discuss other people's work, even if you're not presenting anything yourself."

"I didn't know there were any rules," said Adam. He'd been so quiet for the whole ride, Virginia had almost forgotten he was there.

"Not rules," said Bernard, "moral obligations."

"You didn't say anything about moral obligations when I signed up," said Nancy.

"The moral obligations of the Leopardi Circle are subtle," said Bernard. "They sneak up on you. Like this, for example, our field trip to the Big City to support the launching of Gillian's book."

"Gillian's book hardly needs our support," said Nancy.

"Then why are you going?" asked Bernard.

"Because it's the right thing to do," said Nancy.

"Only you, dear Nancy, would say something like that," said Bernard.

"She's going for the same reason the rest of us are going," said Adam. "Because Gillian expects us to, and she'll see it as a betrayal if we don't."

"Ah, the truth at last," said Bernard. "No one wants to risk having Gillian as an enemy. Still, I think your motives may be rather different from the rest of ours."

"What's that supposed to mean?" asked Adam quickly. He turned now so he was facing Bernard.

Virginia feared which way this was going, but it was too late to head Bernard off.

"It's all right to be in love with Gillian," said Bernard. "We all were at one time or another."

"For God's sake, Bernie," said Virginia. "Speak for yourself, if you must, but have the decency not to assume anyone else shares your particular obsessions."

"That's uncharacteristically harsh of you!" said Bernard.

"Well, you deserve it," said Virginia, and she couldn't help her voice rising. "You say things that are hurtful and you seem totally unaware of it."

"It's okay," said Adam. "Bernard's right. I am in love with Gillian."

"Oh dear," said Virginia. "You have that perfectly lovely girlfriend."

"Tell me about it," said Adam.

Even Bernard was silenced. Good, thought Virginia, it's about time. The old affection she felt for Bernard, which had been eroding ever since his cruelty at Rachel's Thanksgiving dinner, was nearly entirely gone. He was insufferable. She wished she weren't in his car, wished she wasn't in this physical proximity to him, wished she didn't have to drive all the way back with him after the event.

In the front seat, Adam put on earphones. Beside her, Nancy closed her eyes and feigned (Virginia assumed) sleep. Virginia turned so she wouldn't have to stare at the back of Bernard's head. Above the armrest on the car door was a panel of burled walnut veneer. Virginia traced the whorls of dark grain with her forefinger. It seemed strange that this piece of what was once a living tree should be traveling with them now, should be party to their conversations.

They were driving through the South Bronx now. Virginia would have preferred for Bernard to enter the city through Riverdale and the West Side Highway, but he'd taken the Major Deegan Expressway. This section of the elevated highway went through the part of the Bronx that made Virginia the saddest. She turned away and tried to keep her eyes on Nancy sitting beside her—Nancy with her opal earrings and her blond hair newly cut so it was perfectly chin length—yet she couldn't stop herself from looking out the window. Someone in the city had come up with the idea of painting curtains in walled-up windows on abandoned buildings so it would look as if people were still living in them. They looked as if they were a stage set for a play. A dog on a chain in a scrap metal lot, guarding nothing worth stealing, barked at the sky.

BOOKCASES HAD BEEN PUSHED ASIDE on the second floor of Borders for the reading, but the space was inadequate for the crowd. There were several stacks of *Transcendence* sharing a table with a novel called *Restitution,* by M. G. Findlay. The name Findlay sounded familiar to Virginia for some reason, but she didn't think she had ever heard of the author. Chris, who had arrived ahead of them, had nabbed extra seats in the front section, marked "Reserved." It was a good turnout for any new book; for poetry it was remarkable. People obviously were sniffing out a Pulitzer here. Gillian's success was even greater than Virginia had realized. Bernard raised his eyebrows and made a face at Virginia to show that he was impressed.

Gillian, flanked by her agent and editor, was off on the side. She was wearing a long, sleeveless dress, and her shoulders looked white and vulnerable. When she looked over and saw them, she gave them a nod and a smile, the smile of a goofy kid whose two front teeth had grown in crooked. Virginia saw Gillian's husband, Jerry, in the front row, that poor boy, Paul, stuck next to him. Virginia, Nancy, and Adam sat in the row with Chris. Bernard chose a stool along the bookcases on the side rather than one of the chairs that Chris had saved. He sat there now, the Buddha's father, with his moleskin pants tight around his portly thighs. His fleshy hands—the hands of someone who had never done much physical labor—were pale and freckled. Those hands had touched Gillian's shoulders, thought Virginia. There had been a time when she had assumed that Bernard's affair with Gillian had occurred after she and Bernard were no longer together, but now she was not so sure. Because of Joe, because of her being so happy, it hadn't mattered. But maybe it did matter, after all.

The bookstore manager fiddled with the microphone at the podium, sending, inadvertently, two shrill whistles that made the crowd jerk to attention. She was a squat, short-haired woman with a few too many piercings in her ear. She gave a summary of Gillian's poetic career, mispronouncing Coit, as well as one of the titles.

"Before we begin the reading," she said, "Gillian's editor at Knopf, Rob McInnerny, has a few introductory remarks he'd like to add."

Virginia had spoken with Rob at the Christmas party. He was no older than Rachel, yet he had risen to the top ranks and camouflaged his extreme ambitiousness under an air of casual boyishness. He was good-looking, though his chin was small and feminine. Adam must hate him, thought Virginia.

Rob was tall, and he twisted the mike up towards his mouth. "I have a little surprise announcement for you," he began. "Some of you may have been wondering why there's a novel sharing the table with Gillian's new collection, *Transcendence*. The name M. G. Findlay is new to you, I'm sure, but the author is here with us today." He was smiling so excessively that Virginia knew, immediately, what was up.

"I've had the extraordinary great fortune to be the editor of Gillian's three most recent poetry collections. You can imagine the elation I felt—and I don't use that word lightly—when she confided in me that she had written a novel, on the side, for the fun of it."

Findlay, thought Virginia. Gillian's aunt had come from Findlay, Ohio, and Gillian had spoken of visiting her there. This must be the novel Gillian had been writing in secret that Paul had told Rachel about.

"Wheels turn slowly in publishing," continued Rob, "but there are exceptions, and this is one of the remarkable ones. We were able to bring this novel out just in time for Gillian's new collection—it's a miracle—in fact, I didn't know till this morning that we'd have early copies available at this event today. It's a breathtaking novel, a style so different from Gillian's poetry that you will be dazzled by her variety. *PW* called it 'a virtuoso performance by a new novelist,' since Gillian chose to publish it under a pseudonym, but now the secret is out."

A PR scheme to create buzz, Virginia thought, not just for the poetry but for the novel as well. A brilliant move: the poetry followers would buy a novel Gillian had written, and people drawn to the novel might end up buying the poetry as well.

When Gillian stepped up to the mike, it was the perfect height. She didn't make any introductory remarks, just gazed out across the audience and began to read. She was a seductive reader, and Virginia tried to analyze how much of it was her voice—a whispery quality, as if the air stayed in her mouth and never made it down into her chest—and how much of it was Gillian's presence—her slender figure, thin, bare arms, and her impossibly long hair held back so tenuously that a dramatic line might loosen the noose's hold. A number of the poems had been brought to the group, and Virginia remembered early drafts of a few of them, and in one case a suggestion of her own that Gillian had actually taken. It was entirely appropriate, she thought, that they were all thanked in the front of the book.

After the reading Gillian was thronged by fans, and a line quickly formed for signed copies of the books. Virginia and the other Leopardis, who were planning to go to the party afterwards, hung around on the side.

"What a coup!" said Bernard. "I guess she rose to your challenge, Chris."

"That editor of hers is so besotted," said Chris. "He'd publish a cookbook of hers if she wrote one."

"I'm impressed," said Virginia. "And how like her to keep this as a surprise." Virginia looked over at Adam and realized, from the expression on his face, that he hadn't known about the book either. "I wonder what it's about," she said.

Nancy had left the conversation and gone over to the table at the side. She was leafing through Gillian's novel.

"While we're waiting for our star to disengage herself," said Bernard, "I'm going to see what they have in children's books. I've been building Horace's library."

"Every book I've given Ben and Sam that they took home with them got chucked by their mother," said Chris. "I have to keep all their books at my house now."

"Aren't you curious to see what Gillian's novel's about?" asked Virginia.

"Something precious," said Chris. "She'll give us all copies, and then we'll have to read it."

"You're just miffed because she's honing in on your territory," said Bernard. "She's going to beat you at your own game."

"Hardly," said Chris. "Gillian may have hammered poor Nancy about the plot for her novel, but I can't imagine Gillian knows how to turn out a plot of any sort."

Virginia looked over at Nancy. Nancy was holding Gillian's book in one hand. Her other hand was cupping her mouth. She was staring at the open pages as if there was something there both hideous and fascinating. She snapped the book shut, stuck it under her arm, and headed towards the escalator.

"Excuse me, you need to pay for that up here," the bookstore manager called after her, but Nancy ignored her. She was running down the escalator now.

Gillian was still signing books at her table. Her dark hair was over her shoulder as she leaned down.

"Pay for the book," said Virginia to Bernard. "I'm going to try to catch Nancy."

"Why should I pay for Nancy's book?" asked Bernard.

"Pay for the goddamn book, Bernie," said Virginia, and she thumped Bernard in the chest. "Just pay for it." Then she ran off after Nancy.

ɴANCY

ɴANCY RAN OUT OF THE BOOKSTORE, CLUTCHING THE BOOK, and turned left, downtown. She'd forgotten her sweater behind, a blue cardigan draped over the armrest of her chair, but there was nothing she would have gone back for. She ran down the sidewalk, pushing her way through the press of pedestrians, jogging in place at the corners where she had to wait for the light, or for turning taxis that didn't pause to let her pass. She didn't know where she was headed— she just ran. She didn't look back, didn't notice that Virginia had started after her, then given up, a sad-looking presence on the side- walk, breathing heavily. All she knew was that she needed to find someplace where she could read, someplace private. She passed coffee shops, a church, a branch of the library, considered each quickly, but none of them seemed right. She ran, desperate, and then she thought of Bloomingdale's and headed there. She'd worked in Junior Dresses one summer when she had been in college, years ago, living with a friend whose parents had given them the use of their apartment while they summered in the Hamptons. She knew Bloomingdale's had changed dramatically since then and was now a trendy reincarnation of its for- mer self, but she thought she'd still be able to find an out-of-the-way dressing room. She took the escalator upstairs to a department where the clothes were for older, less fashionable women and the customers were few. She managed to get into the dressing rooms without being spotted by a saleswoman. The dressing rooms were deserted, and she hurried to the one at the end of a row. She closed the door behind her and sank to the floor. She called Oates on her cell phone but got his voice mail.

"Call me," she said.

The dressing room had peach-colored carpeting and a delicate chair upholstered in peach-colored velvet. There were no clothes on the hooks, just a tangle of bare hangers. Nancy brushed aside a few straight pins, some tissue paper, and an envelope that said "extra buttons." She sat with her legs straight out and leaned back against the locked door. She closed her eyes and gave herself a few moments to catch her breath. She'd run for blocks and blocks. She was safe now. No one would find her here. She had not loosened her grip on Gillian's novel, almost as if she were afraid it would take off and escape from her. When she opened her eyes, she saw a mirrored triptych of herself. Three versions of herself to bear witness.

Nancy took in her breath and turned to the back flap of the novel in her hand. There was no photo of the author. The copy was brief: "M. G. Findlay is the wife of a prominent surgeon. This is her first novel." Then Nancy turned to the opening chapter. She had always been a fast reader, but now her eyes sprinted over the pages, not so much reading them as taking them in whole. It was uncanny, this novel, like seeing a strange version of herself, as if the mirrors in front of her were fun-house mirrors and everything had been distorted. The first chapter was nearly identical to hers, a paraphrase so close that at first she mistook the words for her own. But then the novel went off on a different course, taking Nancy's character, the character based on her father, and turning his story inside out. In Gillian's novel the young doctor was responsible for the baby's death, and he was brought to justice. After a sensational medical malpractice trial, he was proven guilty because of his incompetence, condemned, and stripped of his license to practice. In shame and humility, he eventually became a teacher of small children, as if, through working for these young lives, he could do penance for the one life he had taken away. In every child's face, though, he saw the face of the child the baby would never become, and his career became his punishment. He was a character out of Hawthorne, a guilt-ridden, twisted man. Not a man of conscience, but a man who had conscience forced upon him.

Nancy's own father, the hero of her novel, had felt no guilt, because there was no reason for it. He hadn't been denied the right to practice medicine, he had stepped away from it to do something he was better suited to. He had moved to a new career so he would not be confronted with such loss, such sadness, a career where the odds were better. Nancy's novel was all about someone who had chosen what he believed was the happier course. It was a novel about choice, not punishment.

What Gillian had done was defile the very man he'd been, taken the character whom Nancy had revered and celebrated, and made him a man of shame rather than honor. She had written a dramatic trial scene—a scene she had suggested Nancy write. But stealing Nancy's novel wasn't the deepest treachery, the treachery was how she had used Nancy's father, done with him what she wanted, maligned him to fit into her plot.

It was strange the way the anger built. It started in Nancy's arms, as if they, and only they at first, had been attacked, and then spread to her shoulders, then her chest and neck. It was defined and certain, not so much something that happened to her but something that she became.

In a dressing room closer to the entrance, a woman with a cough had taken up residence with another, younger-sounding woman, most likely her daughter.

"Don't worry about whether you'll get another chance to wear it," the daughter urged, "just concentrate on finding something that will look good for the dinner."

"At my age, nothing looks good," said the woman with the cough.

Nancy felt dizzy; she needed air. She got carefully to her feet. Outside of the dressing rooms, it was mercifully cooler. She saw a saleswoman threading her way around the racks towards her, and, before she could be accosted, she made her way to the escalators and out of the store.

Outside, on the street, she realized that it was approaching evening. She had no idea how long she had been in the dressing room. An hour at least, more likely, two. In the closet-sized, windowless room, she had been in a timeless zone. She looked at her watch now and saw that it was close to six o'clock. The book party for Gillian would still be humming. She tried Oates again, but she still couldn't get him. She couldn't wait; she'd have to go ahead without his counsel, without his comfort. She spotted a taxicab that was letting someone out and darted into the street and lunged for it.

"That's mine!" shouted a woman beside her with her hands full of shopping bags. But Nancy pushed right past her, dove into the cab, and slammed the door shut.

$\mathcal{P}$AUL

$\mathbf{P}$AUL WENT TO HIS MOTHER'S ON ALTERNATE WEEKENDS, AND this should have been a weekend in Connecticut, but his parents had worked out a trade so he would be able to attend Gillian's book launch. He wondered how his dad had pulled this off, since his mom would never be generous when it came to anything that had to do with Gillian. He wondered what his mom must have extracted from his dad in exchange. The idea of being traded back and forth by his parents made him furious, but the thought that his mom had capitulated to his dad upset him, too. He hated it when his mom stood up to his dad and they fought, but he hated it more when she gave in.

Paul would rather have spent the weekend hanging around his mom's dull house than be dragged to New York for some big deal thing for Gillian's new book, but his dad had not really given him a choice. Sure, it was cool to go to New York City and have his own room in the Waldorf-Astoria, where he could stay up all night and watch movies, but he'd had to wear a coat and tie and sit through Gillian's reading. Jerry, sitting beside him in the front row, had a proud, proprietorial look. He kept smiling over at Paul as if he expected Paul to share in this, as if he imagined that Paul took pleasure in Gillian's success.

The reading was long and boring enough, but then they had to hang around so Gillian could autograph books. She was set up at a table stacked with copies of her poetry collection and her novel, and a long lined formed in front of her, as if she was a celebrity. She cocked her head—it was her way, Paul thought, of looking sincere—and smiled at each fan, listening to their praise. Although she took an interminable time with each person, no one in line was deterred. Paul wandered off and found the graphic novel section, pulled one off the shelf, then settled in a corner to read.

He was well into the book when Jerry appeared suddenly. "I was looking for you," he said.

"Well, here I am," said Paul. "Can we finally leave now?"

"The line is thinning," said Jerry.

"I thought we were going to a party," said Paul.

"We are," said Jerry.

"So when are we going to get dinner?"

"There'll be plenty to eat at the party," said Jerry. "And we'll be going out to a restaurant after that." Jerry held out a copy of *Restitution.* "So," he said, "what do you think? Quite a surprise, huh?"

Paul didn't say anything immediately. He had taken a quick look at Gillian's novel before the reading. It didn't seem like the kind of thing he'd be interested in reading. Everyone was making such a big fuss about it—as if Gillian were a concert pianist who'd been discovered to be a world-class tennis star as well—and even if he had been interested, he wouldn't have let on. It occurred to him, all of a sudden, that maybe his father hadn't known about the novel in advance, that it was possible Gillian had kept it a secret even from him, right up to the end. He was struck with a sense of power, with the feeling that once, for the first time, he was one up on his father.

"I wasn't surprised," said Paul. "Were you?"

Jerry laughed. "Nothing Gillian does surprises me," he said. "But I hadn't expected her to produce a novel."

Paul savored the moment. It made him almost tremble. "I knew she was working on it," he said slowly. "Didn't you?"

The expression on Jerry's face shifted from confusion to something else—doubt? fear? He obviously wasn't sure if Paul was kidding him or not. For a second Paul felt sorry for his father and wished he could reclaim what he'd said, but that feeling didn't last. He liked his father's uncertainty, liked having this small bit of power over him. Jerry had his hand on Paul's shoulder, but someone came up and interrupted them, and Jerry had to leave unasked the questions Paul knew he was forming. Once or twice, before they left the bookstore, he could tell his father was trying to catch him alone, but the moment didn't arise.

In the limo to the party, Paul sat across from his father and Gillian. Gillian tilted her head back and shut her eyes. Her lashes were long and black and public, but her naked eyelids were delicate and reminded Paul of a newly hatched bird he'd once seen. Jerry put his arm around Gillian and drew her closer to him, as if he were laying claim to her, asserting his right to her after she had been on loan, among her fans. When he looked across at Paul, there was that flicker of uncertainty on his face.

The party was at least better than the reading. It was being thrown for Gillian by somebody rich, in their Fifth Avenue apartment overlooking Central Park. Five million is what the place had cost, Jerry had said. Sure it was ritzy and all that, Paul thought, but you probably couldn't take a walk in the park across the street after dark without some guy clobbering you on the head with a rock and helping himself to your wallet. Jerry stuck by Gillian's side, as if unwilling to relinquish his claim on her, and Gillian, looking wan and dreamy, moved among the crowd. Voices rose with excitement around her, but her own voice was consistently soft. Paul looked around for Adam. He was hoping he might have brought Kim to the party. Paul hadn't seen Kim since the Christmas party, but he often thought about her. His sketchbook was filled with drawings of her—how he remembered her—his superhero, Tark, rescuing her from a variety of perils. He finally spotted Adam, but Adam was alone, and he looked as if he didn't want to talk to anyone.

The event was catered by some fancy place that pretended everything was organic, right off a farm. Waiters with trays of suspicious-looking hors d'oeuvres slipped among the crowd. The goat cheese really smelled like goats, and Paul saw Gillian's editor taste a bit of it on a cracker and then dispose of it in his paper napkin when he pretended to cough.

Paul wandered around, looking at things on the walls and artifacts on the shelves. There was a collection of ancient-looking clay figures including one of a guy—a satyr maybe?—who had a hard-on that was longer than his arms. Paul had seen pictures of something like that in his art history book but couldn't remember if the statues were Greek, Roman, or pre-Columbian. He wondered if these were actual artifacts or just copies. If they were the real thing, they must be pretty valuable, yet they were on an open shelf, and if somebody swung a champagne glass too close, it could clip that penis and knock the figure to the floor.

Gillian was talking with a short man with a laugh loud enough it carried across the room. Jerry, no longer in tow, had been cornered by a woman who was wearing a theatrically wide-brimmed hat. Paul thought it was ridiculous for someone to be wearing a hat indoors, and in the evening, too. When Gillian noticed Paul she beckoned him with a single finger. When he walked over to her, she reached out her arm towards him and took his hand, drawing him close.

"This is my stepson, Paul," she said to the man and then, turning to Paul, said, "This is my dear friend Richard Weinberg, who has so generously provided this venue for our gathering."

"It's an honor," he said, smiling at Gillian. Then he gave Paul a "so, what do you have to say for yourself?" look.

"Cool stuff you've got over there," said Paul, gesturing with his head towards the shelves.

"Nice to meet a connoisseur," said Richard. "You know, Paul, you're never too young to start collecting."

Gillian didn't smile, but she gave Paul's hand a little squeeze. "Paul just got his learner's permit," she said. "He's taking driver's ed classes and has his eye on my truck."

Paul was surprised Gillian knew about his learner's permit. She was often totally unaware of things like that in his life. The comment about the truck was even more surprising. He'd had his eye on it, but he'd never said a word.

Richard gave a loud laugh. "Don't settle for a truck," he advised Paul. "Ask your stepmother for a sports car. A Ferrari, a Bugatti."

"As much as I would love to give Paul any car he'd want, I think a Bugatti may be out of my reach," said Gillian.

Richard scowled and shook his head. "Just wait till after the Pulitzer," he said. "And I expect your novel will be a bestseller, too."

Gillian released Paul's hand and held her finger to her lips. "We're not mentioning any prizes," she said.

A couple next to them, sensing a temporary lull, joined the conversation. Paul stood awkwardly next to Gillian. She seemed to forget that he was still there. After a while he slipped away unnoticed. At the buffet table he copped a handful of olives—a stretch for a farm theme—and sampled some of the ham. The bread had so many herbs in it, it looked green.

Paul kept his eye on the bar, and when the bartender went back to the kitchen to get more ice, he refilled his ginger ale glass with champagne.

"How're you doing?" somebody asked, and Paul swung around.

"Chris," the guy said, holding out his hand. He obviously had observed Paul's transaction at the bar and gave him a conspiratorial wink. "I met you at your folks' house," he said.

One of Gillian's writers' group, Paul remembered. "Right," he said. "They're not exactly my folks," he added. "I mean my dad's my dad, but Gillian's just his wife, not my mom."

"Sorry for the semantic insensitivity," said Chris. "I should know better. If my ex-wife got remarried, I wouldn't want people calling her and her husband my kids' folks."

Paul shrugged.

"So, you must find this sort of thing something of a drag," said Chris. It wasn't what Paul had expected him to say. Everyone who had come up to him had mumbled something inane about how excited he must be to be part of all this. He didn't know quite what to make of Chris. It occurred to him that Chris might have had too much to drink.

"I can think of about fourteen hundred things I'd rather be doing," said Paul.

Chris laughed. "You have to hand it to your stepmother," he said. "She knows how to keep the literary world on its toes."

"I guess you don't like her very much," said Paul. The champagne hadn't yet had sufficient time to embolden him, but he felt daring now anyway.

"I admire her without reservation," said Chris.

"My point exactly," said Paul, echoing a phrase he'd heard from someone. Perhaps it was Gillian herself.

A plump, older woman who looked familiar came over.

"Virginia," said Chris. "What's become of Nancy? She was coming here, wasn't she?"

"I don't imagine she'll be coming now," said Virginia.

"What's up?" asked Chris.

"You didn't see Gillian's novel yet?" said Virginia.

"No," said Chris. "Am I missing something?"

Virginia gave a great sigh. Then she pointedly turned to Paul, her voice bright. "You probably don't remember me," she said. "I'm Virginia, Rachel's mother. She's told me all about you."

"Now that could be a problem!" said Chris. He obviously thought himself to be a comedian.

"Oh no, not at all," said Virginia, seriously. She looked at Paul and smiled. "She's very fond of you."

Paul looked down at the rug. He was afraid that Chris would see his face—he didn't mind about Virginia—betraying the happiness he felt hearing this. He had sort of guessed that Rachel liked him, but it was different having it said aloud this way. Though maybe Virginia was just being kind—she seemed like the sort of person who would be kind. But when he looked up at her quickly, almost as if to check, she gave him a little nod of confirmation.

"Is that Rachel's dad over there?" he asked. A man with long, grey hair and a whiter beard was lecturing and gesticulating, drink in hand.

"Yes, that's Bernard," said Virginia.

Paul tried to imagine his own two parents at the same party. Both of them having a perfectly good time, content to be in each other's presence.

"How's that ham?" Chris asked Paul, pointing to the half-eaten piece on Paul's plate.

"I've tasted worse," said Paul.

"Oh dear," said Virginia, and her voice was quick and alarmed, "here's Nancy."

"I wish you'd clue me in to what's going on," said Chris. But Virginia didn't say anything. Paul's eyes followed where she was looking. He remembered Nancy, too, from Gillian's Christmas party. She was one of the writers in the group. She looked different, though, her hair ruffled as if she had been caught in the wind and hadn't had a chance to smooth it down.

Nancy entered the room and, rather than meandering through the crowd, the established choreography of such parties, headed straight through, like a hockey player cutting across to the puck. She was wielding a copy of Restitution.

Virginia pursued her. "Nancy!" she called, but Nancy didn't slow down, and when Virginia reached for her arm, she shook it free. No one except Paul and Chris seemed aware of what was happening. Jerry was a few paces away from Gillian, no longer attached. Gillian was facing them, talking to someone. She noticed Nancy approaching her, but the look on her face was merely curious.

Nancy went right up to Gillian and stood in front of her. "You stole my book," she said. Her voice was just loud enough for Paul to hear her words.

Gillian looked somewhat amused. "What are you talking about, Nancy?" she asked.

"You stole my novel, and you published it as your own."

Jerry swung around now and moved close to Gillian, but Gillian pressed her hand against his chest, as if to hold him away. She gave a little laugh. "Nancy, you obviously haven't read my novel," she said.

"You're a plagiarist," said Nancy, and now her voice was louder, or perhaps, Paul thought, it sounded louder because the conversation around them had stopped.

"Plagiarism's a serious accusation, Nancy," said Gillian. "I suggest you be careful of what you say."

"I am careful," said Nancy. "And it's not just the plagiarism, it's what you did to my father."

"Your father? What does your father have to do with it? I thought we were talking about a novel here. Fiction."

"He never made a mistake," said Nancy. "He was not forced to leave the medical profession, it was entirely his choice."

"That's the plot of *your* novel," said Gillian. "If you call it a plot. If you call it a novel. I offered you the plot of my novel, but you refused to take it. It was too good a plot to waste. *Restitution* is quite different from your novel. Which is perhaps why mine got published, and yours, I believe, still has not."

"Oh, God," said Chris.

Paul watched Nancy lift her arm, saw the skin pulled taut with tension over the top of her hand as she made ready to strike. He remembered the time his mother had smacked his father. The sound of the flat of her hand against his father's face. His father's quick exclamation. He willed Nancy to strike, willed her hand to move through the air, willed those fingers to make contact with Gillian's cheek. For all the things she had done to him and not done, he wanted suddenly to have skin hit skin. He felt a thrill that he was the one about to strike, that Nancy's hand was as good as if it were his own hand.

But Nancy's hand retreated through the air, descended beside her body and reclaimed its position by her side. Nancy backed away from Gillian, as if she was something too horrible to touch.

CHRIS

AFTER THE BOOK PARTY, CHRIS SPENT THE NIGHT WITH AN old flame, Amelia Sonnenberg, who had an apartment on East Ninety-sixth. She'd been an editorial assistant at Random House when his first book was published there. Now she was in textbooks, an executive editor. She had been too young for him then, and was too young for him still. Their affair had ended when she had fallen in love with a writer from Argentina, but their good feelings for each other had persevered—a rare situation for Chris. They remained in touch, and they reconnected on occasion after the Argentinean had returned to his native terrain and while Amelia was still in turmoil about whether she wanted to follow him there or not.

When Chris arrived at Amelia's apartment, they debated about going out for dinner but ended up eating leftover Chinese food and finishing off an almost-stale coffee cake along with the bottle of dessert wine that Chris had brought. Chris was upset by what had happened at the book party, but he was too tired and had had far too much to drink to want to talk about it now. When he and Amelia headed down the hallway to her bedroom, the walls seemed to be leaning in towards him, and the floor seemed to buckle. They took off their clothes and got into bed, and Amelia nuzzled close to Chris, her cheek against his chest. He stroked her hip. She was small and wiry, with a nervous energy that made her sexy, but Chris was relieved when he realized that neither of them really felt like making love. They didn't want to hurt each other's feelings, though, so it took some cautious investigation before they discovered this. They lay companionably, in the pleasant proximity of each other's body. Chris listened to Amelia debate the merits of Buenos Aires, and it wasn't long before he fell asleep.

After Nancy's exit from the party, Chris had snatched a copy of *Restitution* and ducked into the pantry behind the kitchen to take a look. He saw immediately why Gillian's novel had provoked Nancy's astonishing, un-Nancylike behavior. The first chapter was eerily familiar, and even though the book veered off in a fresh direction, he found it unnerving. He was not surprised by Gillian's cleverness or her deviousness. But he was surprised at the smoothness of what she had done, and the speed. She had produced a novel in less time than it took even him to write one—and he'd always prided himself on his ability to knock things out.

He wondered how the rest of the Leopardis viewed what had happened. Virginia had left soon afterwards, with Nancy, and he hadn't had a chance to talk with her. Bernard had been out of earshot, holding forth on his own, and Adam had merely looked confused. Adam was an odd duck anyway, Chris thought. He was probably pissed that Gillian could turn out a novel in less than a year when he had been working on his for several years and there was no end in sight.

As for Gillian, she merely shook her head and turned from the sight of Virginia putting her arm around Nancy, and them walking away. Jerry came forward from the crowd and guided her away from the spot as if Nancy had left something still dangerous there. The crowd around Gillian moved in close, protectively, tittering concern.

"Who was that woman?" someone asked.

Chris caught a glimpse of Paul. He looked amazed and excited, the same way Ben had looked the time he had gotten a strike at the bowling alley. Chris made his exit from the party without saying good-bye to anyone. A headache was starting behind his eyes, the way it did, moving up across his right temple and progressing over his ear. He grabbed a taxi up to Amelia's apartment, thrusting a ten at the driver, too depleted to try to figure out a proper tip.

IN THE MORNING Chris sat on a stool at the counter of Amelia's small kitchen. She'd inherited the apartment from her parents, who'd bought it back when it was worth a fraction of its current value. From the window he could see a slice of the East River. It probably wouldn't last long. It was an old brick building, tall for its time, but new, taller buildings were going up all around, claiming the airspace.

Amelia poured them each a cup of coffee and perched on the stool across from him. She was wearing a T-shirt and pajama bottoms, and had her hair clipped up with an oversized barrette. She looked like someone's kid sister.

"Why are some women so treacherous?" Chris asked.

"You're not talking about me, I hope," said Amelia.

"Not you, sweetie," said Chris. "Someone in my writing group."

Amelia stirred her coffee. "Probably starved for success. Has to depend on her wiles."

"This is someone successful. Gillian Coit. That book party I went to last night. You must have heard of her."

"The poet?"

Chris nodded. "She's pretending to be a novelist now, too. Except she lifted part of her book from someone else's manuscript."

"Wow," said Amelia. "Whose?"

"Another writer in our group, Nancy Markopolis."

"Then she'll get her comeuppance," said Amelia. "Yummy."

"I hope so," said Chris. "But Gillian has amazing sangfroid, and I'm not sure Nancy has the guts to really take her on. She freaked out and confronted Gillian, but my guess is that she's now restored to her genteel, diffident self."

"Then you'll have to come to the rescue," said Amelia. She clinked her spoon against the edge of her coffee mug and laid it smartly on the counter.

"Not I," said Chris.

"Am I missing something?" asked Amelia. "Are you and Gillian Coit involved?" She made little quotation marks in the air with her fingers.

"Not on your life," said Chris.

"How about this other writer—what did you say her name was?"

"Nancy. And no, again. Though in her case, not because I don't find her appealing; she's very much spoken for."

"You've always liked to champion a worthy cause," said Amelia. "And this is a worthy cause, isn't it?"

"You bet," said Chris. "But I've got enough crises to deal with in my own life."

"I'm sorry," said Amelia, and she got off her stool and gave him a kiss on the side of his face. "More coffee?" she asked.

"Thanks, no," said Chris. "I'd like to try to make it to the boys without having to do a pit stop."

THE TREES ALONG THE HIGHWAY were turning their fall colors, more reds and brighter yellows as Chris drove farther north. It energized him, as it always did, this ridiculous display of color, and made him feel optimistic. He had recently sold movie rights to his second novel, and now he decided it would be fun to buy a convertible. Then he could really suck up these fall colors. Not a sports car—he already had that—but a vintage American car like a Cadillac or a Lincoln Continental with cushy seats, the kind of car he would have liked his parents to have owned when he was a kid growing up, but they never did. The boys would love it, he was sure.

When he drove up to Susan's house, Ben and Sam weren't watching for him out the window the way they usually did. After sitting in the driveway ten minutes, he began to get nervous. He gave it five minutes more. When they still hadn't appeared, he called the house. Susan answered the phone. "They'll be out shortly," she said, without waiting for him to speak, and hung up right away.

When the boys came out to the car, they were strangely sullen. It wasn't their usual reticence, which wore off quickly, but something else. Chris felt anxiety spread across the muscles of his back, up into his neck. Only fifteen minutes before, he realized, he had been calm and happy.

Even when they got to Jimmy's, the boys barely spoke to him. They slung down in their seats. A new waitress, with hair dyed a dark, unnatural red, came to take their order.

"I don't see Jimmy around today," said Chris.

"He tore a muscle in his shoulder," said the waitress. "Needs to have surgery on it. His wife won't let him come in."

"I'm sorry," said Chris. "So, what'll you have, boys?" he asked.

"I don't want anything," said Sam.

"Me neither," said Ben.

Chris ordered the spanakopita special for himself and then looked at his sons across from him.

"Should I just order the usual for you guys?"

"I'm not hungry," said Sam.

"How about we start with the ice cream, then?" asked Chris.

"No thanks," said Sam, but Ben's face had brightened a little, and given that inroad, Chris plunged ahead. "One strawberry sundae with chocolate sauce, peanut butter chips, and marshmallow topping."

"So you're really not hungry?" Chris asked Sam.

"We already ate lunch," said Ben.

"Well, then, let's get you a sundae, too, Sam, and if you can't finish it, I'll give you a hand after I've eaten my lunch." He looked up at the waitress. "Two of those sundaes," he said.

When she had left, Chris leaned across the table towards his sons. "How come you ate already?" he asked.

Ben slumped down farther in his seat. "Mom made us," he said. Sam turned and gave his brother a look of reproach.

"I see," said Chris, trying his best to keep his tone light. "Didn't you know I was taking you out to lunch?"

"We weren't sure," Sam said.

"Why not?" asked Chris. "We planned it."

"We weren't sure you'd come," explained Ben.

"Why wouldn't I come?" asked Chris. "It's the highlight of my week."

"You didn't come yesterday," said Ben.

"No," said Chris. "But I wasn't supposed to come yesterday. We made a date for today."

"Mom said you were coming yesterday," said Ben. "We waited for you. We waited all day, and you never came."

"Ben," Sam said, "sh! We weren't supposed to say!"

Chris's heart lurched. He knew that he hadn't confused the dates. Trained as a journalist, he'd always been precise about dates, and when it came to the boys, he was obsessively punctual because he didn't want to give Susan anything legitimate to complain about.

"Your mother must have made a mistake," he said. He pulled out his pocket calendar and showed them the week where "Lunch with Sam and Ben" was there, clearly, in ink, under Sunday. "Hey, guys, listen, I would never, never miss a chance to be with you."

"Mom said you forgot," said Ben, "but I thought maybe something happened." His face quivered; he struggled against tears.

"If anything happened and I couldn't get here, I'd call," said Chris. "I'd never not show up. I promise you that."

The waitress came with the spanakopita and the two sundaes. The spanakopita looked as if it had been burnt and someone had scraped away the black filo pastry on the top. The sundaes looked garish; the red strawberries almost glowed.

Chris forced a smile. "Save some for me!" he said, pointing his fork at the sundaes.

Ben took a bite of his sundae and smiled up at Chris, a brown mustache of chocolate sauce decorating his face. Sam poked at his sundae but didn't actually lift the spoon to his mouth.

Chris tried to catch his eye. "Sam," he asked, "is there something else going on?"

Sam shook his head and looked down.

"Sam?" asked Chris, and when Sam reluctantly looked up at him, he said, "Come on, something's got you down in the dumps."

"Mom got tickets for the circus for today, and now we can't go," Sam said.

"We can't?" asked Ben. "Why not?"

"It's too late," said Sam, turning to him.

"What time is the show?" asked Chris. "Maybe we can still make it." He was ready to bolt up out of his seat.

Ben shook his head. "No, Mom said we'd have to miss it because you came the wrong day, but we had to go to lunch with you."

Chris could barely keep his voice level. "Boy am I sorry about the mix-up, guys," he said. "That really sucks, doesn't it? But I'll figure out a way to get you to the circus next time you come to my house."

"It's just this weekend," said Ben.

"I'll take you into the city to the Big Apple Circus," said Chris. "You'll like it even better."

When the waitress came to clear the plates, she saw that he had barely touched his spanakopita. "Want me to wrap that up for you to take?" she asked.

"No thanks," said Chris. "I'll just take a coffee to go."

In the car driving back, Ben, somewhat mollified, was more like his usual self, but now Sam was nursing his grievance about the circus. When they got to Susan's house, he barely let Chris kiss him good-bye, and then he scampered into the house without looking back again. Chris sat for a moment in the car and then he pushed the car door open, and got out and charged up the steps to the front door of the house. Screw the legal warning. Susan must have been standing right in the foyer looking out from the narrow window by the front door, because she opened the door before he had a chance to ring. Her eyebrows were very thin, as if she had been plucking them and hadn't known when to stop.

"What are you doing here?" she asked.

"You fucking bitch," he said. "Don't you ever lie to them again."

"Hit me," she said, calmly. "I dare you."

His hands filled with heat. He wanted to punch her. He wanted to flatten her. He wanted to pummel her so hard she could never rise again. He wanted to take her by the shoulders and shake her until she couldn't breathe. But strangely, instead of provoking him, her voice called him to his senses. It was as if his arms were caught between two competing magnetic forces, and they trembled in the air and then, finally, were drawn back down to his sides. He had once described a character in one of his novels as "shaking with impotent rage," and that hyperbolic phrase came to him now, a description of himself. He walked back to his car, got in, turned the key, and backed out of the driveway, saving himself from Susan, from himself, from all he most wanted to do.

CHRIS WASN'T ABLE TO get in touch with Nancy until eight the following night.

"I'd like to see you," he said. "May I drop by now?"

"I just got back from New York," she said. "I'm kind of tired."

Chris knew Nancy was chronically polite, but even so, he didn't give her an opportunity to protest. "We have to talk," he said. "I'll be over in half an hour." He could be at her house in fifteen minutes, but a half hour would allow her time to comb her hair, tidy her living room—whatever it was that women like Nancy needed to do.

Chris had been to Nancy's house only once before, for the wedding, and it seemed more modest and smaller than he'd remembered it. Of course, that day it had been all spruced up, the big white tent in the garden, flowers everywhere. Now it looked plain, like a girl without her makeup on.

Nancy opened the door. She did look tired, but her hair was obviously freshly brushed. She wore clothes that were more casual than Chris had ever seen her in before—corduroy slacks and an oversized sweater, and she had slippers on her feet, shearling leather with fuzzy cuffs that made Chris think of Mrs. Claus.

"What's up?" she asked.

"Gillian."

Nancy let out a sigh. "Come on in," she said. She led Chris past the formal living room at the front of the house, through the large kitchen, to a sitting area beyond. Oates was sitting in an armchair, his stockinged feet up on a footstool. He got up and reached out to shake Chris's hand. His hand made Chris's look small.

"Would you like a cup of tea?" asked Nancy. "Or some coffee?"

"Thanks, no," said Chris.

"How about a glass of sherry?" asked Oates.

Chris spotted a plate of cookies out on the coffee table. Oatmeal cookies were what they looked like, arranged in a circle on the plate. They were probably homemade, he thought.

"Sure, I could do with a little sherry," he said.

Oates brought over a decanter and some glasses. "Will you have some, Nancy?" he asked.

Nancy had sat down on one side of the sofa. "Thank you, sweetheart," she said, "but I'm afraid one glass of sherry, and I'll fall asleep."

Chris didn't think she meant this as a rebuke, but he felt obliged to apologize anyway. "I'm sorry to be coming by this late," he said, "but I've been trying to get in touch with you since yesterday."

"I didn't get back from New York till this evening," said Nancy.

"Make yourself comfortable," said Oates, pointing to the chair across the table rather than the other side of the sofa, where Nancy sat.

Chris sat down and took a sip of his sherry. "I can't believe what Gillian did to you, Nancy. Actually, I can believe it. That's the trouble. I've been feeling pretty steamed up on your behalf and thought it was important to tell you in person that I'm behind you, one hundred percent, whatever you do."

"That's very sweet of you," said Nancy. "But I don't really think that there's anything I *can* do."

Chris set his glass down on the coffee table. "Of course there's something you can do," he said. "Gillian can't get away with this. She stole your book. It's blatant plagiarism. I can't imagine how she thinks she'll get away with it."

"Unfortunately, it isn't exactly plagiarism," said Nancy.

"What do you mean?" asked Chris. "I didn't read the whole thing yet, but she copied your book, didn't she?"

"Only the first chapter," said Nancy. "Then she changed things quite a bit in the rest of it."

"So, the first chapter," said Chris. "She lifted it straight from yours. Word for word."

"Not exactly," said Nancy. "And that's the real issue, I'm afraid."

"What are you talking about?" asked Chris. "I heard you read your first chapter. I remember it very well." He hadn't meant for his voice to get so loud. Nancy seemed to be sinking down into the sofa cushions.

"Here's the situation," said Oates. "Nancy stayed in the city till today so she could talk with her agent in person. They met this morning.

Her agent compared the two texts side by side. Gillian paraphrased Nancy's chapter, but she didn't copy it exactly."

"For God's sake," said Chris. "It's close enough."

"Unfortunately not," said Nancy. She sat up and looked intently at Chris. "It's very clever. It's like an echo, but it's just a beat off. It's much easier to prove plagiarism if the phrases are identical."

"Gimme a break!" said Chris. "You can't let Gillian get away with something like this!"

"I may not have a choice," said Nancy.

"Of course you have a choice," said Chris. "You've got to go after her."

"My agent said it would be a mistake," said Nancy. "Even if I could prove plagiarism—and my agent thought that wouldn't be as easy as I thought—I'd be hurting myself. Gillian is so well-connected, so influential, people will just look at me as some pathetic wannabe who's trying to bring her down."

"Darling, you're not a pathetic wannabe!" said Oates.

"Are you telling me that, because Gillian's hot stuff right now, she can do what she pleases, rip off a fellow writer's text, and blatantly publish it as her own?" asked Chris.

"That seems to be it," said Nancy.

"This makes me sick," said Chris. "Did you know she's in line for a goddamn Pulitzer Prize?"

"That was my agent's point," said Nancy. "Don't tangle with someone who's a shoo-in for a Pulitzer, you'll come off badly no matter what you do. Better to just let this one go. So I guess I'll just have to take her advice."

"I can't let this go," said Chris. "There's got to be some justice out there somewhere."

"That would be nice," said Oates. "But justice isn't that easy to come by these days."

Chris slid his glass back across the surface of the table and pounded his fist on the wood. "I'm going to make justice happen," he said.

Nancy reached out and touched his arm. "It's okay, Chris. I appreciate your wanting to go to bat for me, but your coming over here and
being so supportive is enough. You don't have to do anything more
for me."

"I'd be doing it for myself, too," said Chris. "This stuff really gets to
me. The arrogance of that woman! The dishonesty!" Chris got to his
feet. "Bedtime, folks." He looked at Nancy. "Don't get up," he said. "I
can see myself out." He reached down and snagged a cookie. "One for
the road," he said.

"Chris, thank you," said Nancy. He would have kissed her good-
bye, but Oates had gotten up, too, and walked with him to the door.

"Nancy, I'm not giving up on this," said Chris.

"I appreciate you coming," said Oates and again shook his hand.

Chris got into his car and opened the windows and sunroof before
he started up. No cars drove past this time of night, and it was quiet
enough so Chris could listen to the sound of the river. He sat there for
a moment, looking at Nancy's house. Oates must have turned off the
lights in the front of the house as he walked back to where they had
been sitting. Light from that room spilled out onto the side yard, but
beyond its range everything was dark, the river a presence only because Chris had witnessed it by daylight, knew that it was there. Chris
imagined that Oates and Nancy were talking about him now, talking
about his visit. He started up the engine and turned on his headlights,
opening up a whole new swath of the world with the light. He pulled
out onto the road. He did not want to be watching the house when the
light went off in the sitting room and a light appeared in a bedroom
upstairs. He did not begrudge Nancy and Oates their having each
other—he felt kindly towards them both—but he didn't want to feel
sorry for himself, going home alone to his own dark house.

$\mathscr{B}$ ERNARD

WHEN RACHEL AND TEDDY HAD BEEN BABIES, THE HOUSE had smelled of diaper pail. Not that Bernard had noticed—he had a fine ear but a poorly developed sense of smell—but he remembered guests remarking on it. "It's like cats, I guess," Virginia had said. "Those who own them never smell them."

Aimee had a refined nose. She had no tolerance for body odors of any sort and forced Bernard to engage in a continuing cycle of ablutions, ministering to his body orifices as if they were sources of pollution. Under her tutelage he flossed, he cleaned his ears with Q-Tips, in the shower he spread the cheeks of his buttocks and washed with soap, he filed his fingernails, clipped his toenails, spread petroleum jelly between his littlest toes, where the skin had a tendency to flake, and removed lint from his belly button. After meals that involved sauce or butter, he washed his mustache and the beard hair under his lip; otherwise he wouldn't dare kiss Aimee. Not that she often felt inclined to kiss him since she had moved back in.

Instead of the cloth diapers Virginia had favored, Aimee used disposables. They had special odor-absorbing chemicals, and every night Bernard tied them up in a plastic bag, sealing them off from the air, and deposited them in the garbage can in the garage. When Aimee came home from work, she expected Horace to be clean and bathed and scentless.

Bernard had always found bodily smells sexy. He preferred Virginia's sweaty armpits to Aimee's odorless ones. He preferred a mouth that reeked of garlic to one that smacked of mouthwash. He was fond of the smell of his own shit, and he was particularly partial to the sweet smell of Horace's loose bowel movements. He was partial to anything that Horace produced, and could even tolerate the smell of the white barf Horace sometimes coughed up, which made Aimee feel like retching.

During the week Aimee had been away with Horace visiting her parents, Bernard had lapsed somewhat in his meticulous habits, but he was industrious the day before her return, getting the house and his own aging body up to her standards again. He had missed Horace excessively, though not as much as he had expected to. In fact, he realized, during his trip to New York, he had actually enjoyed his temporary freedom. At Gillian's book party he had reconnected with power brokers in the publishing world whom he hadn't socialized with for a long time. He felt like a man of letters again, and though he had initially brandished a photograph of Horace, he discovered that few were interested. People passed right over the subject so dear to his heart and inquired about his book in progress. And as he began to talk about George Frideric Handel, Horace was nearly forgotten.

Back home again, Bernard felt guilty about this, as if he had betrayed his son by being consolable in his absence. He felt guilty, too, for not having accompanied Aimee, leaving her to manage the plane trip with Horace on her own. This guilt was exacerbated when Aimee and Horace returned the next evening and Bernard discovered that Horace had developed a diaper rash while he had been away.

"I'll take him in to the pediatrician tomorrow morning," he said.

"Don't overreact, Bernard" was what Aimee said, and she passed along to Bernard a tube of Desitin ointment, which her mother had given her.

The smell of the ointment—fish oil!—rekindled memories of Bernard's two grown children as babies. And the tube even looked the same. Was it possible that this ointment hadn't been altered in all those years? The sight of Horace's red thighs and genitalia filled Bernard with remorse. He would have liked to blame Aimee and his mother-in-law for this—for surely it was a result of neglect—but he didn't dare. Aimee could certainly point out—and no doubt *would* point out— that it was he who had been the neglectful parent, absorbed by his monologues on Handel while his darling baby son's most vulnerable flesh had been placed in jeopardy.

Aimee took off for work the morning after she was back. She had gone to bed early the night before, and they had not yet had an opportunity to talk. She had known Bernard had driven to New York with his writing group for a book event, but Bernard had not actually told her whose book was being celebrated. He always did his best not to mention Gillian's name. He was hoping he could get away with not having to mention it now.

Bernard had just succeeded in getting Horace down for an afternoon nap when Virginia called. He had been planning to snatch some time to work on his book, but he hadn't made it to his desk yet. Exhausted from carrying around a fretful Horace, he had sunk into his old leather armchair—the one piece of furniture he had not let Aimee get rid of when she did the house—the baby monitor still gripped in his hand.

"Virginia!" he said. "I'm glad to hear from you. How come you decided to spend the night in the city rather than drive back with me after the book party? I was devastated."

"The events of the evening had tired me out," said Virginia.

Bernard sensed, from Virginia's tone, that there was something more going on here, but he wasn't sure he wanted to know what it was.

"Nancy didn't ride back with me either," said Bernard. "Which meant I was left with just Adam, who is hardly scintillating company when awake and, in this case, even less so because he fell asleep."

"I'm sure you can understand why Nancy wasn't up to a car trip back with the Leopardis."

"What was that fuss all about?" asked Bernard.

"Did you read Gillian's novel?" asked Virginia.

"I glanced at it."

"You need to do more than glance at it," said Virginia. "And then we need to discuss what's happened. That's why I called. Are you free to meet me for lunch tomorrow?"

"I'm afraid not," said Bernard.

"Thursday? Friday?"

"I'm not free for lunch at all," said Bernard. Reluctantly he added, "I take care of Horace then."

"Then let's meet for a cup of coffee, in the morning or late afternoon," said Virginia.

"I would dearly love to do that," said Bernard. "But I'm on duty here while Aimee's at the office."

"Are you telling me that you're never able to leave your house during the day?" asked Virginia.

"It's just somewhat difficult at the moment," said Bernard. He stretched out the top of his turtleneck and rubbed his collarbone with his knuckles. He knew what Virginia was thinking. "But why don't you come over here? Tomorrow?"

If Aimee found out that Virginia had been over while she was away, that might arouse suspicions, yet it would be more awkward to leave Aimee home in the evening to go meet with Virginia. Especially if they were talking about something that had to do with Gillian.

Virginia hesitated. "I'd really prefer to meet somewhere else," she said finally, "but if that's the only way, I suppose I'll come. What time?"

"Horace takes his afternoon nap around two."

"I'll see you then," said Virginia.

It had been a long time, Bernard realized, since Virginia had been to the house. "We've disconnected the doorbell," he said. "But don't knock. Horace is a light sleeper. I'll leave the door open."

After he hung up, Bernard went upstairs to check on Horace. He didn't fully trust the baby monitor, and the house had solid walls. He wasn't sure if Horace woke up crying he'd be able to hear it from his study. He stood at the doorway of Horace's bedroom and watched, for a moment, the small lump in the crib. The room was a pale green, the color, Aimee had said, of willow leaves in early spring. Bernard would have preferred the robust green of the great green room of *Goodnight Moon*, but he hadn't dared say so. It looked as if Horace was sleeping soundly, and with luck Bernard would have two hours. He was itching to get back into the world of George Frideric Handel, but with Virginia descending upon him tomorrow, he knew he had no choice but to take a look at Gillian's novel. When he'd brought it back with him from New York, he'd slipped it right into the bookcase in his study. He found it now and settled in his armchair to read.

It didn't take him long to realize why Nancy had been upset. He remembered when she had first read her manuscript to the Leopardi Circle. She'd dealt with her nervousness by reading fast and keeping her face down, and he'd had to interrupt her and tell her they couldn't hear and she needed to start again. She'd looked up, her face stripped of color, and had gone back to the beginning, reading louder this time but still too fast.

He was halfway into the book and must not have heard the kitchen door open, because suddenly Aimee appeared. He sprang from his seat.

"I left early," she said. "I'm coming down with a cold. I think I picked it up on the plane."

"I'm sorry, dear," he said. "Let me make you some tea."

Aimee sank into his vacated armchair, and he trotted to the kitchen and turned on the kettle.

"Chamomile?" he called from the kitchen.

"Whatever," said Aimee.

While the water boiled, he got out a tray and arranged a teapot and cup. He worked to remember the way Aimee liked things. Blue linen napkin. Honey jar. Slice of lemon on a small glass dish. Spoon laid parallel to the edge of the tray.

"Here we go," said Bernard when the tea was ready. He was setting it on the table by the armchair when he realized that Aimee was hold-ing the copy of *Restitution* that he'd left there. Open, facedown.

"What's this?" she asked.

Bernard realized, as he looked at the jacket, that the author was M. G. Findlay. There was no need to tell Aimee it was Gillian, no need to bring up Gillian's name, especially now that Aimee was obviously not well.

"Just a novel," said Bernard. And then, because when he was caught in any sort of lie he had a tendency to go on more than he needed to, he said, "It's a new novel. Someone gave it to me." He was about to add "in New York" but wisely stopped before he did so. He didn't want to have Aimee asking about his trip to the city.

"I didn't know you read fiction," said Aimee, and to Bernard's relief she laid the book on the table.

"Now and then," he said.

Aimee turned her attention to her tea, checked that it had steeped sufficiently, then poured it into her cup.

"You don't put lemon in chamomile," she said.

"You don't have to use it," said Bernard.

The tone of his voice made Aimee alert. "I'm sorry, Bern," she said. "It was very sweet of you to fetch me tea. But I feel like shit. I'm going up to bed."

Bernard leaned down and kissed her brow. "Poor darling," he said.

"Don't catch my cold," said Aimee. "We need you on your feet to take care of Horace."

After Aimee had gone upstairs, Bernard carried the tea tray into the kitchen, then settled back into reading Gillian's novel. He didn't have much time before Horace woke up. It wasn't until later that night, when everyone had been fed, and both Horace and Aimee were asleep, that he was able to finish the book. He was annoyed with Gillian for what she had done—it seemed insensitive at the very least—but he did have to admire the finished product.

In the morning, Aimee decided not to go in to work. Bernard brought her breakfast in bed. He couldn't decide what to do about Virginia. While Aimee ate, he gave Horace his bottle, then, after Horace was changed and dressed and settled down for a morning nap, Bernard went back for Aimee's tray.

She was lying on her stomach, her face to one side, her arms under her cheek. "I could use a back rub," she said.

Bernard set the tray back down on the nightstand, kicked off his slippers, and stretched on the bed beside her. She threw the covers off, and he was jolted by the sight of her unblemished skin, her small, white buttocks. He bent and ran his tongue along the shallow concave stretch of her spine. He rubbed his hands to warm them, and then he kneaded her shoulders and pressed the heels of his hands into the wings of her back, the way she always liked it. She mmmmed with pleasure.

He stood up and unbuckled his belt and slipped his pants off, unbuttoned his shirt and took it off, and took off his undershorts. He lay back down on the bed. He massaged Aimee's lower back now and slowly began to move down lower, to her buttocks and her inner thighs. She reached around and gave his hand a nudge, and then he noticed the short white string of a tampon against her skin.

Virginia had never minded having sex when she was menstruating. They used to slide a towel under her back at such times, but even so, their sheets and mattress were always stained. And there was a girlfriend in college, Molly, Bernard remembered, a Catholic who refused to use birth control and felt the only safe time was when she was bleeding. But Aimee was fastidious about such things, and Bernard's hands retreated. Still, it was enough to touch her back, to lie close beside her, to feel full, to throb.

Suddenly he heard Horace crying in his room next door.

"Fuck," said Aimee.

Bernard got up and ran to him. He plucked him out of his crib and held him against his chest. Was it possible that he had been crying for a while and Bernard hadn't heard him? He carried Horace into their bedroom. Aimee was sitting up in bed, the covers pulled up to her shoulders.

"Don't bring him close to me," she said. "I don't want him getting my cold."

Horace had ceased crying, and Bernard dangled him and danced around.

"Do you think that's healthy?" Aimee asked. "Holding him like that when you don't have any clothes on?"

"Do you mean because he'll catch germs from my privates?" asked Bernard. "Or do you mean because he'll be warped by having witnessed his father's nakedness?"

"I don't know," said Aimee. "It just looks perverted, you stark naked like that, holding a baby against you."

"I'm giving him material for when he writes a memoir," said Bernard.

"You are ridiculous," said Aimee, and she sank down in the bed and closed her eyes.

Bernard's dilemma about Virginia, which had escaped his mind while he was caressing Aimee's back, reasserted itself, and as it drew closer to two o'clock, Bernard realized there was no way he could avoid speaking to Aimee about the visit. After he got Horace settled down for his afternoon nap, he confronted Aimee, who was in bed still, but dressed in jeans and working on her laptop.

"Virginia phoned and said she wanted to meet with me to talk about something," he said, "and since I can't leave you with Horace, I asked her to stop by here. I hope that's all right." He didn't exactly lie, but he thought that Aimee would guess that Virginia had recently phoned, most likely when Aimee had been sleeping.

Aimee hit a few keys and looked up at him. She usually wore contacts, but because of her cold she had her glasses on now, and they made her look even younger.

"When is she coming?" asked Aimee.

"Sometime soon," said Bernard.

"Is something going on with Rachel or Teddy?" asked Aimee.

"No," said Bernard. "It's about the writing group. Something about Nancy."

"Oh," said Aimee. "It's not the best time for company. But I suppose it's best you stay around in case Horace wakes up."

"I don't expect you to come down," said Bernard. "Virginia's not really company." He stood in the doorway, his hand on the doorknob. "Why don't I close this, so we won't disturb you," he said. "Anything I can bring you from downstairs?"

"No thanks," said Aimee. "I'm fine. Just keep your ear out for Horace."

Virginia came at a quarter after two, and Bernard offered her a cup of coffee.

She waved him off. "Thank you, Bernie, but this isn't really a social visit. We have a serious problem here, and I think you're the only one who can help with it."

"Me?" asked Bernard, as they walked into his study and sat down. "You want me to reconcile the warring factions of our group?"

"Reconcile?" asked Virginia. "Bernie, you must be out of your mind. There's no way the Leopardi Circle will ever be meeting again."

"No?" asked Bernard. He hadn't thought of that possibility, and the prospect of the loss of his group seemed acutely painful to him. He needed the support of the Leopardis to keep his Handel project going, but it wasn't just that; their Sunday meetings were one of his few activities on his own. And he liked seeing Virginia, he liked the relationship they had settled into together. "What if we told Gillian she could no longer come?"

"Bernie, it's gone, over. Gillian ruined it for everyone."

Bernard was about to ask, "But what about my work in progress?" but wisely caught himself in time. He could just imagine Virginia scowling at him and saying, "This isn't about you, Bernie."

"Your prediction about the Leopardis seems rather dire," said Bernard. "And, Virginia, it's unlike you to be so pessimistic."

"Nancy's certainly never going to come again, and Chris says he's finished with it. And I wouldn't be surprised if Adam is, too."

"You just need to give them time," said Bernard.

"Time?" asked Virginia.

"Writers require their groups," Bernard said. "The Leopardis—sans Gillian, of course—will rise again." Bernard's voice swelled with these words, but, aware that Virginia would accuse him of pontificating, he added, less dramatically, "You'll see."

"Oh, Bernie!" said Virginia.

"So," said Bernard, "what's to be done then?"

"About the Leopardi Circle, nothing," said Virginia. "But about Nancy, I'm hoping there's something we can do. Chris came to see me about it—he's as incensed as we all are, but he's also better connected. He has a friend from Columbia Journalism School who's on the Pulitzer Committee, and he's ready to rush in there if we can give him something to work with."

Bernard had made note of the word *incensed*. It didn't describe how he felt, and he was surprised by Virginia's assumption that it did.

"What do you mean 'we'?" he asked. "What are you talking about?"

"Chris talked with Nancy," said Virginia. "Apparently she spoke with her agent about what had happened, but her agent counseled against bringing a charge of plagiarism against Gillian. She said it would be difficult to prove and in the end would only hurt Nancy's career."

Bernard was relieved to hear this. He had been afraid Virginia was cooking up something where all the members of the Leopardi Circle would join as a body to testify to what they had heard of Nancy's novel.

"That sounds wise," he said.

"Perhaps," said Virginia. "But you have to admit that something needs to be done."

Those words brought up a familiar sense of unease. Virginia's sense of social justice had always been more extreme than his, and during the years of their marriage she had often dragged him into things he would rather have let pass by.

"I think that would be Nancy's department," he said. "Not ours."

"It's ours, too," said Virginia. "We're responsible for what happened to Nancy—you in particular, since you brought her into the group. Gillian broke the rules, she destroyed the trust. We're all implicated, whether we like it or not."

There was a sound on the baby monitor, and Bernard held up his finger for a moment and leaned close. Unfortunately, it was just the noise of a passing truck, and he had no excuse to take a break from the conversation.

When he looked back at Virginia, her eyes hadn't left him. "Well, Virginia," he said. "I understand why you're upset about this, but I think you are overstating the case a little."

"Overstating it?" cried Virginia, and Bernard raised his finger to his lips fearfully. "Whose side are you on, anyway?"

"I didn't know we were choosing sides," said Bernard, and he leaned towards her, hoping to get her to lower her voice.

"How can we not?" asked Virginia. "After what Gillian did?"

"What did Gillian do?" ask Aimee. Neither of them had heard her come downstairs. She stood in the doorway, barefoot.

"I'm sorry we disturbed you, dear," said Bernard. "I'll tell you about it all later."

Virginia was obviously surprised to see Aimee, and Bernard felt obliged to explain why she was home. "Aimee took the day off to nurse a cold," he said.

"I'm actually feeling a lot better," said Aimee, and she came in and sat on the arm of Bernard's chair. "Tell me what's going on."

"Gillian plagiarized part of the manuscript of Nancy's novel," said Virginia, "and published it herself, under a pseudonym."

Alas, the book Bernard had foolishly left out on the side table was still there, and Virginia picked it up and waved it in evidence. It would be hopeless to pretend he hadn't known who the real author was.

"For a variety of reasons," continued Virginia, "Nancy won't bring a case against her for that, but I came by today to talk with Bernie about something else that's worth looking into."

Bernard didn't know what Virginia could possibly be thinking of, but instinct told him whatever it was, it wasn't something he wanted to hear, and not something he wanted Aimee to hear either.

"I can't imagine what you have in mind," he said.

"Remember when we were putting the group together I was somewhat concerned about inviting Gillian to join us because of something in the past you had told me about, an incident of unethical behavior she was involved in years before?"

Bernard remembered Virginia's reticence, but he thought it had to do with feelings she'd had about Gillian—suspicions, which he hoped she had never been able to confirm, that he and Gillian had once been lovers. But there was no way he could say anything like that now. Anything he said about Gillian, anything at all, was likely to get him in trouble with Aimee.

"I'm not sure I remember," said Bernard.

He was afraid Virginia was on a roll. Was it possible that she was seizing on Aimee's presence to embarrass him in some way? But why?

"Well, you should," said Virginia. "Your friend Martin Jacobson, who'd been her senior thesis advisor, told you she had stolen some lines of poetry from another student, a Russian exchange student the year before, and included them in her own work. And when she was confronted with the evidence by Martin, her defense was that it had been unconscious. She admitted she had heard the other girl read her poems aloud at a student presentation but insisted any imitation was accidental, she had never actually copied them. If I recall, you told me Gillian said that even if she had actually copied part of the poems, it would have been all right because she had improved them. Martin had been so bowled over by her chutzpah that he let her thesis get highest honors nevertheless."

Bernard now remembered it all too clearly. Virginia had argued at the time that Martin had been so snowed by Gillian he'd let her get away with something an unattractive student would have been expelled for. "I told you that in confidence," he said. "And besides, I can't see that it's relevant now."

"It's absolutely relevant. It's the same writer we're talking about, with the same questionable morality."

"Even so," said Bernard, "I don't see what's to be done with it."

"What's to be done is that you tell Nancy all about it, get the information she needs to document it, and let Chris use it in any way he can."

"I'll do nothing of the sort," said Bernard quickly. "That was something that happened many years ago, when Gillian was an undergraduate, a girl. It's not right to drag it up now."

"Not right?" said Virginia. "We're talking about Gillian here. And if you don't tell Nancy about it, I will."

Aimee shifted her weight on the arm of the chair. If she weren't there, he would plead with Virginia to let him off somehow, plead with her to keep him out of this. But Aimee was there, staring at him, waiting for him to speak.

"I'll get you what I can," he said. Mercifully, there was some more noise on the baby monitor. Bernard stopped to listen. Horace wasn't crying, but he was stirring and soon would be awake. "But I'd appreciate it if you'd be the one to tell Nancy about it. Let Chris do what he wants with it, but please, keep the source anonymous."

Virginia stood up. "I'll do my best," she said.

ᴀDAM

ADAM HAD SPOKEN TO NO ONE FROM THE LEOPARDI CIRCLE
since his return from New York. He'd gotten two messages from
Chris, one from Virginia, and even one from Bernard, and when he saw
from the number that it was Virginia calling him again, he still didn't
pick up. She didn't leave a message this time. He didn't mind ignoring
Chris, but he felt guilty about Virginia. He could imagine her sigh of
disappointment when she hadn't been able to get through to him. She
obviously wanted to talk to him about what had happened with Nancy,
and, given Virginia's rapier quick empathy, she would be wanting to know
how he was doing, since she now knew how he felt about Gillian—
most likely, Adam guessed, she had known long before this. He wasn't
ready to talk to anyone yet, not even to Virginia. From the moment at
the reading when he learned about Gillian's novel, he didn't know
what he thought, didn't know what he felt.

In the car riding back from New York with Bernard, he had been
able to avoid conversation, first by pretending to doze and, not long
afterwards, by actually falling asleep. He'd drunk more champagne at
the party than he'd drunk at any wedding—and he'd certainly put away
plenty of champagne at weddings. He had sat on an upholstered bench
by the window, drinking and watching Gillian.

Ever since her Christmas party, he had been waiting for Gillian to
get in touch with him. He held on to her words exactly as she had spoken them: "Sometime, when I'm in Truro, you can come have supper

with me again." He knew she had been to Truro on her own since then, but the invitation had not come. It would be too awkward for him to have to remind her of her promise—if, maybe, she had forgotten it. It was painful to think that she might have changed her mind and now regretted having raised his hopes. It was worse to think that she'd never meant the invitation seriously in the first place, that it had been mere conversation and she'd never imagined he'd expect anything to come of it.

He did not want to go up to her now, he wanted her to come up to him, but she hadn't done so. He wanted her to say something to him about the fact that she had not told him she was writing a novel. He understood why she had not let the Leopardis know anything about it, but why hadn't she confided in him, a novelist, too? She would know that he would keep any secret she entrusted to him absolutely safe. He wanted her to apologize to him—or at least explain to him. At the very least, he wanted her to acknowledge him. He hadn't taken his eyes off her. He didn't want to watch, but he couldn't stop observing Jerry's hand on her shoulder, the way he steered her from behind, as if they were dancers on a dance floor, couldn't stop watching the way Gillian was embraced by everyone around her, those wealthy New Yorkers, those well-connected publishers. Chris had come by to talk with him and suggested he should be networking, that the lush party was the venue an aspiring novelist would dream of, but he did not have the stamina for it.

When Nancy had attacked Gillian, he'd sprung to her defense, but he never even got close to her. Jerry and their friends circled around her, and Adam's protective move was ignored. It was so unlike Nancy to flip out that way, and Adam had no idea what she might be so furious about. He had been too far away to hear most of what was said. All he'd caught was Nancy saying something about her father, but he couldn't imagine what that had to do with Gillian.

Adam had bought a copy of *Restitution* at the reading, but he post-poned looking at it for two days. His curiosity was intense, but he had a gut feeling that there was something in the book that he would prefer not knowing. And when he did read the novel, breathlessly, first with shock, then, in spite of it, with admiration and jealousy, he knew what everyone in the Leopardi Circle was calling him about. He had been absorbed by his hurt that Gillian had not confided in him, but now, without her telling him, he understood why she hadn't. He forgave her for the hurt he'd felt, and all he wanted to do now was protect her. They'd come down hard on her, everyone in the group. They'd side with Nancy.

And the worst thing was that he sided with Nancy, too. Not just because he was also a novelist, and could so easily imagine how she felt, but because what Gillian had done wasn't quite right. If it was anyone else but Gillian, he would have rallied to Nancy's side. But it was Gillian. And he couldn't reject her because of it. Strangely, it only intensified his feelings for her. Her flaw made her more vulnerable, and stoked Adam's devotion. She'd need him now, especially as the forces of the Leopardi Circle were marshaled against her.

KIM WORKED ON SATURDAYS at a pet store in the strip mall. They didn't sell puppies there—the owner was against puppy mills that sup-plied them—just smaller animals, but the sidewalk in front had a row of doghouses, wooden, with shingle roofs, in four, graduated sizes. The store was deep and narrow, and although Adam put his face to the glass window to look in, he couldn't see Kim. She wasn't at the register when he entered, just a young man with a face so pimpled Adam wanted to look away. Inside it was hot and smelled of rodents and amphibians. In the high ceiling area above the fluorescent light fixtures, sparrows flew; below them, flocks of colorful parakeets chattered, imprisoned in cages.

Adam made his way down an aisle towards the back of the store. The dog toys looked like children's toys, stuffed animals and rubber creatures with silly faces. Along the wall were tanks with gerbils and snakes and lizards, on the other wall, tanks overfilled with fish. A fat girl in a red apron looked up from a handful of studded dog collars she was pricing on a rack.

"Something I can help you with?" she asked.

"No thanks," said Adam. He walked deeper into the store.

Kim was in the far corner helping two customers, a boy and his mother. The boy's hair stuck up stiff as a hedgehog's. Kim had on the red store apron, and she looked as if she could be helping out in Santa's workshop. She did not notice Adam, and he stepped back into the aisle, watching her, unseen. She was leaning down over a tank to scoop crickets up and put them in a plastic bag she had filled with air. Her glowing hair, silver blond under the fluorescent light, fell forward, and because her hands were both full, she had to shake it back over her shoulders.

"Here you are," she said to the boy.

The boy held up his balloon of crickets. "Are these the small ones?" he asked. "They look pretty big to me."

"Yes, they're the small ones," said Kim. "The big ones are over here. Take a look." She squatted down by another tank and tapped on the glass. The boy squatted behind her.

"Those are really big," he said. "My snake's kind of little. I think he'd be scared by them."

"We certainly don't want to scare the snake," said the boy's mother. She smiled at Kim. "I'm actually afraid of snakes, and now I have one living in my house. The things we do for our children! You'll see, some-day, when you're a mother."

"How much are these?" the boy asked, holding up his bag of crickets.

"They're a dollar twenty-five for a dozen. I think there are a few more in there than twelve, but tell them up front you've got a dozen."

"Thank you," said the mother, and she followed her son towards the registers in the front of the store.

"Adam!" cried Kim happily, noticing him now. Her face was so round—a moon face—so suffused with smile, that he took a step back from her. She ran towards him but stopped just short of embracing him when she realized his arms were at his sides.

"What are you doing here?" she asked.

"I just needed to talk to you about something."

"Is everything okay?"

"Yeah, sure," he said.

She scowled a little. "Aren't we going to be doing something to-night? It couldn't wait till then?"

"Well, that's it, I mean, tonight's not really going to work for me."

Kim tilted her head, a question. Her perfect white teeth were small, like his mother's cultured pearls.

"You think you could take a break and come outside so we could talk?"

"Sure," said Kim.

The woman who had been hanging up dog collars was at the front of the store now, at the second register.

"I need to take a few minutes, Shirley," said Kim. "Could you cover for me?"

"Sure," said Shirley. She was clearly bursting to ask who Adam was, eager to be introduced. She watched them shamelessly as they left the store.

Outside the mall it was cold, and Kim rubbed her shoulders. She had on only a short-sleeved blouse under her apron. Another time Adam would have taken his denim jacket off and put it around her.

"So what's the matter?" asked Kim.

"I'm just not up for this anymore," he said.

"What do you mean?" asked Kim.

"I mean I'm just not in a position to be going out with you right now."

"Are you talking about tonight?" asked Kim. "Or are you talking about . . . about always?"

"I guess I'm talking about— Well, not just tonight," said Adam.

"What are you saying, Adam? I don't understand what you're saying," said Kim.

"I've gotta take a break from things," said Adam. "I've got to stop seeing you."

"But why?" asked Kim.

"I don't know," said Adam.

"There's got to be a reason," said Kim. "You can't just do this and not have there be a reason. There's got to be a reason." As if by insisting, she could make it not true.

Adam looked around him. The store next to the pet food store was called Mattress King, and in the window was a deeply quilted box spring and mattress in ivory-colored satin, designed for a sultan. It looked bare, stripped of its sheets, like someone in underwear.

"I'm in love with someone else."

Kim's smooth face was broken up by lines now, like a globe that had been smashed.

"Who?" she asked after a while, her voice a child's.

"It doesn't matter," said Adam.

"Who?" Kim asked, louder this time.

"I can't say," said Adam. "I'm really sorry, Kim," he continued. The word *sorry* seemed so inane, but he didn't know what else to say. "I didn't want this to happen."

Kim didn't say anything, she just kept looking at him.

"Are you going to be all right?" asked Adam.

But Kim didn't answer. She just stood there, hugging herself more tightly, her shoulders hunched around her pale neck.

"You better be going back in," said Adam. "It's too cold for you to be standing out here." He didn't want to leave Kim standing there on the concrete in front of the lineup of doghouses, but he felt desperate to get away. "Please," he said, "go on inside, you're going to freeze out here."

There were two doors to the pet store—one marked "in," one "out." He pushed the "in" door open and held it for Kim. She stepped into the store, and he followed behind her, but he was careful not to touch her.

She turned to him. "Adam?" she asked, but he shook his head and backed out of the other door.

ON THE WAY TO GILLIAN'S HOUSE, the gas tank warning light flashed orange on Adam's dashboard. There was no way he would stop for gas, though, now. He couldn't even imagine "afterwards, on the way home, I'll stop to get gas," because he could not imagine "afterwards," could not imagine "on the way home." His mind was filled with the image of Gillian's house. He saw it exactly as he had seen it that one time, months before, when he had taken Kim to the Christmas party. He wasn't picturing Gillian, just her house, his destination. He knew the way there exactly, because he had driven to her house many times before—driven past the entrance to her long driveway, the number, not the name, on the mailbox, the house not visible from the road.

It had been winter when he had last driven up Gillian's driveway. Now, three seasons later, the maples had begun dropping leaves, the oak leaves were brown but firm. The gravel on the driveway was thin in places—almost just a dirt road—but deep closer to the house. Adam was aware of the noise his tires made in the deeper gravel. There were no other cars in the driveway, and the garage doors were closed so he could not tell who might be at home. For a moment, he felt hesitant, but once he turned off the engine and stepped out of the car, he was swathed once again in his purpose, in the immovable clarity of it.

He was not surprised when Gillian finally answered the door. But she was clearly surprised to see him.

"Adam?" she asked.

"I came as soon as I could," he said.

She looked puzzled. "Because of what?"

"I had to talk to Kim first. I had to end things with her."

"I don't know what you're talking about," said Gillian.

"Don't you think we should be inside?" asked Adam.

"I don't like to be disturbed at home when I'm working," said Gillian, "but since you've obviously driven all the way out here to tell me something, I suppose you should come in and sit down for a moment." She led the way through the kitchen to the dining area that looked out across the lawn, and sat on a Breuer chair at the glass table, nodding at another chair for Adam. "It's something important, I hope."

The kitchen looked austere, as if no one had ever cooked a meal there. The glass table was perfectly clear, as if it had never borne even a crumb of food.

Adam sloughed his jacket off so it fell over the chair back. The glass table was so cold to his touch that he pulled his hand back to his knee.

"I ended things with Kim," he said. "I told her I couldn't see her anymore."

Gillian waited as if she expected him to say something additional. "What does that have to do with me?" she asked.

Adam leaned towards her, his arm on the glass table. "Everything," he said.

"I'm sorry, Adam," said Gillian, "but I'm not following you."

"When I read *Restitution*, when I saw what you'd done, I realized why everyone in the group was going crazy. I wanted to be here for you, entirely. And I couldn't do that if I was, in any way, still involved with Kim."

"What do you mean by what I'd done?" asked Gillian. Her voice was sharp.

"What you'd done to Nancy," said Adam. "They're all up in arms about it. But I'm with you. I'm with you all the way."

"What have I done to Nancy?" asked Gillian.

Adam pulled back a little. For the first time he actually took a breath. "The book," he said. "Her book."

"What about her book?" asked Gillian.

"That first chapter that you took from her."

"Took from her? Is that what you think?"

"I mean, I know what you were doing, artistically, that is. But naturally Nancy didn't, I mean—"

"Nancy's novel was self-indulgent and myopic and unpublishable. I gave Nancy the entire plot of my novel, but she refused it, and she refused all my advice about how to shape hers into something publishable. I didn't take her first chapter. I used what I remembered of it, and brought it to a new place. Are you telling me you think there's anything wrong with that?"

Adam closed his eyes for a second and ran his tongue over his bottom lip.

"I'm not judging you," he said softly. "They've judged you, and they're all up in arms. But I love you, Gillian. It doesn't matter what you do. That's how I knew that it wasn't just some casual infatuation thing I felt but something with"—Adam held his hands out, as if holding an invisible loaf of bread—"with substance," he said, "with longevity. And I realized as long as I was involved with Kim—involved with anyone else—you'd never take me seriously."

"You expect me to take you seriously?" asked Gillian.

Adam couldn't tell from her tone exactly what she meant. He felt he was blundering but didn't know how to rescue the situation.

"I thought you might need me now," said Adam. "To stand up for you."

"Stand up for me?" cried Gillian. "Am I on trial now?"

"Not exactly," said Adam. Everything was going so wrong, he didn't know how to save it, any of it.

"You judgmental little prick," said Gillian.

Adam blinked. "I love you," he said. It was the only thing he was clear about. Nothing else quite made sense.

"Get out of here," said Gillian, and she stood up.

Adam looked up at her. "I love you," he said again, his voice close to a whimper.

"You are such a bore," said Gillian. "I was a fool to ever be nice to you."

Adam stood up slowly. He thought he might puke. He leaned on the glass table. Through the clear surface he saw the shiny chrome base of the table and Gillian's bony toes, two ridges of blue veins across the top of her foot.

There was no way any of this could be undone. Even if she hadn't meant what she said, had said it only in a moment of anger. But she had meant it. He was pretty sure of that.

NANCY

THE CLUES THAT NANCY GOT FROM VIRGINIA WERE SIMPLY these: a college literary magazine, *Ailanthus*, and a Russian exchange student. Virginia didn't say where she got her information from, and Nancy, sensing that Virginia preferred to keep her source secret, did not ask. But Nancy guessed that it was Bernard. She had no idea that he would never have provided the information if Virginia hadn't wrested it from him. She wondered if the clues were slender because it was all Bernard had been able to come up with or if, in his perverse way, he didn't want to make it too easy for her.

When Adam called to offer his assistance, Nancy was surprised and a little suspicious. He'd gone to Virginia first, he said, and she had explained what Nancy was trying to do.

"I don't really need your help," Nancy said. "It's just a matter of me tracking down that publication—I'm assuming it's a literary magazine at Gillian's college—then hunting for a Russian-sounding name."

"But once you find it, you'll need someone like me," said Adam. "I know all of Gillian's poetry. I'll be able to spot anything familiar."

This was true. Nancy had been daunted by the size of Gillian's new collection, which included not just a section of new poems but selections from her six previous ones.

"I thought he was in love with Gillian," Oates said when Nancy told him Adam wanted to join her on her trip to Bolton College.

"He was—at least he said he was—but I guess he isn't anymore."

"It's hard to love a plagiarist," said Oates.

"No," said Nancy. "That's not true. People love plagiarists in spite of the fact that they are plagiarists."

"What then?"

"I don't know," said Nancy. "But something's changed. Adam's all fired up about this. He said he wanted to 'bring her down.'"

"Whoa!" said Oates. "In that case, I'd say it was a lovers' quarrel."

"I don't think they were lovers," said Nancy. "I can't imagine that Gillian would sleep with anyone as insignificant as Adam."

"He's young, he's handsome."

Nancy shook her head. "No. Gillian is too calculating to go simply for youth and looks. I'm sure it was all unrequited love on Adam's part."

"So why would he turn against her now?"

"Because of what she did."

"But you yourself said people love plagiarists in spite of what they do. So it must be a case of him finally wanting his revenge."

"Revenge?" asked Nancy. She thought for a moment. "Is that what I'm doing, Oates, seeking my revenge?"

"No, not revenge," said Oates. "What you're seeking, to use your champion Chris's word, is justice."

"Thank you," said Nancy.

"Wait a second, sweetheart," said Oates, and he caught her by the arm. "What's so wrong with revenge?"

"It's just not who I am," said Nancy.

AS THEY STARTED OUT ON THE CAR TRIP, Nancy felt a rush of excitement. It was the thrill of the hunt, the exhilaration she always felt when she was tracking down something for her newsletter, when she went after any scrap of information. But maybe there was something more now. Maybe I *am* seeking revenge, she thought, and it upset her to realize this about herself. Is this what I'm becoming? she wondered. Is this what Gillian's turning me into?

Adam had wanted to drive, but Nancy was too wound up to be a passenger. She gave Adam the AAA map and asked him to navigate. Adam threw his briefcase on the backseat of the car. He'd brought several of Gillian's poetry collections along for reference. As they drove, he seemed no more relaxed than she. He chewed on his cuticle the way a girl would.

"Have you ever been to Bolton?" Nancy asked.

"Once, a while back," he said.

"Friends who went there?"

"No," said Adam. "I just wanted to see Gillian's college. I wanted to picture her there."

It was the first reference he'd made to Gillian since they'd started out.

"A bad crush," said Nancy.

"I guess you could call it that," said Adam.

Nancy had a desire to reach out and touch his arm, a Virginia gesture, but she kept her hands on the steering wheel, gave it squeeze to keep them rooted there.

"How is Sonia doing these days?" she asked him.

"Sonia?"

"Your character," said Nancy. "Your novel."

"I haven't been writing," said Adam. "Not for a long time."

"How come?"

"Too much shit going on," said Adam.

Nancy took her eyes off the road a moment to look at him.

"I broke up with my girlfriend, Kim," said Adam.

"That's too bad," said Nancy. "I met her at that Christmas party. She seemed very nice."

"She is nice," said Adam.

Nancy was tempted to ask what had happened but guessed that Adam had already revealed more than he was comfortable with.

"If you're available for dating now, I have a lovely daughter," said Nancy. "She'll be home from college for vacation. Of course she'd be mortified if she knew I was fixing her up with anyone."

"Sure," said Adam.

Nancy was immediately angry with herself for offering up Aliki this way. It was difficult talking to Adam. She steered the conversation into safer territory.

"You should get back to your novel," she said. "It's worth working on."

"Yeah," said Adam. "I know."

They drove for a while without talking, and then Adam turned to her.

"Here's something I don't understand," he said. "How come you gave a copy of the manuscript of your novel to Gillian? We haven't been doing that in the Leopardi Circle, we've just been reading."

"I didn't."

"Then how did she get the manuscript?"

"She never had the manuscript."

"Then how did she copy your first chapter?"

"She must have remembered it from when I read it."

"But she got it almost exactly."

"It's very close," said Nancy, "but it's not exact."

"You think she ran home after the meeting and quickly wrote it all down?"

"I don't think so," said Nancy. "I don't think she decided to write a novel herself until months later."

"That means she remembered your first chapter all that time," said Adam. "That's pretty remarkable."

It was pretty remarkable, Nancy thought, though she hated conceding any compliment to Gillian. Adam, she could tell, was struggling with his admiration.

"She's pretty extraordinary," he said, but then, to Nancy's relief, he added, "But what a bitch."

NANCY KNEW HER WAY around college libraries, and, as the editor of her newsletter, she had access to any collection she wanted. Nowadays she did almost all her research online, but there had been a time when she relied on actual journals. She loved libraries, the smell and heft of books. She loved the feeling of mystery each time she entered the stacks, their profound quiet and stillness, the sense that there were secrets—ideas, information—that had been buried there for years.

The Bolton College library had been renovated recently, years after Gillian had graduated. The main reading room, part of the original 1850s building, still had the aura of a church, with stained-glass windows and a vaulted ceiling, but half of the reading tables had been taken over by computer terminals, and the current periodicals were now arranged alphabetically on severe grey metal shelves.

The online catalog turned up nothing for *Ailanthus*, but Nancy found that the college literary magazine, *The White Mountain Review*, went back to Gillian's day.

"Maybe Virginia got the name wrong," said Adam.

"Virginia wouldn't get it wrong," said Nancy, "but maybe her source did."

"Who do you think her source was?" asked Adam.

"No idea," said Nancy. "Virginia knows a lot of people." She did not mention her hunch that it was Bernard, wanting to shelter him if he were the source—though her instinct to protect Bernard puzzled her. What was it about Bernard that called for her protection?

The bound back issues of *The White Mountain Review* were in the most subterranean level of the stacks, on rolling shelf units that were sandwiched together. When Nancy had located the right shelf, she and Adam had to move seven of the units to the side to make an access corridor. The overhead light was on a timer that clicked out the seconds, measuring the time before they would be left in darkness.

"Chris could use this as a crime scene," said Adam.

Nancy shuddered. When the shelves were pressed together, someone could easily be crushed between them. It looked as if no one had ventured into this part of the library for years.

They carted the volumes to a table at the end of the room. A gooseneck lamp gave them a circle of light to read by. The timer on the light in the stacks counted off the minutes as they worked through the tables of contents. It reminded Nancy of the sound of crickets in her basement.

"I haven't seen anything remotely Russian," said Nancy when she was nearly through her half of the pile.

"No Russian names here either," said Adam.

When the timer reached its final moment, the overhead light snapped off.

"I'll get that," said Adam.

Nancy watched him make his way to the shelves, a dark, ursine shape. He wound the timer fully clockwise, then returned to his seat, and Nancy was aware of his smell—a comforting fragrance of wool and bacon—in contrast to the odor of the stacks: concrete floors and forgotten books. She turned back to the volume she was studying. It was the last one. Her finger stopped midway down the table of contents.

"This may be it!" she cried. "Minsky. That's Russian. Something called 'Homilies.'"

Adam got up and came behind her to look on. But when Nancy turned to the pages, they weren't poems but dreary lithographs of womb-like shapes.

"Fuck," said Adam.

"Have you been through all of yours?" asked Nancy.

Adam gave the stack of bound volumes a nudge. "Nothing here. So now what?" he asked.

Nancy smiled at him. "You didn't expect it to be that easy, did you?"

Adam shrugged. "We've been here all morning," he said.

"Let's put these back and get some lunch," suggested Nancy. She was beginning to wonder whether it had been a good idea to have Adam along. Nancy was used to the slow pace of research, and she didn't want to be influenced by his quick discouragement. She had trained herself to believe that all information was there, somewhere, and it was just a matter of meticulous searching until you finally uncovered it. She had never let herself entertain the thought that the information didn't exist. She explored in an almost dreamlike state of investigation, and uncovered clues that would never reveal themselves if she didn't allow herself time to meander. She loved handling printed matter, the feel of the edges of the paper, like touching the wing tips of birds.

But what if the clues she had been given were false? What if there were no *Ailanthus*, no Russian exchange student?

"Let's go eat," she said.

THE DELI ACROSS THE STREET from campus had a menu board posted over the counter. Every sandwich had a cute name—some insider reference, no doubt.

There were some fresh-baked cookies on a serving dish by the register. "Want one?" Nancy asked.

"Trying to cheer me up?" asked Adam.

"You bet," said Nancy. Adam actually smiled.

They ate at a table by the window. Bolton was one of the Seven Sisters that was still all women. Outside, students ran back and forth across the street, some waiting for the crossing light, others darting out between bursts of traffic. Adam was watching them as if he were searching for Gillian among them.

"So," said Nancy, "what do you think our next step should be?"

Adam turned his attention back to her. He shrugged and licked some mustard from his lip. "I don't know," he said. "Do you have any ideas?"

"Talk to a reference librarian, for one," said Nancy. "Look through the old card catalog. Check the yearbooks from when Gillian was here."

"Sounds good," said Adam. The food had improved his disposition.

The old card catalog had turned up no *Ailanthus,* and the reference librarian had never heard of it. In the yearbook they found a photograph of the staff of *The White Mountain Review* but no *Ailanthus* among the pages of campus organizations. Adam was clearly disappointed that Gillian's photograph was not included. The listing for her on a page in the back offered no information beyond her home address. Nancy was not surprised. It seemed quite like Gillian to feel disdain for the yearbook mentality. She probably had had contempt for the entire world of undergraduates and had slipped through Bolton without belonging to any organizations, without anyone knowing her. While other student writers were vying to get their work published by *The White Mountain Review*—or, if it existed, the mysterious *Ailanthus*—Gillian was submitting to *Poetry* magazine and *The New Yorker,* not getting published yet but collecting handwritten notes of encouragement.

There was no point in checking out students with Russian-sounding names. An exchange student wouldn't have been in the yearbook; she'd been at Bolton for only that one year she was in the United States.

Adam flipped back to the page where Gillian Coit's photograph would have appeared, ran his fingers over the white space between Mary Beth Cochrane, a serious-looking young woman who had chosen to be photographed against a brick wall, and Judith Cole, who peered down at the photographer from the branches of a tree.

"Didn't they have color photography back then?" asked Adam.

"Of course they did," said Nancy, "but black and white was considered more artsy."

"This one is so artsy," said Adam, pointing at the bottom of the page, "she's entirely in shadow."

Elenah Cooper was, indeed, practically obscured, except for a bit of illumination on the side of one eye. She was, not, however, an obscure undergraduate, and had several lines of activities listed under her name, including the Gold Cup Society, the Drama Club, and *Ailanthus*, editor.

Adam's forefinger tapped the spot. "We found it!" he cried. "This is phenomenal."

"We didn't find it," said Nancy, "but at least we know it exists."

"Do you need a cookie?" asked Adam.

Nancy laughed. "You're right," she said. "This is great."

Knowing that *Ailanthus* existed, however, was quite a different matter from finding it. It was nowhere in the archives of the library, and aside from spotting that one mention in the yearbook, they weren't able to uncover a reference to it anywhere else.

"You might try the English Department," the reference librarian suggested. "Someone there might know something."

They made it to the English Department office only fifteen minutes before closing time. The department secretary had never heard of *Ailanthus* but told them old literary magazines might be found in the reading lounge upstairs. "No one has cleaned that place out for years," she said.

The reading lounge was deserted except for a lone student stretched out in a chair, listening to something on earphones. She wore argyle-patterned tights and a skirt much shorter than any Nancy had dared to wear when she was in college. She barely noticed Nancy, but took in Adam and repositioned her legs on the coffee table. Not long afterwards, she left. Nancy was relieved to have the room to themselves. It

wasn't as if they were doing anything illegal, but it was more comfortable working without worrying that someone might question them.
Even so, Nancy couldn't shake the feeling that Gillian herself would
appear at the door and ask, "What do you think you're doing?" But
Nancy was fired up now. She'd confront Gillian. She'd stand her ground.

The bookcase-lined room was two stories high, with a library ladder
for access to the upper shelves. At one end was a stone fireplace worthy
of an English manor house. It looked as if it had never been used. Ceramic ashtrays, back from the days when smoking had been allowed,
were stacked on the mantel. Nancy and Adam divided the room and
worked towards each other. The shelves housed a hodgepodge of dis-
carded books, periodicals, old student newspapers, and bound student
theses. There was no order to the collection; critical studies on now-
unfashionable writers were shelved beside out-of-date bestsellers. It
didn't look as if anyone had consulted any of the books for years. When
it started getting dark, Nancy found the light panel and turned on the
overhead lights that dangled from metal chains. A janitor poked her
head in and emptied a wastebasket by the door.

"How late is this room open?" Nancy asked.

"We lock the building at ten," said the janitor.

"Are you getting hungry?" Nancy asked Adam.

"Getting there," he said.

They found a pizza place near campus. The front window was
steamed up, and the neon letters spelling out "Apollo Pizza" had a mysterious glow.

They sat in a booth along the wall. The pizza had so much melted
cheese it resembled a lunar surface. Adam bit into his without waiting
for it to cool. A web of cheese connected the piece in his hand with
the one on the plate. He went through three pieces of pizza before
looking up at her.

"There's something I've been meaning to ask you," he said.

"Yes?"

"At Gillian's book party, when you went up to Gillian . . . remember?"

Nancy waited. She hadn't expected Adam would remind her of that evening.

"I overheard you say something about your father. What was that about?"

"Oh," said Nancy. She hadn't been thinking about her father; she had tucked him away in a safe place in her mind, far from any taint of revenge. She hadn't wanted to talk about this to anyone—except Oates. But in this pizza place, miles from home, on this hunt that Adam had teamed up with her for, it seemed she might as well.

"The doctor in my novel was inspired by my father," she said. "He decided to stop practicing medicine because he felt inadequate. It wasn't his lack of skill as a doctor, but the profession as a whole. Gillian took him and turned him into an incompetent—a doctor convicted of malpractice."

Adam was listening intently. Nancy leaned toward him across the table. "She sensationalized him, she maligned him. She *used* him."

Nancy hadn't realized it, but while she had been speaking, her hands had tightened into fists. Adam's hands covered them now. His warm palms encompassed her knuckles.

"She used me, too," he said.

WHEN THEY RETURNED to the reading lounge, they picked up where they had left off. They worked for two hours more. They were in the middle section of the main bookcase, Adam on the ladder, Nancy on her knees going through a low shelf, when someone from campus security came by. He was an older man in a grey uniform that looked a size too small for him.

"Building closes in half an hour," he said. He took another look at Nancy. "Mind if I ask what you folks are doing here?"

Nancy stood up and smiled at him. "I'm a visiting scholar, and this is my research assistant," she said. "Would you like me to show you some identification?"

"Nah," he said. "Nothing worth stealing in this place."

After he left, Adam came down the ladder. "Your research assistant is done up here," he said.

"I'm done, too," said Nancy. She sank down on the sofa facing the fireplace. Adam sat down beside her.

"I guess we might as well head home now," she said. "I don't know where to go from here. I was so sure we'd find something in this place."

"We've still got half an hour," said Adam.

"But we've been through every shelf," said Nancy.

"What about those cabinets?" asked Adam.

"Where?"

"Beside the fireplace," said Adam.

Nancy looked where he pointed. There were leaded-glass windows on either side of the fireplace, and below the windowsills were wooden panels with barely visible knobs. She hadn't noticed before that they were cabinet doors.

Adam took the cabinet on the left, Nancy the one on the right. She opened the door and squatted to peer inside. The cabinet was deep, and there was no light. The upper shelf was packed with old journals. She lifted out an armful. They were all back issues of *The White Mountain Review*.

"Anything there?" she asked Adam.

"So far it looks like there's nothing but old course catalogs," said Adam.

Nancy wrestled out a cardboard box that was wedged into the lower shelf. It was filled with ancient course handouts of Jonathan Swift's "A Modest Proposal." Behind it was a stack of pamphlets. She reached in and pulled it out. When she set the pile on the floor, it slipped sideways and fanned across the carpet. She lifted the top pamphlet. *Ailanthus* was printed in Bookman Old Style in the center of the cover, and beneath the title was the black profile of a tree. It was nothing more than a slender sheaf of mimeographed paper with an off-white cover, two staples, their prongs now rusty, holding it together. Inside it was all student poems.

"We got it!" she said.

They grabbed all the pamphlets from the cabinet and spread them out on the floor. *Ailanthus* had been published biannually and had survived for several years. There were multiple copies of some issues, only one or two for others.

"We've got only about twenty minutes," said Adam.

They snatched up the issues for the years Gillian had been at Bolton. The year that Gillian was a sophomore Nancy found poems by a student named Anya Kuznetsov listed in the table of contents. She handed the copy to Adam.

"You look," she said.

She watched him read through the poems. The paper snapped as he turned the pages. Suddenly he paused. His head didn't move; his fingers froze. "Bingo!" he cried.

He tilted the page to show Nancy. His finger pointed to the spot. "Translucence is not transcendence," he read aloud. "They come at different times." He shut his eyes and recited: "Translucence, not transcendence. Nor time allows, nor years." He opened his eyes. "Gillian's poem goes off in a different way," he said. Then he added, sadly, "It's one of her best poems."

BEFORE THEY LEFT FOR THE DRIVE BACK, Nancy went down the hall to use the bathroom. The floor was covered with black and white octagonal tiles, an optical illusion; as she moved her head, it was a white floor with black, or a black floor with white. The bathroom was all hard surfaces, and sounds were magnified: the Niagara-sized flush, the metal stall door swinging back into place, the pressing of the plunger of the soap dispenser on the wall.

The hot water felt good on Nancy's hands. She splashed water on her face and blotted it with a paper towel. Her face, in the mirror over the sink, looked like that of a woman who'd been up all night. She started to take out her makeup, but decided she didn't really care enough. It really didn't matter what she looked like, it didn't matter at all. She stepped out into the hallway, the bathroom door closing slowly behind her. Gillian had walked down this hallway when she'd been a student here. She'd sat in these classrooms, wandered into the lounge.

"I've got you," Nancy wanted to crow at her—through time. "I've got you at last!"

NANCY WAS SO TIRED she considered asking Adam if he wanted to drive back, but he was so keyed up she was afraid he would suddenly collapse. He chose a radio station that had rock music she would never listen to on her own and hummed along, poorly, out of tune, tapping a beat on the armrest.

When they were getting close to his house, Nancy turned off the radio.

"You know, Adam," she began, "we do need to be a little realistic here. A few words—that's all we really have—it might not be enough."

"It's not just those few words," said Adam. "We've got something more."

"But there was only that one poem."

"Yes, but there are about fifty in Anya Kuznetsov's thesis."

"Her thesis?" asked Nancy.

"When you were in the bathroom, I checked out those bound theses in the bookcase. I found hers and glanced through it. I spotted some other stuff. I have it, right here, with those copies of *Ailan-*

thus," said Adam, and he patted his briefcase on the floor between his feet.

"You took it?" asked Nancy. "You just took it from the shelf?"

"Don't worry," said Adam. "You have nothing more to do with this now. I'm delivering all this to Chris myself."

GILLIAN

CHRIS HAD HIS FRIEND, BUT GILLIAN HAD HER FRIEND, TOO. He wasn't able to rescue the prize for her, but he did leak to her what had happened. The Pulitzer Committee saw her as a potential liability—those few echoes of lines from the poems of another student many years before were insignificant in themselves, but everyone was nervous there might be something more. A Pulitzer Prize winner was high-profile, a choice target for the jealous and resentful. They'd go after those skeletons, they'd deconstruct the closet itself.

Gillian was upstairs at her desk when the call came. She had been expecting very different news. She was so astonished she was barely able to respond, to protest. She sat for a moment, running the words over again in her head, trying to find some opening in them, some contradiction that would render them untrue, but the fact they conveyed was irrefutable. Her wrists felt cold against the edge of the desk, and the cold spread upwards through her arms, to her shoulders. She reached for the sweater that was usually slung over the back of her desk chair, but it wasn't there.

She got up and walked to the door. Jerry was downstairs in the kitchen. When she opened the door to call out to him to come up to her, she heard him talking to Paul. She hadn't realized Paul was home. She closed the door and looked out the window at the darkening meadow. A blue jay coasted across the open expanse, seeking refuge in the woods beyond.

Anya Kuznetsov. She had not thought of the name for so many years, had pushed it away, cleaned her mind of it. She worked to remember what Anya had looked like. Lank, blond hair tucked behind her ears. Big ears, and a narrow face. She'd never read Anya's poems—she saw no point in reading student magazines, pretentious, shallow stuff—but she had once heard her read them. It was at the department's poetry competition, which Gillian had entered only because there was a hundred-dollar prize. That was a lot of money for her then, and when she won she'd used it to buy course books and one frivolous luxury, an Indian silk scarf, lapis blue, with a pattern of swirls and leaves in red and violet and green. It was long enough to circle her neck and flutter to her waist. She'd bought it in Harvard Square when she was visiting a boyfriend there. The shop smelled of incense and teak and brass. The scarf had been the most exotic thing she had owned, proof of a world she was determined to visit someday, far beyond the stark New England landscape. She hadn't worn it for years—if she wore a scarf at all it was a solid black or the green-blue-grey of her eyes—but she was fairly sure she still had it. She found it in a drawer, under the pile of perfectly folded scarves, and pulled it out. The silk in her hand felt thin and light, almost not there at all.

It was two years later when her thesis advisor, Professor Jacobson, accused her of copying Anya's poems. But she hadn't copied them. Some phrases from them had gotten caught in her unconscious—the way the eelgrass at the edge of the bay catches the detritus of the rising tide—and ended up in the poems in her senior thesis. She had been reading so much poetry then, scooping it up like someone starved for words. First, Gerard Manley Hopkins. Then Eliot, Pound, and Wallace Stevens. And, finally, Yeats. She had memorized most of his poems, and would recite them to herself for an hour without pause. She had learned from all these poets: their rhythms, their cadences, their density. But she had never copied them.

Towards the end of the semester, after she turned in the final copy of her poetry manuscript, Professor Jacobson had invited her to meet him for lunch. She assumed they were celebrating the completion of her thesis. The honors committee was meeting the next week, and Professor Jacobson had hinted that she could expect to be awarded a summa.

They ate at the Dorset Hotel, in the restaurant behind the bar. During commencement weekend, the hotel would be packed, even though it lacked the amenities of the two newer hotels closer to campus, but it was quiet now. Professor Jacobson's house was far out in the country, and he sometimes rented a room at the Dorset, he told her, so he wouldn't have to drive home when he worked late on campus.

They sat in a curved booth in the back of the restaurant. At dinnertime the table would be covered with a tablecloth, but now it was a half circle of black Formica, shiny as patent leather. Even so, it had seemed like elegant dining to her. The silverware came rolled up in a white linen napkin. Gillian unrolled hers carefully; Professor Jacobson yanked at the corner of his napkin, his silverware clattering on the tabletop.

They had finished their lobster bisque and sandwiches, and were waiting for their blueberry cobbler when Professor Jacobson explained that the reason for this meeting was to discuss a problem that had arisen with her thesis. He told Gillian that a line in one of her poems had struck him as familiar, and he had finally hunted down the thesis of a student whom he had worked with two years before and compared the poems side by side. Gillian insisted she had never read Anya's poetry, only heard it that one time, but he made it clear he didn't believe her. When he showed Gillian Anya's poem for proof, she was surprised but unapologetic. She had no reason to apologize, and would not have apologized even if she had done something wrong. She never apologized for anything. Professor Jacobson suggested she resubmit her thesis and remove the poem in question. But she argued that her poem was a different poem entirely, and even Professor Jacobson had to admit it was better than the original.

THE ELEVATOR WAS small and creaky and gave a little bump when it landed on the fourth floor, jostling them closer together. He took her hand as he led her down the corridor, which turned the corner twice before they reached the door of his room.

It was the first time she had made love with someone who was this much older than she. Naked, under the covers, she had watched while he shed his shirt and took off his pants and his undershorts. He'd kept his eye on her while he massaged his penis back and forth. He pulled the blankets back off the bed and looked at her.

"You are so beautiful," he said, "so beautiful." Her skin had pebbled with cold, but he hadn't noticed. He knelt beside her on the bed, and she rolled towards him as the mattress sloped under his weight. He touched her small, flat breasts. He parted her legs with his fingers, then parted her labia with his tongue. It was the first time anyone had sucked her there. She closed her eyes. She heard the sound of him ripping a condom wrapper with his teeth. She lifted her knees, and he lumbered on top of her. Her arms went around him, and she could feel the hair on his shoulders.

"I want you to come," he told her, and she tried to keep herself from coming just because that was what he wanted. But she lost the power to do so. Her body shook loose on its own.

"Blanche, my princess," he said. "My beautiful white princess."

THE SCARF LAY ON HER DESK, a swath of vivid color across the plain wood surface. The label, held by a single blue thread, stared up at her. HANDWOVEN PURE SILK MADE IN INDIA. She crumpled the scarf and pushed it off the side of the desk, to the floor.

NANCY

NANCY COULD NOT FALL ASLEEP. BESIDE HER IN BED, OATES slept purposefully, inhaling slowly, as if his breath had a difficult journey along the corrugated roof of his mouth. She tried to think of images to occupy her mind, something benign, soporific, but she kept coming back to Gillian. She did not feel sorry for Gillian. Pity had always come so easily to her, and she was unnerved by its absence now.

She cuddled close to Oates and put her arm around him to hug him closer. She would not wake him, but she wished he would wake, and when he finally stirred, she kissed his upper arm. He rolled towards her, onto his back, and woke up.

"You still awake?" he asked her.

"I've been trying for hours," she said, "but I can't sleep."

"What's the matter?"

"I don't feel like myself," she said. "I think I've lost my moral center."

He blinked and rubbed his forehead. "What time is it?" he asked.

"Nearly two." The lace on the neckline of Nancy's flannel night-gown felt scratchy. She undid the tie and opened the buttons.

"Can't this wait until morning?"

"I wish it could," said Nancy.

Oates took in a generous mouthful of air and held it for a moment before letting it out. "I thought you'd be feeling great," he said. "You finally accomplished what you hoped to do. You aren't sorry you did it, are you?"

"No," said Nancy. "And that's just the point. I don't like me this way."

"For God's sake, Nancy," said Oates. He freed the pillow from under his head, gave it a shake, and rolled it in half before he let his head sink into it again. "Gillian plagiarized your book. She stole your father's story and turned it upside down. If she loses the Pulitzer Prize, if her reputation is damaged, it's exactly what she deserves. Isn't it?"

"But she's not being done in because of my novel, she's being done in because of something else."

"So it's indirect justice," said Oates. "Sometimes that's the best we can do."

Nancy heard the tone of exasperation in his voice. She didn't want to aggravate him, but if she couldn't explain to Oates, then there would be nobody she could explain to. Everything about them, their future, depended on this.

"Here's what I realized," said Nancy. "Gillian has an incredible memory. She absorbed my first chapter just hearing it that once and was able to reproduce it, months later, almost exactly. Maybe she didn't deliberately copy Anya Kuznetsov's poems but read them once and then unintentionally absorbed them."

"So?" asked Oates.

"So, then she isn't really guilty. And yet I don't care, because I got what I wanted."

"I don't see the problem then," said Oates.

"The problem is I don't like the person I've become. I'm not good."

Oates held Nancy by the shoulders now. "You are the craziest woman in the world," he said. "You get yourself into these moral tangles. Stop worrying about being good all the time."

She felt off balance, as if she were a boat in the sea and her cargo were words, shifting from side to side. She pressed her head against Oates's chest to steady herself.

She worried about being good because that was what had mattered to her father. She had inherited a moral compass from him, and she had always worked to keep the jiggling needle pointed right. Without that, she was someone he wouldn't respect.

"Gillian has turned me into this," she said. "So she's the one who has the final revenge."

"Let her have her revenge then," said Oates.

"Do you still love me?" asked Nancy. "Do you love me the way I am?"

Oates settled back down in bed and pulled her close to him. She wanted to hear the words, but she knew that he was done with talking, and had to accept, as an answer, the pressure of his arm across her hip. She closed her eyes and tried to fall asleep.

Oates listened to her, he loved her, but he didn't truly understand her. No one had ever really understood her, except her father. And she was the only one who had really understood her father—her mother hadn't, his parents hadn't. She'd explained her father in her novel, she'd set things right. But her novel would never be published.

But that wasn't the worst thing. The worst thing was the incontrovertible fact that her father was dead, and she'd never be able to talk to him again.

$\mathcal{P}$AUL

$\mathbf{P}$AUL WAS DOWNLOADING MUSIC WHEN HIS FATHER KNOCKED on his door. Instinctively he slid the biology textbook he was supposed to be studying to the center of his desk as he called out, "Yeah?"

Jerry closed the door behind him when he came into the room, and this gesture made Paul sit up straight. Even with the door open, you could barely hear anything upstairs from here. A closed door guaranteed that.

"Can you manage here on your own for a few days?" Jerry asked.

"Sure. I guess," said Paul. He knew that his father was worried about something because Jerry didn't comment, as he usually did, on the disorder in the room, didn't even seem to notice.

"Gillian wants to go out to Truro, and I don't want her to be driving down there alone. I'm on duty at the hospital tonight," Jerry said. "But I've persuaded her to wait until I can go with her tomorrow morning."

"What's going on?" asked Paul.

"She didn't get the Pulitzer," said Jerry. "She just heard."

"So," said Paul. "Lots of people don't get the Pulitzer. What's the big deal?"

"Paul!"

"Yeah, okay. I get it," said Paul. "So it's a big deal for her." It was hard for him to sound suitably sorry. It wasn't that he didn't want Gillian to get that silly prize—she was always nicer to live with when she got what she wanted—but he liked the idea that expectations didn't always pan out. Everyone had described her winning the prize as a sure thing. He was glad that things weren't that predictable.

"I'll need you to hold down the fort until I'm back late tonight," said Jerry.

"Sure," said Paul. "What do you want me to do?"

"Don't let anything disturb Gillian. Keep your earphones off so you can hear the phone. And if you find out that she's decided to head out to the Cape on her own, page me."

"You want me to go up there and check up on her?" Paul asked.

"No," said Jerry. "I don't want you to bother her at all. Just get in touch with me if she tells you she's leaving."

"Okay," said Paul. His father looked tired and old. He looked like a man who needed a good night's sleep, not a doctor who was heading off to be on call for emergency appendectomies.

"Are you afraid she's going to off herself?" asked Paul.

"God no!" said Jerry. "Whatever gave you an idea like that?"

Paul shrugged. "People kill themselves over major disappointments," he said. "It happens all the time."

"You don't have to worry about Gillian," said Jerry. Not that Paul was worried, it was Jerry who was obviously worried. But as Paul thought about it, Jerry was right. Gillian didn't fit the profile of someone suicidal. He knew all about that from some website on depression.

Paul looked at his biology for a while, until he saw Jerry's car head down the driveway, then he went upstairs to scrounge something for dinner. He heated a frozen pizza in the microwave and brought it downstairs to his room. He put his earphones on, but he kept the music low enough so he figured he could hear anything important. It was dark out now, and the windows, instead of offering a view of the sloping lawn down to the driveway, offered only a mirror image of his own room, and his own face. He went upstairs to get some ice cream for dessert. The freezer had been set too high, and the ice cream was so hard he couldn't get it out with the scoop. Chubby Hubby was the flavor. He took the container of ice cream over to the glass table by the kitchen and used a spoon to shave off pieces, eating directly from the container.

It was hard work digging out the ice cream, and when he jammed in his spoon to extract a piece, the ice cream flew out and landed on the floor. He got down to pick it up. The floor was so clean that he called out "five-second rule!" and popped the chunk into his mouth. He was still on his hands and knees when he heard the doorbell ring. He hadn't heard a car drive up the driveway, and was surprised. He raced for the door, grabbing it open so whoever was ringing wouldn't hit the doorbell again. The outside light wasn't on. He could barely make out the woman standing there. He opened the door wider, illuminating the front entrance.

"Kim!" he exclaimed. She was wearing a dark sweatshirt, the hood circling her face. She had come out of nowhere, a fantasy suddenly turned actual. He had not seen her for months, not since the Christmas party Adam had brought her to, but he thought about her all the time—barely daring to fantasize doing more with her than just hang out, talk. He kept trying to capture her in his drawings, but he'd never been able to get her quite right.

"I want to talk to Adam," she said.

"What?" asked Paul.

Kim pulled the hood back off her head, and her long white-blond hair burst out, like an exploding dandelion.

"Adam. He's here, isn't he?"

"No," said Paul, trying to keep his voice low. His father would give him hell if Gillian were disturbed. "Why would he be here?"

"I thought he might be," said Kim. She looked as if she were going to cry.

"Well, he isn't," said Paul.

"You're not just lying to me?" asked Kim.

"No. I wouldn't lie to you," said Paul. "Where's your car?" he asked. He didn't see anything there in the driveway.

"I parked out on the road," said Kim. "I walked up the driveway."

"Are you okay?" asked Paul.

Kim pulled in her bottom lip and shut her eyes. She'd obviously been crying for a while. Either that or she had a cold.

"Come on in," said Paul. "But we've got to go downstairs. We can't talk here."

He closed the door behind Kim and led the way down to his room. For a second he saw it through her eyes: the bed strewn with papers and clothes, the dirty plates and cutlery stacked precariously on the desk. She was definitely crying now. Little, burpy sobs. He closed the door behind them and pushed some clothes off a chair so she'd have a place to sit down. He sat on the bed across from her.

"What happened?" he asked.

Kim shook her head.

"Can I get you something?" asked Paul. "Something to drink or eat? I could run upstairs to the kitchen and be back in a minute."

Kim was still looking down at her lap.

"Hey, you can talk to me," said Paul. "I mean, I'd like to help you, if I could."

"Adam broke up with me," said Kim. She looked up at him now.

The idea that anyone who had achieved the acquisition of someone as unattainable as Kim as a girlfriend would ditch her seemed so preposterous to Paul that it took him a moment to say anything. He had never had a girl sitting in his room before. Never had a girl in his room, with the door shut, just the two of them. And this was Kim! At the Christmas party, when he'd shown her around the house and brought her down here, they'd stood briefly at the door and she'd looked in. "Cool," she'd said, but he had guessed she just said that to be nice. Standing close beside her then, he'd seen the edge of her white bra strap, the metal clasp that adjusted its length. The skin over her collarbone was pulled tight, and he would have given anything then to be able to touch her there, touch her with just a single finger.

"Why would he do that?" asked Paul.

"He's been seeing someone else," said Kim. "He told me he was in love with her."

"He's nuts," said Paul. "But why did you come here?"

"I just found out who it was. I thought Adam might be over here. I wanted to tell him how sick I thought it all was." She was animated now. The blood under her skin had inundated her face unevenly, continents of red on the white skin. Still, she was beautiful. God, she was beautiful!

"But why would he be here?" asked Paul again. He felt there was some essential thing that he must have missed.

"Because," Kim said, "it's Gillian."

"Jesus," said Paul. It was quite wonderful, this news, something he would never have imagined. If his father found out, that would finish things between him and Gillian, or would it? Or did his father already know? It seemed suddenly unbearably sad that his father might love Gillian so much he was willing to put up with anything she did, even something like this.

"He told you that?"

"No," said Kim. "He wouldn't tell me who it was. I would never have guessed her—I mean, she's old."

"Then how did you find out?"

"I couldn't stand it any longer. Not knowing. I still had the key to his apartment. I went over there when he was at work. He leaves his laptop at home. I went through his files. He writes about everything."

Paul remembered now that Kim was a computer person. She'd be able to access Adam's stuff without much trouble.

"But why would you think he'd be over here now?"

"I was going to catch him after work in the parking lot, when he came out. But he didn't come out. This guy I know who works in his office told me he'd said he was leaving early to meet with someone in his writing group."

"It must have been someone else," said Paul. "Gillian's here, upstairs. Do you want to say something to *her*?"

"Oh no!" Kim looked frightened. "I just want to find Adam," she said. "I want to tell him what I think of him."

"I could get you something to eat first," said Paul. "There's some more pizza."

"No, thanks," she said. She stood up. "Look, I've got to go." She pulled her sweatshirt down on her hips and pulled the hood up over her head. Her hair was pushed forward and stuck out on both sides. Paul wanted to tuck it back in, smooth it against her head. "This whole thing was pretty stupid," she said. "Pretty pointless."

There was no way he could get her to stay longer. He could see that.

"You can leave from down here," said Paul. He pointed to the sliding glass doors that went straight outside.

"Okay," she said. He opened the slider and stepped outside with her.

"Want me to walk to your car with you? It's a long way out to the road," he said. He was wearing only a T-shirt and the night was cold, but he didn't consider going back into his room to grab something warmer.

"No, that's okay," she said. She turned towards him now. "Thanks, though," she said. "And thanks for listening to me."

"Sure," he said. He reached to touch her. The tips of three fingers brushed the sleeve of her sweatshirt. He could have held them there forever.

"Bye," she said, and she set off, cutting down the hillside to the curving driveway. He could barely make her out in the darkness, with her black hood up. The black absorbed the black, absorbed her. Made it as if she had never come.

THE GARAGE WAS ON THE FAR SIDE of the house, so Paul had not heard the garage door open. And he did not hear the engine until

Gillian's pickup truck came around the side of the house. Gillian had not turned the headlights on. It took Paul a second to note this. He figured Gillian must have guessed that Jerry had asked Paul to call him if she left, so she was trying to drive off without being detected.

Paul had a split-second vision of Kim, invisible in the dark driveway. He took it all in, in an instant; factored in speed and time and consequence. His body acted instinctively. He flew down the hillside, crying out Kim's name. He plunged out into the driveway, just below the curve, where no driver would have been able to see him, even if they had had their headlights on, and even if they had been able to see him, would not have been able to stop in time.

GILLIAN

THERE WAS NO TIME TO TAKE THE BACK ROADS NOW. GILLIAN pulled onto the highway without glancing in her rearview mirror, without giving herself a chance to think. Semitrailers thundered around her, and she sped along, caught in their wake. Her hands trembled on the steering wheel, and, although her fingers were icy, the steering wheel was slick with sweat. She had no idea how fast she was driving—certainly faster than she had ever driven before—and only when she looked down and saw that the orange needle was pointing straight up, noon on a clock face, did she realize that she was going well over eighty. I can't do this, she thought, I can't do this. But there was nothing else she could do. Trapped in a center lane with traffic on either flank, she was a small fish in a school of fish in a rushing stream. She dared herself to shut her eyes, and then, she shut them. She drove straight ahead, sightless, for a minute—was it a full minute?—her hands on either side of the steering wheel, her foot steady on the accelerator. She forced herself to open her eyes, and she bit on the inside of her mouth, hard enough to make it bleed, so she could steady herself with the pain.

At last she reached the Cape Cod Canal. A sign on the side of the Bourne Bridge read "Desperate? Call the Samaritans." It was ironic that she'd hardly noticed it in the past, yet it seemed prominently displayed right now. Surely it was intended for people who were walking across the bridge, not driving, or did it include everyone? It seemed unlikely there was a sufficiency of desperation among travelers to the

Cape to warrant such a sign. *Desperate,* she thought, no doubt from the Latin *desperare,* "to despair." She played with the word in her head, worked to dull its sting.

When she had crossed over the canal and headed out on Route 6, she finally eased her grip on the steering wheel and allowed herself to breathe. Her breath came in quick gasps at first, like the breath of someone who had nearly drowned, and then, finally, it slowed.

It must have been a deer she hit. What else could it have been? It was not a tree branch or a rock—she was sure of that—it was something softer, something alive that had darted out in front of her. But she could not stop the truck and get out to look; she could not bear to see a creature injured, possibly even killed. Surely there was nothing she could have done to help it. She was desperate to get away from the house, and even if there had been something she might have done, she could not have stopped. She could not wait around for Jerry. And she did not want Jerry with her at all. She did not want his kindness, his sympathy, his understanding. Once, early in their relationship, he'd said, "I understand how you feel" about something that had happened to her, and she had snapped at him, "No one, not even you, can understand me." He'd never used the word again. Jerry was quick that way.

At last she made it around the rotary in Orleans and headed north, the last segment of the journey, where her little house, Button, awaited her, where her marsh and the night air from the sea awaited her. She ticked off the towns in her mind: Orleans, Eastham, Wellfleet, Truro. Beyond lay Provincetown, the end of the road, the last town before the ocean, the dead end of the Cape. Truro was safely one town farther back. A town on the way to somewhere else, a town most of the traffic on Route 6 would pass by.

When Gillian got to the end of her dirt driveway, she parked the truck farther than usual from the house, its front end nearly buried in a thicket of blackberry bushes. She got out and closed the door behind her but did not slam it. She walked quickly to the house and did not look back at the truck. She did not want to check to see if her bumper had been dented, if there was anything there, any mark from the creature she had hit.

Gillian had brought nothing with her except the key to her house. She could not see the lock in the dark, but she could work the key by feel alone. She leaned against the door, and it opened, forgiving. She entered her house's embrace. The electricity had been left on from her last visit. She ran her hand along the wall beside the door and found the light switches for the small yellow outside light and the wall sconce in the front hall. She looked out towards the marsh before she shut the door. She had parked the truck at a distance from the house, but she could still see it now, a dark shape, a speck of light glinting on a curve of chrome. It was not she who had hit the deer but this dark shape, this intermediary. *Intermediary,* she thought. She let the word loose, and a poem began forming itself in her head. She closed the door and went back into the house, turning on lights as she walked room to room, letting the poem grow, undisciplined, in her mind as she went about her tasks: turning on the heat, removing the spread from her bed in the studio, finding a box of unopened crackers in the pantry, pouring herself a glass of sherry, getting out a pad of unlined paper from her desk, selecting a pencil with a decent point. She circled the downstairs again, this time extinguishing the lights, leaving on only the standing lamp by her armchair in the study. She curled up there and began to lay the words on the page. *Intermediary:* something between two other things, something that connected. Driver and animal. Person and person. Man and nature? Man and God? The fenders caressed by the blackberry leaves, pricked by the thorns. The light glinting on the edge of the chrome around the taillight, as if a match had been struck there.

A flash of something like light. A flash of something moving. Not the white tail of the deer—not snout, or flank, but something like a limb flung up, the whiteness of a hand.

But what she had seen—that flash—had been off to the side; it was not what she had hit. It could not be. Two deer perhaps? But even as she phrased this in her mind, a reckless thought broke through that it had not been a deer, but something else. What it was, was too terrible to imagine, and so she shoved it away. She took a sip of the sweet sherry, held it in her mouth, and pulled herself back to the poem flickering on the page in front of her.

Intermediary: the air between the cry and the ear that heard it.

But there hadn't been a cry, or if there had, she had not heard it. The windows had been up, and all she'd heard was the truck's engine. If there had been a cry, surely if there had been a cry, she would have stopped. Even if she had not wanted to, she would have stopped.

Intermediary: a mediator, an agent of compromise. The marsh between the sea and the land. *The diurnal swelling. Land becoming sea. Sea distorting land.*

When the phone rang, she moved towards it numbly. It took her a moment to recognize the voice of her lawyer, an old friend. She listened to what she was being told. She did not say anything, she just listened. She did not cry. She did not make any sound at all. When he was done, she said simply, "I'm not going anywhere. I'll stay right here." She hung the phone up. It did not look like it would ring again.

It was not leaving the scene of an accident, was it, if you thought that what you'd hit was just a deer? If your headlights were not on because you needed to drive away without being spotted, that might be negligent, but it was not criminal. The law recognized the difference. People forgot to turn on their headlights all the time.

She had lost Jerry. She was certain of that. He had given up too much for her already, accommodated too much. This was beyond even his foolish devotion. She would have to make her way without him, without his unflagging support and praise and patience. She'd done fine on her own before Jerry, and she'd do fine without him now. She'd live here, and she would never have to see Jerry again. She would not play with the possibility that he was still so in love with her that even now, with this, he could not give her up. She'd live here in Button. She would not have to return to that other house.

She stumbled back to her chair and lifted the pad to her lap. She would write. No matter what happened, she always had her poetry to write. Her poem now would take it, turn it, so it would become the way she wanted it to be. She could change anything with her poems.

Intermediary. The hand between the leaf, the mind that knows the leaf, its intricacies, predictable, its fierce, green will.

It was that girl, who had seen the truck, who, it seemed, had been a witness to what happened. That girlfriend of Adam's, with her shining white-blond hair, her high forehead. Gillian remembered her name: Kim. If she hadn't been there, if she hadn't told, no one would have known. Gillian would be safe in Button, and whatever tragedy had happened would be far away.

"I love your house!" Kim had said that night at Gillian's Christmas party. "Adam, don't you just love their house?" and she had taken Adam's arm. She was young, so young.

And Paul, young and foolish, had rushed out into the darkness to pull her back to safety. Gillian did not love Paul—she did not love anyone—but Paul was someone she had come quite close to loving.

Paul! It was impossible now to wall off the thought of what had happened to him, the thought of what she had done. She worked to keep herself from imagining it, but she could not escape the images: darkness and a flash of white.

Paul.

Gillian squared the pad of paper on her lap. She clenched her pencil. She stared at what she had written at the top of the page: *Intermediary*. She did not know what more to do with it. There was nothing left about the poem. It had never failed her before, but now, she had nothing to write. The poem was nothing, just an exercise in words.

ACKNOWLEDGMENTS

I am grateful to many brilliant and generous people who were instrumental in the making of this book, including my editor, Sarah Landis; my agent, Rebecca Strauss; fellow writers Betsy Hartmann, Karen Osborn, Stefan Petruchka, Robert Redick, and, especially, Anita Shreve; my friend Elaine Lasker von Bruns; my family members Artemis Demas Roehrig, Austin Bliss, Gary Van Deurse, and, as always, Matthew Roehrig.

My thanks to Mount Holyoke College for a faculty fellowship, to the writing groups who have nurtured me, and to my current writing circle: Barbara Diamond Goldin, Anna Kirwan, Patricia MacLachlan, Lesléa Newman, Ann Turner, Ellen Wittlinger, and Jane Yolen, who lived with this other writing circle, chapter by chapter.